BERKLEY UK

THE VAULT

Emily McKay is the author of *The Farm* and *The Lair*, which are also published by Penguin. She loves to read, shop, and geek out about movies. When she's not writing, she reads online gossip and bakes luscious desserts. She pretends that her weekly yoga practice balances out both of those things. She lives in central Texas with her family and her crazy pets.

The Vault

EMILY McKAY

BERKLEY UK
PENGUIN

PENGUIN BOOKS

UK | USA | Canada | Ireland | Australia
India | New Zealand | South Africa

Penguin Books is part of the Penguin Random House group of companies
whose addresses can be found at global.penguinrandomhouse.com.

First published in the USA by the Berkley Publishing Group,
part of the Penguin Group (USA) LLC 2014
First published in Great Britain by Berkley UK 2014
001

Printed in Great Britain by Clays Ltd, St Ives plc

A CIP catalogue record for this book is available from the British Library

ISBN: 978–1–405–91870–1

www.greenpenguin.co.uk

MIX
Paper from
responsible sources
FSC® C018179

Penguin Random House is committed to a
sustainable future for our business, our readers
and our planet. This book is made from Forest
Stewardship Council® certified paper.

ACKNOWLEDGMENTS

Last year, when *The Farm* won the RITA award for Best Young Adult novel, I blanked and totally forgot to thank my husband and family. So this time, that's where I need to start. Thank you, Greg, Adi, Henry; you guys are the best! Thanks, Greg, for reading the series and loving it. Thanks for never hesitating to pimp the books, and for calling friends on a Saturday to ask them questions about what kind of fuel single propeller planes take and how hard it will be to find in the apocalypse. Henry, thanks for telling everyone you know that your mommy is a famous author and for thinking it's cool that I have blue hair. And Adi my dear, thank you for helping me brainstorm things you can kill a vampire with. It's a disturbing predilection in a nine year old, but it's somehow proof you're mine.

Thank you to my completely fabulous editor, Michelle Vega. Have I told you lately how much I love working with you? You are a joy to chat with, to bounce ideas off of, and to hang out with. These books would not be *these* books without you. Also, thanks to everyone at Berkley who has worked on the series, and this book in particular. Thanks to Martin Karlow, my copyeditor, for keeping me honest and grammatically correct. Thank you to Courtney Wilhelm Vincento, production editor. Thanks to Lesley Worrell in the art department for working tirelessly to make this cover amazing! I love you guys!!!

Jessica, I hope that after our nine years together, you don't need me to tell you how much I love working with you, but if you do need to hear it, well, here it is: you are fun and you get me and I could never have written these books without you. You are tough and unflinching in your criticism, but you know when it's right. Plus, you're so dang fun to work with. Thanks for putting up with me!

Thanks to my writer buddies: Robyn DeHart, Tracy Wolff, Shellee Roberts, Sherry Thomas, Hattie Mae, Skyler White, Karen MacInerney, and Jax Garren. You guys rock. I wouldn't have the strength to come back to the keyboard day after day without you. How did Jane Austen do it alone?

And this time around, I owe an extra-big thanks to my beta readers: Carine, Melanie, Joey, and Brandi. You guys were great! Thanks for the feedback. Joey, when I really needed a boost in confidence, you were there, cheering me on and loving the book. Brandi, thank you for taking such good care of my baby! I love the playlist you made. I love that you love my characters so much. When the writing got tough and I despaired of ever getting the revisions just right, I'd flip through the notes you made and remember that there are fans who love the characters as much as I do, and I'd know that I needed to keep working. I hope you all love the final version. You guys made this book!

And finally, thanks to my good friend Misty Baker. You are the only person I know who loves Pemberley Digital like I do. I feel like we're soul sisters! Let's plan that sleepover soon, okay?

THE VAULT

CHAPTER ONE

CARTER

Texas hadn't fared well in the apocalypse.

Some parts of the country had fallen by inches. Places where the virus spread slowly and the human population held their own against the Ticks and against the fear for at least a little while. Those places lost their battles incrementally. Not Texas. In just a few short weeks, Texas went from being the second-most-populated state to being the least. Texas fell in a blaze of blood and gunfire.

It wasn't just the genetically mutated monsters that did Texas in. It was the Texans. We turned on one another.

I'd told myself over and over again that I wouldn't make the same mistake. That if it had been me, if I'd been the one with my finger on the trigger, staring down a friend or a relative, I would do things differently. I would have a little faith in humanity.

Turns out, I was wrong.

There in the basement of Genexome Corporation—the company that engineered EN371, the virus that created the Ticks—I finally got it. When the life of someone you love is on the line, trust is almost impossible. Under the right circumstances, anyone will crack. Yeah. I admit it. I cracked.

The deserted hallway with flickering lights and spooky cobwebs creeped me out. I got that hairs-up-on-the-back-of-the-neck sensation that I wasn't alone. And, oh yeah, the pile of dead bodies that I'd had to haul out of the way to clear a path down the hall? Those didn't help.

Which is why I pulled a gun on Mel when she crept up behind me. One second I was staring at the LCD panel for the storage facility's security system. Tech stuff, wasn't really my thing, but I was trying. That's when I heard it, the faintest scuff of a shoe behind me. Too subtle to be an animal or a Tick. Too soft to be someone who wasn't trying to sneak.

Somewhere down the hall, someone was coming up behind me and whoever it was didn't want to be heard. I deliberately kept my breathing steady as I slipped my hand into the coat pocket where I kept my Glock. I wrapped my hand around the grip and pulled it out, spinning as I thumbed off the safety.

My finger was already on the trigger when I realized it wasn't some unknown enemy sneaking up behind me. It was Mel.

My girlfriend's twin sister. My friend.

I pulled the gun up, finger off the trigger, and held up my other hand. But she was faster than I was. My aggression provoked something in her. The instant she saw the gun, she dashed down the hall and rammed into me. The force of the impact knocked me off my feet. I tried to roll into the fall, but ended up just getting slammed to the floor with her on top of me. My hand hit the floor again and I instinctively let go of the gun. It skittered away from me. Agony flared out through my back and chest. Damn, she moved *fast*.

Mel bounced back up and landed in a crouch maybe five feet away, hands curled into claws, fangs bared and gleaming in the fluorescent lights.

I got my hands under me and tried to sit, but my whole body pulsed with pain and it was all I could do not to groan. My neck

2

throbbed. When I brought my hand up to the spot, my fingers came away sticky and damp with blood.

Panicked adrenaline shot through me and I scampered back. Yeah. I know. Scampering isn't exactly manly, but trust me, when your neck is bleeding and a hungry vampire is crouching five feet away from you, you do anything you can to get away. Even when it probably won't make a difference.

Heart pounding, I pressed myself against a concrete support beam in the hallway. I didn't have any weapons. My gun—even if it wasn't closer to her than to me—would barely faze her. I didn't have anything handy that would actually stop her. No stake. No blade.

Besides, it was *Mel*.

There was no way I was going to hurt her, let alone stake her and chop off her head. Which was a moot point, anyway, because if she wanted to kill me she would have done it already.

Pressing one hand to my neck to stanch the flow of blood, I held my other out in supplication. "Mel," I said slowly, persuasively. "Calm down. It's me. Carter."

Jesus, I hoped this would work.

Theoretically, I was an *abductura*. Which meant I had the power to superimpose my own emotions over hers. Theoretically.

Problem was, I didn't know jack about how to actually use my powers. At least not consciously. So either this would work, or I'd end up as a midnight snack.

God, I just love the apocalypse.

CHAPTER TWO

MEL

Blood lust—the uncontrollable need to consume the food before you—isn't my favorite thing ever.

In the Before—when I was a human girl—I clung to my control. Even though I was autistic, even though I sometimes spiraled out of control, I somehow always held on to the thread of myself. I was always able to pull myself out.

My vampire's blood lust is new to me. It's not only about hunger, but about need. The need to dominate. To protect myself. To feed. Its embrace is violent and jagged and I'm not myself when I'm in its grasp.

But this blood is all wrong.

Its sweetness sours my stomach. I nearly retch. Instead, I spit it out, then wipe off my mouth with hands clenched in feral claws. A false peace floods over me, washing away my fear and need. I stand, blinking away the blood lust.

That's when I see Carter crouched against the wall, like a scorpion backed into a corner. He's fierce and deadly, even though I could squash him like a bug.

"Calm down, Mel. Just . . . calm down."

The words seem to echo in my brain. Like he's been saying them over and over again and I'm only now hearing them.

Only then do I see the way he's holding his neck.

4

I run my tongue over the fronts of my teeth, my mind racing.

I was walking up behind him, hungry, yes, but in control. Then I felt this burst of fear. He whirled around. I saw the gun and then . . .

What?

My mind was blank. Blood lust. That's what.

Carter must sense that his efforts to calm me are working. That I'm more myself, because he changes the script.

"Are you are okay, Mel?" he asks, his eyebrows slightly raised. "You good?"

"Yes," I say shortly. "I'm fine."

I turn away from him. My mind still racing, because I know I'm not fine.

Carter is Lily's boyfriend. Her love. Her *savior*. They are meant to be together.

And I almost *ate* him.

I swish my spit around in my mouth, using my tongue to scrub the last of the blood off my incisors, and then I spit out the mixture of blood and saliva.

I exhale a deep breath and try to bring my mind back into focus. My vision clears a little. I blink again and make myself look at the hall around me.

This is it. What we're here for: the underground vault of Genexome Corporation. The storage facility where we will find the cure to the Tick virus. The cure we need to save my sister's life.

But I'm still struggling to make sense of what I see.

There's a door. Thick steel set straight into the concrete. An LCD panel in the wall beside it bigger than most people's computer screens. Somehow our presence in the hall has triggered it, because it's alive with swirling colors. There's a digital keypad

5

on one side and a rectangle about the size of a handprint on the other. Then to the left of the whole panel, there's a retinal scanner.

And there, on the floor in a pile on either side of the door, are dead bodies. I do a quick head count—literally counting heads because the arms and legs and torsos are so jumbled I can't count the bodies any other way. There are sixteen people. They all look similar, so I focus on one. He's got the bulky look of hired muscle. He hasn't been dead that long and it's cool enough, here underground, that his body hasn't started to rot, but my nose and stomach are more sensitive to that kind of thing than they used to be and their stench makes my stomach churn. It's all I can do to focus my attention away from him.

Whatever's beyond this door is what we came for. Of course, whatever's beyond that door is being protected by a security system strong enough to kill the sixteen people who got here before us.

"This is it," I say softly. Sebastian—the vampire that made me and mentored Carter—told us that the cure to the Tick virus was here, at Genexome Corporation, in the company's underground storage facility.

"You think these are Sabrina's people?" Carter asks.

The corpse is dressed in full SWAT gear, but they aren't police or even military. I point to the emblem stitched on the front of the jacket. "That looks like the Smart Com logo to me."

"I don't suppose when Sebastian told you about the cure, he mentioned how to get past all this security."

"No, he didn't." Of course, I'd just staked him through the heart in a fit of vampire rage, so neither one of us was feeling super communicative at the time.

Carter walks up behind me. Slowly and loudly. Like he's waiting for me to freak again.

He studies the setup, shaking his head, his hand still pressed to his neck.

"This is a dead end."

That's when I see the seam in the wall about three feet back from the doorway. I run my fingers along the seam on one side and then the other. On the ceiling, the seam bulges out slightly. On the other three sides, the seam is indented. Guide tracks for a door. But it's the vents in the ceiling above the LCD display that make me nervous.

Carter clearly sees everything I do. Maybe more, since he knows a lot about this kind of thing. "I'm guessing if you trigger the security system, a door drops down, trapping you in." He points to the pair of vents. "And then you get gassed."

"I could probably live through it," I point out. There's not much that can kill me.

"You don't know that. Sabrina threw a lot of people at this and none of them made it."

"None of them were vampires." I glance at him, looking pointedly at his neck. "How bad is it?"

"Not bad." He pulls his hand away and glances at it. There's a smear of blood on his fingers, but it's already clotting and the smell of it is repulsive to me. He wipes his fingers on the sleeve of his coat and then presses the back of his other sleeve to his neck to wipe off the last of the blood there. Then, as if he hasn't just been cleaning up the wound I gave him, he says, "The point is, we need a plan B."

"No. Sebastian must have thought we could get in. He wouldn't have sent us here otherwise." I look at Carter's neck again. "I'm, um . . . sorry. About that, I mean."

"Don't worry about it." He shrugs, still studying the security system. He holds out his palm, maybe five inches from the LCD screen, like he's sizing it up. "What do you think? That look about the size of my palm?" Then he shakes his head, muttering a curse. "We need Sebastian."

My heart gives a strange little thud. "He could be dead by now."

Carter shoots me an odd look that I have no trouble interpreting.

Carter and I talked about this. When we left Sebastian with a stake through his heart, pinned to the ground on the green in the middle of El Corazon, we hadn't really killed him. The only way to be sure a vampire is dead is to chop off his head. No, Sebastian is most likely still alive. Either he is clinging to life or he's already freed himself. Somehow I know this. Sebastian is stronger than death.

He is the vampire who made me, who trained me, who manipulated and lied to me. He lied to everyone.

Suddenly a horrible thought occurs to me. "What if there is no cure?"

Carter doesn't even look at me this time, but I know he heard me because his entire body goes tense. "There is a cure."

"He lied about everything," I say. "What if he lied about this, too? What if—"

Carter whirls to face me. "There is a cure."

"You don't know—"

"Yes, I do know. You know how I know? Because if there is no cure, then that means Lily is lost. Maybe forever. I'm not willing to believe that."

"But what—"

"We just need a new plan. That's all." He takes in a breath and I sense him struggling with his own doubts and fears. "Here's what we're going to do. We'll split up. You go back to El

8

Corazon and find Sebastian. If the cure is still here, he's the one who can get us in."

The idea of going back there sends panic skittering along my nerves. But I will do it. I have no choice, because it's like Carter said, the alternative is to give up hope. "What are you going to do?"

"I'm going to Sabrina's. If the cure isn't here, then she has it."

"We don't know that for sure," I tell him.

"What did you see in the rest of the lab? Did you see any sign of a cure? Any sign Sabrina got there first, too?"

"Yes."

Sebastian had brought me to meet her, just before he'd sent me to El Corazon. But vampires are territorial and it had been a risky move on his part. She could have killed us both. Instead, he'd bought our freedom with information about the location of the cure.

The same information he'd given Carter and me after the battle at El Corazon.

When we'd first arrived at Genexome, Carter and I had split up. He'd gone to search for the underground storage. I'd searched the rest of the industrial compound. I was faster than Carter and could cover more ground in less time, so it had made sense.

"I found the labs. It looked like someone or something came through there recently just like here." I reach into the pocket of my jeans and pull out a glass vial. I hold it out to him carefully. "I did find this."

He takes it and rolls it over to read the white label imprinted with the code EN371.

"Jesus, this is the virus?"

"Just like he said it would be," I say. "But that only proves they created it here. It doesn't mean—"

"What is it you want me to do? Just give up?" That's when Carter turns to face me head-on. No longer cocky. Just determined. "Humans are losing this fight against the Ticks. If this cure doesn't work, then Lily will finish her transformation. Maybe you're right. Maybe the chance is slim that Sebastian is telling the truth. Maybe there is no cure. But the alternative is to just accept that Lily is going to be a Tick. Are you really ready to do that? Because I'm not."

With Carter here, pinning me with his glare, coaxing me with his resolve, I realize that no, I'm not ready to give up.

But I still have doubts. Can Sebastian be trusted? Can Sabrina? Can *any* vampire be trusted? Even me?

I want to believe that there might be good in Sebastian. That maybe there is a reason he created the Tick virus. Something I don't yet understand. Something beyond his seething need to exact revenge on Roberto. I want to believe there is goodness in him and that that goodness drove him to create a cure. Because if he might be redeemed, then there is hope for me, too.

I want to believe, but it's hard.

"Any chance you have a plan C?"

He ignores my sarcasm. "Yeah. You and I go to the Farm, where your father took her. We bring her out of the medically induced coma and you bite her."

"What?"

"Just like Sebastian did for you when you were dying, after you'd been attacked by that Tick. You bite Lily. You save her life."

"If I bite Lily, she becomes a vampire. Like me."

"Exactly."

"No!" Every cell in my body, every functioning brain cell, recoils from this idea. "No! I'm not turning my sister into a vampire! You don't know what you're asking me to do!" Because the thought of turning my sister into a vampire—into a thing like me—it's repulsive. It's like a poison in my blood. "You're asking me to do this to her—to turn her into a monster—without her consent."

"If it saves her life, then yes."

"No!" That's what was done to me. In a darkened parking lot, after a horrible attack by Ticks, I sacrificed my life to save my sister, and she repaid me by begging Sebastian to turn me into a vampire. And Carter strong-armed him into it. I'd had zero say in the matter. I'd died a hero and woken up a monster.

"You don't know what you're asking me to do," I say again. "She wouldn't be Lily anymore. She'd be . . ." There are simply no words to describe the transformation she would go through. All I can come up with is "something else."

"She would be alive."

"She would want to eat you."

"She would fight the urge," he insists.

"It's not an urge. The need to kill isn't like a craving for Taco Bell. It's not just something you fight."

"You fought it," he says, gesturing toward his neck. "You didn't kill me just now."

"It would be months, maybe years, before she could actually be with you. Longer before she could be comfortable around you."

"You think I wouldn't wait?" he asks. "You think I want Lily now and only now? You think I'm going to lose interest if this takes too long? I'm not," he says fiercely. "I am in this for her. I don't want her just when it's easy or convenient. I love her. Forever. No matter what."

My heart twists itself into a knot, because I almost believe him. What would it feel like to be loved like that? To love like that? Unconditionally. Forever.

My family loved me like that. When I was human. But no guy has ever felt that way about me. And now? Now that I'm this monster? I couldn't even be with a guy without wanting to eat him. Not quite the all-consuming love of girlish fantasies.

I can't contain the jealousy that slices through me. Lily always seemed to have it all compared to me. I hadn't minded. I'd had order and music and power I didn't even understand. I had never wanted what she had. And now I do.

It shouldn't bother me. I don't want it to bother me.

Carter is just looking at me. Waiting for a response.

I say the only thing I can think of. "I would *never* have chosen this for myself. This was forced on me. I won't force it on her."

"She's been exposed to the Tick virus!" he yells, like I don't understand. "Don't you think she'd rather be a vampire than a Tick?"

"No," I snarl back. "I think she'd rather be dead than a Tick."

"Are you threatening to kill her?"

Suddenly Carter is right in my face, and now I have more to contend with than just his anger. The desperation. The fear. The love. It's all right there, ready to shove my own will out of his way.

But what would it hurt, really? Would it be so bad? My sister as a vampire? As a murderer? My sister, who has always been so determined to do the right thing. To make the world a better place. To protect the weak.

It would kill my sister to become a vampire. To see humans as kine. To feed off the people she loves.

But maybe she'd be stronger than I am. And Carter would be with her. He could help her control herself. He could . . .

What he could actually do is force me to change my mind.

His determination is already swaying my will.

He is so dangerous and he doesn't even seem to realize it.

I back away, slowly, palms raised. "No. But I won't turn her. Not as long as we have any other options."

"Okay then," he says firmly. "Let's go get those other options."

I take another step back and another, because I can still feel it, tugging at my mind. Biting Lily is the only solution. The only way to guarantee her safety. And I know I need to get out of there before he's convinced me.

"I get Sebastian, you go to Sabrina's." Suddenly, sending him far, far away from me doesn't seem like such a bad idea.

Before Carter can say anything else, I turn and run. Not just from him and this strange power he holds over me, but from myself as well.

Because I know, deep inside, that it wasn't my restraint that saved his life just now. It was something else. Not something within me, but something within him. I didn't stop because I got control over myself. I stopped because his blood tasted wrong. Horribly repugnant. Deadly.

The truth is I was dangerously close to killing one of the few people I've ever really considered a friend. And he is *Lily's*. He is her love. He may be the one person who can save her. Killing him would have risked her life and destroyed her happiness.

Those are things I didn't even consider when his throat was in my mouth. They wouldn't have stopped me. That is the kind of monster I am.

I can't do this to her. Not as long as there's another choice.

Out in the parking lot, far from Carter, I consider my options. There are plenty of cars, but I pick the one we came in. I only learned how to drive in the last three days. I need familiarity.

I don't even know how to hot-wire a car, but we took this one from El Corazon and we have the keys, so I slide into the driver's seat. Except—dang it—the dog is in the passenger seat. It's nearly as large as a wolf, but fluffier. Chuy, Carter had called him. The dog of a friend.

I reach past the dog and open the passenger-side door. "Get out," I tell him.

The dog just stares at me, his thick black tongue lolling out of his mouth.

"Get out," I say again. I move to give him a push, but he just nuzzles my arm. "I don't like dogs."

He looks up at me from under his eyebrows and makes a little whining noise—like he wants to stay with me. Like he's begging to do it. This is why I don't like dogs. I have trouble believing the truthfulness of anyone who claims to want my company.

But even when I give the dog a shove, he just shifts his weight and then settles back into the seat. Finally, I snarl, "Fine." I turn my attention back to the car. I start the engine and shift into drive before pushing my foot on the gas hard enough that the car lurches forward, momentum shutting the door on Chuy's side of the car. Beside me, Chuy lowers his chin to his paws and lies down.

Carter has plenty of options left to choose from and I've seen him hot-wire cars before. He'll be fine. Worst-case scenario, he has to stay at Genexome until I can return with Sebastian. That wouldn't be a bad thing.

CHAPTER THREE

CARTER

Moving a lot slower than Mel's vampire sprint, I followed her out to the Genexome parking lot, only to realize she'd stolen my ride. Which shouldn't have surprised me. My suggestion that she bite Lily and turn her into a vampire had freaked her out. Hell, it freaked me out.

As plan C's went, it was crap, but it was all I had. I just hoped to God I wouldn't have to use it.

Maybe, just maybe, plan B would be enough to save our asses. Plan B started with me going back to San Angelo, where a large chunk of the rebellion was trying to wrestle control of one of the Farms.

Hopefully, from the Farm in San Angelo, I could figure out where Lily's dad had taken her. I knew they'd been headed to a nearby Farm, but I didn't know which one. But the Farms had ways to communicate, and hopefully, once I reached San Angelo, I'd be able to figure out where the helicopter had gone. Once I knew where Lily was, I'd need to go get the cure from Sabrina. As much as I didn't want to drag anyone else into this mess, I wasn't stupid. I couldn't take on Sabrina all by myself. Not when Lily's fate and the fate of all humanity rested on my success. I needed backup.

I looked around, cursing. In the Before, Genexome had been

a sizable company—not huge, but certainly one of the major employers in this South Texas town. Unfortunately, it was one of the epicenters of the outbreak. The company, the grounds, the town, had all been hit hard by the Ticks. The upside was there were a lot of cars left in the lot.

Yeah, I know that sounds callous as hell, but once you've seen what I've seen, and done what I've done, you can't think about the people who are already gone. There's only enough room in your head to worry about the people who are still here. The people you can still save.

When I looked out at the parking lot, I didn't let myself think about the people who'd driven those cars. Instead it was: What can I hot-wire? What will have gas? What will get me to San Angelo? Fast.

At the far end of the parking lot was a long building so low to the ground I'd almost missed it. In this barren part of Texas, the featureless horizon and the dust have a way of messing with your perception. But that building, it almost looked like an airplane hangar. Or a private garage. Exactly the kind of place an eccentric vampire would store his collection of sports cars.

True, I didn't know whether or not Sebastian had a collection of sports cars, but if I was rich as hell and couldn't die, that's how I'd spend my money.

I took off at a jog toward the hangar, glancing at my watch as I did. Fifteen minutes and a couple of miles later, I stopped, panting, in front of the hangar. It was farther away than it had looked and a lot bigger, about as big as a football field. All four sets of bay doors on the structure were locked from the inside, but when I circled around back, I found an open window. Because Alpine was ground zero, there hadn't been enough humans around to loot it and Ticks didn't care about anything they couldn't eat.

I jumped up, caught the edge of the window, pulled myself through, and dropped down on the other side. Light drifted in from the windows on the bay doors and from skylights. Dust motes filled the air, giving each beam of sunlight tangible weight as it fell on the line of cars. There were seven in all, each looking fast and sleek. A Lotus. A Pontiac GTO. An Aston Martin. A couple I didn't even recognize. Any one of them would get me to San Angelo a hell of a lot faster than the crossover SUV Mel had taken. Then, glancing into the shadows at the far end of the hangar, I saw something even better. A pair of planes.

I walked down to that end. I ignored the bigger plane—a passenger jet that was way out of my league—to focus on the smaller one. A little single-engine Cessna Skyhawk.

Strictly speaking, I hadn't ever flown a plane. But I had spent two years at Elite Military Academy, which was owned and managed by Sebastian. We'd learned all kinds of crazy shit at Elite that probably should have tipped us off that it wasn't just an ordinary school. We'd learned mixed martial arts and how to pick locks. We'd learned battle tactics and strategy. And, in our free time, we'd logged hours in the academy's flight simulator.

Knowing what I knew now—that Sebastian had founded Elite because he was looking for an *abductura* and because he was building his own army—it seemed obvious that everything at the academy—every lesson, every course, every pastime— had been designed to equip the people in Sebastian's empire with the skills to survive and to protect him during the apocalypse. And if need be, to fly him around.

Because the plane I'd learned to fly in that flight simulator was a Cessna Skyhawk. And now I'd get to fly one for real.

I did a quick run-through of the preflight maintenance, opened the bay doors, and climbed inside the Cessna. Despite my fears, my doubts, my anxiety—despite all that, adrenaline pumped through my body. First time in the cockpit of a real plane. The layout of the instrument panel was exactly what I expected. I could do this.

I'd spent less time getting this puppy ready than it would have taken me to hot-wire a working car and I'd get to San Angelo in a third of the time—assuming I remembered how to navigate, which I was pretty sure I did.

They say you never forget your first flight, but mine wasn't filled with exhilaration and joy, but with nerves and desperation. I will say this: if I didn't survive the apocalypse long enough to fly again—when I could actually enjoy it—I was going to be pissed.

* *

I landed the plane—badly but safely—in the deserted airstrip outside San Angelo. I didn't have any trouble finding a car. When civilization had collapsed, everyone with a plane or money for a ticket had booked it, which meant airports were the easiest place to find cars and gas.

That was a tip I'd learned from Ely Estaban. Ely had gone to Elite also, but he hadn't joined the rebellion. Not really. He'd spent his time searching for his family and he'd been better at surviving on his own, outside the Farm system, than anyone else I'd ever met. That was why I'd trusted him to keep Lily and McKenna alive when they'd left the safety of base camp to search for a hospital where McKenna could have her baby.

I didn't bother doing anything to secure the plane once I

landed it at the small regional airport. I found an older Toyota that I was able to hot-wire easily enough. It only had a half a tank of gas, but that was more than enough to get me from the airstrip to the college. Even though I'd only been to San Angelo a couple of times, it wasn't hard to find a midsize college in a town that small. It wasn't until I was almost there that I thought about what I was going to say.

There's no easy way to return in defeat.

I left the Farm in San Angelo just two days ago, determined to save Lily and bring her back safely. Instead, she'd been exposed to the Tick virus. She'd practically been kidnapped by her own father. Oh, and the vampire who we'd all thought we could trust—the person who had been our greatest source of information—turned out to be a lying bastard.

I had no good news to bring back to San Angelo. Zip.

Having a plan helped, but I couldn't sugarcoat things. Not to people I liked and trusted.

Of course, that was assuming the good guys—my people— were still even in control of the Farm in San Angelo. I'd left to go get Lily and baby Josie thinking that I'd only be gone for six or seven hours. That had been two days ago. We'd just taken over the Farm when I left. For all I knew, while I was gone it had fallen back into the hands of the Collabs we'd wrestled it away from. In a perfect world, I could have used the satellite phone to call Zeke or Tech Taylor for a sitrep when I'd landed in San Angelo. But—no phone.

Have I mentioned how much I hate this crap?

It was close to dusk when I parked a block away from the campus behind a fast-food place and went in on foot, keeping in the shadows of the building until I was close enough to scan the fence line.

The good news was, the gates were still standing, and secondly, there was a security detail up in the guard tower. Moreover, the security detail was made up of a single beefy guy in a Collab uniform with a rifle and three other people, all wearing hoodies and carrying tranq rifles. The three people in hoodies were obviously Greens. They were thinner and smaller than the Collab and they held their tranq rifles with caution rather than arrogance.

The fact that they were on the security detail and had rifles to hold meant that the takeover at the Farm hadn't collapsed after I'd left. The fact that the security detail included a Collab and Greens meant things were going well enough that the two groups were actually working together. Which seemed like a friggin' miracle given how bad things had been at this Farm before we'd taken over.

I walked out into the open, hands raised and clearly visible. I made it to within a hundred feet before the Collab swung the rifle around and got me in his sights. I'd spent a lot of time in Farms over the past year. I'd spent time pretending to be a Collab so that I could help people escape and I'd spent time around weapons. Even from this distance, I was pretty damn sure that the weapon that Collab had trained on me was not a standard Farm-issued tranq rifle, but something much more powerful.

I stopped and waited. There wasn't much I could do. The Collab looked trigger-happy, and if he was even a halfway decent shot, I was a dead man.

Then one of the Greens in a hoodie placed a hand on the arm of the Collab. There was a short exchange, and finally the Collab lowered the rifle. The Green who'd been arguing in my favor waved me forward before dashing down the stairs for the gate.

I blew out a relieved breath as I jogged the rest of the distance to the gate.

I made it just as the Green was pushing back her hood. It was Dawn, the nurse from Elderton who had come down with me from Utah. Dawn wasn't actually a nurse. She'd been home on break from nurses' school when the Tick outbreak had happened. Still she knew a hell of a lot more about medicine than anyone else at Base Camp.

She threw open the gate to let me in. The second it closed behind me, she gave me a fast hug.

"Man, am I glad to see you!"

"Likewise."

I nodded in the direction of the guardhouse and the asshole Collab. "Things okay here?"

She pulled back. "Better than they were when we first arrived, but still . . . tense. As you can see. Everyone's been freaking out because we saw a plane."

"Oh. That was me." It hadn't occurred to me, but yeah, it would have been months since anyone had seen a plane. When martial law had been declared, all commercial air travel had been suspended. For a month or so after, you'd see a plane here and there, but since then, since things got really bad, there'd been nothing. I shrugged. "Sorry. I didn't think about it freaking people out."

"You're a pilot?"

"I am now."

She laughed at that, shaking her head. "Let's get you inside. I know Zeke and Joe want to talk to you."

I was sure they would. I just wish I had better news. Things here were tenuous. We obviously needed every good person we

21

had to keep things stable, but now I would be asking them to send at least two people with me, quite possibly on a fool's errand. On the other hand, if we succeeded, we'd save Lily. And possibly the human race.

Yeah. No pressure there.

CHAPTER FOUR

MEL

The last time I was here, I felt only rage and purpose. I had come to kill Roberto. I was focused and determined. I was in the grip of a vampire berserker frenzy. Here, in the middle of Roberto's territory, I'd been unable to control my natural hatred for other vampires. It wasn't aimed only at Roberto, but at Sebastian as well. It was a thing beyond mere anger. A thing beyond and apart from me.

It that state, I'd stabbed Sebastian. I'd rejoiced in doing it.

Now I need him alive. Will I be able to control my rage? Even for the cure? Even for my sister? Or will my new nature win out?

It had been less than twenty-four hours since I'd left El Corazon, but the time had taken its toll on the tiny village. El Corazon looked like a Victorian-era Texas county seat, with one massive building in the center of a town square and other businesses flanking the building on all four sides. Though, of course, it hadn't been the county seat, since it wasn't part of a county and wasn't on any maps. It was quaint and lovely if you could overlook the fact that it had been owned and run by a monster. And now it is overrun by the Ticks who flooded the town when the fences came down. They swarmed and they devoured all of Roberto's kine.

Here at El Corazon, the people who lived under the protection

23

of Roberto and Jonathan Price had believed completely that they were safe from the Ticks. They had stood by—protected—while other towns were ravaged, while countless lives were lost, while the government fell and major cities had been blasted to dust. They had been safe and they had believed they always would be because my father promised them that.

When the fences around the city came down, when the Ticks swarmed in, the citizens of El Corazon had been slaughtered wholesale. By the hundreds.

I couldn't help feeling like they'd deserved it.

But that didn't make the carnage at El Corazon any more palatable.

Ticks—mindless pack animals that they are—are efficient killers, but inefficient eaters. It's like their prefrontal cortex is just gone—or maybe cut off from the rest of the brain. They are incapable of logic or reasoning. They are driven only by the need to consume and the contradictory fear that they can't consume it fast enough. They don't drain the blood from a human the way a vampire does. They crack open the human's chest. They drink right from the heart itself. Bones shatter. Viscera spew.

They are greedy and wasteful. They don't eat. They gorge.

They leave the dead still twitching where they killed them. They move on to their next kill, eating until they can hardly move. When they've eaten their fill, they satisfy other needs. And then they sleep, huddled like dogs in whatever dark, warm place they can find.

Nature would never make a killer like this. And I know nature will not allow this killer to reign for long. A vampire could have lived indefinitely on a population this large. But the Ticks ate their way through it in less than a day. Far less, based on how badly the bodies are already decomposing.

This is the scene that awaits me when I return to El Corazon. I don't want anything sneaking up on me, so I park a couple blocks away from the square and walk in. I hope to get a sense of where the Ticks are—something I would never be able to do from the moving car.

When I climb out of the car, Chuy hops out after me. I point back to the front seat. "Stay."

He just looks at me.

"Whatever." Maybe I would be able to make him obey, but I have bigger things to worry about. "I don't like dogs," I remind him. "And if you lag behind, I'll leave you here."

He must understand, because he falls in step beside me, close enough that his fur brushes against the backs of my fingers as I walk. It's weirdly comforting, as I face the scene before me, the senseless death. The waste of precious resources. I don't mourn the people. They were their own kind of monsters. But I'm disgusted nevertheless.

Beside me, Chuy stops, his fur bristling, in the same moment my own internal warning bells go off. We are not alone.

Sebastian is still alive. I can hear his buzz in the air. Faint, low. Weak. But still there.

And of course there are the Ticks, too. They have not traveled on, even though they are out of food. They are too sated to bother moving. I work my way through town, stopping every once in a while to triangulate their position. They're in a house. Outside the square. Maybe more than one. It's still day, so they are sleeping. I can't get a sense of how many there are, which probably means there are too many for me to easily take on.

Which means I will try to deal with Sebastian first. The devil I know before the monsters I don't.

The stench of day-old blood churns my gut. I would retch,

but my stomach is empty. I haven't eaten since I killed the girl outside the Farm. Soon the air is thick with flies, and their buzzing drowns out the hum of the Ticks where they sleep. A block from the square and the buzz is like a roar in the air, overpowering even Sebastian's sounds.

I can only hope he is where I left him, pinned to the ground on the green by the gazebo. If he has managed to free himself and crawl away, I don't know how I'll find him.

I keep waiting for my vampire berserker rage to kick in. For the fury that dances along my nerves and lights my blood. I keep waiting for it to guide me to him, but it doesn't.

What if it's gone? What if he's gone?

I can't hear him anymore over the buzz of the flies. I can't feel his presence. No pulsing anger driving me to ferret him out. To stab him through the heart and rip him limb from limb. Not even a tingle of annoyance.

Is he dead?

In the time it's taken me to walk through El Corazon, has he died?

Something like grief hits me. How is that possible? How can I grieve for someone that I barely knew? How can I mourn him when I haven't even mourned the life I had before him?

My pace quickens. I run the last block, which is better anyway, because then I don't have to see the carnage and waste. I round a corner, nearly stumble on a body, but catch myself before I can fall and then I'm leaping over the patches of ground where the bodies are too thick to walk through. Did anyone in town make it? Anyone at all?

I slow down as I reach the center square, dread pulling at my feet. There on the green, beneath the sprawling live oak, I can see the two bodies. Roberto's petite and headless body is sprawled out. In life, he was as fragile and as lovely as an angel. Or maybe one of Tolkien's elves. Now he is headless and lifeless. I can't make myself look at him, knowing that when I die—someday in the distant future—this is how I will go.

It's Sebastian's body I've come to see or save if I can.

He is still there, as I somehow knew he would be, the stake I thrust through his heart pinning him to the ground. His eyes are closed, his always pale skin paler than pale, as white as the ghost I feel like I'm seeing.

This—apparently—is the limit of Chuy's friendliness. He stops maybe fifteen feet away, letting out a low, tense growl. "Stay," I tell him, and this time he listens. He lies down, submissive, but not relaxed, wiggling backward without taking his eyes from Sebastian's form.

Instinctively, I take a cue from Chuy, and move forward slowly, crouching down by his body, my eyes searching for that final proof that he is truly dead. I hear no music from him at all. No annoying buzz. He seems as lifeless as Roberto's headless corpse. And yet I can't believe that's true. How could Sebastian be dead?

I lay a palm on his motionless chest. It doesn't rise and fall with breath, but when I rock back onto my heels, his eyes are open. The gleam of life in them is dulled by pain and blood loss, but somehow he still lives.

Relief surges through me.

I didn't kill him. As much as I wanted to, I didn't. Somehow, through some miracle—if vampires can be granted miracles—he has survived.

I keep my hands on his chest and lean over to study him. It's almost as if I'm seeing him for the first time, not with the eyes of the autistic girl or the angry fledgling vampire, but with eyes made new. His pale skin is smeared with grime and blood and too hot to touch. The spark of his eyes is faded. And despite all that, the sight of him fills me up with something unfamiliar and so big it is almost uncomfortable, like it is squeezing out all the soft tissue of my body, making me both harder and more vulnerable.

"You're still here," I say softly. "You haven't taken out the stake."

He draws in a deep breath and I can almost hear the wheezing in his chest. "I was just getting around to it," he says. "But you see, it's ever so comfortable."

His gaze stays on mine long enough that I start to feel shaky. I don't know what to say. How to excuse what I've done. I don't know if he's glad to see me or angry at me and simply too weak to kick my ass. With his normal strength, he could easily dominate me. I would never have been able to stab him at all if he hadn't been distracted and drained by his fight with Roberto.

Not sure what to do, I lean closer and say the only thing that comes to mind. "I don't want to kill you."

His lips twist in that familiar sardonic smile. "Then you probably shouldn't have stabbed me through the heart."

I frown as it takes me a second to get his point. "No," I say. "I mean I don't want to kill you now."

"I know. I was"—he pauses and sucks in a pain-laced breath—"just teasing you, Melly."

"Why?" I ask.

"Because you're fun to tease."

I nearly smile at that and can't help wondering when the last time was that I did smile. Certainly not since I've turned. And only rarely before. Music made me smile, back when I was Mel, but since then? Nothing until now.

"No," I say gently. "I should want to kill you, shouldn't I?"

He quirks an eyebrow. "Because I lied to you about Roberto?"

"Because of the vampire berserker rage. I wanted to kill Roberto. I wanted to kill you before. Why don't I want to kill you now?"

His shoulder twitches, almost like he's thinking about shrugging, but it must send a bolt of pain through his body, because he writhes with it. After sucking in several deep breaths, he says, "Well, off the top of my head, I'd say it might be because I'm an inch from death."

I lean a little closer. "Does it work that way?"

"I don't know. First time I've been staked." His lips twist again, but it looks more like a grimace than a smirk. "Let's take the stake out and we'll see, shall we?"

I look then at his hands. His fingertips are scratched and bloody from trying to get the stake out. I realize now that the stake did not just go through his heart, it went deep into the ground. How much force must I have used when I did that? How much hatred had fueled that single action? How much anger?

I have many reasons to free Sebastian now. He's the only one who can get us into the underground storage where the cure is stockpiled. He is the only living expert on the Tick virus. He may have been the one to engineer humanity's downfall, but he is also the one who could save it. He has it in his power to save Lily. To keep her from turning into a monster even more horrible than I.

Yet despite all those very good reasons, I fear the real reason I want to save him is more personal. In the end, it doesn't matter why I save him. All that matters is that I do. That I succeed.

But first, we have to get out of here. Fast. I'll worry about his wound later. For now, I need to get him off the ground. I can't bandage him here, not when there are Ticks sleeping nearby.

I crouch back down beside him. "I'm going to try to move you."

He meets my gaze, but his eyes are foggy. "You know, it would be much easier, my dear, if you would just finish the job you started and kill me. I understand Roberto had quite the weapons collection. I'm sure he won't mind now if you borrow a nice katana."

"Shut up," I mutter, trying to think of options.

"Do it quickly," he murmurs, his voice almost seductive. "This can all be over soon."

"Too bad. I need you alive. To help me get the cure for the Tick virus."

He almost smiles. "Ah, it's good to be wanted."

I lean over him again and wrap my hands around the head of the stake. I hadn't looked at it before, but I do now. It has a rounded top and intricate carvings on the sides that bite sharply into my hand when I grasp it. I remember the anger. The blunt-edged fury that drove me to it. More importantly, I remember the reasons.

Sebastian carefully molded me into the perfect assassin. He trained me to kill. He fed my need to seek revenge. He convinced me that I was the only one—the only person in the world—who could kill Roberto.

And I had bought it all. I had believed completely that killing Roberto was my destiny. That it was my gift.

However, when I'd arrived at El Corazon, nothing had been as I'd expected. By the time Sebastian had showed up to stage his own assassination, I'd realized the depths of his betrayal.

I know the truth now. I had only been a decoy. A distraction. There's nothing unique about me. I have no special destiny.

There's another truth I know. Sebastian will do anything to get what he wants. He will tell any lie. He will trick any fool.

I have no interest in being his fool again and I don't know which of his lies to believe. I can't trust him, but I need him. Alive and conscious.

I grab the stake and give a sharp tug, wrenching it free from his chest and from the blood-soaked ground beneath him.

He lets out a sound that starts as a gasp and ends as a scream. A sound that makes the hairs on the back of my neck spike with fear and makes Chuy whimper in distress. It's the sound of death and agony. It's the sound of torture. His whole body bucks off the ground.

His scream fades into echoes, yet there I stand, leaning over him, watching him draw in shuddering painful breaths. Watching what's left of his blood pulse out of his body.

I reach out a hand and he takes it in his own. His hand barely has the strength to grasp mine. His skin is so cold he might as well be a corpse. He's visibly shaking as he struggles to stand and I feel a burst of regret. He's wounded and now that I've pulled out the stake, he's dying more quickly. And I'm about to stab him in the back. Literally.

"I'm sorry," I say.

Still holding his hand in mine, I plunge the stake back into the hole I'd pulled it out of.

CHAPTER FIVE

CARTER

"Is Josie okay?" I asked as Dawn led me across campus to the Dean's office.

"She's fine." Dawn's expression went all gooey as she said it. "We found infant formula in the storage center. Lily was right. The Farms were well equipped to care for babies."

Before I could ask any more questions, Dawn showed me into the office, giving me one last worried look as she shut the door behind her.

Joe and Zeke were both waiting for me in what had once been the Dean's office. Joe had always seemed like an old soul. Even though he was about my age, he'd always seemed wise. And I trusted him. That was important. I'd only known Zeke a handful of days, but we'd traveled across the country together to pull off a risky as hell coup at this Farm. So even though I didn't know him well, I knew he was as determined as I was to stay in the fight. And that counted for a lot, too.

Since neither was much for bullshit and we didn't have time for that anyway, as soon as the greetings were out of the way, I launched right into sharing the bad news about Sebastian's betrayal. "I'm not going to sugarcoat this. We're up shit creek. This betrayal didn't help, but—"

Before I could continue, Zeke held out his hands. "Look, I know it sucks, but I didn't know what else to do with him. Joe wanted to just leave him outside."

"Yeah," Joe said belligerently. "After what he did—"

"Wait." Now I held out my hand. "What are you talking about?"

For a second we all just stood there, staring at one another as it sank in that we were having two different conversations.

"What are you talking about?" Joe asked. "Why are we up shit creek?"

"Sebastian lied to us. Roberto didn't have the cure. In fact, Roberto didn't create the Tick virus. Sebastian did."

Zeke just sort of shrugged. He'd never met Sebastian, but Joe had known him, had fought side by side with him. He ducked his head, shaking it slowly. "Dude, I'm sorry. And Lily?"

"She's with—" I hesitated before mentioning her father. Yeah, my own dad was no prize, what with the general disinterest interrupted by the occasional beatings, but at least he'd never helped launch the apocalypse. If Jonathan Price was my dad, I wasn't sure I'd want my friends knowing. So instead of mentioning him, I said, "The doctors at El Corazon induced a coma to slow the progression of the disease. Then the doctor took her and some of the other patients to one of the nearby Farms. It bought us some time to find a cure."

"But there is a cure?" Zeke asked, a note of awe in his voice.

I nodded. It wasn't that I wanted to lie to them, I just still wasn't ready to consider any other possibility.

"What were *you* talking about?" I asked.

Zeke and Joe exchanged a look. Finally Zeke cleared his throat and admitted, "Ely showed up yesterday afternoon. Joe wanted to leave him outside the fence. I had him brought in and locked up."

For a second, I couldn't even think. My vision tunneled as my blood pressure spiked. Ely was here?

How the hell had that happened? Ely had kidnapped Lily. He'd tried to abandon baby Josie in the desert and turn Lily over to Roberto. Lily—being Lily—had fought back and had won. The last anyone had heard from him, he'd been left in the desert with a gun and a single bullet. So how the hell had he survived?

But, of course, I knew the answer to that question. When it came to staying alive on his own, Ely was the best there was. Besides, he was too much of an asshole to die.

"Where's he being kept?"

"Now wait a second," Zeke said, palms out again, in a placating gesture.

I turned to Joe. "Where is he being kept?"

"In a copier room, just down the hall."

I didn't need Zeke to tell me which room Ely was in. There was only one room with two guards standing outside of it. They were guys I didn't know and had never seen before, but either they knew who I was or they were too scared to get in my way, because they stepped aside and let me pass.

The mammoth copier sat silent in one corner. Cabinets lined three walls. Boxes of paper reams lined the other. There was no furniture, but Ely had stacked a couple of boxes near the copier and he was sitting on them, legs sprawled in front of him, head tipped back.

Some tiny part of me knew that I had to be logical about this, but when I saw him—in that split second that I first laid eyes on him—there was nothing in my brain except Lily. The fear in her voice when she'd first called to tell me he was working for Roberto, that he'd tranqed her and left baby Josie to die. The quiet desperation after she'd been exposed to the virus. The way her voice quavered when she asked me to kill her. To make it quick. Because she didn't want to become a monster.

What the hell was I supposed to do with that?

My girl, asking me to kill her quickly, because of this guy. How was I supposed to be logical?

Ely barely opened an eye in the time it took me to get across the room and haul his ass to his feet. I whirled him around and slammed his back into the wall and held him there.

In that instant, logic didn't matter. None of it mattered. Because Lily was sick. Lily was dying. Maybe lost forever. Because of this guy. This worthless sack of shit. This traitor who was supposed to keep her safe and didn't.

I hauled back and punched him square in the jaw just once, then dragged him back up. There was nothing I couldn't do to this guy that wouldn't be fair. That wouldn't be reasonable. I wanted to take him apart. Every instinct I had yelled at me to destroy him.

Instead, I just held him there, seething for a moment before I could even speak.

"I am going to kill you," I said slowly. He made a strangled choking sound, but didn't struggle to get free. He was shorter than I was, stockier, and I held him dangling several inches off the floor. "I am going to tear you apart with my bare hands. Whatever Roberto threatened you with to coerce you into betraying us, I will do worse." Then I let go of him and he crumpled. "But I'm not going to do it today."

He sat sprawled on the ground and brought his thumb up to wipe away a single drop of blood. "Why not just kill me now?"

"Because I'm going to go save Lily's life and I don't have time for you."

And with that, I turned and walked away. I would make him pay, but not right now. Now I had more important things to do.

CHAPTER SIX

MEL

Sebastian writhes in agony as I thrust the stake back into his heart. I've killed him again, in hopes of saving him.

"I'm sorry," I whisper once more. He's deadweight against me and I struggle to get my arms around him. I heft him up so he's leaning on me and his face is inches from mine. "You're bleeding too much."

"So you stabbed me again?" he gasps out.

"We have to get out of here. I don't have time to bandage your wounds here. We have to get out of here before the Ticks wake up and—"

I break off when I hear a desperate howl rend the air. From behind me, Chuy lets out a panicked yelp. I glance over my shoulder. He has stayed precisely where I told him to, but he's standing now, tense and poised to attack, staring off into the distance.

Sebastian nods toward the town. "Those Ticks?"

I turn and look out across the green. In the half-light of dusk, dark shapes loom at the edge of the square. Hulking, clumsy shapes. And they're moving toward us.

The Ticks. Those lazy, sleeping beasts I was sure were too blood drunk to notice my arrival. Sebastian's screams have woken them and they are clearly not morning people. Or dusk people as the case may be.

My gaze scans the town square. A dozen. No, two dozen. Maybe more. Chuy clacks his teeth together, too nervous to be still.

"You think we can take them?" I ask.

Sebastian laughs. "Ah, I have missed your wide-eyed optimism, dear Kit."

"I've seen you take out a dozen Ticks."

"I'm humbled by your high opinion of me, but I'm not prepared to die for your stupidity."

"But—"

"I can fight a dozen Ticks when I'm well fed and healthy. And you, my dear, are no me."

"Okay," I snap, because I know he's right. "What do you want to do? Just stand here and wait for them to come eat us for dessert?"

Sebastian looks around. All I see are more Ticks. Yeah. We're definitely in trouble here.

Our only clear way out of the square is to go back toward Roberto's house.

"Retreat?" I ask.

"Ladies first."

I wedge my shoulder under his arm and pull him against me. "Come on, Chuy," I mutter, and the dog leaps to my side. Together, we turn and run.

CHAPTER SEVEN

CARTER

Joe was waiting for me in the hall outside the copier room.

"That's it?" he asked. "You just threatened him and walked away."

I hadn't seen Joe when I'd been in the room with Ely, but I guess he'd been listening. That didn't surprise me nearly as much as the vehemence in his voice. "Yeah. That's it. For now."

"He doesn't get any kind of punishment?"

Once I'd made it back into the Dean's office, I turned to look at Joe. The guy wasn't that much older than me. Maybe a year at most, which put him at around nineteen years old, but he looked much older. Older even than he had looked just a few days ago. Losing McKenna—the girl he'd loved and the mother of his child—had done that to him.

Did I look older, too? Jesus, I sure as hell felt older.

"I swear to you, I will make him pay. For what he did to Lily. For what he did to Josie. He will pay. But until I've rescued Lily, until I've found the cure, revenge is going to have to wait."

Joe looked like he wanted to argue, but after a solid minute of clenching and unclenching his fists, he nodded. I exhaled in relief. Joe was a lot of things, but he sure as hell wasn't a killer. "Okay. Then what's next?"

"You have a map of Texas? We need to see where all the

Farms are. We need to figure out where the helicopter might have gone."

Zeke paused in the act of rummaging through a drawer in a desk. "You don't know?"

"Things were . . . a bit confusing when we left El Corazon." The fences had collapsed. Ticks were swarming onto the property. Lily's dad had loaded her and a bunch of other Ticks-in-comas into the helicopter. They'd just gone. "I know the general plan: get to another Farm, but there hadn't exactly been time to submit a flight plan."

Zeke finally found a map and shoved some stuff aside to unfold it onto the desktop. We all bent over the map. I grabbed a pen and drew a big X just north of San Saba. "Here's were El Corazon is. Roughly."

Zeke, the only one of us who'd been a Collab and had actually worked in the Farm system, added circles around Dallas, Austin, College Station, Waco, San Marcos, and Abilene. I leaned over and added a circle at Georgetown just north of Austin and then a few in San Antonio. I'd been in and out of most of the Farms in Texas as part of the rebellion, trying to help people escape and looking for Lily. There were a hell of a lot of Farms in Texas. It had taken me six months to find and rescue her last time. How much longer would it take this time? What if her father went back on his word and tried to hide her from me?

I looked up at Zeke. "I assume you have some sort of directory of all the Farms? The Dean must have had the numbers of their satellite phones. We'll need to find that list and—"

"If the Dean had a sat phone, he guarded it closely and took it with him. And as far as we can tell, it wasn't used for the day-to-day stuff," Zeke said. "But we have a ham radio."

I frowned. I should have thought of that. Operating a ham radio had been one of the many obscure skills I'd learned at Elite, but we'd only spent a couple of days on it. But if the Farms all had ham radios . . .

"Who's operating the radio at this Farm? Is the room secure?" Because if there was some Collab here who was sending messages to the other Farms, by now the guy could have told every Farm within a hundred miles that the rebellion had taken over here. Then our problems might be a hell of a lot worse.

"We secured the room right after you left to go get Lily," Zeke told me. "I didn't even know about the radios until after you'd left. Apparently the Dean didn't want us talking to other Farms and comparing notes."

That made sense. The entire Farm system was built on isolating people and controlling them with fear. "If you take me to the radio room, I might be able to figure it out. If not, we get Tech Taylor in here to help. I'm sure he remembers more about the radios than I do."

"No need," Zeke said, gesturing for me to follow him down the hall. "The Collab who was operating the radio is still here. Joe thought it was better to have someone at the radio. That way if one of the other Farms tried to contact this one, there'd be someone to answer."

Zeke led me past the reception area outside the Dean's office and down a narrow hallway to the radio room. Desks set up with several computers lined one wall. On the back wall, by the windows, were a pair of chunky-looking radios. An old-fashioned typewriter sat in front of the radio. A girl leaned against the counter picking at her nail polish.

I stopped short at the door. "You're the Collab?" Every Collab

I'd ever met had been a guy, and they were all brute force and muscle. It hadn't occurred to me that there might be female Collabs, too.

Her lips curved down at the term and her gaze darted warily to Zeke, who stood just behind me. "Who's this guy?" she asked.

"He needs to talk to some of the other Farms. Maybe even without the Deans of those Farms finding out. You think we can do that?"

Zeke was right. The quieter we kept this, the better. I stepped farther into the room. "Actually, I can probably figure out how to use the radio myself."

The girl stepped up to me, waving a hand in my face. "Whoa, whoa, whoa. Stop right there. This is my radio room. You have any idea how long it took me to learn to use all this equipment?"

"But I can—"

"You want to send a message, it goes through me."

I glanced at Zeke. "You sure we can trust her?"

She answered before he could. "You think I don't know that the Dean abandoned this Farm and everyone in it? You think I don't know we'd all be toast if you guys hadn't gotten here to keep the electric fences up? Yeah. You can trust me."

I guess that was the good thing about Collabs—they would always act in their own best interest. "Okay," I said. "What's your name?"

"Charla."

"Okay, Charla, here's the deal." Then I summed up what I needed her to do.

Only a few seconds in, she was frowning. Again she stopped me with a wave of her hand. "I don't know if it's the helicopter you're looking for or not, but an SOS went out yesterday about a helicopter crash."

My stomach dropped through the floor. "What helicopter?"

She moved toward me. "Are you okay?"

Shoving a hand through my hair, I tried to slow my racing thoughts. "Tell me about the helicopter."

"They had some kind of engine problem. They had crashed."

"Where?"

"I don't know."

"There's no way to tell where the message came from?"

"No. He said they were fifty miles from a Farm, but I don't think it was this one, because he sounded farther away than that."

"You can hear how far away someone is?"

"The radios only transmit within line of sight. Then there are repeater stations set up at intervals between the Farms. There's a slight degradation of the signal every time it repeats. The farther away they are, the more static you hear."

"But there's no way to tell for sure how far away it was?"

She shook her head, dropping her gaze.

Great. Well, that effing narrowed it down, didn't it?

"It might not have been the helicopter you're looking for," Zeke said.

Yeah, I knew he was right, but I also knew statistics weren't on our side in this one. "You seen many other helicopters zipping around the state in the past six months?" There was a moment of dead, awful silence in the room. "Yeah," I said. "Me neither."

Shit.

Lily's helicopter had gone down. With her in it. She could be dead already.

Almost without realizing it, I dropped my hands to my knees and bent over, struggling to suck air into my lungs as panic clutched me.

Everything I'd done, and I could have lost her to this, an accident. God damn it!

The freakin' apocalypse happens and takes out seventy, maybe eighty percent of the entire population. And the one person I really care about somehow survives. And I actually manage to find her. We get a couple of months together before the world starts ripping us apart again. Then she's exposed to the Tick virus, but at least there was still hope. But now?

Jesus, if her helicopter crashed . . .

How the hell was I supposed to keep hoping?

I really was going to kill Ely, because she never would have been on that helicopter if it wasn't for him. If it wasn't for him, she'd be safely back at Base Camp. If it wasn't for him, she'd be . . .

I sucked in another breath.

No. I couldn't think like this. Not while there was still a chance. I pushed myself up to see Charla and Zeke exchanging worried looks. "The message that went out, was it an automated SOS? Something the helicopter would have sent out on its own?"

"No, it was from a person. A guy named Jonathan Price."

I scrubbed my hands up and down my face. So definitely Lily's helicopter. But if he'd survived long enough to send the message, then maybe she had, too.

"When did it happen?"

"I don't—"

"How long ago did the message come through?"

She lowered her gaze again before answering. "Maybe twelve hours ago."

"Are the messages recorded?"

She shook her head.

The helicopter had left El Corazon just a few minutes before

Mel and I had pulled out. That had been just about thirty hours ago. They should have reached the closest Farm within a couple of hours at most. Instead, they'd crashed. There had been a doctor and a pilot, as well as four people who'd been exposed to the Tick virus and were sedated to slow its progress. Jonathan wasn't the type of guy to do a lot of heavy lifting. If he'd put out the distress call, it meant there was no one else to do it. Which meant the helicopter had gone down and there'd been . . . ah, shit . . . at least twelve to sixteen hours where he'd been too out of it to send out a call.

None of this sounded good. At all.

Even if Lily was still alive, those intravenous meds she'd been getting on a drip, those probably hadn't survived the crash. Which meant she wouldn't be sedated anymore. Which meant the Tick virus would continue to progress. And she'd turn into a Tick. Within the next couple of days.

And again, that was if she hadn't died in the crash.

My time line for getting to Sabrina's had just gotten a hell of a lot shorter.

CHAPTER EIGHT

LILY

I wake to pain. That dull achiness from a virus. The chills. So strong I can't stop shaking long enough to ask Mom for a blanket. Or to move me somewhere more comfortable. A strange dizziness that makes the sky above me seem to shift and buckle. A weird scratching, scuffling sound, too. Loud and close and somehow soothing. Despite the pain, I close my eyes and sleep again.

It's harder next time, to drift away again. But I do. I slip in and out with the pain and the scuffling and the jabbing, scratching at my back and the bending, shifting sky overhead. It doesn't stop.

Until suddenly it does.

Then I'm out.

Next time I wake up, the sky above has stopped moving. Why am I outside?

The pounding in my skull and the chills racking my body tell me I'm sick. Very sick. But why am I outside?

Where am I? Outside, yes, but outside where? Not home, where the lawn service keeps our St. Augustine crisp and green. The grass here is patchy and wild, like we used to see by the side of the road on long drives. The dirt is the dull red-brown of Texas clay. I'm far from home. Far from the city.

I twist my head to look around, stopping—not because of the pain—because there's a man near me.

Not just a man. My father.

My father?

That can't be right.

I haven't seen him in years. In almost eight years. But it's him.

He's sitting, leaning against the trunk of a scrub oak. His head tipped back and his eyes closed. Is he dead? Then I see his chest rise and fall with a shuddering, pained breath.

Still, I can't reconcile what I know of my father with the image before me. His hair is graying at the temples and the lines of his face are sagging with age and exhaustion. There's a bloody gash from his right temple to his cheekbone and another, shorter one by his mouth. One of the sleeves of his shirt is missing. The rest of the white oxford cloth is dusty and he has sweat stains under his arms. The last I heard, my father was working at some kind of brain trust in southwest Texas. He was rich and successful and totally not interested in me. What the hell's happened to him? What's happened to me?

I reach out a hand and try to speak, but the sound comes out as a garbled croak.

His eyes flicker open. "Lily," he says on a groan thick with pain.

"Daddy?" This time it comes out clearer. Tears burn my eyes, because I haven't seen him in so long. And I'm in so much pain. All I want is for him to pull me into his arms like he used to when I was child. I want his strength. His warmth. Oh God, his warmth. "So cold," I gasp out.

He pushes away from the tree. Leveraging his weight with his hands, he pulls himself along the ground toward me. That's when I see his leg. He's dragging it uselessly behind him. Something dark brown is tied around his thigh and there's an odd lump under the bulge. No. Not brown. Dark red. And the lump isn't just a lump. It's a compound break. The lump is his bone. The brown fabric is his once-white sleeve drenched in blood.

My stomach flips over and I manage to turn my head to the side before I puke all over the ground.

There's not much in my stomach, but after I empty it, I feel . . . not better. Steadier.

This foggy feeling, the nausea. It all seems familiar. I push myself to my hands and knees and crawl to my father's side. His eyes are closed now, his breathing so shallow I worry again that he's dead. A moment later, his eyes flicker open. He reaches a hand toward my face, but it's icy cold. Again I'm hit with a feeling of déjà vu, but I shake it off. He's lost too much blood. Even knowing nothing else, I know that.

How do I know that?

What happened?

A car crash? But I don't see a car. And why was I with my father? I haven't seen him in years. Or have I?

A memory flashes through my mind of a sterile white room. And Mel was there, looking hyperalert and talking about mice. In rhymes. She hasn't talked in rhymes since . . . I can't remember.

But I get another flash of memory. Mel saying, "Red rover, red rover, let Carter come over."

Carter?

Carter Olson?

"What happened?" I mutter aloud.

My father's too-cold fingertips brush my cheek. "So sorry. I tried."

"What?" I demand, but my voice sounds suddenly harsh. "What did you try to do?"

"To keep you safe. At the Farm. You were supposed to be safe from the Ticks there. Top priority."

And then I get a blast of memories. The Tick outbreak. The virus that mutated people into unstoppable killing monsters. The Farm. Where Mel and I were supposed to be safe, but where we lived in fear and "donated" blood to keep the monsters away. Leaving the Farm, escaping with Carter Olson. And a vampire. Mel nearly dying. Being bitten by Sebastian. Turned into a vampire herself.

I am bombarded by image after image. The terror. The fighting. The camp in Utah where the resistance was. Sleeping curled up against the warmth of Carter's chest. My friend McKenna, dying. Her cold hands handing me her baby. Being shot with a tranquilizer gun.

That's why this feels familiar. Why I feel woozy and lightheaded. Why I puked. Because I'm coming out of sedation. And it's why I have so many patches missing from my memories. Why I'm so confused.

But I still don't remember why my father is here.

We must have gone to the brain trust. We must have thought it was going to be safe, except . . .

No. It wasn't a brain trust. It was Roberto's ranch. My father didn't work for some think tank. He worked for Roberto, the vampire who spread the Tick virus. As fuzzy as my brain is— still struggling to piece together the hours before I ended up here—I do know this: Roberto is evil. The enemy. And my father—*my father*—worked for him. My father helped bring down all of civilization.

I stumble back from him. "Roberto," I gasp out. "You work for Roberto."

"Yes," he says simply, his eyes closing.

"You left us. You left Mom and Mel and me to go work for that monster!"

I know the way I'm saying it is wrong. That somehow I'm equating the leaving and the working for Roberto. As if the sins are equal, when they aren't. And yet, they are related because as much as I've hated my father for leaving, I could forgive it when I thought he'd left to go try to save the world. Then it seemed almost noble. But this? This was monstrous in a way I could barely fathom.

His eyes flutter open weakly and he gazes at me with something almost like fondness. "You don't understand."

"You're right. I don't. I will never understand how you could be part of Roberto's plans."

"You will someday." Weak fingers reach for my hand and clutch it. "Someday your own powers will blossom. You'll become an *abductura*, then you'll know what it's like. Maybe you'll even take my place with Roberto. You'll see the brilliance of his vision."

I wrench my hand from him. "I am not an *abductura*. That's Mel. And she's not one either now. She's a vampire. And we would never follow in your footsteps."

But the words stumble as they leave my mouth. Because there's something there that set off warning bells. Something about Mel being a vampire. Because if she has the gene to become a vampire, that means . . .

And that's when the big missing puzzle piece drops out of the sky and hits me square in the chest. The Tick virus.

I was stabbed in the foot with an arrow covered in the blood of a Tick.

I have the virus.

That's why I was tranqed. To slow down the spread of the

virus until Carter could get to the cure. But something must have gone horribly wrong. Because I'm not in some hospital on Roberto's ranch. I'm in the middle of nowhere. With my father, who is wounded.

What the hell happened?

I don't realize at first that I must have asked the question aloud, because my father's eyes open again.

"The helicopter went down," he chokes out.

"What helicopter?" I demand.

He frowns. "You don't remember?"

Anger edges out my fear. "Why were we in a helicopter? Why was I even with you?"

"Your boyfriend . . ."

"Carter?"

"He thought we had the cure. Brought you to me. But the Ticks breached the fence. We left in a helicopter. Going to a Farm."

But the helicopter went down.

I wait for another flash of memory, being on the ranch. Getting in the helicopter. Anything. But all I have is being in the white room. "Mel? Carter?" I ask.

"They were leaving together. To try to find the cure. They were supposed to meet us at the Farm." His eyes roll back in his head for an instant and I think I've lost him again, but then he forces them open. He grabs my arm with surprising strength, forcing me to look at him. "We've got to get out of here."

"I know," I say. "I'll get you to the Farm. There'll be a doctor or something."

"No." He's shaking his head, but I don't know if it's because he thinks I'm wrong, or if he disagrees. "Have to get away. From the others."

"Others? What others?"

"The other Ticks. On the helicopter. There were four of you."

"Four? Four of me?" He's shaking his head again and I realize that this is just my brain being sluggish. Not four of *me*. Four people who'd been exposed to the virus.

"The others haven't woken up yet. They were sedated longer than you. But they'll wake up soon." He clutches my arm again. The strain of talking is wearing on him. Blood pools in the corners of his mouth. His lips are bright red with it and the rich, coppery scent of it drifts up to me. The blood is beautiful against his too-pale, too-cold skin. I'm so distracted by it I almost miss his next words. "Men like that. They'll probably have immersion delirium, too. They'll be mindlessly violent. That's before they turn into Ticks."

Turn into Ticks.

And that's what I'll be, too.

I will be a Tick.

I'm transforming already. The chills. The aches. They are signs of my body morphing into something else. The sudden fascination with my father's blood.

Oh God.

Oh God.

It's happening already.

I push my father off my lap and scramble away. I have to stop this. I have to.

But how?

I scuttle back to him, almost as fast. "You can't let this happen. You have to kill me. Do it now."

He shakes his head. "No. It's okay. You'll be fine. You just have to get us to the Farm."

"To a Farm?"

52

"They'll protect you. Put you back under. Until the cure."

I rear up and look around. If there is a Farm nearby, I don't see it.

If I knew where it was, could I get there in time? Would they really take me in? The Farms feed the Ticks, but they keep them out. They don't lure them in and protect them. I can't go to a Farm. And I don't even trust them to kill me, because that's not what they do. The Farm system is about controlling the Ticks, not eradicating them.

No. I have to find a way to kill myself. I have to do it before I become a mindless, conscienceless monster.

CHAPTER NINE

MEL

Roberto's house is a Victorian mansion by way of the Addams Family. It's three stories of Gothic gingerbread and frilly wrought iron. It is not a fortress you can hole up in to protect yourself from an angry mob of monsters.

I haul Sebastian up the steps and through the front door, which had been left open during the battle that had happened here the previous day.

"Do you think there are already Ticks in the house?" I ask, almost hesitant to close the door behind me. I *so* don't want to lock myself in with the monsters.

The question is rhetorical, since I'm not sure Sebastian is capable of answering.

I look around the house as I shut the door behind us. There can't possibly be more Ticks inside the house than there are outside it. I glance down at Chuy, who is sniffing the air but not freaking out. To my left is Roberto's "study," where he kept a creepy collection of vampire assassination tools—those I'll pilfer later. For now, I need a place to stash Sebastian while I secure the house. To my right is an elegant living room with—thank God—a sofa and a fireplace, which might prove useful if we live long enough for me to tend to Sebastian's wounds.

I hobble with him into the living room and dump him on the

camelback sofa, too worried about the monsters on the outside to take care of the monster inside. I run back to the door,
Chuy by my side, throwing the dead bolts—there are several. Chuy and I dash through the rest of the first floor. I check
doors and windows, watching him for signs there might be
something hiding that even I can't sense. We check the second
and third floors just to be sure there aren't Ticks nesting somewhere, and I grab a first-aid kit out of one of the bathrooms. A
set of sheets I can tear into bandages. And towels. I bring lots of
towels.

Back on the first floor, Chuy prowls around a little before
settling just inside the front door, waiting. Sebastian looks even
worse than before. Maybe it's the loss of blood, but his skin is
gray. His breathing is shallow and labored. And it hits me—I
could lose him. He could die. Right here.

After all we've been through, after every horrible thing he's
done and I've done, I could lose him.

I'd panic, but there's no time for that. Instead I race through
what needs to be done in my mind: get the stake out, clean him
up, bandage him up, and then feed him. Exactly what I'm supposed to feed him, I don't know. I'll worry about that if he lives
long enough.

I dash back to the kitchen—ignoring the pots big enough to
boil body parts and a terrifying array of food processors. I look
for the basics: soap, more towels, water. But the water must run
on an electric pump, because it doesn't come on. And there's tons
of dish soap—probably for washing all those food processors—
but not a simple bar of soap.

Panic edges into my thinking, moving me faster. Okay. No
soap. No water. Then how do I clean a wound?

My mind races back to the Before and lands on some old TV

show. A western, I think. Where they cleaned a wound with alcohol. I throw open the cabinets and start searching. I don't know if vampires even drink alcohol. I hope so. A couple of cabinets in, I hit pay dirt. Big-time. I'm guessing this stash had belonged to Roberto's valet. If I'd been the human responsible for disposing of Roberto's victims, I'd need to drink a lot, too.

Back in the living room, Sebastian doesn't look any better. His eyes flutter open. "Took you long enough."

I kneel beside the sofa. "What? No sarcastic quip?"

"Quipping takes too much energy."

"I'll try to hold up the conversation for both of us, okay?" I say as I unbutton the front of his shirt. I peel back the right side, but hesitate on the left. The stake went through his shirt, which undoubtedly means there are bits of fabric deep within his heart. Fabric that he'd been wearing for who knew how many days. And who knew how clean it had been when he'd put it on. I think of the bacteria and panic starts to creep back in. Pushing it down, I focus on how to get his shirt off instead of why I need to.

I'll have to slip the shirt off his right arm and around his back, leaving it pinned to his front until I pull the stake out.

"Cuffs," Sebastian gasps out.

"What?"

He raises a hand weakly. "You haven't undone my cuffs."

I feel myself blushing as I realize my mistake, because I wouldn't have been able to get his shirt off at all. I'm helpless at this. I quickly undo one and I'm undoing the other when his fingers grasp mine until I look him in the eyes.

"Whatever it is you're so worried about," he says softly, "it'll be okay. Just get the stake out and feed me. I'll be fine."

There's such confidence there. Such faith.

No one has ever had confidence in me before. No one has

ever trusted me to handle things. As much as I want to argue with him, to warn him about my incompetence and the bacteria, this time I really do put them out of my mind and I just move. Quickly.

I undo the cuff on the other side and raise him enough to get the shirt off and to put a towel down underneath him. I don't let myself look at the smear of thick blood that's pooled under his body. I pull out the stake, careful to tug the fabric with it. The remains of his shirt and the stake both go onto one of the towels. Then I open up the bottle of scotch and upend the bottle over his chest.

When the scotch hits the hole in his chest, Sebastian loses it. He bucks off the sofa, his arms flailing. He knocks the bottle out of my hands and scotch sprays across the room. I go flying back, but bounce quickly onto my feet. I have another bottle open and ready. I lunge for him, ready to pin him down and go again.

But he's got his feet under him now and stumbles back. "What the hell?"

I hold up a hand to pacify him. Chuy has come to stand in the doorway, hackles raised, like he's ready to throw himself on Sebastian. "Calm down," I say, to both of them. To all of us.

"I'll calm down when you put down the bottle."

"I'm cleaning the wound."

"You're . . . ? What the fuck? By pouring scotch into my heart?" He brings a hand up to his chest as if feeling for the stake.

I lunge for him. "Stop touching it! You're only going to make it worse!"

"Make what worse? You staked me and now you're poisoning me. It doesn't get worse!"

"Okay. I'm putting down the bottle. Just . . . just sit, okay?"

He eyes me suspiciously, swaying. He's vertical, but just barely.

"I was trying to clean the wound," I say, trying again to persuade him to sit before he passes out or Chuy attacks. Though maybe passing out would make him easier to deal with. "Look, alcohol kills bacteria, right? I don't want you to get an infection."

He just stares at me like I'm speaking nonsense. Then he laughs, which must hurt, because he has to put a hand on the sofa back to brace himself. Clearly laughing and standing at the same time is impossible, so he sits. I move a step closer, but he waves me away.

"What's so funny?"

"A vampire with an infection?"

I scowl. "Who knows where that stake had been? And your shirt was probably filthy and—"

"When that Tick killed you, she cracked open your ribs and stuck her hands in your chest. I doubt she scrubbed for surgery first and you were right as rain within twenty-four hours. I'll be fine."

"Oh." I hadn't thought of that. I screw the lid back on the bottle. In the doorway, Chuy lies down again, this time angled so he can keep an eye on the door and on Sebastian. Clearly Chuy's not sure about Sebastian, but apparently he likes me. Carter had said Ely was better than anyone at staying alive on his own, but I'm guessing Chuy had a lot to do with that. "But at least let me bandage you up."

He smirks, clearly still amused. "If you must."

I rip the sheet in long strips and then carefully wrap them around and around his chest. Until now, I hadn't thought much about what Sebastian's chest would look like. In fact, this is the first time I've ever seen a man's naked chest. In person anyway. He's lean, but still muscular. I know firsthand how strong he is. How fast his muscles can move. Now that the stake is out, his skin feels warmer beneath my hands. He doesn't complain, even when I pull the fabric tight and knot it. I stop to survey my work. Did I get it tight enough or is it going to bleed through?

"Melly," Sebastian murmurs.

I look up into his eyes. Suddenly he seems very close. His skin very hot.

Oh my God. I'm still touching him. My hand is still plastered to his chest, my palm resting on top of his bandage, my fingers against his bare skin. Before I can jerk away, his hand covers mine, pressing my fingers briefly.

I bite down on my lip, unable to pull my gaze away from where my fingers rest against his pectoral muscle, long and pale against his darker skin. Something warm and delicious stirs in my belly, like the feeling I used to get when I listened to Rachmaninoff, like I am somehow bigger than just myself.

"Thank you for coming back for me," he says softly.

My breath catches and I jerk my hand away.

I should not be sitting here with my hand on his chest and a warm feeling in my belly. And I definitely should not be contemplating Rachmaninoff and Sebastian in the same thought.

"I didn't come back just for you. I came back because I can't get into Genexome without you."

His lips twist into a smile that is both sad and understanding. "I know."

CHAPTER TEN

CARTER

My mind was racing so fast as I turned to leave the radio room I barely noticed that Zeke wasn't there anymore. He must have slipped out first. I had other things to worry about now. I had to get out of here. Go find Lily, find some way to get her back into a medically induced coma—like I could just pull an anesthesiologist out of my ass—and *then* go get the cure from Sabrina. Because—ah, hell—this wasn't hard enough to begin with.

At least I had the plane. Maybe I could search from the air. Maybe I could—

In my mind, I was already gone. So deep and so far into crisis planning that it took me a moment to realize the halls were emptier than they were just a few minutes ago. And there was noise coming from down the hall. It took me a second to recognize the sounds of fighting. The brutal thwumps and crunches of fists hitting flesh. The rumble of encouragement from a crowd of onlookers. The chanting jeer of "Fight! Fight! Fight!"

I rounded the corner in a jog only to stop short. I couldn't even see who was fighting. It looked like everyone on the floor, hell, maybe everyone in the building had crowded into the space. The crowd seethed, surging around the fight in the center raging right outside the copier room, where Ely was being held.

I don't know how, but somehow I could tell that they were

tag-teaming it. Something about the way the crowd shifted tipped me off. It wasn't just one guy fighting Ely. It was a bunch of guys.

I'd been in a lot of fights and I'd sparred with Ely. He was good. Maybe one of the toughest guys I knew. But no one guy could hold his own when a whole crowd was chanting for his blood.

I heard another sickening crunch followed by a muffled "umph" and disgust rolled through me.

I'd wanted him to pay. I'd wanted revenge. But not like this.

I rushed toward the crowd, pushing people out of the way. "Zeke!" I yelled for help. Because he'd be good in a fight and I needed backup if I was going to get Ely out of this alive. Plus he knew these people. He could help calm them the hell down.

The crowd closed around me and I had to shoulder my way through. "Zeke!" I started to call again, but then the crowd shifted and I got pushed forward, right into the center of the fight. And that's where I found Zeke.

Some guy I didn't know had Ely's arms behind his back and Zeke was landing blow after blow to Ely's stomach. Zeke's face was a blank of mindless rage.

Less than thirty minutes ago, Zeke had been the one protecting Ely from Joe. Now he was beating the crap out of him. After standing ten inches from me when I thought about killing him. Shit. I'd done this.

All this anger. All the rage. This was me.

Damn it.

I threw myself at Zeke's back, but he shook me off and just kept pounding on Ely.

How the hell was I going to fix this? How could I save Ely when part of me still wanted revenge?

The answer was obvious. I couldn't calm things down until I calmed myself down. How could I do that when I still wanted to take him apart?

And this was it. They might well kill him. Unless I stepped forward and stopped it, Ely would die. Yeah, maybe he was a lying sack of shit, but he'd done it to save his brother. I had to remember that.

I threw myself between Zeke and Ely. Zeke had momentum behind him and a punch grazed my ribs. I twisted away from the punch so his fist rolled off me and then I danced out of his way. While he was off balance, his hand extended, I locked his fist in mine and twisted his arm up under me, holding it between my arm and my ribs. Zeke twisted so his back was toward me, reaching his other hand over his head and behind him. His hand found my jaw and his fingers dug into the vulnerable skin there. It hurt like hell, but I was taller than him. Not by much, but by just enough that he wasn't able to get the leverage to rip my jaw off.

"Calm down," I said in his ear, practically yelling to be heard over the confusion. The crowd had surged back when I got in the fight, and a rumble of confusion went through it. "Think, Zeke," I said, more quietly. Just for him. "You don't have any problem with him."

"Bullshit, I don't!" Zeke's fingers curved, digging more sharply into my skin. "He didn't just betray you. He used me to get to you. He used everyone in this Farm. He betrayed all of us!"

The other guy, the one who'd been holding Ely—or maybe someone else even, I couldn't quite tell—launched himself at my back, trying to tear me off Zeke. A hand dug into my hair, yanking my head even farther back. Which gave me the perfect view of the angry mob surging forward again, ready to take down me and Ely.

Well, crap, this wasn't exactly helpful.

What was I supposed to do now?

My anger had gotten me into this mess—my pure, driven need for revenge—and my logic wasn't doing jack to get me out of it.

Somehow the person at my back got his arm—but it was a small arm. A small person. Maybe a girl? Whoever it was, she got her arm around my neck and pulled, pressing the hard edge of her tibia against my windpipe.

The last person to put me in a choke hold had been Lily. She'd nearly kicked my ass and I'd fallen even more in love with her. And now she was in danger, maybe dying, maybe dead, and I couldn't help her because of my own anger. God damn it.

It couldn't end like this.

I wasn't going to let it end like this. I would find a way to help her. One that didn't involve a bunch more people getting hurt.

I dropped my hold on Zeke, pushing him away from me as I wedged my hands under the girl's arm and pried it from my throat. She stumbled back. I whirled around, putting myself between Ely and the others.

Crap, the girl was Charla. Three minutes ago, Charla had been a rational human being. Until I'd dosed her with my rage. Great. Just friggin' great.

"Stop!" I yelled, at everyone and no one. "Just stop! We can't do this."

The crowd grumbled with discord, looking unconvinced.

My need to avenge Lily had gotten us into this. Maybe my need to save her could get us out of it. "We can't kill him. I need

63

him alive," I said, a plan just beginning to form even as I said it. "Lily is out there and he's the only one who can track her down."

Most of these people didn't know who the hell Lily was and didn't care, but the fact that I knew, that I cared, that seemed to sink in for them. The fury and rage began to dissipate from the crowd as people blinked, looked around, and seemed surprised to find themselves there. The emotions eased away, but not entirely. There were mumbles of dissatisfaction as they started to drift past me. That rage and fury still lingered. The people in this Farm had been too angry and too hungry and too helpless for too long. Their emotions had been their own. I'd just distilled it. I'd given the rage an outlet.

The change was most obvious with Charla and Zeke, the two people who'd gotten the strongest dose of my anger. And then there were the other two guys who'd been in the fight, the guy who'd been holding Ely and another guy near the edge with bloodied knuckles. They were the two guards who'd been outside Ely's room when I'd first gone in.

I looked at the four of them and then, without really turning my back on any of them, I reached down to where Ely had slumped against the wall and grabbed his arm, hauling him up. I pulled him along with me, down the hall to the Dean's office.

The door was open, the office empty. Thank God there was a bolt on the inside of the door. I released Ely's arm, letting him sink to the floor beside the door as I threw the dead bolt. And then wedged a chair under the knob, just for good measure. Then I sank to the floor myself, back to the door, and buried my head in my palms.

Roberto had told me I was an *abductura*.

I don't know that I'd really believed him. Until now, I hadn't seen any tangible proof. Not like that. Yeah, there'd been times when I'd influenced someone's actions. Maybe. Like when Mel had been dying and I'd ordered Sebastian to bite her, turn her into a vampire and save her life. But that had been just one guy. At the time I'd thought I'd just made a really convincing argument. And then again at El Corazon when I'd ordered people to save themselves. But it was hard to believe you had special powers when you'd just convinced them to do something logical and in their own best interests. It was easier to believe when you'd single-handedly created a lynch mob.

After a minute, I asked, "How bad is it?"

He opened his eyes at least as much as he could. One was already swollen shut.

His lips twisted into a cocky grin. "Bad enough."

"You gonna live?"

"I've had worse."

"I don't believe you."

He tried to shrug, but winced instead. "I deserved it."

"Is that why you came here? Because you think you deserved it?"

This time, Ely laughed, which must have hurt more than shrugging, because he cringed and nearly doubled over. "Nah," he said after a minute. "I got caught. I tried to sneak in and steal supplies. Guess I'm not as good as I thought I was. My boy Zeke took over security and he's got Greens patrolling the fences during the day, too."

"You were right about him," I told Ely. "He's a good guy."

"When he's not trying to kill me."

I could only nod. Maybe Ely could make a joke out of that, but it scared the crap out of me. What the hell was I going to do?

I had to find a way to manage this. Fast. Problem was, I was all out of ideas.

"So," Ely said after a minute. "I'm guessing you're one of those *abductura* things Sebastian told us about."

"I thought you didn't believe in that crap."

In the Before, the academy had been attacked by Ticks, and after we'd fought them off, Sebastian had told us all the truth about vampires and about *abducturae*, the humans who worked side by side with them to control the will of others. He'd described it as a symbiotic relationship that allowed vampires to accrue power and *abducturae* to chart the course of humanity, for better or for worse. The guys who'd believed Sebastian had all banded together against Roberto. The idea was, if we could kill Roberto and his *abductura*, then humanity might have a fighting chance.

Some of the guys, Ely included, had thought Sebastian was full of crap. Ely had had other plans. The rest of us could go save humanity. He was going to find his family and get the hell out of Dodge.

Ely shrugged. "It's a lot harder not to believe in *abducturae* once you've been attacked by an angry mob because you pissed one off."

I couldn't argue with that, so I said nothing.

After another minute, Ely asked, "So why'd you stop them? I thought you didn't have time for me."

"I don't. But that doesn't mean I'm going to let a mob kill you. Hell, those people have no idea you tried to turn Lily over to Roberto. Most of them have no beef with you."

"People want a scapegoat. When someone like you gives it to them, they take it."

I shot a look over at Ely. He was sitting up a little straighter. He sounded less wheezy. "A scapegoat?" I asked.

"Yeah. Someone that's easy to blame when shit goes bad."

"I know what a scapegoat is. I was just—"

"Surprised I knew? What? We were in class together for two years. You think I never paid attention?"

That reminder, of our shared history and years of friendship . . . it only pissed me off all over again. I felt anger boiling inside of me and sucked in a deep breath to cool it down.

As it was, I felt sick to my stomach looking at the damage that had been done to him, not by me but by this force within me that I could barely control.

But I had to control it. I had to. I couldn't let it rule me. I refused to be the kind of person who abused this power. I would not be like my father.

"Tell me something," I asked Ely to distract myself. "Why the hell didn't you come to me?"

He looked at me. "Instead of taking her to Roberto?"

"Yes, God damn it. You had to have known that if I'd realized he had Marcus, I would have done everything in my power to help him."

"Everything except hand over Lily," Ely said flatly.

"I would have found a way."

Ely was shaking his head. "You've been there. You've seen Roberto's compound. You know what the security is like. It's not like breaking into a Farm. At a Farm you can walk right up and they'll just let you in because they need as much fresh blood as they can get. At El Corazon, they're keeping track of every warm body on the ranch. Price sent me out to get his daughters for him and the guards had orders to not even let me back in unless

67

I had Mel or Lily with me. I'd seen what we were up against. There's no way we can defeat that guy. All we can do is try to take care of our own. Stay alive as long as we can, any way we can."

"No way we can defeat what guy? Roberto? Because guess what? He's dead."

Ely looked at me blank-faced for a minute, then he tipped back his head and he laughed. "You are so full of crap." And then he laughed even harder. "And you must be getting damn good at this *abductura* thing, because I almost believe you."

"I'm not full of crap. I killed him. I brought Lily to El Corazon for treatment after she was exposed to the Tick virus and—"

"Lily was exposed?" Ely asked dumbly.

"Yes." I had the urge to curse some more. To punch him again. Something. Anything. I didn't.

Ely was cursing for me. "Jesus, I'm sorry, man. She wasn't supposed to be hurt. That was never the plan."

"Plans never go as expected. You know that."

"So what now?" Ely asked. "You going to throw me back in the copier room so I can wait around for someone else to lose their shit?"

"No." I felt calmer, more centered. And the plan I was cobbling together was clearer in my mind. Maybe it was all about focus and planning. Maybe as long as I didn't lose it, no one else would. It was just a theory, but I didn't have time to test it out slowly. I had to dive in, headfirst, on this. I pushed myself to my feet. I held out a hand to help Ely up. "I really do need you to save Lily."

I told him about the helicopter going down.

He stood, wincing as his ribs shifted. He'd probably cracked a couple of them. He slanted me a look. "Last time you trusted

68

Lily to me, I tried to turn her over to the vampires and I nearly got her killed. Why the hell would you trust me again?"

"Because you're the best person for the job. And because it's probably going to save your life. And because your brother was on that helicopter, too."

CHAPTER ELEVEN

LILY

I don't let myself dwell on what I've just learned about my father. I have more pressing concerns.

I need to kill myself. I'm not even sure if that will work. Maybe I'm already too much of a Tick. But I have to try.

The only other option is to wait it out, suffer through the effects of the virus, and wait for the transformation to happen. And then I'll be one of them. A soulless monster. A killing machine.

I can't let that happen. I've seen what they can do. Up close and personal. I've seen their dumb eyes and thoughtless glazed stare. I've seen the ruthless thirst. I've felt the hot breath of a Tick on my neck. I've watched as a Tick cracked open my sister's rib cage to get at her heart. I know what they're capable of. That's not going to be me.

But out here, in God only knows where, I don't have a lot of options. My father is drifting in and out of consciousness. No help there. I don't even know how much time he has left. He's lost so much blood. He can't survive long with those wounds. That much blood seeping out of him. Blood.

I shake to make myself look away from the blood, but it's everywhere. All over him. On his clothes. On his useless bandage. On the ground. Even when I look away, all I see is the blood.

And then I really do see more blood. A smear of dark brown in the red-brown dirt. A drop here. A streak farther away. More drops.

I follow the trail, stupidly at first, my gut guiding me more than my brain. Slowly I figure it out. This isn't a trail to food. This is a trail away from something. Away from the site of the helicopter crash. Away from the Ticks. This is the blood my father lost when he dragged me here.

At the site of the crash I might find something. A gun. A weapon. A . . . something.

I pull myself step-by-step over toward the rise, following my nose and my instinct. I'm not as cold anymore. I've stopped shaking, but I don't know if this is a good thing.

Beyond the hill, I can see a plume of inky smoke. I follow that when the drops of blood become more sparsely spaced. I hadn't noticed it before, so dark against a line of trees. When I crest the hill, it's there before me. A field of some kind of grain, and in the center of it, the smoking metal heap that was once a helicopter.

It seems huge. Much bigger than the Life Flight helicopters we would sometimes see overhead in Dallas. It must be a military helicopter if it was big enough to bring . . . how many of us had he said there were? Four patients?

Three predators that could awaken at any moment. Starving and mindless. I may want to die, but I don't want to be eaten by a Tick. And I'm not sure that would kill me anyway.

Am I different already? My body feels heavier somehow. And there's a deep gnawing hunger in my belly.

71

As I stumble toward the wreckage, my head spins. The air reeks of smoke and hot metal and something else I can't pin down. Something in the twisted pile of metal is smoking, but the helicopter is too intact for there to have been an explosion. There are bodies littering the ground near the helicopter. I can't tell if they were thrown clear or if someone dragged them out. My father dragged me, but would he have bothered with anyone else?

Two weeks ago, I would have said he wouldn't have even bothered with me. Two weeks ago, I hadn't seen him in nearly a decade.

I am drawn to the other bodies with a kind of twisted fascination. There are two men, both wearing singed and torn hospital gowns. Both large hulking types, with bulky arms and pronounced brows and heavy jaws. Their bare arms and legs are covered with thick, coarse hair. They look like a cross between professional football players and the wax Neanderthals from the natural history museum. Like mercenary soldiers who have almost turned into Ticks but aren't there just yet.

They should be less terrifying unconscious, but they aren't. They are too close to what I will become. Another day? Maybe two? No more than that, now that I'm awake.

I stumble around to the other side of the wreckage; the air is heavy with the stench of fire and blood and singed hair and roasted flesh. I see another body, this one impaled on a hunk of helicopter metal. The pilot. He didn't even survive the crash. I trip backward, desperate to get away. I move up the hill but stop at the sight of another body. A woman, dressed in a white doctor's coat. Facedown in dirt, like she stumbled away from the site and collapsed. Instinctively, I drop to my knees and roll her over. I place my hand on her chest and feel her take a shuddering breath. One of her arms flops oddly, like her shoulder has been dislocated. Her belly is strangely distended. A nasty gash oozes blood on her temple.

She won't make it. Somehow, I know this instinctively. I tell myself this, gazing at the lovely smear of blood on her forehead. It's bright red and fresh. Before I can stop myself, I lean down and lick the blood from her skin.

It's sharp and tangy on my tongue. My eyes roll back in pleasure. I'm so hungry. And she's dead anyway. I know she is. Internal bleeding. Surely. All that blood.

That blood.

I jerk away, throwing myself back from her so hard I roll down the hill, before catching myself and scrambling into a crouch. My every muscle tenses, poised to flee or to destroy. To destroy myself and not to destroy her.

I can't let myself become that. To lose my mind. My will. My everything that makes me human. I cannot lose that. I will not.

That's when I hear it. In that moment that I'm completely still and feel nothing but the thundering of my own heart and the wavering of my resolve. That's when I hear the crying.

It's not my father. I'm sure of that. It's younger than that, but not a baby. Not an animal. Not the mournful keening of someone out of control, but a soft, fearful crying. The noise of someone hurt and hiding.

I tip my head to the side and listen for it again. It's gone. Almost. I hear a sharp, trembling breath from near the helicopter. I lope around the tail and then stop short when I see the kid huddling close to the crumpled end of the helicopter.

He sees me and instantly cringes away, arms upraised to block my attack. He's younger than I am. Maybe fifteen. Maybe younger. Latino. Short cropped hair, dirty clothes. I'm sure I

73

don't know him and yet I do. I know this boy. Or someone who looks like him. Exactly like him. But older.

Ely.

This is Ely's younger brother. It must be.

As sluggish as my brain feels, seeing this boy still brings understanding.

Ely had been one of Carter's best friends from the military academy. Carter had asked Ely to keep McKenna and me safe when we'd left Base Camp to search for somewhere that McKenna could have her baby. Carter had trusted Ely. We had trusted Ely. He'd been so damn good at staying alive on his own no one had thought to ask how he did it. No one thought to wonder if he'd survived by forming an alliance with Roberto. Now I know why he did that. He did it because Roberto had his younger brother.

I crouch down beside the boy, but he cringes away from me, scuttling deeper into the shadows so that he's almost back inside the wreckage. His fear pulls at something deep inside of me. No one has ever been afraid of me. Not in the Before. Not on the Farm. Not even at Base Camp, where people thought I was an *abductura*. But this boy. He fears me and what I'm becoming.

What do I look like that this kid is afraid of me?

Except he's not a kid. He's a teenager. In the Before, he was probably the kind of kid who was scared of nothing. And now I terrify him.

Which means two things: one, he doesn't yet know that he's been exposed also, and two, I'm far enough gone that I must look like a Tick. At least to him.

I should just leave. I haven't found anything in the wreckage that I could easily use to kill myself. Maybe I would be better off just running into the wilderness. Leaving him alone with his fear, rather than making it worse.

But there's this: what is he going to do if I leave him?

No matter how tough he was in the Before, he's just a kid. If he's terrified of me now, then how's he going to react when the mercenary-Neanderthals wake up? And if my father is right, when they wake up, they'll be violent. And they're a lot less human than I am. They'll turn not long after they wake up. Then he's dead.

I can run or I can try to protect this kid. It's not really a choice.

I crouch down lower, ducking my head so my hair falls forward, covering part of my face.

"Hi," I say. My voice sounds lower, rougher than it normally does. The kid doesn't respond, so I add, "I'm not going to hurt you."

He shifts then, to peer at me over his arm.

His palpable fear mingles with confusion, but he doesn't say anything, so I add, "You're Ely's brother, right?"

He jerks back, clearly surprised to have heard Ely's name from me, but after several heartbeats, he nods.

"I'm a friend of Ely's." The lie nearly catches in my throat, choking me. Ely is not my friend. He was Carter's friend. Once. Me, he tranqed and tried to deliver to Roberto.

On the other hand, if Ely had succeeded, I might not be transforming into a Tick right now.

But on the other hand, if he had succeeded, Josie would be dead. There isn't anything I wouldn't do to keep Joe and McKenna's baby alive, including sacrificing my own life.

And on the other hand, wouldn't I have betrayed a friend to protect Mel?

But wait, that's too many hands. Too many ifs and fears and buts for my Tick-ish mind to take. And not enough getting our asses out of here before the mercenary-Neanderthals wake up.

"I'm a friend of Ely's," I repeat, and this time I try to sound like I mean it. "I know he would do anything to protect you. I would do anything to protect my sister, too." This is easier to believe when I say it. "I know you're scared. I won't hurt you."

I know that's a promise I can't keep, but I make it anyway.

I won't hurt him. Not as long as I'm me. Not as long as I can hold on to the shreds of myself.

Finally, he drops his arms, leaning forward to get a better look at me from within the shadows. "Are you one of them?" he asks. "Are you a . . ."

"A Tick?" I ask, when he leaves the question hanging. Jesus. How do I answer that? "I don't know. Not yet." I can't lie to the kid. He needs to know what I'm becoming, what's he's becoming, too. But we'll get to that soon enough. So I tell him what I do know. "I was exposed to the virus. I will turn, but I haven't yet. I was put in a coma. I think you were, too. We were being brought to a Farm, but the helicopter crashed."

I tried to sneak in the bit about him, but he catches on and crawls forward to get a better look at me. "Then I'm one, too?"

"Neither of us is yet."

His gaze meets mine for only a second, then he juts his chin out just a little and nods. There's a quiver to his jaw, but he's trying so damn hard to be tough, it about breaks my heart.

I might hate Ely. I might have been damn close to killing him. Hell, I left him unprotected and without transportation in the middle of nowhere. He may be dead already. But no matter how much he pissed me off, he would have done anything to protect this kid. And now, somehow, it feels like it's my job to do so, too.

"We gotta get out of here," I tell him. "You and I both woke up, that means those other guys will soon. We can't be here when they do."

He nods, but he doesn't come out the rest of the way. "Are you gonna just eat me?"

"No. Not yet anyway."

Either my answer or my honesty must reassure him, because he ducks his head and starts to climb out. He braces his hand on some kind of support beam, and before he can even cross under it, the whole thing shifts. It tips toward me, and instinctively, I thrust up an arm to catch it. The weight of the metal slams into my palms, but somehow I manage to hold it up. My muscles strain and tear, but I keep it from crushing us.

I don't have to tell the kid to get out of there. He scrambles out from underneath the twisted metal, and as soon as I see he's clear, I let go and spring free from the falling wreckage. I fall and roll, landing maybe ten feet away. My heart is pounding, and I'm struggling to suck air into my lungs, but I'm free.

I push myself up and glance around. Ely's brother is maybe five feet away, but from the way he's staring at me, I know he's still afraid. I don't blame him. I glance down at my hands because that's where he's looking. Deep cuts cover my palms from where I grabbed the helicopter. Blood drenches my hands, but I can barely feel the pain. It's nothing. No worse than a scratch. A cut like this, in the Before, and Mom probably would have taken me to get stitches. But it's not like we can just call 911.

For once, I don't bother trying to clean the wound, but just shove my hands in my pockets.

"So, kid," I say, trying for nonchalance. "What's your name?"

"Marcus Estaban."

I realize then that I never even knew Ely well enough to learn his full name. Somehow that makes me sad.

I nod to Marcus. "Hi. I'm Lily."

He nods back, but I can see I haven't exactly won him over. "We need to start moving. You can walk, right?"

He nods again.

I push myself to my feet and start walking. "We gotta get out of here."

"Where are we going?" he asks after maybe fifty feet.

I don't realize until then that I have no idea where we're going. Away from here, obviously. Away from the mercenary-Neanderthals. But where? I had just started walking without giving any thought to it at all.

I give my head a shake and try to think through things. The landscape is unfamiliar. Lots of sprawling live oaks and rolling pastureland. The trees are bigger than I'm used to, which means we're in the eastern part of the state, where the trees get taller. I know we were headed toward one of the Farms in northeast Texas, maybe even the one Mel and I had escaped from. That's probably still our best bet.

I try to guess north based on the position of the sun and start to head northeast.

Except, again my brain is sluggish, so I'm not really paying attention when we crest the rise and I see my father, pale and bloody, leaning against the trunk of the tree. I stop for a moment and just look at him. If I hadn't been here only ten minutes ago, I would swear he's dead. But when I walk up to him, his eyes flicker open and something almost like a smile twists his lips.

"I knew you'd come back for me."

I hate that smugness. I hate his confidence. His belief that I could not abandon him completely, even if he's right. He's a jerk and he's pure evil, but he's still my father. And I can't just leave him here to die.

Still, to him I say, "We need you alive. When we get to a Farm, you have to get us in and tell the doctor how to treat us. That's the only reason I came back for you."

He doesn't say anything, but his smile doesn't waver, either.

I lean down and pick him up fireman style, slung over my shoulder.

My father is a big man. Not overweight, but tall and solidly built from a lifetime of having plenty to eat. I should not be able to lift him, but I can. That scares me so much I can't even think about it.

I'm strong enough to carry him, and together, Marcus and I stumble out over the barren landscape, hoping that we'll find a Farm before our bodies turn against us. Praying that our immune systems are strong enough to keep the virus at bay until we reach the Farm. And praying that the mercenary-Neanderthals don't find us first.

CHAPTER TWELVE

CARTER

I left Ely alone to ponder my news about his brother for a minute and went out to check on things in the hall. Most of the crowd had dispersed. Only the two guards and Zeke and Charla were hanging around. I pointed to each of the guards. "Go wash up and then patrol the outer fences." I wanted them as far away from me as possible. They looked to Zeke to confirm the orders. He frowned but nodded.

Unfortunately, I couldn't send Zeke or Charla out to the fences. To her, I said, "Go back to the radio room. I want you to try to get that helicopter back on the wire."

She looked confused for a second, but then nodded. "Okay."

"Don't leave your post. Short of the building burning down around you, I don't want you to leave that radio unless you're bringing me good news. If there's anyone still in the helicopter, we need to know where they are. Got it?"

This time she nodded quickly and hurried off. Apparently specific directions helped. Now I just needed to avoid the specific thought of killing someone in a vengeful rage.

I looked at Zeke. "Go find Joe, figure out where he disappeared to and bring him back."

We could use a little of Joe's peaceful Zen vibe. After all, he had the best reason of any of us to want Ely dead and he hadn't caused a riot.

I was about to head back in to talk to Ely more, when Dawn and Darren came hurrying down the hall.

"What happened?" Dawn asked. "I heard something about a fight, that it got really bad."

She looked from Zeke to me and back again.

Zeke didn't say anything, but he ducked his head and he tucked his bloodied hands into his pockets. "I'm going to—" He bobbed his head toward the stairwell and dashed off without saying another word.

I nodded to Dawn and Darren. "Come on in. I'm going to need your advice."

A few minutes later, we were all standing around the map, which was still spread out on the Dean's desk. Still trying to figure out which Farm Price would have headed for. A hell of a lot had happened in the past hour, but I was right back where I'd been. Only the pile of shit was bigger.

"What kind of facilities would he need?" Dawn asked.

"Enough space to keep the patients isolated from the rest of the population and enough meds to sedate them indefinitely." I circled three other spots on the map. "I figure the Farms with those kinds of resources are here in Waco, here in College Station, and the Farm up by the border where Lily was when I first got her out." I exed out that last one. "But this one is almost exactly three hundred miles from El Corazon. With the helicopter loaded up like that, that puts it at the very edge of the copter's range. Price probably wouldn't want to push it like that."

"That's a big assumption."

I ignored Darren. "For now, we have to assume he was heading either for the Farm in Waco or the one in College Station."

Dawn pointed to a pair of spots on the panhandle. "What about Lubbock and Amarillo? Aren't there Farms there?"

"Yeah. But Amarillo's too far and Lubbock is also three hundred miles away. Plus, Price left El Corazon heading east. We have to assume he'd head to one of the closer Farms." And if one more person gave me hell about the assumption, I'd lose it. Because I was barely holding on as it was. Yeah. This was all based on assumptions. And Texas was friggin' huge. Finding a downed helicopter would make looking for a needle in a haystack seem like an afternoon at the park. Even if all our assumptions were right, only an idiot would think he could wander out into Tick-infested no-man's-land to find a downed helicopter. An idiot or an arrogant ass.

Thankfully, I had an arrogant ass who owed me.

Just then, Joe, Zeke, and Ely came in. I gave Zeke a hard look when he walked in the room. He seemed to know just what I was looking for, because he nodded slowly to let me know he was himself again. Beside him, Ely tensed and eyed Zeke, but didn't say anything.

Joe pushed past Zeke. "Zeke said Lily's helicopter went down and—" Then he stopped short. "This is your big plan? You're sending *him*?"

"Look—"

"No, you look. This guy's an asshole. He betrayed us all. He tried to kill Lily. He—"

"He's also better at staying alive on the outside than anyone I know. He's a good fighter. He's been all over the—"

"I don't care if he has a squadron of winged monkeys who

can fly around and spot the copter from the air. You're not sending him."

"He's the obvious choice. He's the only one good enough to find them without getting killed and he's the only other person with a dog in this race. His brother was on that helicopter."

"No." Joe took a step toward me, anger radiating off him. "Not just no. Hell, no."

Okay, so much for Joe being the reasonable one. "Look, Lily is out there. She is turning into a Tick. We only have a few days to find her. If we lose track of her now, she's gone. Forever. And he is the only guy who has a shot of getting to her."

"McKenna might be alive if it wasn't for him! Have you thought of that?"

"I have," I said calmly, trying to soothe Joe's grief. "But McKenna was bleeding out. It wasn't Ely's fault. I'm not saying he was right. He wasn't. But we need him now."

"He left my baby to die!" Joe yelled, tears pooling in his eyes.

"I was—" Ely tried to chime in.

Joe whirled around as if he'd almost forgotten Ely was standing there. He took a step toward Ely.

I threw myself between them. Ely was built like a pit bull—stocky and all muscle. Joe was thin and wiry. I'd never seen him in a fight, but if I had to guess, Ely could beat the crap out of him one-handed.

"Look, let's just—" I said, trying to calm everyone down.

But neither of them listened. And apparently, Ely had taken one too many punches to the head. He stepped up, getting right in Joe's face. "What was I supposed to do, man?"

"Anything but that. You left her to die, you shithead."

Joe tried to take a swing at Ely; again I got in the way.

83

"I was going to Roberto's. Do you have any idea what a sadistic prick he was? I thought I was protecting her. It's what I would have done for my own kid, okay?"

Joe stepped back, shock written on his face.

But Ely was still pissed and he kept coming. "You think my brother on that helicopter is the only family I found? I had my sister and two other brothers with me when Roberto's crew found us and brought us in. The gene or whatever it is that lets someone turn into a Tick? Marcus is the only one of us that has it. So Roberto shot him up with the Tick virus while I watched. The other three . . . Roberto just ate them. I had to watch him butcher my brothers and sister. So, yeah, I left your baby to die in the desert, because it would be fast. Can you even imagine what he would have done to a baby? Because I can and I—"

Ely broke off. Like he'd just realized how much he'd revealed. He stepped away, then bent over, palms to his knees like he didn't have the energy to stand anymore. Joe had gone pale. He stared at Ely for a second and then dashed back out into the hall. A second later, I could hear him puking.

I felt my own stomach flop over. Joe was a good guy. Too sensitive for the world we now lived in. Sure as hell too sensitive for the job I was asking him to do, but I knew he'd step up and do it.

"Look, here's what it comes down to," I said to Zeke. "I'm taking Ely out of here. I'm giving him the plane so he can search for the helicopter from the air. And then I'm going to Sabrina's to find the cure. I need good people to stay here. Keep things under control." I pinned first Joe and then Zeke with a serious stare. "You think you can do that?"

I saw it in his eyes, that flicker of doubt. That shame, but then Zeke nodded. "Yes, sir."

When I'd first arrived, I'd hoped to bring Zeke out with me, because I knew he'd be good in a fight. Now . . . well, now I knew he could fight, but I also knew how susceptible he was to my talents. He seemed too vulnerable to my sway to risk that. I needed good people, but I needed people who wouldn't follow blindly. I needed people who would stand up to me. And maybe what Zeke needed was a chance to redeem himself.

Joe still stood aside, glaring sullenly at Ely, but looking less sure of his hate. Finally, he nodded, too.

I turned back to Ely, who was standing up now, clenching his teeth and trying to look like he hadn't been crying. I looked over at Dawn and Darren.

I didn't want to ask them. Honestly, I didn't. If it was only Lily's life on the line, I would have gone to Sabrina's all on my own. I hated the idea of Dawn and Darren risking their lives because I asked them to. Especially because before they'd met me, they'd been living in relative safety in the small town of Elderton—the only place I'd ever been where people were still living somewhat normally. But Dawn and Darren had come down to Texas with me because they'd wanted to join the fight.

And this? Sneaking into Sabrina's compound to steal the cure? This was bigger than just me. And even if I wanted to do it by myself so I could keep the people around me out of danger, I couldn't. Because if I failed, all of humanity would pay the price.

Besides, Dawn had more medical training than anyone else I knew. If I was going to actually find the cure when I got to Sabrina's, I needed her with me.

I looked at Dawn and Darren. "Any chance I can talk you two into—"

"Absolutely," Dawn said simply. "We're with you. You don't even have to ask."

Darren grinned. "It's not like I'm going to let her have all the fun."

"Okay. Then let's go find a car."

The four of us headed down the hall to the elevator. By the time we climbed inside, Darren was bouncing up onto the balls of his feet, channeling his nerves into ideas. "We should stop on the third floor. It's where the supplies are. We can snag a couple of sat phones and then head down to the maintenance garage for extra gas."

"We'll need a lot for the drive from here to Albuquerque," Dawn said. "That's what? Five hundred miles?"

"I can take you as far as Lubbock," Ely said. "It'll shave at least three hours off your drive and we can look for the crash site. Just in case they did head for the Farm in Lubbock."

"Okay," I agreed. "We'll leave first thing in the morning."

Even though my instincts were screaming to get out there and start looking for Lily, looking for the cure, I knew there was no point in that. It would be dark soon and we wouldn't be able to see anything then anyway.

Dawn nodded reluctantly and I could tell she didn't fully trust Ely. Which was fine. I didn't trust him, either. I probably never would again.

Yes, I needed him. I didn't have time to find Lily and bring her to Sabrina and I couldn't be in two places at once. Ely was the only one with the skills to find that helicopter and rescue Lily and Marcus. But I certainly didn't trust him to keep either of the Armadale kids safe.

On the third floor, Darren and Dawn got off to go scrounge up the sat phones. Just outside the elevator, I turned to Ely.

Before I could speak, he said, "Everyone thinks you're an idiot for trusting me."

"Maybe," I agreed. "But I'm trying to save your life here, so you should try to be gracious."

"You're sending me out there, not so I can stay away from Ticks, but so I can actually track them down, and you think that's saving my life?"

"Try to think of it as giving everyone here a reason not to kill you right now."

He nodded, like he saw my point. "I still don't get you, man. Most people? They wouldn't give me a second chance." He leveled a look at me, very serious, very hard-core. "And I'm not sure you should, either. Maybe I'm not the good guy you seem to think I am."

"None of us are." I returned his look. "But the people we love are in danger. We don't have any options except being the good guys they need."

He seemed to consider this for a moment. Then he nodded solemnly.

"Besides," I said, "if you betray me again, I will find you. And I will kill you. Myself. Got it?"

He nodded. "I wouldn't have expected anything less."

CHAPTER THIRTEEN

MEL

There is no surprise when I tell Sebastian why I came back for him. No disappointment. Who exactly was I reminding: Sebastian or myself?

Then, as if he is no more comfortable than I am, he looks down at the towels I placed on the sofa and the table to absorb the blood. He arches a disdainful eyebrow.

"What?" I ask.

"You were very careful to keep the blood off the furniture."

"So?" I ask, not mentioning the nasty stain under the towel.

"We're trapped in the house of a psychotic murderer, surrounded by a horde of marauding Ticks. I don't think preserving the upholstery is our top priority."

Yes. This is better. I can handle sarcastic Sebastian more easily. At least I'm used to him.

I bend down to pick up the towels and the stake—anything with blood on it—and I carry the items over to the fireplace and toss them all in. There are matches on the mantel and the towel catches quickly.

"I don't want the blood to attract the Ticks. I don't even know if they'll drink our blood, but we can't take any chances."

"I doubt we need to worry about them. Not just yet anyway."

"I made sure the doors and windows were locked," I tell him. "But I don't think that will keep them out for long."

"I wouldn't be so sure about that," he says. "This house may look like a Victorian clapboard, but I'm guessing that's a veneer covering the bones of a concrete bunker. Don't forget, Roberto's been preparing for the fall of humanity for a long time. He wouldn't live in a house that wasn't strong enough to withstand a direct hit from a bomb."

I look around the room at the oak paneling and the large windows. Then I notice that the windows are set deep in the walls, like in a castle. "What about the glass?"

"Probably bulletproof. Or something even newer that hasn't been released to the public yet. Roberto was heavily invested in the military-industrial complex."

The stench of burning blood is heavy so close to the fire, so I walk to the window and tap on the glass, trying to gauge just how safe we really are here. Up close, I realize there are multiple panes, and when I tap, it doesn't ring quite like glass does. In the Before, when I was autistic, I could determine the strength of glass by the way it sounded. Like the flaws in the glass actually vibrated in my ears. What would this glass sound like? Surely not high-pitched and fragile. Maybe low and resonant. Strong.

Then I look beyond the glass, expecting to see the Ticks. Expecting to feel their anger and hunger.

I don't hear any of that. I don't feel or even see them.

"Where did they go?" I ask, the hair rising on the back of my neck. If I can't see them, they could be anywhere.

"Don't worry," Sebastian says. "They won't attack tonight."

I turn to see him leaning back against the sofa, his head resting against the dip in the camelback, his eyes closed.

"Why? How can you be so sure?"

"I can't. But this is the very heart of Roberto's territory. Even though he's dead, it still reeks of him. Can't you sense it?" He opens his eyes just long enough to see me nod. I do sense it. It's why I'm so jittery. "Their instincts will keep them away."

"If that's true, then why did Ticks attack the academy? Wasn't that the heart of your territory?"

"Doubting I'm as strong as Roberto, are you?"

"No. Just trying to understand."

"The academy was in my territory, but never the heart of it. That was Genexome. The Ticks that attacked the academy were newly made and starving. These are sated and lazy. They'll attack us if they feel threatened or when they get hungry. Probably not until then."

"Probably?"

"Just a theory."

I nod. It might be just a theory, but I hope it is true.

"How does this whole territory thing work? Now that you've killed Roberto, does that mean this territory is yours?"

"I didn't kill Roberto," he points out, a stab of anger in his voice. "Carter did."

"So then this is Carter's territory?"

"No. Even as an *abductura* he can't claim territory. He's not a vampire, he doesn't get to play."

"So then this could be *your* territory, if you claimed it?"

"According to the Meso-Americana Accords of 1409, yes. I could claim it."

"What would you need to do? To claim it, I mean?" Because he's still looking weak, and despite his faith in Roberto's house, I am not sure how much longer we can keep the Ticks at bay. He'd told me long ago that a vampire was strongest in his or her own territory. Maybe making this his territory would solve both those problems. "What do you need to do? Do you go around scenting trees and pissing in the woods or what?"

"Nothing that animalistic. There are rules. Laid out in the Accords." His eyes flicker closed, like he is too weak to even finish.

Whatever was laid out in the Accords would have to wait because we have bigger things to worry about. Sebastian's wound has been bandaged up for several minutes now, and frankly, he doesn't look any better.

He swears my injuries had been worse. Had I healed this slowly? I don't think so. Then again, Sebastian had started bringing me cups full of Tick blood to feed on almost immediately.

I cross back over to the sofa and kneel down in front of him. "I need to get you some food and the Ticks are the only source of blood around."

His eyes open. "You could feed me the dog."

I recoil back. "Ew!"

"Easy, Kit. I was joking." His lips curve into a wry smile. "Besides, that dog is more fur than blood. He'd barely tide me over."

"No wonder Chuy doesn't like you." I push myself to my feet and go look for weapons to hunt Ticks. When Chuy raises his eyebrows like he's asking if he can come with me, I nod. If I'm going out to face a horde of Ticks, I don't want to do it alone.

CHAPTER FOURTEEN

MEL

I half expect Sebastian to protest. It's not like going out to hunt Ticks on my own—for him, no less—is exactly safe.

Instead, he gives a little nod of acceptance and just sits there with his eyes closed. Which must be a sign he's even worse than I thought.

With some thirty-plus Ticks out there, my odds aren't good, but I can improve them a little. Roberto's library is like a vampire hunter's museum. There are countless wooden stakes, bows and crossbows, swords, daggers, crosses, vials of holy water. All seemingly collected from assassins that hunted him over the years. And who says vampires don't have a sense of humor?

I cross to the wall where the blades are and select a katana, because it's light and familiar. I've lost the katana that Sebastian gave me when he was training me and I miss its easy weight. The one I pick has a scabbard and I strap its ancient leather around my waist. I look at the crossbows next. I run my thumb down their strings. The bow won't work if it's too brittle.

I finally pick out a bow, but when I turn around, I see Sebastian standing in the doorway, leaning against the doorjamb.

"I thought you were smarter than this."

"It's not stupid if it's our only chance. Then it's just desperate." I sling the bow over my shoulder and move to walk past him with Chuy by my side.

He holds out a hand to stop me. "No, it's only stupid if you *assume* it's your only chance."

I stop, frowning. "You know, sometimes your Mr. Miyagi act is great and insightful, but sometimes it's just annoying as hell. It wouldn't kill you to give me just a simple, clear answer."

He pushes off the door and steps over to a nearby umbrella stand. He carefully selects a cane with a curved ebony handle and a rosewood staff. He holds it up looking at the length for a moment before turning around and leaning heavily on it as he walks back to me. "Think about it, my dear. Would Roberto really have built a fortress with no way of feeding himself once he was locked in?"

"No, of course not. You think . . ." I trail off, feeling suddenly sick to my stomach. "You think there are people trapped in here somewhere?"

"Nothing as dramatic as that. And no. We can assume the Ticks already ate up all the live kine. But Roberto wouldn't rely only on them. He'd have a backup supply."

"Refrigerated blood? Like from blood banks?"

"Ding, ding, ding." He gives the cane a twirl. "And the girl wins the prize after all."

"But if it's refrigerated blood, then it will be going bad since the electricity has been off for the past day. Except, if Roberto had been planning for the worst-case scenario, he would have assumed the electricity would go down. He would have someplace safe where he could ride out the storm. Someplace with a generator and locks and . . ." I look up at Sebastian. "Someplace exactly like your underground lair."

He gives an exaggerated wince. "I rather think 'lair' has a nasty, unpleasant connotation, don't you?"

"Really? What term do you prefer?"

"Personally, I like 'vault.'"

"Okay then. If this was your house, where would your vault be?"

"In the basement, of course."

"This is Texas. No one has basements."

He gives me a beleaguered look. "Have a little imagination, will you? If you're an immortal vampire with limitless resources and all the time in the world, you can have a basement if you damn well want one."

"Oh. Good point," I grumble. "Okay, let's go find it, then."

Sebastian dismisses me with a wave. "Well, then, run along. Find the lair of the evil vampire."

I want to growl at him again. This being-treated-like-a-naughty-child bit is really getting old.

Despite that, I do exactly as he says. Chuy and I run through the first floor again, this time opening all the interior doors, looking for a stairway leading down. I find it in the center of the house, just off the kitchen. A set of stairs that indeed lead to a basement. It reminds me eerily of my Nanna's basement in Nebraska—only a lot cleaner. There's a workbench. Enough tools to fix or maintain anything my very unmechanical mind could imagine. Cleaning supplies line the opposite wall. And tucked into the back corner is another door, from which I can hear a faint electrical hum. Though the door looks like it's made of wood, it makes a hollow, metal sound when I knock on it. To the side of the door is a rectangle that opens to reveal an instrument panel almost exactly like the one at Sebastian's.

Sebastian's waiting for me at the top of the stairs. "What did you find?"

His voice sounds strained. He's hunched over and leaning heavily on the cane, like an old man.

"Apparently, all evil vampires use the same security company. The setup is nearly identical to yours. Hand and retinal scanner." I stop just a step shy of him. "Will they work now that he's dead? If I go outside and bring his body back in, would that do it?"

Standing above me, Sebastian is dimly backlit and it's nearly impossible to read his expression. "Possibly."

I nod. "Okay then." I push past him out into the kitchen and toward the front door. I pause only long enough to collect the weapons I'd selected earlier.

"Aren't you going to ask me?" Sebastian says from behind me.

I turn to see him standing in the hall, leaning his shoulder to the wall. "Ask you what?"

"If my system will operate once I'm dead. If you can merely bring back my hand and my head and get into my vault."

I ignore him and sling the bow back over my shoulder.

"Going out there for Roberto is a very stupid idea," he says. "So far, the Ticks are keeping their distance. You shouldn't antagonize them."

Hand on the doorknob, I ask, "Then what should I do? Let you starve?"

"There's an attached garage and probably a dozen gassed-up cars. If you were smart, you would kill me now, take my body, and drive all night to reach Genexome."

"Clearly hypoglycemia is making you irrational. I'm going out. I'll get his body and we can get you some food."

"No," Sebastian says. "Not now."

"Not now? Then when? You need to feed or you're going to die."

"It's dusk. The Ticks will just be coming out."

"I'm not afraid of them."

"Not afraid of a swarm of hundreds of Ticks? You're strong, Kit, but everyone has their limits."

"I've fought Ticks before," I point out.

"Not this many and not at once. No. Better to wait until morning, after they've stumbled off to find nests. Any that are still out will be weaker during the day."

"I'll be weaker, too."

"But you have the mental capacity to understand your limitations. They do not. You have rationality. They do not. We are outnumbered and injured. Please do not throw away one of the few advantages we have."

"You're asking me to just wait here while you starve to death?"

"No, I'm asking you to be just a tad less dramatic. I won't starve to death in the next twelve hours. Get some rest, Kit. You'll need it when you go out to face the Ticks."

"Twelve hours from now, won't it be even less likely that Roberto's dead body will open the security system?"

"It will either work or it won't. A few hours won't make a difference."

Sebastian heads back into the living room and I follow him. Even though I know he needs food, I can see his logic. Right now they're leaving us alone. I should rest while I can. Not twelve hours, maybe, but surely a couple won't hurt. I can go out at dawn.

"Have you always been such a jerk?" I ask, lowering myself to one of the wingback chairs near the fireplace.

"Yes. As a matter of fact, I have." He stretches out on the sofa again. "As you'll learn soon enough, that's the nature of vampires."

"To be jerks?" I could believe that, even though I didn't want it to be true. But was this my fate? To become more and more of an asshole as the years passed?

"No." He chuckles faintly. "To be unchanging. When you become a vampire, that final and massive transformation seals your personality forever. You don't age. You don't change. You are immutable. Which means you will always be this stubborn, optimistic, swooningly romantic fool that you are, and I—unfortunately—will always be the manipulative ass that I am."

I feel my cheeks heat. Is that how he sees me? A stubborn, optimistic, romantic fool? Is he wrong?

I have the sinking feeling he isn't. I am not ashamed of any of those qualities, yet he makes them all sound like insults.

Though what I really should be worrying about is the "always" part of that statement—the idea that I am now immutable. Stuck like this forever. Unable to change or grow.

I can't imagine it. I have spent all my life—both my human life and my vampire life—in flux. In constant change. Slightly out of sync with the rest of the world, always playing catch-up to bring myself and my abilities and my gifts into line, to bring my mind into focus with my world. I can't imagine not changing.

I look down at Sebastian, wanting to ask more questions—needing more answers—but his eyes are closed now, his breathing shallow. He looks as though he's fallen asleep, which is a sign of exactly how exhausted he must be. I know what a strain it is to stay awake and alert through the daylight hours and he has been doing exactly that for several days in a row. For that matter, so have I.

I tuck my legs up on the chair beside me and rest my head on one of the chair's wings. Despite the fact that dusk is falling and I should be wide-awake, my eyes drift closed.

I still don't know what to think of Sebastian. I doubt I can trust my own instincts to guide me. When I was autistic and an *abductura* I could trust my gut about people. I just knew the ones who were trustworthy, because I could *hear* it. But I'd never gotten a reading on Sebastian. He'd been silent to me.

I have one final thought as sleep takes me: if it truly is the nature of vampires to be immutable, then Sebastian is either a very bad man who sometimes pretends to have good intentions or he is a very good man who can never forgive himself for the mistakes he's made. I have no way of knowing which he is.

CHAPTER FIFTEEN

CARTER

Early the next morning, Ely dropped us off just south of Lubbock at an airstrip outside of Brownfield that had been used for crop dusters in the Before. We found an old truck right away but traded it for a sedan as soon as we found one in town. From there, it was just tiny Texas towns. The kind of dusty, one-stop-sign towns that probably hadn't looked much better in the Before than they did now. We saw hardly any indications of Tick activity. This wasn't the type of landscape where anything thrived, not even scavengers.

We skirted Lubbock. There was a big Farm there. One of the biggest in the state. I'd broken in twice before, so I knew just how good the security was. They would certainly notice a car passing by or a plane flying overhead. Darren was asleep in the back and Dawn was driving when she asked, "So tell me about this vaccine you got?"

I'd been nearly asleep—despite the fact that I was riding shotgun and felt obligated to stay awake, too. I figured she was probably getting sleepy and was talking to keep herself alert. I stretched a little. "How did you hear about that?"

She rolled her eyes. "Neither you nor Ely whispers as softly as you think you do."

"I see." Ely and I had talked about the vaccine when he'd

landed the plane in Brownfield. "I got it at El Corazon. Right after I arrived. Why?"

"Did Ely get it, too?"

"I don't think so." Though Ely had never answered me directly when I asked him. "To hear him tell it, he's way more worried about a Tick ripping his heart out than being exposed to a virus."

"He has a point." She was silent a minute and then asked, "When you got the vaccine, did they say why it wasn't more widely distributed?"

"Cost, I think. They said it was time-consuming to make."

She made a hmm sound, one that was more speculative than in agreement.

"A vaccine works by exposing your body to a weakened version of a virus, right?" I asked. "And then your body makes the antibodies."

"Right," Dawn said.

"Then, theoretically, I have antibodies against the Tick virus. Right now. In my blood. Could we somehow use those to make our own cure?"

"No," Dawn said, without even giving it much thought. "That's not the way the Tick virus works. It's not like a normal virus."

"It's not?" I mean, of course I knew it wasn't. A normal virus, your nose ran for a couple of days and you felt a tad achy. With this, you were pretty much out cold for four days and woke up to the worst hangover in history.

"No. The problem is, the thing that causes humans to mutate into Ticks isn't a virus. It's a retrovirus. A virus that's already encoded in your DNA. The vampires, I guess, call it a regenerative gene, but it's not a single gene at all. It's lots of bits of DNA intermingled with your own. Obviously, not everyone has it. And it lies dormant until some other virus comes along, wakes it up, and causes all those bits of DNA to start throwing switches in your epigenetics."

"So the virus—EN371—that's the virus that woke up the retrovirus?"

"Exactly. Lots of retroviruses work this way. Multiple sclerosis, for example. And schizophrenia. They're diseases caused by a retrovirus being exposed to some new virus. So in reality EN371—the virus you have immunity to—isn't the Tick virus at all. It's just the alarm clock."

Frustration brewed in my chest. "So even if we did find a cure for EN371, it wouldn't do jack for the people who've already transformed into Ticks."

"No, it wouldn't."

God damn it!

I'd known there was a chance Sebastian was full of shit. I'd *known* it. Yet there'd still been some hope, until Dawn's biology came along and squashed it.

"But that doesn't mean there isn't a cure," she said hastily. "Or that there won't be one someday. The cure for the Ticks would have to be a whole new virus. Something completely different from EN371 that goes in and turns off the retrovirus. And it's entirely possible that the scientists at Genexome were working on it. The media portrayed this like it was all an accident, but someone at Genexome had to know what was going on. They were in deep. If anyone would know how to tailor-make another virus that would undo what EN371 did, it would be Genexome."

"So you're saying there could be a cure?"

"Yeah. I wouldn't be in this car with you if I didn't think

there was a cure." She gave a baffled-sounding laugh. "I mean, you're a great guy and all, but it's not like I'm going to risk my life—let alone let Darren risk his—just because you need backup for this dumb-ass stunt."

I let that soak in for a minute. Until now, I hadn't given a whole lot of thought to why they'd volunteered to come. I guess I'd just assumed it was some *abductura* thing. Like I'd unwittingly drawn them into my cause. Knowing this—that she actually thought there was a cure—well, it took the pressure off a little. Yeah, I was still going to do everything in my power to keep them safe, but at least I didn't have to keep them safe believing I'd suckered them into danger in the first place.

Plus, Dawn believed there might be a cure. Dawn—who'd never even met Sebastian, Dawn who was smart and capable and had a medical background—actually thought it was a possibility.

"You know a lot about this stuff, don't you?"

She shrugged, but gave a smile that looked just a little smug. "Yeah. I do."

"You're not just a nursing student, then?"

"The nursing thing, that was something my dad encouraged. For me, it was just a jumping-off point. Nowadays, you can go from being a nurse to being a physician's assistant to . . ."

Her words trailed off. When I glanced over, she was screwing up her face like she was trying to keep from crying. I doggedly looked back at the road. I never knew what to say when girls started crying and I especially didn't know what to say about this, because—shit!—there was no *nowadays* anymore. Not like there used to be. Not where she could even finish her nurses' training, let alone go on to be a doctor or a researcher or whatever she'd planned in the Before.

I wondered sometimes if it was easier for a guy like me, a guy who hadn't had much in the Before. I'd had money and connections, yeah. I'm sure that if the Tick-pocalypse hadn't happened, my dad would have pulled strings to get me into one of the Ivy League colleges. A ten-million-dollar donation and admissions would overlook a lot. But I hadn't had hopes or dreams of my own. In the Before, the only thing I'd really wanted was Lily.

"I don't know how," I said suddenly. "But we're going to get through this. We're going to kick this thing's ass and get humanity back on track."

I whispered the words, fiercely, pushing all my will into them, wanting Dawn to believe them. Wanting to give her hope. And wishing that my powers would also work on me, because just then, driving through the night to face down a monster to save the one person I really cared about, I needed to believe, too.

CHAPTER SIXTEEN

CARTER

We rolled into Albuquerque after an uneventful three-or-so-hour drive. One good thing about the Tick-pocalypse? No traffic and even fewer cops. If you've ever wanted to punch a Toyota sedan up to a hundred, the highways in New Mexico were the place to do it. We had stopped to siphon gas once in the town of Roswell. There, I'd loaded up a duffel bag of supplies and stashed it in a safe place. When we made it out of Sabrina's with the cure, I wanted to have some resources waiting for me.

Mel hadn't been able to tell me a lot about Sabrina's lair. She hadn't even known where it was located, but she had seen the Smart Com logo on all the buildings. And it just made sense. A lot of the vampires were aligned with major corporations. I'd remembered Smart Com was headquartered in Albuquerque, but once we got there, we had to stop and look for more info. We found a library on the east side of town and I had Dawn and Darren wait in the car while I went in to look for a phone book or something.

Libraries—along with churches and universities—were the kind of places Ticks usually avoided. They didn't like those obvious reminders of what they'd once been. Still, there was no way I was going to send Dawn or Darren into a building I hadn't scouted first. I came back out after only a few minutes and slid into the backseat.

"Did you find the address?"

"Even better. I found maps and some brochures about the company." I held them out to Dawn. While Darren drove, Dawn started reading aloud as I unfolded the map to pinpoint where we were.

"It says here that Smart Com's headquarters are located in a state-of-the-art, seven-building campus sitting on two hundred and forty-seven acres in the suburbs north of Albuquerque. They have an on-site health clinic, a day care, and a cafeteria capable of feeding all twenty-five hundred employees."

"You gonna send them your résumé or not?" Darren asked.

"Shut up. I'm doing research," Dawn grumbled.

"You think you could sound a little less impressed?"

"Probably not. They even have their own greenhouses."

"What?" I asked.

"They grow their own vegetables for the cafeteria. And— looks like we have a winner." She waved the pamphlet around. "They also claim to have an underground disaster shelter."

"Wow," Darren said from the front seat. "An underground disaster shelter? In New Mexico? It's not exactly tornado alley. Or hurricane central."

"Yeah," I said grimly. "Sounds like Smart Com was prepared for something a little outside Mother Nature's pay grade."

"Someone was prepping for the apocalypse long before prepping for the apocalypse was cool," Dawn added.

"Exactly."

Dawn gave me a pointed look. "This is obviously it, right? We found Sabrina. Shouldn't you be excited or something?"

"Yeah. Or something." Sabrina not only had all these resources, but she was ballsy enough to advertise it in a friggin' brochure. I had the feeling that Smart Com was going to make El Corazon look like child's play.

Suddenly I was feeling very unprepared. You know that nightmare where you find out you're late for a final for a class you didn't even know you were taking? Like that. Except the final is a battle to the death and the lives of everyone you know are at stake.

For Christ's sake, I didn't even know what Sabrina looked like.

I thrust the map up to the front seat. "Switch with me."

Dawn handed back the brochure and I started flipping through it. On the second-to-last page, I found a picture of Smart Com's upper management, smiling and standing arm in arm in front of one of the buildings. Beneath was a blurb about how the company was founded.

The picture must have been old, because the company's former CEO, Paul Workman, was standing there, front and center. Paul Workman was *the* tech guru of his generation. People practically worshiped him. When he'd been diagnosed with some rare cancer about six months before the fall, Smart Com's stock price had plummeted. But in the picture, he looked hip and healthy as he smiled serenely for the camera.

Beside him was a beautiful woman with long dark hair. The photo was captioned with job titles, not names, but I figured that had to be Sabrina. She was the only person smiling with her mouth closed. Which, I'm guessing, you'd make the habit of doing if you had incisors the size of hypodermic needles.

"How much farther?" I asked, leaning forward in my seat to get a better view out of the windshield as we inched through town.

"Hang on," Dawn muttered, squinting out the windows, trying to catch the names on dusty street signs as she glanced back and forth between the map on her lap and the worn signs.

Darren slowed to a stop at an intersection. "We're at Baker and Parkland."

"Hmm . . . okay . . . that's . . ."

Darren gave his sister a playful punch in the arm. "Hurry it up. We don't have all day."

"We've got time," I said. Actually, we did have most of the day. We'd gotten here early enough to find Sabrina's compound, do a little recon, and hopefully approach the front gate well before dark.

"That doesn't mean she's not being a slowpoke," Darren grumbled.

Without looking up from the map, Dawn reached over and thumped Darren on the forehead. "Shut up. I'm doing the best I can."

Darren snorted. "Yeah, right."

"Okay, when was the last time you read a map? Dad got the GPS for both the cars when you were ten. So it's not like you know what you're doing." Before he could say anything else, she held up a hand. "Wait. I found it. I mean, I found us. We're right here." She pointed to a crinkle in the map. "I think we're about three miles away. Here's where I think Smart Com's headquarters are." She pointed to a pale pink splotch that took up a sizable swath of the map. Then she shrugged. "But that's just based on the street address."

"And we have no way of knowing how far out Sabrina's territory extends. Pull in here," I ordered Darren.

He guided the car into the parking lot I'd indicated and I had him park behind the strip mall next to an abandoned Corolla covered with a layer of dust thick enough to choke on.

"Great!" Darren said. "Who ordered a pizza?"

"What?" I frowned, looking around and trying to hide the way my stomach grumbled at the thought of pizza.

"He's just being an idiot," Dawn said, pointing to the sign over one of the doors. "Domino's Pizza." She turned and scowled at Darren. "Dork."

He shrugged, smiling. "Don't tell me you wouldn't fight a honey badger for a slice of pizza."

Dawn and I both ignored him.

I turned to Dawn. "You two, wait here. I'm going to do some recon."

"This far away?" Dawn asked. "We're still a couple miles from Smart Com."

"Maybe," I muttered. "But I don't like the looks of this. It's too . . . clean."

"Too clean?" Darren leaned forward between the two front seats. "What do you mean? Looks like the typical alleyway. Back behind the typical strip mall."

"Yeah," I said grimly. "Exactly." Dawn and Darren exchanged a look, so I expanded. "This place doesn't seem any different from any other city in the Before."

"So?"

"So, this isn't the Before anymore. There isn't anywhere in the U.S. that looks like this now. At least not anywhere I've been."

"Elderton looks like this," Darren said stubbornly.

"Sure. Elderton. That's like never-never land. But out here . . ." I couldn't repress a snort of disgust. "Out here, things are a lot worse than they are in Elderton." It was easy to forget sometimes how sheltered Dawn and Darren had been.

108

When it came to the big cities, here's the way I saw it: shit went bad in Texas fast. I mean, fast. From life as we knew it to fire-bombing Houston in a couple of weeks. The wreckage from that—the sheer number of bodies—was bad enough in the smaller towns I'd been sticking to. I'd seen mass graves with what looked like hundreds of bodies, dug by backhoes—graves that hadn't even been covered up. As if, midburial, Ticks had swarmed through and ripped the guy operating the backhoe right out of the driver's seat. In the big cities? I couldn't even imagine. The Dallas metroplex had eight million people. If I was optimistic and guessed that only half of those were dead . . . still, what did you do with four million Tick-ravaged bodies?

Nothing. You did nothing with that many bodies.

There weren't enough living people to bury the dead.

My guess was, the big cities, like Dallas, were literally filled with rotting corpses.

So, yeah, I avoided them.

Until now.

"This place," I summed up, "looks too normal. Someone's been doing regular patrols. Keeping the Ticks away. Probably keeping away looters, too." I twisted in my seat. "I'm going to get out and scout. Try to get the lay of the land. See if I can figure out how regular the patrols are."

"Why does it matter if there are patrols?" Dawn asked. "I mean, don't we want them to find us anyway? We're not planning on sneaking in. I thought we were planning on just driving up and turning ourselves over."

"Eventually, yes. But I'm kind of hoping we can also get back out. I'm not planning on being Sabrina's pet *abductura* for the rest of my life. I don't want to go in there until I have some ideas about how to escape."

Both Dawn and Darren nodded. They were smart kids even if they'd been sheltered. And, yes, I knew it was stupid to think of Dawn as a kid when she was three years older than I was.

"You guys wait here," I said as I reached for the door handle. "I should be back in twenty minutes or less. If I'm not, you take the car and head back to San Angelo."

I climbed out of the car and crept to the edge of the buildings, looking in either direction for some sign that Sabrina's people might be out there. The strip mall was L-shaped and we'd parked at the very back. I crept around the corner and behind the other side of the building. I stopped at the edge of the wall and considered my options. I had a decent view of the street in one direction, but not the other. There was a freestanding ATM about twenty feet away. I'd have a better view from there—in both directions—and I'd still have decent cover. I made the dash to the ATM and then looked around again, keeping my back to the wall.

Albuquerque might as well have been a ghost town. Across the road was another strip mall, equally unexciting. A half block down was a school. There were a few cars on the road, but they were all parked. Like they'd been left there deliberately.

Not like Ticks had swarmed through and ripped the drivers out of the cars while they were still running. I shuddered, giving my head a little shake. There was no point in creeping myself out any more than I needed to.

I studied the street in either direction. Though the sun was nearly at its zenith, the full moon was low on the horizon, so pale against the milky blue sky it was almost transparent, like a water spot on a glass. The air was cool on my heated skin, but I knew that wasn't the only reason for my jitters.

There was something not quite right. Something other than the fact that I was deep inside the territory of some badass vampire and I was about to hand myself over to her like a lamb to the friggin' slaughter.

Then I heard it, a car door closing. Not softly, either.

I briefly closed my eyes, shaking my head.

For once, would it have been too much to ask to have someone—anyone—just follow my directions?

With all the things that sucked about leading the rebellion, you'd think the one perk—being the guy in charge—would occasionally pay off. But no.

I heard Darren and Dawn trying to sneak up behind me. You'd expect someone who's as good a shot as Darren to have a little—I don't know—coordination or something. But I swear the guy stepped on every twig and piece of trash in the alley. Jesus, was he *trying* to make noise?

Yeah, I knew I was being paranoid. There probably wasn't anyone nearby to hear but me.

I turned around and was surprised to see Dawn step out of the alleyway first. I'd pegged her as a follow-the-rules kind of girl.

"Got bored waiting in the car?" I asked. There was no point in staying quiet when anyone in the vicinity would have already heard us.

"You know, it's really annoying when you just leave and expect other people to follow your directions," she said.

"Yeah. I've been told that."

She bit down on her lip and shot me an apologetic look. Then she stepped away from the building. Stumbled, really.

She caught herself, and straightened. Taking a big step out into the open, revealing the guy behind her holding a semiautomatic shotgun right at her back.

A second later, Darren stepped out, too, another guy with another gun right behind him.

The second guard studied me for a second and then must have decided I was the bigger threat, because he shifted to point his gun at me.

Collabs always had a problem looking cocky but being lazy. They were always a little too comfortable with their rifles because they'd never had enough training to really respect what their weapons could do.

These guys didn't look like that. Both guys looked very much like the hitters that Roberto had hired. They were big, muscled-up guys. Guys who knew their shit. They'd been well trained, either by the military or by some private organization, like the Elite Military Academy that I'd gone to, only a lot more hard-core. Sabrina had obviously hired the best. Or she'd trained them herself.

"We need you to come with us," Muscles Number One said. He gave me another expressionless, steely-eyed glare before glancing at his companion and nodding in my direction. "He's not going to give us any trouble. Are you?"

Muscles Number Two read between the lines and shifted his gun back to Darren. Which was a smart move. They were still maybe twenty feet away from me. Close enough that he certainly might have hit me—if he was as good and as well trained as he looked—but far enough that I might have tried to charge him. Maybe he'd take me out, maybe he wouldn't. As long as I had surprise on my side, I would have a shot. But, at point-blank range, there was no way either Dawn or Darren would walk away from a firefight. Obviously Muscles Number One had figured out that I wasn't about to do anything to endanger them.

Fortunately, there was one thing Muscles One and Two didn't know.

I'd planned on getting captured all along.

CHAPTER SEVENTEEN

MEL

I wait until well after dawn before I head outside alone, feeling queasy and light-headed. I'm not sure if it's hunger or revulsion. It's been almost three days since I've eaten. Three intense, physical days.

I need to eat almost as badly as Sebastian does.

I don't know what I'll do if Roberto's hand and eye won't open his vault. Or worse, if I go to all this trouble and it's filled with something useless like money instead of blood. I do know this: I can't feed off Ticks anymore. Or rather, I don't want to.

Any Tick I feed off of will regenerate as a vampire, something I cannot risk. I would have to kill any Tick I feed directly from.

Could I kill a Tick, knowing how close we are to having a cure? Knowing that somewhere out there, my sister is slowly transforming into a creature just like this? That this Tick is someone else's sister or brother?

If it comes down to my life versus theirs, will my resolve hold?

I guess I'll find out.

Crossing from the house to the green where Roberto's body is, I choose stealth over speed. The Ticks are as fast as I am. I can't outrun them. In a fight, my big advantage isn't strength or speed but intelligence.

Though it's too bright for me, I can see okay. The Ticks have retreated from Roberto's house. I'm not sure if it's his lingering presence that keeps them away or mine and Sebastian's. Though they aren't close, they're still out there. I can feel them, like the buzz of a computer fan, whirring in the background. They're groggy and sated—overfed, like guests at Thanksgiving.

When I reach Roberto's body, I pull out the katana. His body is already sprawled on the ground, arms stretched out like he died while making snow angels. I aim for his wrist, but miss. The blade hits bone, which shatters and splinters. My stomach roils. I think of my Nanna again and the hours I used to spend in her kitchen watching her carve chickens for frying and the easy way her knife sliced between the joints. My butchery would not impress her.

Of course, my blood lust wouldn't, either.

My stomach squirms as I pick up the hand. It's as cold as raw meat, but I can't shake the fear that his fingers are going to grab me, and when I look around for his head, I'm afraid his eyes might still be open. Blinking at me. Knowing.

I fear him, but I fear my own fate as well. Because what if Sebastian has lied to me? What if chopping off a vampire's head doesn't kill him? What if there is no death? What if there is only eternity lived in smaller and smaller pieces?

Suddenly I'm desperate to find that head. To confirm that Roberto really is dead. That it will be possible to kill me. That I won't be trapped like this for eternity. That I *won't* live forever.

Tucking Roberto's hand into the pocket of my hoodie, I look around for the head, but I don't see it.

The final battle took place on a rise in the green. I see the discarded swords Roberto and Sebastian fought with. I see Roberto's body. But his head is gone. Did it roll away?

Was it here when I came back for Sebastian? I search my mind, but can't remember. Not for sure. I think so, though. Wouldn't I have noticed if it wasn't?

I dash back to the rise and turn in circles, looking for any sign of Roberto's too-pale hair. He was so blond, his hair was as pale as corn silk. Surely I should be able to see that in the morning light. His hair should practically glow. I spin until my head swims, and then I close my eyes, dropping my hands to my knees.

Standing there, eyes shut, I force my mind back. It wasn't that long ago. I kneel by Sebastian's side, checking for his pulse, listening for him. My head on his chest, my eyes open. And, yes, I saw Roberto's head off to the side.

I stand up. If it was here last night, then where is it now?

There's only one explanation: one of the Ticks took it.

A shiver of disgust runs through me. Why would someone take his head? Ticks eat hearts, not brains. They're not zombies.

But who knows what goes through the mind of a Tick. Whoever has Roberto's head may not have eaten it, but that doesn't mean they're not doing something else with it. I need it—intact. Eyes in place.

I shudder again and this time I can't keep my revulsion down. My stomach threatens to crawl up my esophagus. I bend over and retch. Nothing comes up and I'm left shaking and even weaker than before.

Only after I straighten do I hear it. Or sense it. That primal screech that the Ticks make. I look around, certain there's one nearby.

And then I see her. She's sitting just down the hill at the base of the sprawling live oak in the square. She's small, but I can't tell if she's petite or if she's just young. I haven't seen any Ticks

116

who are children, but that doesn't mean there aren't any. I have no idea what she's doing out here in the morning, when she should be asleep. The roots of the tree stretch out around it, and she's nestled against the trunk. Her hair is a wild mass of blond tangles. She's sitting cross-legged with Roberto's head in her lap, running her fingers through his blond hair.

Her touch is both gentle and clumsy. The way a toddler finger-combs the hair of a beloved doll.

I have nothing left to vomit, but my stomach churns away, and my heart clenches in sorrow. This girl—for she must be a child—has lost so much. Whatever family she had in the Before is dead now—for surely if her parents were here, they wouldn't let her sit outside alone. For all I know, she killed them herself. Whatever childhood innocence she once had is gone forever. Yet clearly she still aches for what she's lost, because she seems to be stroking his hair to soothe herself.

My throat closes over my own loss. I think of the things that comforted me in the Before. My Slinky. My squirrel Beanie Baby. My pink backpack. They were my holy trinity on the Farm. My magic talismans. They kept me calm and grounded. With Lily by my side and my backpack of magic, I could do anything.

Now I have none of those things. But I still need to keep moving. Unlike this girl, I can't take false comfort from a mere stand-in.

I creep down the hill to her. She doesn't look up until I'm right in front of her. Her eyes are dark and feral, her too-big teeth have twisted her mouth into a snarl. I have to bend her will to mine, just as Sebastian once bent my will.

I bare my teeth at her, growling low in my throat, until she looks down, giving a faint whimper before thrusting her fingers deep into Roberto's hair and clutching his head tighter to her body.

I hold out my hands and growl again.

She ducks her head, looking at me with barely restrained anger. I lean in, forcing her to rock back slightly. I growl again, and this time, when I thrust out my hands, she pushes his head forward into them. I hold up Roberto's head and look at his eye. It's still there. I fist my hand in his hair like it's a handle and I stand.

Apparently, this is too much for her. She launches herself at me, aiming right for my middle so she knocks me down. I go flying back, with her on my chest, the head in between us. I roll out of the tackle and hop back to my feet. She's now unwilling to let her prize go. She throws herself at me again, this time howling. Which is sure to attract the attention of every Tick at El Corazon.

I elbow her sharply in the sternum, cutting off her cry, but it's too late. Other Ticks are already yelping in return. She's woken them, and they're pissed off. I don't know what their howls mean, not precisely, but still I understand. She's called for help. And they're on their way.

I spin on one foot and kick hard with the other. She staggers back a step. It's all the advantage I have or need. I run for it. Roberto's front porch is only fifty yards away, but there are Ticks melting out of the shadows from everywhere.

I clench my fingers more tightly in Roberto's hair and sprint for the house. I don't look back. I can hear thundering footsteps behind me, but still I don't look back. Hands are reaching for me, grabbing me. I fling out an arm, trying to swat them away while running, but there are always more hands.

Then I hear the familiar twang of a bow firing. The phffft

thump of an arrow lodging in someone's chest. A set of hands falls away as I hear someone stumble to the ground. But there are more hands, more Ticks, ready to fill in the gaps. They're stronger and faster than I remember. Maybe stronger and faster than me.

Then I hear another arrow shot and another.

Maybe they are stronger than I am, but I'm not alone. Sebastian is with me. Fighting for me. And he's only fifty feet away. Then twenty. Then I'm on the porch. I reach him and whirl around, pulling out the katana as I spin. I slice and jab, trying not to aim for the hearts, trying only to knock them back.

Sebastian and I are shoulder to shoulder as we back through the door. I have to grab Chuy to keep him from launching himself at one of the Ticks. Sebastian fires one last arrow before I slam the door shut and throw the dead bolt.

I look down at myself. I hold the katana in one hand and a severed head in the other. I am splattered with blood and grief and regret. Chuy wedges himself under my sword hand, whimpering. He buries his nose in my pants, like he's trying to hide from Roberto's head. I wish I could do the same.

Sebastian is beside me looking as war worn as I feel. There's a crossbow at his feet and a rapier in his hands. He pulls a handkerchief from his pocket and wipes the blade clean before sliding it back into the sheath. Suddenly the rapier is once again a cane.

Outside, the Ticks throw themselves at the door. One loud thud follows another.

"Good job not getting their attention."

I just stare at him. "Seriously?"

"You can thank me for saving your life later."

CHAPTER EIGHTEEN

LILY

The yelping in the distance stirs a fear deep inside. This bothers me, but I can't remember why. Something about safety. About movement. About night.

We've been walking for so long I no longer know where we are going or which direction we came from. Marcus stops, looking over his shoulder in one direction and then the other.

"Is that them?" he asks.

"Keep moving." I practically growl the words, even though I don't mean to.

My father is a deadweight across my back, a heavy burden I'm tired of carrying. He must have passed out, but I can't remember when. I shift him but the new hold feels no better on my burning muscles.

"We have to run!" Marcus says frantically. "We have to hide."

"No," I bark. "We can't run. Just keep walking."

Marcus stops. I turn to find him glaring up at me, his jaw jutting out stubbornly, his eyes filled with challenge. "You don't know where we're going, do you? We're just wandering. We need to go back."

"Back where? To the—" But my mind blanks. Back to the . . .

the what? "The crash? *They* are back there. The others. We can't fight them. But we might still make it."

"Where?" he asks. "Where are we going?"

Where? Where are we going?

Why can't I remember?

We're going to . . . the place. With food. And safety. And hope.

Where, though? And why can't I remember?

"A Farm!" I say as the word suddenly comes to me. "We're going to a Farm. When we get there it'll all be okay."

"A Farm?" he asks. "No, Farms are bad. They hurt people."

"No, Farms have food and safety. We'll be safe there. I promise."

He believes me. Almost.

Then someone howls in the distance. Someone calling to us. Demanding we join them. Others answer. And the call beckons to me, pulls at me, moves me like nothing I've ever known. And I want to . . . I want . . . to.

Marcus has already turned to the calling. He's almost out of my reach when I drop my burden and run after him. I yank him around, grab his arm, and shake.

"No!" I command. "We can't go! We can't go back! We have to move forward." He pulls away, but I throw myself at him, pull him to the ground under me. "We can't go back! We have to keep walking!" I'm on top of him now, my weight on his, my hand on his neck, holding hard to this control, to this one thing, to this hope. "You're coming with me."

"Yes!" he yelps. "I'm with you!"

His obedience soothes me. It dances along my nerves like peace and food and warmth.

I back away from him, a growl low in my throat, but he doesn't fight back, only whimpers. I growl again and stand. I move forward, and he falls in beside me, on my left, one step behind, where he belongs and it feels good.

The land around me is suddenly clear—not the glaring too-bright of day, but the soothing gray of silver and black. I can see so clearly. I can see the path before me. I feel the way to go. The way home has never been so certain.

CHAPTER NINETEEN

CARTER

I nearly cried when I first saw Sabrina's compound.

I'd been picturing something like El Corazon, part fortress, part archaic snapshot from Texas history. It had been this dusty, quaint little town, as creepy and atmospheric as the set of a Coen brothers movie. The whole thing had been one clown short of a horror novel. Except, wait, it already had its own bloodsucking monster.

Smart Com was nothing like that.

It was—quite literally—a shining beacon in the desert. From the gleaming skyscrapers to the acres of greenhouses, this was the product of modern human invention. This was civilization.

In the nine months since the Tick virus had been released, everything had fallen. Every city, every town, every insignificant blip on the map had been ravaged by the Ticks' mindless rage. Now even Roberto's fun house of torture was gone. Ten thousand years of human accomplishment and it was all destroyed.

Except this.

If I looked past the three razor-wire-topped fences, the guardhouse at the gate, and the—oh, forty or so guys with Uzis—if I looked past that, then Smart Com was the prettiest thing I'd ever seen.

Unfortunately, I only saw one way in. And no way out at all.

Muscles One drove us through the gate in a Hummer that looked like it had been purchased from paranoid-rich-jerks-r-us. My father had had that model. But, seriously, who could afford to drive something like that now? Every drop of gas was a precious and limited commodity. That alone was a clue to Sabrina's wealth. She had to have a massive stockpile of gas somewhere.

Even though we were clearly in a company-issued vehicle, we were still stopped at the guardhouse. Everyone piled out of the Hummer and was searched. Again. As if we could have smuggled in a toothpick after the last search.

A few minutes later, the Hummer rolled through the last set of gates into the compound. The relatively barren landscape of Albuquerque meant that there weren't a lot of trees on the compound. Nothing blocked the view but the buildings themselves. A few years ago, back before I'd been shipped off to Elite, before I first met Lily, my parents had brought me on a vacation to Mexico. My dad wasn't really the relax-on-the-beach type, but I guess my mom had badgered him into it. Even though the part of Mexico we were in was basically desert, the resort had still been manicured up like it was Disney World or something. Smart Com looked like that. There were stretches of native grass interspersed with islands of sparkling gravel and cacti. Huge spiky agave nestled up against the buildings. Golf carts zipped around transporting VIPs from one corner of the property to the other.

Needless to say, we weren't considered important enough to warrant the golf car treatment. Muscles parked the Hummer just inside the gate and marched us right across the lawn. I didn't know where all of Sabrina's people were—hell, for all I knew, Smart Com was still manufacturing phones and tablets—but there weren't many people out on the walkways. Those who were out eyed us suspiciously and walked purposely around us in wide, distrustful arcs.

"Where is everyone?" I asked.

"Keep moving," Muscles One grumbled.

"This compound is huge. There's got to be room for thousands of people here." Instead I saw maybe twenty—not counting the muscle.

This time, instead of answering, Muscles One gave me a jab in the back with the nose of his rifle. Good thing I didn't bruise easily.

Still, I filed away the observation as well as Muscles's non-committal response.

Maybe this was a sign that things were not as sunny here in paradise as Mel had thought. Or maybe when you were on the dinner menu for a vampire, you had the option of sleeping in. Sebastian and Roberto had acted like earning a spot on a vampire's compound was like getting the golden ticket to the Wonka factory. But maybe it was different here with Sabrina. Smart Com's resources had obviously served her well. How many people exactly could she house here? If Smart Com had employed thousands, how many of those thousands had made it?

At the door to one of the buildings, Muscles handed us off to another guy. This one was a little older, but no less fit. If possible, this guy was even bigger and more muscle-bound. He was roughly the size of an industrial freezer and looked about as warm and fuzzy as one, too. Based on the way Muscles deferred to him, I'd guess this was either Muscles's immediate boss or maybe even the commander in charge of the whole operation. The handoff went smoothly enough that he'd obviously been expecting us. Which told me someone had called ahead. Which told me that strangers showing up in Albuquerque was a rare occurrence.

The Freezer supervised as a couple of muscle clones escorted us through the building, up an elevator, and into a waiting room.

At El Corazon, Roberto had had cells set aside to hold prisoners. Okay, so they hadn't been barred, but that had obviously been their purpose. He'd held us in an otherwise completely empty room with a cushionless bench built into the wall. There'd been nothing I could have used as a weapon.

I'd expected Sabrina to have a similar setup.

Once again, she surprised me.

We were shown into a room so luxurious that it could have been the VIP lounge at an upscale hotel. There was a sprawling sectional sofa. A TV and gaming system big enough it put my dad's media room to shame. There were a couple of open doors on the far wall. If I had to guess, I'd say they led off to a bathroom and possibly a full kitchen. There was a wall of windows that overlooked the rest of Smart Com's campus. A table laid out with a bucket of chilled cans of Coke. And—get this—a friggin' fruit and cheese plate.

By the time I was done gawking at the spread, the Freezer had disappeared. The guy moved so quietly, I hadn't even heard him vanish. I gave the doorknob a twist, but it had been locked behind him, of course. We were all alone in the VIP lounge.

Darren bolted for the TV like a kid on Christmas morning. He ran his hand over the spines of the games displayed on the bookshelf beside the TV. "Check it out! They have the latest *Assassin's Creed*. I didn't even think they'd released this one before everything happened. And—holy crap—a PS6? I had no idea this was in development nine months ago."

126

Dawn went straight for the food. She popped open a Diet Coke and took one long gulp, eyes closed, savoring the taste. A moment later, she opened her eyes, practically blinking back tears, and looked embarrassed. "Dad was always so strict about the no-caffeine thing. He refused to waste any storage space on soda, but, man, I've missed it."

I didn't tell her not to drink it. Part of me wanted to. That cautious part that didn't fully trust that this was going to end well. There was a chance—and I didn't know how great that chance was—that the food was drugged. Or poisoned.

Okay, probably not poisoned. If Sabrina was going to kill us all, she probably wouldn't waste our blood. Unless she was going to have our bodies dumped far beyond Smart Com's grounds and she wanted to use our poisoned blood to kill off a few Ticks. But, if that was her plan, Muscles One and Two probably would have just shot us out on the street. Why waste the gas to bring us back or the Diet Coke?

Besides, chances were good we'd be here for at least a few days. We couldn't refuse to eat during that time. None of us had the fat stores to turn down food. It was possible to justify just about anything when you were hungry enough.

Dawn took another gulp of Diet Coke and then seemed to see the rest of the spread. "Bananas? They have bananas?" she asked, her eyes wide as she looked at me. "Do you think that means they have trade relations with Central America?" She picked up an apple, brought it to her nose, and inhaled deeply. Then a kiwi. "These are fresh. Okay, maybe an apple could last nine months in refrigeration, but not a banana. Not a kiwi. What do you think this means? Does that mean there's still organized agriculture in other parts of the country? Or other parts of the world? Are there still governments?"

"You ask such excellent questions, my dear," a warm female voice said from behind me.

I turned to see a woman standing in one of the open door-ways. She had to be Sabrina.

She appeared older than I expected, given that both Sebastian and Roberto—the only two vampires I'd ever met that I knew of—both looked so young. The picture in the brochure was too small to even guess at her age. Sebastian had been in his early twenties when he'd been turned, so he still looked about twenty-four. Roberto had looked even younger, maybe sixteen or seventeen. And of course there was Mel—frozen in time at eighteen.

Sabrina reminded me of my father's first wife, a beautiful but older woman clinging to the fading shreds of her youth. She obviously took meticulous care of herself. She was lean and fit, with a willowy athlete's body. She was tall for a woman, which still put her a few inches shorter than me. Her black hair fell straight to her waist. Only her skin gave her away. The grooves on either side of her mouth. The sagging just under her chin. The too-taut appearance of her cheeks, as if she'd been carved from wax for a display at a museum. There were some signs of aging that no amount of cosmetic enhancement could cover, and Sabrina had them.

But if she felt self-conscious about those signs—as my dad's first wife clearly had—Sabrina didn't show it. She was as confident as a queen.

"I'm so impressed," Sabrina purred as she strolled toward the table, "that you're forward-thinking enough to consider such questions. I do have trade agreements with several empires throughout the former United States. Such arrangements have proved to be very"—her lips twisted in a lascivious smile—"beneficial."

She stopped close to Dawn and looked her over, running the back of her fingers down Dawn's face, clucking her tongue appraisingly.

I couldn't tell if she was merely admiring Dawn's youthful skin, or trying to figure out how to make a coin purse from her cheeks. Obviously Dawn wasn't any more comfortable with Sabrina's touch than I was, because she leaned back, arching back over the table to get away from her.

Sabrina made a mewling, disappointed sound—though I couldn't tell if her predatory interest in Dawn was genuine or if she was just messing with her.

Sabrina gave Dawn's cheek a final pat—one sharp enough to almost be a slap—and then turned her attention to Darren. She walked toward him, her hips slinking seductively.

"How about you, my dear boy?"

"Pardon, ma'am?"

She chuckled. "You like games, I take it. We have lots of games here. More than you can possibly imagine. I'd love to introduce you to all of them."

Darren swallowed nervously, doing a piss-poor job of hiding his panic. Darren was an impossibly young sixteen. He'd been sheltered in the Before. The obvious sexual connotation of Sabrina's words seemed to freak him out even more than it did Dawn. I didn't blame him. My dad's first wife had come on to me once. It had squigged me out, too, and she probably didn't want to suck my blood afterward.

"What about Mexico?" I asked loudly.

Sabrina's attention snapped over to me. She raised one chilling eyebrow. "Excuse me?"

"You said you had agreements with empires across the former United States. What about empires in Mexico? What about

129

Central or South America?" I pointed to the fruit laid out on the table. "Bananas. Pineapples. Grapes. In the Before, bananas and pineapples came from Central America, right? Maybe Hawaii. Do you have trade agreements with them or are these things grown in your greenhouse?"

Her expression hardened infinitesimally. "Well, aren't you the curious little kitten?"

"I'm more of a dog person, actually."

I crossed my arms over my chest and met her gaze. It had been a risk, asking such pointed questions. If she hadn't guessed it already, she now knew that I was the leader of this little bunch. I wanted her to understand that if she should mess with anyone, it should be me.

After eyeing me for a long moment, she extended a hand toward the table. "My men said they picked you up earlier this morning not far from the compound."

I nodded. "That's right."

"Then you must have driven through the night to get here. You must be simply starving." She gestured toward the table. "Please, help yourself."

"No thanks."

She tilted her head as if trying to figure me out. "Is there perhaps something else you'd prefer? We have excellent chefs on staff. I could order something for you." She looked over at Darren. "Perhaps a burger? Some fries? Maybe a chocolate shake?"

From more than ten feet away, I heard Darren's stomach growl.

Sabrina smiled, turning her attention back to Dawn. "A slice of cake, perhaps? Or a dish of ice cream? There's a brand—Ben and Gerald's, I believe—that's quite popular among girls your age."

"You have Ben and Jerry's?" Dawn asked softly.

"Yes, yes. Ben and Jerry's. Precisely."

Sabrina smiled and again I got that sense that she was just messing with us. That she had changed tactics. Now, instead of acting the part of sexual predator, she was playing the part of sweet, nurturing mother. Not only was she well aware of Ben & Jerry's real name, but there probably wasn't a single pint of anything on this compound that she hadn't personally picked out herself.

Still, she smiled at them. "You've spent months out there in the wilderness." Sabrina gave an exaggerated shudder of disgust. "Please, just tell me what you desire and I will do everything in my power to accommodate you."

When no one answered her, she asked, "Are you sure you won't eat something?"

"Quite sure."

"Are you worried that it's poisoned? I guarantee you, it isn't. I wouldn't dream of doing something so Machiavellian."

"Yeah. I'm sure."

"Because the selection of cheeses is—"

"Yeah. I bet it's all great. The best money can buy." Darren was still gazing longingly at the food and I swore he'd inched closer to the table. His hand kept drifting out like he might snatch up a snack without meaning to. Poor guy didn't know quite what he was dealing with here. "And if we eat it, it'll be the best meal we've had in months. Maybe years. There we'll be, full and content. Our blood will be pumping with the serotonin that you vampires find so yummy and delicious. That's the whole point of this spread, right?"

"Whatever do you mean?" she asked, hand pressed to her chest like she was offended.

131

"The point of this room, stocked with all the things that delight humans. The foods we love. The entertainments we've been missing. What if I wanted a blow job? What if that's what I needed to really relax me? Would you get a girl in here to give me one of those? Because I'm guessing that hormone release tastes really good in the blood."

Her smile turned a bit cruel. "True. But it's even better if you care about the person giving it, and I didn't sense that you feel that way about either of these two. But shall I give you a few minutes alone?"

"No thank you. If you're going to drain me, you'll have to take blood that's drenched in anger and adrenaline."

I half expected her to be offended, but again she laughed, deeply amused by my outburst.

"Of course I'm not going to drain you. Silly boy! Why would I do that when I have every intention of keeping you around for quite some time."

"What's your point?"

"I have so many points." Still smiling, she ran her tongue over her needle-sharp incisors. Then she cackled. "I've never been able to resist a good pun!" She dropped her hand and turned away from me. "Wordplay is such fun, don't you agree?"

"Excuse me?"

"Banter? Witty conversation? Repartee?" She gave a disappointed sigh. "Oh dear. I was so hoping that you'd be clever. You seemed to be with all those questions about Central America."

"I'm not an idiot, if that's what you mean." Though, frankly, I was starting to feel like one. Where the hell was she going with all this?

"Oh, no. Of course not. People with your traits tend to be far above average intelligence. But you can't blame me for hoping for something a little bit more"—she tipped her head to the side, considering—"refined. Urbane even. My current *abductura* is so focused on accruing tremendous power and wealth. He's always blah, blah, blah, strategy. Blah, blah, blah, global positioning. Do those things interest you?"

She sent me an odd, piercing stare that gave me the impression she could see into my very soul.

"Money?" she asked. "Wealth? Political power? The fate of nations?" She paused again, than waved her hand in a give-it-to-me-straight gesture. "Any interest at all?"

I shook my head.

"Good," she snapped. "It gets so very dull. I really miss decent conversation. But I suppose you can't all be Oscar Wilde. Now there was an *abductura* all the other vampires envied."

She kept prattling on, but my mind was stuck on that one stunning revelation. She knew I was an *abductura*.

CHAPTER TWENTY

MEL

Just inside the door, Sebastian sways on his feet. I lunge for him, dropping both the head and the blade to catch him in my arms. He's a deadweight against me. I can feel him trying to get his feet under him, but they don't seem to be working.

"You shouldn't have come out." Fear makes my words harsh. "It was too much for you!"

"What was I supposed to do?" he asks, his words slurring. "Let them pull you to shreds? Besides, your dog was throwing himself at the door. I thought he was going to break the thing down trying to get to you."

I don't argue. I want to say that I didn't need him, but clearly I did. Clearly I can't do any of this on my own. Besides, when Sebastian left the safety of the house, he didn't let Chuy out. If he had, Chuy would have thrown himself into the mix and been taken down by one of the Ticks. Sebastian may be a jerk, but for some reason, he saved Chuy's life. Even though I keep saying I don't like dogs, I'm thankful.

Instead of mentioning that aloud, I say, "Let's just get downstairs."

There's another troop of Ticks hitting the door. The whole doorframe seems to shake.

"I hope you're right about this house being as strong as a bomb shelter."

"I hope I'm right about the blood."

"Yes. That, too," I agree.

Trying not to drop Sebastian, I lean down to grab a handful of hair. I can't think about the grisly package I'm carrying or about the butchered hand tucked into my pocket. I can only shove aside my emotions and put one foot in front of the other. I can't fail. I can't lose Sebastian. I can't let either of us starve.

In the basement, I leave Sebastian leaning against the workbench. I leave Chuy to watch Sebastian and go back up to the kitchen to find food for the dog, too. If we're going into this safe room, I don't know how long we'll be there and Chuy has to be hungry by now. Roberto's kitchen is well stocked with human food—for his valet presumably. I grab an armful of canned meat and stew and grab a can opener as well. I wrap it up in a towel to make it easier to carry and head back down to the basement.

"Head first or hand?" I ask after I've set my bundle down on the workbench.

"Hand first. At least on my system. The palm print pulls up the retinal file."

I pull the hand from my pocket, but before I can place it against the touch screen, Sebastian stops me.

"Warm it up."

"What?"

"It . . . body temperature."

"Oh." Cringing, I rub the hand between mine. It's clammy and awful, but I do it anyway. This isn't the worst thing I've done as a vampire. When I press the hand to the pad, the machine makes a series of beeps and then an unhappy blurk.

"Again," Sebastian says.

"I know, I know." I rub more this time, massaging the fingers between mine, trying to get warmth into dead flesh. I press the palm to the pad again and this time all the beeps are happy.

"Now the head. Open the eye first. But be fast."

I make myself look at Roberto's head. His eyelid is almost closed. I have to practically pry it open and then I hold up the head, feeling like Perseus with Medusa.

The retinal scanner casts laser red crosshairs over his face. My heart is pounding and my hands are trembling so much I'm afraid I won't be able to hold it still long enough. I grab the head on either side and hold it closer to my body, which puts it right in front of my face.

There are more beeps. Another blurk. And finally the happy beeps and the sound of a lock releasing.

The door swings open as the sound of breaking glass echoes through the house. I look back over my shoulder to see Sebastian pushing off from the workbench. He can barely walk, but he's holding the bundle of food for the dog.

I start to reach for him, but he gasps out, "Don't let the door close. And bring Roberto. We might need him later."

I hold open the door and step aside for him to hobble through. Chuy files in after him. I hear more breaking glass followed by several loud thuds.

"I thought you said the house was impenetrable."

He shrugged. "Nothing lasts forever."

I give one last look at the basement, refusing to consider how we will get out of here when the time comes, and let the door slam shut behind me.

CHAPTER TWENTY-ONE

CARTER

For a long moment, my mind just reeled. Being an *abductura* was the one advantage I had. The one ace up my sleeve. Now that she knew, was I completely screwed?

"How'd you know?" I asked stupidly, my mind still pedaling to catch up. Dawn and Darren exchanged nervous looks and I saw Dawn take a step closer to her brother.

Sabrina's too-plump lips curved into a smile that made her look vaguely catlike as she slithered closer to me. "I think the better question is why you thought I wouldn't know. I know you're young, so I'll go easy on you." She grasped my jaw in her hand and twisted my face so I had to look at her. "Do not underestimate me merely because I'm a woman."

I tried to jerk my head away from her, but her hold was so tight the action only wrenched my muscles.

"There you go again. Making the mistake of seeing me first as a woman and forgetting that I am also a vampire." Her fingers bit into the soft tissue of my face, scraping the inside of my mouth against my teeth. I could almost feel the bruises forming and could taste the blood seeping into my mouth. "Sebastian knew you were an *abductura*. If he sensed it, did you really think I would not?"

"No," I choked out. "I didn't think—"

I broke off when she jerked me even closer, pulling me down so our faces were mere inches apart. And then she sniffed my breath. It took me a second, and then it hit me. The blood in my mouth. Her eyes fluttered closed as she savored the scent of my blood on my exhalation.

Her grasp on my face loosened, but she snaked an arm around my neck and kissed me.

It was a kiss only in the loosest meaning of the word. Her mouth was covering mine. Her tongue was in my mouth. But there was nothing sexual about it. Nothing sensual or erotic. Just her tongue stroking the inside of my cheeks. Harvesting the tiny drops of blood.

Then, abruptly, she pushed me away. I stumbled back, tripping over the ottoman of the sectional sofa before I caught myself. I was just glad I hadn't landed flat on my ass.

Sabrina took a big step back, pressing the back of her hand to her mouth as she watched me, and I got the distinct impression she had to fight to control her blood lust.

She must have won that battle, because after a moment she wiped at the corners of her mouth with her fingertip, the way some women do when fixing their lipstick, and she said crisply, "You're correct. Your blood tastes like fear and sorrow. Hardly even worth drinking."

I couldn't tell if I should take that as a compliment or an insult.

"I'm not going to apologize for being a bad meal."

I tried to make that sound like a smartass quip. I also tried to hide the fact that I was practically shaking.

Because, yeah, I had underestimated her. She looked older and feminine. She was tall, but so thin she seemed delicate. In reality, there was nothing delicate about this woman. There was nothing weak. Nothing fragile.

The fact that I'd let myself forget, even for a moment, that she was a bloodsucking monster, that she was stronger and fiercer than I was, that she was a remorseless predator . . . well, that mistake was all on me.

"I had higher hopes for you," she said, almost sadly. Then she turned her gleaming gaze on Dawn and Darren. "Perhaps one of your companions will be more . . . obliging." She waved a hand to gesture the Freezer over.

"Yes, m'lady?"

"Bring me the girl."

The Freezer gestured behind him and another pair of Muscles came in and grabbed Dawn and Darren. Dawn was faster than she looked. She tried to duck under the Freezer's arm, but he managed to snag her hand and gave it a sharp twist and spun her around. She yelped, dropping to her knees as he yanked her arm up behind her.

I lunged for them. "Let her go!"

He did and she dropped to the ground, cradling her arm, but then the Freezer shoved a palm to my chest. It was like being hit in the sternum with a log. I flew backward, the air knocked right out of my lungs, and everything went black.

* *

I don't know how long I was out, but when I woke up I was sprawled out on the sofa, alone. No sign of Dawn or Darren or the Freezer. Even Sabrina, the wackadoodle queen of the damned, was nowhere in sight.

Wincing, I rubbed my sternum, which I hoped the Freezer hadn't cracked. If Sabrina was going to drain me, I didn't want to make it any easier on her. But maybe that's what the Freezer actually was. A can opener.

I was still struggling to suck air into my lungs when I heard noises from the other room. I pushed an elbow under me and tried to sit up, despite the aching in my chest.

I sucked in a deep breath and was hit with the unexpected scent of . . . was that fresh-baked cookies? Christ, had I had a stroke?

That was the medical condition that made you smell things that weren't there, right? Or maybe a brain tumor? I inhaled again. The cookie smell was still there.

I sat up, swung my legs down to the floor, and rested my head in my palms.

"Oh good, you're up."

I came to my feet and spun around—too quickly. I felt my head wobble and had to lean against the sofa. And then I squeezed my eyes closed and pried them open again, convinced I wasn't really seeing what I seemed to be really seeing.

Sabrina was walking toward me from whatever room lay beyond that door. She was no longer dressed in her slinky black leather. Now she wore high-heeled black boots, jeans, and a tank top. And an apron.

Not like a white, blood-splattered butcher's apron. That I could have wrapped my brain around. No, she wore a kitschy little housewife's apron. It was bright red with white and pink blossoms and a frilly white trim.

As she got closer, I realized she was carrying a plate of cookies. She set the cookies on the coffee table and came around to stand just a few inches away.

She studied me, her head tilted just to the side, her gaze perfectly sane. Perfectly reasonable. Not at all bat-shit crazy.

"Did he hurt you?" she asked, her eyes searching my face with apparently genuine concern. "I'll have to discuss that with him. I'm afraid Mr. Marek tends to be very protective. As any good leader is." Her lips twisted into a charmed smile. "As you are."

For a second, I just flat-out didn't know what to say. Finally, I burst out, "What the hell?"

She blinked as if surprised, then tilted her head back and laughed. Not the crazed, psyco-bitch laugh of earlier, but a genuine laugh. A little husky, a little bit embarrassed.

Then she noticed I wasn't laughing along with her. She sat, looking chagrined, and patted the sofa beside her.

There was no way I was sitting down with her, but I couldn't exactly refuse, either. Instead, I sidled down to the end of the sofa and twisted so that when I sat, no part of my back was to her.

She noticed that and nodded like it was no more or less than what she expected. "Would you like a cookie?"

"I'd like to know where my people are."

"They're fine. I had them removed." Then she hastily added, "To another room. They are perfectly safe and being well cared for."

Yeah. And I'd believe that when I saw it with my own eyes.

Or maybe I wouldn't, because my own eyes seemed to be messing with me right now. I mean, this had to be a hallucination, right?

Aloud, I said nothing, because when you're having a psychotic break in the presence of a predator, you don't exactly want to advertise it.

She continued, "I'm sure you understand that being a woman in my position requires . . ." She seemed to be searching for the right word. "A certain amount of awareness about perceptions and appearances."

She paused, arching her eyebrows like she was waiting for me to respond.

"Okay," I said slowly.

"A certain amount of showmanship is essential for maintaining power. You understand, I am sure."

"Showmanship?" I asked. "That's what that was? When you threaten to eat one of my people?"

She waved a hand. Her nails still flashed bright red, but the gesture carried with it a whiff of vanilla.

"Oh, no. That wasn't showmanship. I was referring to the clothes. The blood licking. The cackling. That is showmanship. I'm merely conforming to people's expectations. No, the threat to eat Dawn was a test."

"A test?"

"Yes." She frowned. "I'm sorry I had to do it, but it was absolutely necessary."

"A test?" I said again, sounding more clueless than I wanted to. "You threatened to eat my friend as a test? For me?"

Sabrina leaned forward reassuringly. "Dawn was never in any danger. I want you to know that."

"Except for when the Freezer nearly broke her arm twisting it behind her back."

"The Freezer? Oh, you mean Mr. Marek? No, I assure you Mr. Marek is quite skilled. She was never really in harm's way." Sabrina paused to gesture toward the plate. "Did you want a cookie?"

"No."

"Mr. Marek assures me they're quite good. Are you sure you won't have one?"

"Quite sure."

She almost looked disappointed, but smiled faintly. "I'm

going to assume that Sebastian has been his normal uncommunicative self and hasn't told you much about your gift."

"I know enough."

"I doubt that. I was an *abductura* my entire human life and I never felt like I knew enough." For a second, her gaze drifted away and she looked both pensive and nostalgic. Then she offered me a bracing smile and said, "Did you know, for example, that your powers will always be strongest when you're unable to physically act yourself? The less you are able to carry out your own will, the more sway you will have over others. And every *abductura* is slightly different. Some are extremely powerful, some less so, but the one thing they all have in common is that their powers vary depending on their motivations. Some are motivated by greed. Some by the desire to nurture others. Or by the need for power or control." She pierced me with a look. "Are you going to ask me what I think motivates you?"

"Am I supposed to care what you think?"

"You're motivated by the need to protect others. I mentioned money and power, but you barely blinked. I was starting to doubt you had any power at all, despite Mr. Marek's very excellent instincts. But then I threatened dear Dawn and you lit right up."

"Huh." I gave a grunt without meaning to.

Sabrina was right. There was a lot I didn't know about being an *abductura*. About this power I had. And if I trusted her more, she might be a person I could learn from.

She scooted closer on the sofa and reached out a hand to pat my knee. "I am so very sorry," she said softly, "for everything you've been through these past months. As driven as you are to protect people, things must have been unbearable for you since the Before. To make matters worse, you've been with Sebastian."

Her voice took on a note of exasperation. Something in

my expression must have given me away, because she smiled ruefully.

"Don't forget I was his *abductura* once, too. I know how he works. The way he manipulates people. The way he isolates you from others. That way he has of telling you you're special and making you feel worthless all at the same time. Even now, even after all he's done, part of you still trusts him. You still believe that if you return to him, he'll get you out of this." She slanted an assessing look at me and her lips twisted into a bitter smile filled with regret. "He's like that, isn't he? He argues with you just enough to make you believe that you've convinced him to do something, when it was really his idea all along. That's what he did with you, isn't it? With this rebellion of yours. He made you think it was your idea, but it's still gotten him exactly what he wanted."

Shock raced through me. Was that what he'd done?

No. The rebellion had been my idea. My plan. Sebastian had been against it from the beginning.

Or had he?

I wasn't sure anymore and talking to Sabrina was only making it worse. And I wanted a cookie, damn it.

Not that I was going to take one from her, but still it had been a long time since I'd had a fresh-baked chocolate chip cookie.

"You shouldn't feel bad about it," she continued. "Sebastian may not have any powers of his own as an *abductura*, but he's been alive a very long time. That's what two thousand years of life gets you, I suppose. The most advanced degree in human psychology ever. He is a genius when it comes to understanding people and he's even better at getting them to do what he wants."

That's when I gave in and reached for the cookie.

Damn, it was good. The best cookie I'd ever had. Still warm from the oven. Gooey and sweet. And there was a whole plate of them. And no one here to eat them but me.

I put the cookie down and nudged the plate away. "I didn't come here for a therapy session. If you want to get into my head, you're going to have to work a little harder than that."

"I'm not trying to"—she made air quotes with her fingers—"get into your head. Not all vampires are as bad as Sebastian. I'm just apologizing. For baiting you like I did. You understand why I did it, though, don't you? You understand that I had to do it. I had to know how strong you were. I had to know what kinds of things would motivate you. If you weren't strong enough, or if your motives and mine were at cross purposes, this entire endeavor would fail."

Suddenly I got it. Everything she'd done since I'd gotten here—every weird affectation, every eccentricity, maybe even the blood thing—had been her way of taking my measure. Like some elaborate, interactive Rorschach inkblot test. She hadn't merely been trying to figure out whether or not I was an *abductura*, she needed to know if I could do the job she needed me to do.

"So this was all just some sort of audition?"

"Exactly. And you passed. With flying colors."

An audition? All the creepiness? The blood licking, the threatening, the weirdness . . . she'd been testing me. "What do you want from me?"

"The question isn't what I want from you," she said simply. "It's what we want from one another."

"What makes you think I want something from you?"

"You came to me."

"Your men picked us up miles from here."

"Potayto, potahto. In a hundred and fifty years as a vampire, how many times do you think an *abductura* has simply wandered into my territory?" She raised her hand, her fingers curved in a graceful zero shape. Then she stood and strolled over to the bank of windows on the far wall and looked out them. "No. *Abducturae* are sought out. Cultivated. In the best of all possible worlds, bred. But you never simply happen upon one like a four-leaf clover." She turned, pushing herself off the glass, and strolled toward me, her gait smooth and controlled. "You're the one who said no games. What is it you want from me?"

There was really only one way I could play this. If she hadn't guessed I was an *abductura*, I might have used my powers to sway her. I had convinced Sebastian to bite Mel. I might have been able to bide my time until Ely brought Marcus and Lily here and then convince her to bite them. But since she knew the truth, it was time to move on to plan B.

B as in ballsy and desperate.

"Two of my friends have been exposed to the virus. I want you to give me the cure for them."

CHAPTER TWENTY-TWO

CARTER

"You honestly think that even if I have the cure to the Tick virus, I'm just going to hand it over to you?"

"Yes. Because you need me. You give me the cure. I take it to my friends and treat them. If it works, I'll come back and I'll work as your *abductura*."

She eyed me and I hoped she couldn't see past my poker face. Hell, I hoped I had a poker face. *Abductura* or not, I didn't know enough about how this all worked to have any faith in my ability to even nudge the emotions of a vampire who'd once been an *abductura* herself.

"You've come here to ask me for the cure, but you don't even believe it works?"

"Look, I don't know what to believe anymore." Ah, hell. Maybe straight-up honesty was better than a poker face. "I've been lied to and manipulated so much by you people, I don't have any faith in anything you say. But if there's a chance the cure works, I need it."

"It seems we're at an impasse." She gave my cheek a maternal pat, then stood and crossed to the media center. She selected one of the remotes and clicked on the TV. "Perhaps this will convince you that you can trust me."

I stood there—terrified of what I was about to see, of what

she thought might sway me—as she clicked through a series of menu screens. It could be a live video feed of Dawn and Darren. Probably being tortured. Maybe killed. Or maybe something even worse. Someone I cared about even more. Maybe somehow—against all odds—she'd found Lily first. But how?

Before my imagination could go even crazier, the image on the TV flickered into view. And it wasn't anything I expected. Not Dawn or Darren or Lily.

It was a Tick. A male. Strapped onto a table in a hospital room somewhere. The table was in the middle of the room, well out of range of the cabinets lining the walls and the trays of surgical equipment. What looked like a refrigerator was just barely visible on the left-hand side of the screen.

The Tick was awake and alert. And clearly both angry and terrified. He bucked against the thick restraints holding him in place. The straps bound not just his wrists and ankles, but his calves, his thighs, his waist, his arms, even his head. They really wanted him to keep still. The volume had been lowered so I could barely hear his howls of rage.

I took a step closer. I'd never seen a Tick. Not like this.

Yeah, I'd fought and killed plenty of them. But in the heat of battle, you didn't really have time to take a good look. When a Tick was bearing down on you, ready to rip your heart out of your chest, you didn't have time to do anything but aim a stake at his heart and pray your brains might trump his brawn. I'd been lucky. Mine always had.

Now, watching this guy on film, I really looked at him. The transformation from human to Tick was incredible. He was naked—which meant either he'd been a Tick awhile or they'd taken off whatever scraps of clothes he'd had on. Ticks didn't bother with clothes. They didn't put them on, but they usually didn't take them off, either. The longer a person had been a Tick, the more likely it was their clothes had simply been ripped off at some point. This guy's muscles bulged beneath his skin, making him look bulkier than even the biggest professional bodybuilder. His very bones looked bigger. As always, it was his face that creeped me out the most. His brow ridge was thick and distended. His jaw was huge. His enormous, leonine teeth made his lips protrude. Everything about him repulsed me.

Despite that, I felt pity nudge through me. He was a monster, but strapped down like this, he was pathetic.

Then there was movement on the left. The refrigerator door swung open and then closed. A second later, a pair of doctors walked into view. They wore white lab coats, surgical gloves, and masks. I got the feeling from the way the Tick roared at them that they'd been there all along, just offscreen. They spoke to each other, but it was impossible to hear them over his cries. One of them held a syringe. The other used a piece of surgical tubing to tie off his bicep. Just as the second doctor approached with the needle, the strap holding the Tick's head in place slipped and he reared up off the table. The straps on his upper body had more give in them than they should have, because he was able to buck maybe five inches off the surface—enough to bite into the arm of the doctor closest to him. The doctor wrenched away, but he wasn't fast enough. The Tick left a bloody hole in the doctor's white sleeve.

The second doctor plunged the syringe into the Tick's arm and then dashed to safety. The wounded doctor stumbled out of the frame clutching his bloody arm.

I opened my mouth to speak, but Sabrina held up a hand to

silence me. Then she clicked a button and the video started fast-forwarding. "I assume you don't want to watch this in real time," she said. "It gets a little tedious."

On the screen, the Tick jerked and spasmed at superspeed. His already quick movements—the ones he was capable of while still mostly strapped down—slowed and stopped as he apparently fell asleep.

With Sabrina fast-forwarding the video, it was impossible to tell how much time was passing or to see the minute changes transforming his body. At some point the camera shifted positions. Other than that, it ran on fast-forward for maybe ten minutes before Sabrina clicked it to normal speed.

The Tick's arms and legs were bloody where he'd struggled so hard against the straps. The blood was dried and crusted. His skin looked chafed and raw. But the creature on the table was no longer a Tick. He was a man.

A doctor came in, still wearing gloves and a surgical mask, and undid the man's straps. Slowly, the man sat up. The doctor moved in front of him as if checking his vitals. Then the doctor stepped out of view again, leaving just the man, staring at the camera, haunted and hollow-eyed.

Sabrina paused then, leaving the image of that man on the screen, leaving my heart pounding and my mind racing.

"And so you see," she began. "I am more trustworthy than—"

"When was that?"

"Approximately three days ago. I sent a team to Genexome to retrieve the cure immediately after Sebastian and Mel left here. They found the cure and—"

"In the underground vault?"

She blinked, looking a little startled. "You know this might go faster if you stopped interrupting me."

"Yeah, I guess when you're the grand empress supreme people don't interrupt you a lot, but if you want me to work with you, you'll answer my questions."

"If we are going to work together, I expect you to learn some manners."

"And I expect you to stop treating me like a child and plaything."

"Very well." But her eyes glinted with annoyance as she reached her hands behind her and untied the bow on her bright red apron. She slid it off and folded it neatly as she spoke. "No. Not from the underground vault. Marek couldn't access that."

So the dead bodies outside the vault had been Sabrina's men.

"The sample of the cure that Marek found was right where Sebastian told me it would be—in the research facility on the fifth floor. There were five samples of the cure stored there in a refrigeration tank. I suspect Sebastian has a much greater supply in the underground vault as well as the documentation about how the cure was manufactured in the first place."

"So you still have four samples left?"

"No. Three. The man you saw was our second test subject. The first time my doctors tried to administer the cure to a Tick when he was sedated. The results were . . . less successful."

I didn't bother to ask what she meant by that. I could only assume it was bad. Probably very bad.

"I want to meet that man. Talk to him."

"I'm afraid that's impossible."

"If you want me to cooperate—"

"You can't meet him because he's dead."

"The cure killed him?"

"No." She blinked before turning away, and for an instant, I would have sworn I saw regret in her expression. "The doctors failed to supervise him properly. I didn't speak to the man myself, but it seems he was rather distraught. He was left alone in the hospital room while the doctors tended to another patient and he cut his own wrists." She held up the remote again. "There is footage of that as well if you'd like to see it?"

"No," I managed to choke out past my nausea.

I couldn't help but imagine the confusion, the anger, the grief that man must have experienced. He'd spent months living like an animal. Only to awaken as a human again. What had that been like? Had he—dear God—had he remembered?

That would certainly explain his suicide. I'd seen the things the Ticks did. I wouldn't want to live with those memories, either.

What if living with the cure was worse than living with the virus?

But it didn't matter. I pushed aside the dread coiling within me. I wasn't going to let this happen to Lily. I'd get to her before it was too late.

"This happened here? At Smart Com?"

"Yes."

"Then I want to see the doctors. The room. Everything."

Sabrina clicked the remote and the TV went blank. She turned back to me with an expression that was almost sad. "Were you always this distrustful?" But then she held up a hand. "Never mind. Of course I know the answer. It's Sebastian who did this to you. Who turned you against all vampires. Who made you think we're monsters. We're really not."

"Right. I'm sure you're just like everybody else. Just trying to get by in the Tick-pocalypse."

Sabrina smiled then, giving a delighted chuckle. "Oh, you do have a sense of humor. That will make working together so much more pleasant."

Had she thought I would simply forget that she'd been manipulating me? That she'd been acting bat-shit crazy and then weirdly maternal?

"You forget, I haven't agreed to anything yet."

"You still don't trust that I have the cure? Even after the video?"

"Special effects may be new to you, but I spent my whole life watching dinosaurs destroy Costa Rican forests and aliens invade earth. Anything can be faked well enough to make a convincing video. Until I see the room where that was filmed, the doctor who was injured, and the body of the guy who killed himself, I won't believe there's a cure."

CHAPTER TWENTY-THREE

CARTER

"Very well, you want to see the room where this happened before you agree to my offer, fine. But I have something to show you on the way. Something that may sway you further in my favor."

Before I could even agree, she swept out the door. I followed her. Unless I wanted to seem like a pouting child, I didn't have a choice. The Freezer—what had she called him? Marek—was still waiting right outside, along with a second guy who could have been his twin. As she and I walked past, Marek peeled off the wall and fell in line right behind us, staying several steps away to give us privacy in case she kept talking. She didn't.

As she led me silently through the halls, I was struck again by how empty the building seemed. In the Before, this building would probably have held the company's executive offices. We passed a couple of doors that were closed and may have had someone behind them, but we passed far more that were open and revealed empty rooms.

And okay, sure, Smart Com probably wasn't doing a lot of marketing these days, but surely a vampire like Sabrina had an empire big enough that she could have used the space for something.

She led me to the elevator and down to a basement level that seemed to connect the buildings, which would have explained the lack of people on the upper levels, except that there seemed to be few people down here as well. What the hell was going on?

Before I could ask, we'd reached a reception area set up like a doctor's office, right down to the fish tank and the selection of dated magazines. Sabrina breezed through the doors, past a few people dressed in scrubs, and into one of the rooms. Obviously, this was her compound's clinic, but I couldn't imagine why she'd brought me there until I saw the man laid out on the bed. He was hooked up to an IV as well as all kinds of machinery, including a ventilator. He had a sizable bandage around his arm.

"This is Dr. Bonard. We've been treating him for the Tick virus. He doesn't appear to be succumbing to the transformation, but he is very sick. Needless to say, you can't ask him any of your questions."

When she led me into another room, I expected this one to have the body of the man who'd killed himself, but instead it was a different man.

He was about my father's age. Maybe a few years older. It was hard to tell for sure with the web of tubes and equipment that covered his face. He had thick dark hair, graying at the temples. I would have recognized him even if it hadn't been for the Smart Com brochure, because his picture had been all over the media just a few months before the Tick outbreak. He was Paul Workman and he'd been the CEO of Smart Com. Until his death, that is.

"I thought he was dead."

"He was." She crossed to stand on the other side of Workman's bed and gazed down at him. "Or rather he is. Sort of."

I looked up at Sabrina. "So this is Paul Workman?"

"Obviously." Her hand fluttered over a bare spot on his arm, almost as if she wanted desperately to touch him but was afraid it might hurt him. Then with infinite care her fingers grazed his skin.

"And he's not dead."

"Dead, not dead?" She shrugged. "That's a gray area."

"Not for most people it isn't. Even for vampires. Even with all the mythology about being the undead, it's still pretty clear when one of you actually dies."

"True. However, circumstances being what they are . . ." Her fingers trailed down his arm. She'd done the same thing to me just a few minutes ago.

"You're going to have to connect the dots for me, because right now this all seems very random."

But even as I said it, the pattern was becoming clearer in my mind. Paul Workman hadn't just been Smart Com's CEO, he'd practically been a celebrity. He was handsome and intelligent, and his charisma had created something of a cult following. People bought Smart Com's products in large part because they trusted him. They believed that any product he had helped design would be good and the shopping population had blindly handed Smart Com a stunning share of the market.

Knowing what I now knew about *abducturae*, it seemed so obvious that he was one.

Sabrina hadn't said a word, but when I looked up from Workman's face, I could see she'd been waiting for me to make the connection on my own. She smiled faintly, her expression almost proud.

"Okay," I said. "So, obviously, Workman was your *abductura*. He worked for you and for Smart Com. What went wrong? I thought he had cancer. He died from it."

She waggled her hand in a "maybe" gesture. "Yes, he had

cancer. Still has cancer, technically. Unfortunately, his decline couldn't have come at a worse time."

That's when the rest of the dots joined up. "Oh sure," I scoffed. "Nothing sucks like having your pet *abductura* die a month before the apocalypse. That must have really blown. What choice did you have but to keep him alive on life support, regardless of his personal wishes?"

Her gaze hardened infinitesimally. "You may make light, but this issue is far more complex than you understand."

"No. I think I understand exactly what's going on here. You don't have an *abductura*. Without one, you have no way of convincing your kine to stay here and feed you. Which is really inconvenient now that the apocalypse has happened and you can't just go hire more people. So, instead of just letting Workman die, you hooked him up to the ventilator in hopes that he still has a little bit of juice in him. You are literally sucking him dry. And now you want—"

"Yes," she said sharply. "Now I do want. In fact, I will lay all my cards on the table. I don't just want an *abductura*. I need one. Desperately. The population here is dwindling and—"

"And you can't convince people to stick around long enough to open a vein without Workman here to do your dirty work."

She didn't look shocked or offended, but something else flickered in her gaze. Something harsher. Something ugly. "Do not mock me. People are leaving the compound."

"Good for them."

"They are putting themselves in danger." She slammed her palms down on a tray and leaned over Workman's body. "It's not safe out there—"

"You think I don't know that?! I know it's not safe out there. But maybe they'd rather be in danger than be your next meal. If

157

they finally have a chance to think for themselves, kudos to them for doing it."

"No," she said sharply. "Not kudos to them. They are my people and I've been protecting them."

"They're not your people. You don't think of them as people, do you? You think of them as kine. As livestock."

Again her gaze took on that hard glint. "Fine. My kine are in danger. They are leaving the security of the compound, which is one thing I can't allow. Here they would be safe."

"Here they would be food."

"They would be alive," she said fiercely. "You think they will fare so well out there? You—with all your military training and your knowledge—you are barely surviving. Do you think they have a chance?"

"Do you expect me to believe you genuinely care about whether or not they survive?"

"Believe or don't believe. But it is the truth. If you think I only care about them the way a human would care about her cattle, then fine. I care that my cattle are in danger. They are mine. I had promised to protect them. I have the knowledge and the power to keep them safe. But they are fearful and they have scattered. I cannot imagine what has happened to them nor can I devise a plan to get them back. Now the best I can hope for is to hold on to the remaining kine I have. But you can help. You can convince them to stay. To stay here where it's safe. Where we can protect them."

"Right," I said bitterly. "Because once Workman finally keels over, you'll need another brainwasher to convince them not to be afraid of you, even though you're a bloodsucking monster."

She ignored my jab. "As long as Paul remains alive, they

will stay. Probably. But he has been dying by inches for years now."

Almost as if he'd heard his name, Workman let out a low groan, a sound of pain torn from deep within his hollowed chest. Jesus, maybe he had heard his name. Or maybe he'd just responded to the anger in her voice.

I recoiled from the bed and stared down at him in horror. His limbs shifted weakly and an expression of agony seemed to cross his face. And for one brief second, I felt it. First pain and confusion. Then a moment of alertness that was swept away by a sense of calm resolve.

When I glanced back to Sabrina, I didn't see the face of a monster. I saw only love and concern. Complete benevolence. Of course I would stay. Of course I would help her. Why would I ever want to do anything else? We both desperately wanted to protect people. Why couldn't we work together? Why wouldn't—

I tore my gaze away from her and looked down at the man on the bed between us. His eyes had flickered open. They were filmy and gray. And desperate. And full of agony.

Jesus.

And somehow—still, despite the agony—he'd made me believe. Was still making me believe.

I whirled away and damn near ran from the room. Out into the hall, pushing past the doctor or nurse standing there. I took a wrong turn, which I knew because I didn't end up in the waiting room, but in another section of the clinic. The kind of place where they drew blood to do lab work. There were chairs and sturdy workbenches and the little rubber-topped vials for collecting blood.

Without the table in the middle, it took me a moment to

recognize the room where the film had been made. But this was it. The room where a Tick had been transformed back into a human. And there, just a few feet away from me, was the refrigerator where the cure was being held.

Before I could search the fridge, she was there behind me, her hand on my arm.

I jerked out of her grasp.

"Is that what you want from me? To suck the life out of me until there's nothing left?"

"You think I want him to be like that? I'd much rather put him out of his misery. I hate seeing him in so much pain! He begged me to keep him alive until I found another *abductura*. He won't even let the doctors give him pain meds because it would dull what little power he has left. It's why he refused traditional cancer treatments. No one has ever been more devoted to this cause than Paul. You felt that. In the state he's in, even the most powerful *abductura* that ever lived couldn't project something so strong unless he believed it himself."

Was she right?

Did Workman really believe helping Sabrina was the right thing to do?

I didn't know what to think. Sebastian had told me that a powerful *abductura* could convince people of anything, but it took tremendous effort. It was far easier to convince someone when it was an issue you believed in yourself. It only made sense that for Workman to sway me now, when he was dying and in pain, he had to believe Sabrina was right. Believed it enough that he was willing to spend the last days of his life racked with pain. Tortured. If I had any faith in Paul Workman, that would be a powerful endorsement of Sabrina's intentions.

Which mattered only if I trusted his opinion. And I didn't.

Yeah, I was letting my daddy issues show again, but I didn't trust any CEO with money and power and the ability to force his views on others.

But that didn't necessarily mean I wouldn't help Sabrina.

Maybe she sensed I was about to cave, because she started in on me again.

"Don't you see what I'm offering you? I have the room here to house and feed and protect thousands more people. Everyone you know. Everyone you love. Everyone you want to protect. I could accept them into Smart Com. Once you get me the information from Genexome, we can work on the cure together. You and I can cure the Ticks. Save civilization."

As I stood there in the lab, with Paul Workman still sending me wave upon wave of adoration, my imagination took over. Lily, yes. I could save her. Mel could take over one of the nearby vampire territories. If we combined the two, there would be even more room. Space enough for all the rebels at Base Camp. All the Greens and Collabs in San Angelo. Even all of Elderton if they wanted to come. Joe would never again have to worry about baby Josie. Lily and everyone else I know would be safe. All I had to do was convince them to come.

CHAPTER TWENTY-FOUR

CARTER

"An *abductura* is only as strong as his convictions," Sabrina said softly. "You're no good to me if you believe I'm a monster. You must accept that I can help people. And I *can* help people."

She looked like she genuinely believed it. Which was baffling. In the past hour, I'd seen her go from total nut job to nurturing sweetie to practically Joan of Arc. I didn't know which Sabrina was the real one.

And, yeah, I got that she'd been testing me at first, but there was a kind of crazy that couldn't be faked and she had it. Or did she?

"This isn't going to be easy," she said firmly.

"Well, if we have the cure, it's going to be a lot easier than if we don't."

"True, but we still have an uphill battle. One that could take years to fight. First you'll have to get Sebastian's research about the cure from Genexome. We'll have to manufacture the cure and then find ways to distribute it. And if you don't agree to help me, more and more of my people will die in that time. Since we retrieved the cure, we've been working around the clock, but if I don't have anyone left to do the work, the cure will simply never get made."

I didn't have the right to control other people. That was a no-brainer.

But what choice did I have? If I didn't help Sabrina, I had no way of getting the cure for Lily. For all of humanity.

If I was honest with myself, I hadn't thought as far ahead as Sabrina had. I'd spent so much of the past nine months just staying alive, I hadn't thought about the big picture.

Hell, I had no idea—literally no idea at all—what went into producing a drug. If I hadn't seen it in *The Bourne Legacy*, it didn't exist in my bank of knowledge. Lily was way smarter about science and chemistry than I was, but she was lost to me right now. Tech Taylor was smart enough to figure out damn near anything he put his mind to. And Dawn at least had some medical training. But when it came down to it: we were all still just kids. Even Dawn, who was twenty-one, I'm pretty sure didn't know off the top of her head how to manufacture a drug that we could distribute to however many millions of Ticks were out there.

That's what it came down to: no matter how good our intentions were, we couldn't do this on our own. There was just no fucking way a bunch of kids were going to save the world.

We needed help. And maybe the help we needed had to come from a vampire.

I made myself look at Sabrina. Made myself study her face in hopes that some hint of what she was really feeling would come through.

She must have sensed I was waffling, because relief flickered across her face. Not the satisfaction I'd been expecting, but relief. Like she really would have been screwed if I'd refused.

She reached out and took my hand in hers. "I know you don't

want to trust me. That after the way Sebastian treated you, you never want to trust a vampire again. But not all vampires are as bad as he is."

And that's where she was wrong. Because I did want to trust her. Desperately. So bad I could taste it. And I was pretty sure it tasted like chocolate chip cookies.

But how could I truly trust a vampire, especially this one?

After her performance as the Most Wicked Vampire Queen of the Damned when we first arrived, I knew she could act. Either that or she was actually psychotic. Neither possibility was reassuring.

And she'd said it herself. A vampire didn't need to be an *abductura*. The extended life of a vampire was one long course in how to win friends and influence people. She clearly excelled at it.

I took a step back, putting some distance between us. Trying to wedge some head space between me and Workman's influence. I needed to think. Not just about what I would want for the people I cared about, but about what they would choose. What would Lily want? What about Joe and Zeke? Even if I could trust Sabrina, even if she turned out to be the kindest, most benevolent vampire of them all, would anyone I knew want the safety she was offering?

I didn't even have to think about it very long.

"I'm gonna have to pass."

"Excuse me?"

"On your offer. I'm going to have to turn it down."

Her lips curved down at the corners just slightly. Not quite a frown yet. "I don't understand."

"Don't get me wrong. It's a generous offer, but I can't turn people into kine. No one I know wants to live like a cow."

"But you'd be protecting them!"

"I'd be controlling them. There's a difference."

Her expression hardened. "You don't understand what you're—"

"I understand exactly what I'm saying no to."

"The chance to save humanity."

"Or the chance to enslave humanity. All depending on how you look at it."

Her expression twisted, and for an instant, she looked like a child who'd had her favorite toy smashed. "Even if I handed you the cure right now, you'd never be able to reproduce and distribute it. Not on your own. Not without my resources. You are damning yourself and everyone you care about. You will all die."

"We were all going to die eventually. And the people I know, we'd rather die free than die like cattle."

Her mouth settled into a hard frown. "No. I refuse to accept this. You'll change your mind."

"I'm pretty sure I won't."

She ignored me, and instead looked up toward one of the corners of the room, and gave a nod. I followed her gaze to the line of faux-wood cabinets near the ceiling. There, in the far corner, was a security camera. The lens—the only visible part— was no bigger than a dime and blended almost seamlessly into a cabinet. I realized then that although it had seemed like we were alone, she had known all along that there was a security camera watching our entire conversation. An instant later, Marek and his twin appeared.

"Mr. Marek, please show Mr. Olson to the guest room adjoining that of his travel companions. He needs some time to consider his options."

As I followed Marek back through the underground tunnels of Smart Com, I thought about what Sabrina had said about how

165

not all vampires were as bad as Sebastian. I thought about Roberto and the instruments of torture he'd collected over the centuries. And I thought about Paul Workman being kept alive just barely—despite his obvious physical pain. I didn't care whether he wanted her to do it. The obvious affection between them made it more horrific, not less.

No. Not all vampires were as bad as Sebastian. Some of them were worse.

CHAPTER TWENTY-FIVE

LILY

The pull is stronger with every step. We are almost there. It's so close.

We had to stop to sleep when the sun got too bright. But we are moving again. Toward . . .

Toward what?

Safety.

I have to remind myself, over and over, we are moving toward safety. Safety and food and warmth and hope and food and peace.

And we'll find it at a Farm. It's all there.

They will take care of us. Though I can't quite remember why we need them.

I feel fine. Great. Faster. Stronger. Hungrier than ever before.

But the Farm will have doctors and I know we need doctors. I just can't remember why.

So we keep running.

Then it's morning and the too-bright sun casts flares across the world. I can't see anymore, but we can *be* seen. We are too vulnerable and the open makes fear crawl across our skin.

We stop running and search for hiding instead. I can smell food in the deep distance and other things more near. The grassy dirt in the now, the other pack that passed here in the near now. And the moist smell of animals from the deep past. That's the smell that pulls me. The smell of hay and heat and wood and sleepy animals. It pulls me past the road, the grass, the field, to the barn where animals slept and where we sleep now.

Then the too-bright sun is gone and we wake to catch what food doesn't scurry away. It is as dirty and moist as the hay, but at least it's warm and it keeps us. Another scent pulls us forward. Marcus at my side keeps me moving, because I'm in charge. Without me, he'd dart off to the other pack. And I have to keep him safe. That's important. Keeping Marcus safe. And getting to a Farm. Where there's food and safety and . . . food and safety . . . and . . .

And then we're there. At the Farm, with its tiny suns and its heavenly food. So much food the air is thick with it. Only there's another pack already there. Marcus runs for the food, but I pull him down to the ground and shush him with a growl. The others are dangerous. They were here first and must eat first. Our two can't fight their ten.

So we wait, whimpering, hoping for scraps left when they're done.

They eat and eat and hunger burns in us. We could fight them. Maybe. If they are slow and stupid. They are only ten and we are such a hungry two.

We creep closer. Wanting more. Just breathing in the food.

I watch the pack for our chance and count their ten over and over. The big male—we can't fight him, but males are easy. He won't hurt me and Marcus is too young to challenge him. The female—like me, she is strong and fast. I can't fight her. But there are other, weaker ones. And they are only ten. Maybe we don't have to fight, maybe there is food enough for twelve.

We creep closer still, low to the ground, ready to bow down to join.

168

Then there's a noise, loud and crunching and metal moving. And a food smell so much better and fresher than this food. The others smell it, too. They turn—noses up and leading—and run for the food. The male is smart and the female cautious. They howl a no, but the others don't hear. The male and female move as one to save who they can. But the others go down in an endless blur of noise and angry metal. I throw myself on Marcus and cower. The roar goes on and on—blat, blat, blat, blat, blat, blat.

When it finally stops, we look up. The pack is small now.

The fresh food is moving toward us, their angry metal is hot with death and hungry for us. We slink away before they find us. We follow the scent of the pack. Far away at first, until the female smells us.

More pack? she yelps to the male.

He waits. *Come out*, he growls.

We want to hide, but can't disobey. So out we come. We are new and hungry and untried, but he doesn't swat us away, and when the pack moves on to hunt again, we follow.

We are his now.

The Farm was not food and safety. It was blood and death and we choose life.

CHAPTER TWENTY-SIX

MEL

The door closes, encasing us in total darkness.

"Okay," I mutter. "I know vampires are nocturnal, so we're supposed to be able to see in the dark, but this is ridiculous."

Almost before I can finish the sentence, a flame flickers to life. Sebastian is holding a lighter. He's just a few feet away, leaning against a support column. "I'll trade you the lighter for the head. I think you'll have better luck finding a light switch."

Handing over the head is not a problem. I thrust it out in front of me. "By all means."

"Careful there," he says, flicking the lighter off. "Let's not singe the hair, shall we? I have no interest in having burned hair be the last thing I smell before I starve to death."

I feel Sebastian weave his fingers into Roberto's hair and I let go of my repulsive prize. I keep my hand out in front of me. "Lighter?"

"Hang on a second." He must be reaching around, because his fingers graze mine before finally latching on. His hand is nearly as cold as Roberto's and his grasp is weak. I have a strange compulsion to grab his hand. To cling to him. To beg him not to leave me alone in the dark.

I know I'll feel better when we have the lights on. When I can see his face. Not to mention get him some food. I fumble with the lighter. I've never even held one before. Let alone used one. Sebastian must hear my ineptitude because he tells me what to do. It takes several tries before the tiny bright flame flickers steadily.

I give the room a quick survey. Sebastian is standing against the column, his eyes closed. I don't look at him too long. It's scary how weak he appears. I turn my attention to the walls on either side of the door. I find a panel with too many buttons to be just lights. I push them all with the flat of my hand. Lights blaze on. On the opposite wall, a TV comes to life, and somewhere a stereo blares, playing "Boléro," in midsong.

I click buttons more judiciously this time until the TV and the stereo are silenced, but most of the lights stay on, then I turn to survey the room. Roberto's vault reminds me of a New York bachelor pad from one of the 1960s Doris Day movies I used to watch with Nanna. There's a fireplace tucked into one wall right beside an expansive entertainment system. There's a bar with enough alcohol to outfit a nightclub. In the center of the room, there's a sectional sofa big enough to seat a basketball team. There's even . . .

"Is that a hot tub?"

"Apparently." Sebastian's eyes flicker open. "Being a vampire is very stressful."

"Tell me something I don't know," I mutter. "Like where the damn blood is."

"Try checking the refrigerator."

"Duh." But other than the minifridge in the bar, I don't see one. There's a doorway in the wall behind the fireplace/TV extravaganza. It leads to a hallway, which splits off in two directions. I find the lights and turn them on. I see a bedroom and ignore it for now. Unless Roberto was a midnight snacker, I don't think that's what I'm looking for. The other direction leads to a kitchen with—hallelujah!—a walk-in refrigerator, the kind you see in restaurants. Except instead of fresh produce, it's filled with bags of blood. I don't bother selecting a vintage, but grab an armful of bags and haul them out to the living area.

Sebastian is sitting on the sofa, looking wan, head tipped back, a lock of dark hair draped over his eyes. His breathing is so shallow his chest barely rises and falls. Chuy is at his feet, looking up at me balefully. Almost accusingly. Like he's chiding me for taking so long.

I drop all but one bag on the occasional table and sit next to him. "Sebastian?"

He groans, but doesn't open his eyes.

"Come on, wake up. I found it."

Again, there's almost no response. I shake his arm hard enough to jostle him and his head lolls over, the hair dropping away from his eyes. They aren't closed, like I'd thought, but open and glazed to senselessness.

Shit.

I'm out of time. I have nothing with which to open the bag. I'd been counting on him biting it. I look around for a knife. A toothpick. Anything. In the end, I bring the bag to my own mouth and sink my incisors through the polyurethane. Blood pours into my mouth, it's sweet and rich against my tongue. Like chocolate mousse. A shudder of pure pleasure skips across my skin as saliva coats my mouth. I suck in a deep desperate gulp. Desire floods me. Disarming me. Crippling me. I fall to my knees, crumpling over, almost insensible with the need to devour. A need that is stronger than everything else. Everything except . . .

Except what?

I gulp again and feel the bag empty, feel it collapse and run

172

dry. The bag falls away and it's not until I've dropped it that I realize what I've done. That I've drunk the whole pint of blood that was meant for Sebastian. He is starving. Dying. And I ate first.

I search the ground, find another bag. I can't even tell if Sebastian is still breathing. If he's still alive. I don't trust myself not to drain this one, too, even now that my hunger is slaked. Instead, I dash for the bar. I yank open first one drawer and then the next until I find a corkscrew. Back at the sofa, I jab it into the bag. The precious blood beads at the hole. I kneel over Sebastian and let it dribble into his mouth. At first there's no reaction. I squeeze the bag. More dribbles out, but I fear it's not enough. I jab a second hole in the bag, at the other end, and hold it tilted up, so air can flow into the bag as blood flows out of it. Finally, I see him swallow. See him suck in a shuddering breath and then swallow again. Then, suddenly, his eyes fly open. He tenses. And pounces.

He launches himself at me and we both fly back off the sofa and onto the plush carpet. The bag of blood slips out of my hand, landing on my chest. He is on top of me, cradled between my legs, his teeth in the bag, sucking on it, feeding off my chest. I push up onto my elbows, relishing the feel of him, suddenly warm and bristling with life.

He gives one more pull on the bag and then it's empty. But some of the blood sprayed out across my shoulder and neck. His lips follow the trail of blood. I sweep a hand across his forehead, pushing his hair out of his face, fascinated by the sight of his darker skin against the paleness of my chest, of his inky lashes against his cheeks. His tongue brushes my skin, lapping up the blood in long, luxurious swipes that send shivers coursing through me almost as powerful as the blood lust I felt just a moment ago. My whole body trembles as need floods me. Not just hunger but something else. Something rooted even more deeply inside of me. Something I've never felt before.

Then his mouth is on my neck, nipping with painful tenderness at my flesh, tracing the line of my jaw, capturing my lips. This kiss—my first kiss ever—is achingly beautiful. It's as soft as it is relentless. Just his lips on mine, his tongue tracing the seam of my mouth and then dipping gently inside. His kiss is full of tender hope.

I shiver uncontrollably and wrap myself around him, pulling him even closer to me, wanting to absorb him into me. Except for the bandage, his chest is still bare and I can't stop running my hands across his shoulders, down his back. Suddenly I can't stop kissing him and I don't want to. I want this to go on. Forever.

But it can't.

We both know it, even though he's the first to pull away.

He wrenches himself away from me, leaving me lying on the floor, feeling exposed and abandoned. My heart is pounding, but it's not desire pushing through my veins. It's not even hunger. It's shame.

Because this wasn't supposed to happen. I know that.

I scramble to my feet, turning away so he doesn't see me wiping at the last tendrils of blood that mark my chest.

"I'm sorry," I say clumsily.

"Don't apologize." His voice is hard and strained. Probably from hunger, which still burns inside of me as well.

"But I shouldn't have—"

"I said don't."

"But—"

"If anyone's to blame, it's me. I"—he laughs harshly—"should

174

be old enough to know better. If you're going to blame anyone, blame me."

I turn, just enough to glance over at him, trying to get a read on his expression, but it's impossible. "No," I protest. "I don't blame you. You're . . ." I struggle for words.

"Right," he snaps. "I'm the immoral vampire. The master manipulator. The one with no boundaries at all. That's what you think, isn't it?"

For once, there's no suave cunning to his words. Only raw emotion. Anger tinged with self-hatred. I've never heard him like this and it unsettles me.

I'm drawn back over to him. I put my hand on his arm, a gesture that's supposed to be comforting but that stirs decidedly uncomfortable feelings in me.

"I was going to say that I don't blame you, because you're hungry. Our control isn't particularly strong right now. Not for either of us."

His lips twist bitterly. "Exactly."

If I didn't know better, I'd say the easy out I've given him wasn't what he wanted.

I drop my hand and the subject. I cast around for something to do and see Chuy, whom I'd forgotten about entirely. Chuy is pacing circles from the door to the sofa. I'm not sure if he's nervous because of the Ticks on the other side or if he's upset about the fight between Sebastian and me.

But he's got to be hungry—I do know that much. He hasn't eaten a lot in the time he's been with me. Carter had fed him some granola bars in the car and I had done the same, but he needs more than that. I open a can of the stew and the canned chicken and dump both into a bowl I find in the wet bar. Chuy laps up the food eagerly. When he's done, I give the bowl a quick rinse in the sink and then fill it with water. Suddenly tired, I sit down beside Chuy, taking comfort in the dog's warmth. His fur is soft and running my hands through it calms me, much like I used to calm myself with my Slinky when I was a human girl. At some point I fall asleep.

CHAPTER TWENTY-SEVEN

CARTER

As I followed Marek down the halls, my mind raced to come up with a plan. I'm not entirely sure why I bothered. Plans never worked out for me. I knew that. Still it seemed like a good idea to have some strategy that was more specific than lie, cheat, and steal to get what I want.

The underground tunnels were labyrinthine enough that I couldn't tell where exactly he was taking me, even with the signs. I knew he was leading me away from Building C, but had no idea where we'd started. He led me through a lobby that looked slightly different from either of the previous two. I tried to map the campus out in my mind, but the buildings and furnishings were too generic, so I settled for remembering Building C. That was the one I'd need to get back to. Unfortunately, Marek and his twin weren't the only guards standing around.

Sabrina wanted me to believe she'd had trouble holding on to her kine, and it was true that the campus seemed under-populated because I still hadn't seen that many normal people. Obviously her rent-a-soldiers were well compensated, because she had plenty of them around. She probably didn't dine on them, though. She needed them strong. Unfortunately.

While we waited for the elevator, I said, "Sabrina told you to put me in the room next to Dawn and Darren's."

Marek stood facing the elevator doors, his hands linked behind his back. He didn't even glance at me as he answered. "Yes, sir."

"That's unacceptable." I tried to mimic my father's get-your-shit-together voice. "I want to be in the same room with them at least tonight. I need to see them and make sure they're okay."

"I'll ask."

"Ask now." I put a little push into the words. Might as well see if Marek was susceptible.

He glanced at me and pulled his phone out of his pocket and fell back a step. The elevator doors opened while Marek was still talking to whoever was on the other end of the phone, Sabrina most likely. Marek's twin, unsure of what to do, looked back toward Marek who gave a *wait-here* hand signal. So we waited.

Marek's conversation took longer than I expected, like they were discussing more than just room assignments. Had I made a mistake by giving Marek a push? Had he sensed it? Was that what he and Sabrina were discussing?

But then Marek hung up and crossed back to us. He nodded us into the elevator and then followed us in. "Your request is reasonable. For tonight, you will be billeted with your people."

Okay. So that gave me the rest of today and tonight to figure something out, because I sure as hell wasn't leaving them behind. And frankly, Sabrina was so damn crazy she scared the crap out of me. We needed to get out of here.

* *

Dawn practically threw herself into my arms the second Marek closed the door behind me. Which surprised the hell out of me because I didn't know her that well and I wasn't really the huggy type.

178

"We thought for sure she'd killed you," she said as she let me go. Darren put his arm around her and she leaned into him, looking genuinely scared for the first time.

I felt another jab of guilt. I should not have let them come. Not that I'd had a choice, but still.

It was obvious that the encounter with Sabrina had freaked them both out. Yeah, me, too.

"Nah," I said lightly, not wanting to spook them any more. "I'm too valuable for that."

They both frowned and I realized my mistake. Neither of them knew I was an *abductura*. I was pretty sure neither of them had any idea what one was anyway. Well, wouldn't that be a fun conversation: Yeah, I have the ability to control your emotions and I brought you along on a dangerous mission and we might all die. Instead, I took the obvious way out.

"All of us are too valuable. Did you notice how few people are around?"

"Lots of guards," Darren said, sounding more serious than he usually did.

"Yes. Hired guards. And she needs them strong and fit, so she's probably not feeding off them. But not a lot of normal people."

I let the implication hang there. Not a lot of people she could feed from.

Dawn nodded and then asked, "Did you find the—" Then she broke off awkwardly. "You know . . ."

Yeah. I did know. Way to be subtle.

If Sabrina's goons were watching—and I was sure they were—then there was no way they hadn't caught that.

"The cure?" I asked. We weren't going to fool them anyway. And Sabrina already knew I wanted the cure. Might as well pretend I had nothing to hide and no idea I might need to hide it if I did. "No. But she admitted she has it."

"Does it work?" Darren asked.

I told them everything that had happened. I glossed over the bits about Paul Workman and Sabrina needing me to fill his shoes. I figured she would understand why I hadn't told them more. Hell, she probably expected it. Otherwise, I was honest and open. Nothing to see here.

If I was really lucky, whoever was watching the surveillance feed would get bored.

I glanced around the room while I talked, trying not to look like I was searching for the surveillance camera. For the record, it's damn near impossible to look for a camera without making it obvious to whoever is watching you that you've found it. There's always this one instant when you're looking straight at the camera. So instead, I didn't look for the camera. I looked for places it might be.

The room was a much less fancy version of the conference room we'd been shown to when we first arrived. There was a smaller table. No big basket of fruit, but a bowl with some snack bars and some cans of soda. The furniture was sturdy and drab. There was a sofa and a couple of chairs like you might see in a doctor's office. A cheap-looking media cabinet with a TV and Blu-ray player flanked by bookshelves. No cable—not that there still was cable. No computer. There was a phone, which I assumed either had no signal or—more likely—connected only to other phones here on campus. Things looked a little worn around the edges, which told me this room had been set up in the Before. Obviously, Sabrina had planned ahead. Not that I didn't know that already.

There was an open doorway through which I glimpsed a

made bed. The walls of both rooms were white, which meant the cameras were hidden out of sight somewhere, most likely somewhere along the top of the media center or the bookshelves. That's where I would put them.

There would be part of the room along the wall on either side of the bookshelves that surveillance wouldn't see. Of course, there was no natural way for us all to go stand in the corner and chat.

Besides, when Sabrina told Marek to come get me when she and I were in the lab, she hadn't raised her voice, which meant the audio surveillance equipment was very sensitive. Probably too sensitive to be the standard stuff included with the camera. If it was me, I'd want a separate feed for the audio. And I'd put at least one microphone in the corner the camera couldn't see.

Darren sat down on one of the chairs, looking defeated. "So what are we supposed to do?"

"We wait," I said simply, leaning against the edge of the table. "And we rest a bit. We've all been going nonstop for a long time." I nodded toward the food. "And we eat. It's not fancy, but—"

"Hell no, I'm not eating their food." Darren crossed his arms over his chest.

"Dude, don't act all tough," Dawn said. "You already ate a banana."

"Well, that was before you said it might be drugged."

"I'm not going to make you eat," I told them both.

"Good."

"But you really should eat while you can. Yes, there's a chance it's drugged, but not a very big one. If we're her meal later, she needs to be able to drink from us without worrying about what's in our blood."

"Do they think about things like that?"

"Sebastian always did. If there's tranquilizer in a person's blood, that kind of thing metabolizes very slowly. She wants us comfortable. Relaxed."

"Because they don't want us to fight back?" Darren asked.

I almost let him believe that. But I'd gotten him into this; didn't I owe him honesty? "No. Because your blood will taste better. All the hormones associated with fight or flight, adrenaline, that kind of thing, those taste bitter. Serotonin. Dopamine. Oxytocin. Those hormones taste delicious." Darren and Dawn had both gone pale with shock, so I added, "Or so I'm told."

Darren blew out a breath, like he was trying to stay calm. Dawn just looked grimly nervous. Like she was trying to be braver than she felt. Shit. I should not have brought them with me. They both thought they were prepared to die for this, but were they really?

And what right did I have to ask them to?

"Look," I said—brutal-honesty time here. "I'm sorry I got you into this."

Dawn bumped up her chin. "I'm not."

"Well, you should be. I know this isn't what you signed up for." They both looked like they wanted to protest, but I held up a hand to stop them. I didn't want them saying too much for the cameras and microphones. I didn't want to say too much, either. I just wanted them to know they had options. "Look, I know this isn't exactly what you thought you were getting into, but it's not bad here. Sabrina's population is down, that means she needs people here. Maybe lots of people. And her rent-a-goons will keep the Ticks out, you can count on that. It's not a bad place to wait things out."

I pushed away from the table. "Look, I'm going to see about

getting a shower. Just hang out here for a while. Maybe watch a movie or something."

I only hoped they got the message. Just watch a movie. Do not sit around and talk about how strangely I'm acting. Do not speak clearly for the camera and say anything stupid like "Do you think he found the cure? Why is he worried about a shower at a time like this? Shouldn't we be trying to find a way out?"

I pretty much ignored Dawn and Darren as I checked out the bedroom. It was just what I'd predicted: living room, single king-sized bed. There was a bathroom just beyond, thank God, because I wasn't joking about the shower. It had been too long since I'd had a real shower. Base Camp had outdoor showers set up, but you have to really want a shower before you're willing to shower outside in the winter, in water that hasn't been heated.

Before hitting the head, I went back and opened the door to the hall. Sure enough Marek and company were standing in the hall on either side of the door. They looked up when I opened it.

I felt a burst of panic. I'd known they'd be there, but I'd needed to double-check.

"We need more towels," I said to Marek.

He scowled.

"There are three crappy towels in the bathroom." He shrugged like that wasn't his problem, so I stepped closer and turned up the arrogance in my voice. "Look, you've been safe and secure behind these fences, but we've been out there for the past nine months. That means it's been nine months since I've had a hot shower. The least you can do is get me some goddamn towels."

Marek scowled and his twin actually took a step toward me, anger flickering across his face. I raised my eyebrows in a what-do-you-got expression. Marek put out a hand to stop the other

183

guy. But I could see that it bugged the shit out of Marek, too, this reminder that they'd had it easy here with Sabrina while other people had been out fighting the good fight.

Still, Marek pushed his hand into the other guy's chest. "Go get them some towels out of one of the other rooms."

The other guy glared at me, but turned and stormed off.

When he came back, I smiled, and I didn't even have to try hard to look grateful. If it had been months since I'd had a hot shower, it had been just as long since I'd had clean clothes. Then I saw what was on top of the clothes. The towels I'd requested, a bar of soap, a couple of small bottles of shampoo. Three toothbrushes. New toothbrushes! Hell—I almost would have come here just for the toothbrushes. But the cherry on top was a can of shaving cream and a razor.

Marek must have seen me smile, because he looked more closely at the stack of stuff. He frowned, like he was debating whether to take it away.

"Man, am I glad to see this," I said with enthusiastic innocence. "My girl is always giving me hell about not shaving often enough." I scrubbed a hand across the stubble on my jaw.

I looked back at Marek and the other guy. "Thanks," I said.

Back in the room, I tossed the clothes and most of the toiletries onto the table. "See if any of the clothes fit. I'm going to take a shower."

Alone in the bathroom, I put the toiletries I'd kept—the shaving cream, the razor, and one of the toothbrushes—on the counter. I shaved first. Partly because Lily really did give me hell when I didn't. I hadn't had the time or the razor to shave with in the past week or so. Somehow, doing it now gave me . . . I don't know, the feeling that I could actually pull this off. It made me feel like I really was going to find her. Soon. And that when I did, she'd be human enough to care whether or not I was clean shaven. And it helped clear my head.

Here's what I knew.

I had to get out of here. Soon. This place, with its luxuries and exotic fruits and hot showers . . . this place had the potential to lure me in and never let me go. If it wasn't for Lily out there, fighting for her life—alone—I might be tempted to stay.

But Lily was out there. If Ely had found her and Marcus, and if he was able to stay close enough to keep an eye on them without attracting their attention and if I could get there in time, then I had a chance.

The longer I waited the more likely it was that something bad would happen to them. After all, there were plenty of people out there right now who would be interested in killing a Tick.

No, I didn't have time to wait around here for Sabrina to get together a team of people to go find Lily and bring her back. If Sabrina needed an *abductura* as badly as she said she did, then she would do everything in her power to keep me here. To string me along indefinitely.

No, I had to get out. Soon.

The only question was whether or not I had to bring Dawn and Darren with me. And whether or not they wanted to come. I thought I knew the answer, but I wanted them to know they had options.

As I rinsed off the razor, I looked around the tiny bathroom. The shower was utilitarian. The cabinetry functional, but not fancy.

I tried to imagine Smart Com's offices in the Before. Obviously, this stuff had been here then. How many living spaces did they have on the compound? How many families could it hold? What reasoning had Sabrina given for wanting extensive living quarters in their offices?

Of course, I'd read something once about how high tech companies had expected their employees to work such long hours, they basically lived there. I guess that was the explanation.

I did a surreptitious search of the room, looking for another camera. When I didn't see an obvious place for one, I did a second, more thorough search that turned up a tiny mic but no camera. Good to know Sabrina's people were paranoid but not pervy.

I did a quick look around the room, just in case someone had left a pen and paper in here, but of course I was never that lucky. I took the bar of soap out of its box and used the corner of the soap to start writing. If the bathroom was the one room in the place without a camera, then notes on the mirror were the only way I had to actually communicate with Dawn and Darren.

I was a few words into my note to them when there was a knock on the bathroom door. It swung open before I had a chance to respond. Dawn stepped inside, quickly shutting it behind her.

I put a finger to my lips to shush her and then cupped my hand to my ear and pointed to the mic, which was just visible above the medicine cabinet. She nodded, rolling her eyes in a well-duh expression.

Before I could ask her what she was doing, she said, a little loudly, "Thank God you're okay. I was so worried."

"What are you doing? Darren—"

"Darren's watching a movie. I'm sorry," she said, still talking loudly. "I know you said you didn't want them to know about us, but I had to see you."

Then she squeezed by me and reached past the shower curtain to turn on the water.

"Please. Just hold me," she begged. "I'm so scared."

But instead of throwing herself into my arms again, she jumped up and sat on the counter beside the sink. And then winked at me.

And I just stood there, holding a bar of soap in my hand like a dumb-ass.

In the background, just over the roar of the water in the shower, I heard an explosion from whatever movie Darren was watching. The shower plus the movie would cover the sound of any conversation she and I had.

Dawn was brilliant.

"So what'd you find out?" she asked in a whisper.

"Not much that I didn't tell you already," I admitted.

"But you did find the cure, right?"

"I think so. I won't know for sure until I can poke around a little, but I'm pretty positive the samples are in a refrigerator in the lab. In Building C."

"Near the clinic?" she whispered, swinging her legs back and forth.

"Yes."

"Cool. Then we just need an excuse to go to the clinic, right?"

"Look, it's not that simple." By now, the water had warmed up and steam was billowing out from behind the curtain.

"Of course it is."

"The security here is heavier than I thought. There's a real chance I'll get caught or hurt when I'm trying to break out."

"Wait, what do you mean, when *you* try to break out?" Her voice rose in proportion to her suspicion. Which she must have realized as well, because then she said loudly again, but with more emotion than I could have faked, "Don't make me leave. I love you so much."

Despite her words, she looked completely bored. "Jesus," I whispered. "Are you some kind of actress?"

She grinned cheerfully. "Just three years of drama in high school. I played Anne Frank. But seriously, we are all leaving together, right?"

"Look . . ." I leaned closer, because I hadn't had three years of drama in high school, and if anyone heard my voice, I wouldn't be able to act my way out of it. "I know it's not ideal, but I honestly believe Sabrina needs more people. Yes. She'll be pissed when I leave, but you and Darren would be safe here."

Dawn frowned. "You want us to stay?"

"If you're here, there's three layers of electrified fences between you and the Ticks. There are countless armed guards. And there are fresh pineapples."

"You *do* want us to stay."

"I want you to have the option." My gaze flickered to the note I'd been writing on the mirror. Enough condensation had formed on the glass that my message was legible. The soap-on-the-mirror trick had worked, even if my handwriting was crap.

Dawn glanced over her shoulder and saw what I'd written. *Seems safe. Please think about staying. I'm leaving at*

That was as far as I'd gotten. Dawn squinted at the mirror, trying to decipher my handwriting. Then she turned back to me, glaring.

"You were just going to ditch us?"

"No. I was going to give you the option of staying here where you'd be safe."

She poked me in the chest. "You know you have issues."

Yeah. Like I didn't know that.

She leaned closer and whispered fiercely, "I thought my dad had issues about trying to keep everyone safe. But you make him look like—" She squinted. "I don't know. Someone really chill."

I had met her father only a handful of times, but the idea that I might be crazier than that gun nut terrified me.

"Look, I'm not being paranoid. I just want you to know what you're getting into."

"Darren and I both know what we're getting into. So, you know, screw you for asking." She sounded more annoyed than angry. "We're coming with you."

I held up my hands to ward off the protest I knew she'd make. "If they try to stop us—and they will try to stop us—they'll shoot first and ask questions later. If one of you gets hit—"

"Then one of us gets hit."

"If they catch us and one of you is hurt, there's a good chance they won't bring you back to the infirmary." I'd seen it happen on Farms. Someone got hurt and medical supplies were too precious to waste, when fresh blood was just as valuable.

Dawn seemed to consider the issue for only about half a second. "You forget. I have medical training. If Darren is wounded I'll patch him up. If I'm wounded, then I can talk him through it." She eyed me shrewdly. "I notice you're not worried about what's going to happen if you're wounded."

"No." I didn't know what else to say to that.

"Because you're one of those abductor things?"

"*Abductura*," I corrected automatically. "You know about that?"

She shrugged. "Zeke told me."

"I didn't think Zeke knew."

Jesus. Was there anyone who didn't know?

Yes. There was at least one person who didn't know. Lily.

And once I did finally manage to save her, then I had to tell her the truth about me. And I'd have to face up to the very real possibility that our relationship was . . . weirdly one-sided. But I couldn't think about that now.

Dawn hopped down off the sink. "I don't know. He said that some of the guys from Base Camp had known all along and I guess someone told him."

Some of the guys? "Who?"

"I don't know." She took a washcloth and started scrubbing the soap off the mirror. Then she dropped the washcloth on the floor and turned back to face me. "So what's the deal? Are we going to shower first?"

"What?"

"Before we break out of here? Are we going to take turns showering or what? Because you seemed pretty jazzed about the idea of taking a hot shower."

"I'm . . . yeah. I guess." Hell. I could certainly use the time to clear my head.

"Take your shower," she told me. "But when you get out, be prepared."

"For what?"

She shrugged, giving a little smile. "Well, if the cure is in the clinic, then we need a reason to go there, right?"

"Yeah," I said, still not making the connection.

"So be ready."

"What are you going to do?" I demanded.

"I'm going to take care of it. I'll be creative."

CHAPTER TWENTY-EIGHT

CARTER

I showered quickly because I still wasn't sure what I should "be prepared" for.

I considered and dismissed the possibility that she was going to tell Marek about her nurse's training. That would pique his interest, but wouldn't necessarily get her taken to the clinic. Or Darren and me.

I dried off and got dressed. The first actual hot shower I'd had in months and I didn't even get to enjoy it. I was just pulling my hoodie over my head when the bathroom door slammed open. Darren stood in the doorway, hands clenched, jaw twitching.

Darren, who was easily one of the nicest guys I'd ever met— looked pissed. This was a guy who'd smiled and laughed after I'd nearly beaten the crap out of him. When we first met, his entire family had pointed guns at my chest, but he'd been one of the voices of reason.

And now he launched himself at me. He grabbed me by the front of my sweatshirt and swung me around, flinging me out of the bathroom. I stumbled back into the bedroom and caught myself just before I landed on the bed.

Here's the thing about fighting that a lot of people don't get. Yeah, it's a little bit about size and muscle. It's a little about surprise. It's a lot about training, practice, and experience. But more than any of those things, it's about will. In a fight, a lot of times it comes down to how badly you want to hurt the other person. Are you mad enough or scared enough, do you want to hurt them badly enough that you don't care if you get hurt? That you don't even notice?

I had Darren on height and muscle. I don't know, maybe I had him on training and experience. I'd been to the academy and fought my way out of a lot of tough situations, but he had like five older brothers, so I figured he'd been defending himself against them since he could walk.

But when it came to will, he had me beat. Times ten. He wanted to rip me limb from limb and I didn't even know why.

I liked the guy. I needed the guy on my side. I sure as hell didn't want to hurt the kid. So all I could do was defend myself.

He lunged toward me, swinging at my jaw. I managed to dodge that blow, but not when he brought his other fist into my right kidney. Pain exploded through my gut and I crumpled over. He slammed his fists into my exposed back, which hurt way more than it sounds like it would. I managed to sweep my legs around, scissoring his and toppling him to the ground. I tried to scramble back, but he grabbed my leg with one arm and brought his fist down onto my knee. I rolled away from the punch— which was good, because I so didn't need a broken kneecap. This was getting serious. I kicked my foot out toward his gut, but he rolled out of the way. Somehow the ball of my foot connected with his nose. Blood spewed across the floor. We both scrambled to our feet.

I held my hands out in front of me. "What the fu—"

But Darren wasn't done yet. He launched himself at me again and this time he punched me right on my jaw. I stumbled back a step, tripped on something on the floor, and went down. The back of my head slammed into the floor hard enough that my vision narrowed. I could feel the blood roaring through my brain.

Holy shit, the little bastard had knocked me out. And I still didn't even know why.

* *

I must not have been out long.

When I came to, Dawn was leaning over me, a wet washcloth in her hand. Marek was right behind her. His twin had Darren in a headlock.

Darren looked slightly calmer, but when he saw my eyes flicker open he lurched forward like he was trying to break out of the bigger guy's grasp. Which so wasn't going to happen. Thank God.

"What the hell?" I choked out weakly.

"I can't believe you messed with my sister!" Marek's twin tightened his grip around his throat and Darren stopped struggling against him. But the pure hate in his gaze didn't diminish. "I'm going to kill you!"

"I didn't mess with your sister!" I tried to push myself up, but my head felt like it was going to explode and my vision blurred again, so I lay back down.

Dawn pressed a palm to my shoulder. "Lie down. For God's sake." She ran the washcloth down my cheek, where I guess blood must have splattered.

"If you think you can get away with shit like this—"

"I didn't mess with your sister!"

Dawn looked up at Marek. "He probably has a concussion. Maybe even a broken rib. He needs to go to the clinic."

That's when I got it. Yeah, I was being a little dense. What can I say? I had a head injury.

Marek looked at me critically. "I don't know. You're supposed to stay here until Sabrina comes back tonight."

Dawn shook her head as she stood. "If this kind of injury happened out there, outside the compound, I'd say we could wait and see, but if you have any kind of medical facilities here at all, we need to figure out if he has a concussion. He struck his temple, which is one of the most vulnerable spots on the head."

I'd hit the back of my head. Not my temple. Unless I'd somehow hit something else after being knocked out. But I didn't correct Dawn. Clearly, this was her play.

As far as I could tell, Darren hadn't figured out what she was doing, because he still looked like he wanted to rip the guard's arm off and beat me with it. So I was guessing no.

Marek seemed to be wavering. Dawn walked over to Darren. She refolded the washcloth to expose the clean side and dabbed at his bloody nose. "He probably needs to go, too."

Marek scowled. "What are you, a doctor?"

She met his gaze unflinchingly. "Actually, I'm a nurse. I'm sure you know how serious head injuries are. And this is his second head injury today. We could wait and see"—she shook her head grimly—"but if we wait too long, there might not be anything we can do."

And just like that, we were all on our way to the clinic.

* *

Darren clearly hadn't known what the plan was when he beat the crap out of me, but he must have figured it out at some point. Either that, or I'd done more damage to him than I thought I had, because halfway back to the clinic, Darren passed out. Or pretended to pass out. I was really hoping for the latter.

Marek had been escorting me and his twin was a couple of yards in front of us escorting Darren when Darren stumbled to a stop, paused for a second with his hand to his head, and then crumpled to the ground.

Marek's twin tried to catch him and mostly kept him from slamming his head again. Dawn rushed over and declared that Marek and the twin needed to carry him to the clinic rather than try to revive him. She rushed them on ahead with the reassurance that she'd make sure I was right behind them.

Marek gave me a steely-eyed glare. "There's no way you'll get out of here. You know that, right?"

Dawn stood and glared at Marek. "For God's sake, he has a concussion. Of course he's not going to try to escape. Now go!"

Marek eyed her for another few seconds as if trying to decide if he could trust her. Then he and the twin each wedged a shoulder under Darren's arms and they carried him off. Marek glanced back often to make sure we weren't leaving Darren behind and dashing for freedom.

Dawn put a hand on my arm and guided me along behind them slowly enough that we could talk quietly without being overheard.

"You might have warned me," I said.

"I did warn you. If I'd said any more, you wouldn't have been surprised when he punched you." She shot me a sidelong glance. "I'm assuming there are cameras in the bedroom that probably caught the fight."

"I'm assuming. You took a really big risk."

"Maybe. But we're going back to the clinic, right? That's the goal."

"Yes, but if Darren or I had gotten seriously hurt . . ."

"Darren's not that good in a fight and I knew you wouldn't hurt him." Her steps slowed for a second and she glared at me. "Besides, we need to get out now. It's only going to get harder. The longer we're here, the greater the chance they'll move the cure. Or increase security on us. Or actually tempt us to stay."

"Would you be tempted?" I asked.

She shot me a look I couldn't quite read. "How'd you like that hot shower?"

Hmm . . . Good point. That shower had been amazing. Still, I said, "I'm not going to abandon Lily because a hot shower feels good.

"When we get to the clinic," I said, changing the subject, "you need to insist we get taken to the lab room. That's where the samples of the cure are. In the fridge in the corner."

She nodded, and even though she looked like she wanted to say something else, she didn't. Instead she fell in line beside me.

CHAPTER TWENTY-NINE

CARTER

"We need to get the doctor. Fast."

That drama teacher at Dawn's high school really deserved, like, a medal or something, because when she said it, it convinced even me.

The clinic had been empty when we arrived. I guess the whole compound kept vampire hours, which meant even though it was early afternoon, it was essentially the middle of the night. Surely there was always someone on staff to monitor Workman, but Marek led us past the hall that led to Workman's room, down a short hall, and into a room set up like an ICU, with ten hospital beds, curtains separating each one.

Darren "came to" as they laid him on one of the beds. He groaned and pretended it was a struggle just to bring his hand to his head. At least I hoped he was pretending. Jesus, I'd barely hit the guy. Right?

Dawn looked at Marek's twin. "There is a doctor, right?"

The twin looked blankly at Marek, who answered. "Sure, but she's off shift now. She won't be here for another eight hours."

Dawn made a sweeping gesture toward me. "At which point, he could be dead. You need to go wake her up now."

Clearly, Dawn was trying to get rid of one of the guards, since it would be much easier to take them out one at a time. I approved of the idea, but hoped like hell that it didn't depend on my convincing them I was near death, since I hadn't attended the Elderton High School drama program and couldn't act for shit. The best I could do was hope some of my nerves would push Marek over the edge.

"He looks fine," Marek pointed out.

"Which is a classic symptom of this kind of head injury." She crossed to where I stood and pushed my hair back at my temple. "Look at this."

"He doesn't even have a bump," Marek observed, sounding suspicious.

"Exactly. All the swelling from his head injury is internal. He could be in serious trouble and you're standing here debating it."

Finally Marek nodded to the other guy. "Go wake Dr. Dudzinski."

As soon as he was gone, Dawn lit into Marek again. "Okay, tell me where the supply of meds is." When he looked like he was going to argue, she cut him off. "Look, my brother is in pain. I'm going to go find something to help him."

"I'm not supposed to let you out of my sight."

"Either you can worry about whether or not I'm going to try to escape—which would mean leaving my guy and my brother behind—or you could tell me where the meds are so I can get my ass back here before anyone realizes I'm gone."

Jesus. Dawn was like a drill sergeant when she got going. It was hard not to follow her orders. Marek just pointed toward a door at the back of the room.

"Take a left through there and then another left. That's the lab. The meds are kept in the fridge."

"Thank you."

She headed for the door, but stopped when Marek said, "But

the fridge has a lock on it. You can't get in there without a level-three passkey."

But Dawn didn't panic. She just asked Marek flatly, "Well? Do you have a level-three passkey?"

He fidgeted, glancing in my direction.

I tried to look beaten and pathetic. It wasn't hard.

"Then get over here," she ordered, taking his lack of answer as a yes.

Which it must have been, because he followed Dawn meekly through the back doorway.

The second it closed, Darren started to sit up. Shit.

If he sat up and started talking to me, then whoever might or might not be watching down in security would realize he wasn't hurt as badly as he'd pretended.

"Don't be an idiot," I said. Then for the sake of the cameras, I added, "I kicked your ass once today. Don't make me do it again."

Darren made a sound like a strangled laugh. "You kicked my ass? That's not how I remember it."

"Really? You want an instant replay?"

Before he could answer, the door opened again and Marek and Dawn came back in. She'd pulled on latex gloves and held a nasty-looking syringe, presumably full of painkillers for Darren.

Had she been able to lift the cure while she was at it? She definitely seemed to have a plan here. And I didn't want to get in the way. At this point, all I could do was be ready.

She walked over to Darren, set the syringe on the table beside the bed, and looked down at her brother. She brushed his hair tenderly away from his face. "How are you feeling?"

He groaned dramatically.

"I'm going to give you a shot of Menderall. It'll help with the

199

pain and whatever swelling might be causing it." Then she looked up at Marek. "I need you here. You have to hold down his shoulders in case it causes a seizure."

Marek hesitated again.

"Get your ass over here. We don't have time for this!"

Again, Marek hopped to it. I guess he was used to following orders. She showed him how to brace his hands on both of Darren's shoulders.

"You have to really lean into it."

He looked down at Darren and then puffed out his chest. "I think I can hold down one kid."

"If he seizes, he'll be much stronger than he looks now. Have you ever seen someone on meth? It'll be like that."

Marek blinked and then leaned into it.

And the second Marek's neck was exposed, Dawn jabbed the syringe into it and shot him full of Menderall.

He reared back like a rhino hit with a tranquilizer dart. His arm shot out and he knocked Dawn clear off her feet. She flew maybe five feet through the air right into a cart of medical supplies before crumpling to the ground. The needle was still sticking out of Marek's neck and he ripped it out. A sharp splash of blood sputtered from the wound. He flung the syringe aside and clapped a hand over his neck, before ducking his head and charging at Dawn where she lay on the floor.

Darren and I both launched ourselves at him. I jumped right onto his back like a wrestler, wedging my forearm into his windpipe. Darren threw himself at Marek's knees. The combined force of us brought the guy down. And then, a second after we all landed sprawled on the floor, Marek went limp.

I scrambled back, trying to untangle myself and Darren from Marek's form, rolling Marek over in the process. His eyes were still open, his expression vacant. Darren and I both reached Dawn at the same time, just as she was struggling to sit up. Her hand was pressed to the side of her head and she'd gone pale.

"Jesus, are you okay?" I asked.

"Dawn? Say something!" Darren demanded.

Her eyelashes fluttered for a moment, like she couldn't make herself keep her eyes open. Then she pushed herself to her feet, swaying slightly. "Yeah. I'm fine." She looked around the room, her lips twisting a little when she saw Marek. "That guy was like a bull moose."

"How long will the Menderall keep him out?" I asked.

"Come on, *Mend*-er-*all*? I made that up."

"Then what'd you shoot him with?" Darren asked.

"Ketamine." She swayed again a little, but fought through it. "I gave him enough to knock him out. We don't have to worry about him. Not for a while anyway. It's the old-school version of what's in the tranq darts."

"No, all we have to worry about is whether or not someone is watching the video feed."

"And Dr. Dudzinski coming back."

"Right. So we've got maybe ten minutes to get out of here." I eyed Dawn. "You going to be okay?"

"I'll be fine." But she looked more unsure than she sounded.

"Okay," I said, despite the aches in my side. I was a lot less worried about me than I was about Dawn. Marek had sent her flying. "Come on, get his passkey. We still have to go back and get the cure. Let's get the hell out of here."

Before I even finished the thought, Darren had rifled through Marek's pants and come up with the passkey. It was clipped to his pants by some kind of security wire.

"Hang on," I said, digging through one of the cabinets until

I found a pair of scissors. Which couldn't cut through the wire. "What is this stuff?"

Darren ran his thumb along it. "Some kind of reinforced cording. And the clip seems embedded in his jeans. So it's impossible to get off." He looked up at me. "What do we do? Drag him with us?"

"How far are we from the lab?" I asked Dawn. Between the three of us, we now all had injuries. "I don't want to be dragging around two-hundred-plus pounds of deadweight unless we're out of options."

Dawn just rolled her eyes. "Well, unless his pants are also made of reinforced steel, I'd just use the scissors to cut the clip off his jeans."

Maybe two minutes later, Dawn slid the passkey through the lock on the fridge.

"Okay," Darren said. "Let's grab the cure and go."

I would have agreed. Except I was right behind Dawn when she swung open the door on the fridge.

"It's not going to be that easy," Dawn said.

"Why?" Darren asked.

Dawn stepped back to show him the contents. The fridge contained rack after rack of tiny glass vials. There were hundreds. Maybe thousands of them.

"Shit," I muttered under my breath.

"What?" Darren asked. "So we just take them all. We sort them out later. So what?"

"We can't take them all," I said.

"This is the compound's entire supply of meds," Dawn said. "Vaccines, insulin, painkillers. Whatever they need, it's here. If we take it, people could die."

And I hadn't even thought of that. "Besides," I added. "If we take everything we see, we won't know until we sort it all out whether we actually got the cure. I'm not leaving until we know we have it." Still, in my mind, a clock was ticking. If we were lucky, we had eight minutes left before security came through the door. They wouldn't kill me, because I was too valuable. And maybe they wouldn't kill Dawn and Darren right away. Maybe Sabrina would just torture them to keep me in line.

I couldn't think about that. I couldn't let my fear win out, because panicking wouldn't get the job done.

"Okay," I said, forcing myself to think through it. "We pull out all the trays and start looking through the vials. Hopefully it'll be labeled with the words 'Miracle Cure' or something. Basically look for anything at all that's not labeled with a name you recognize."

We moved quickly after that. Dawn had been right about the medications. There was tons of insulin, and vaccines for all the major diseases and several I hadn't ever heard of. When I found a tray of vials labeled "EN371—VAC," I set them aside. There were maybe twenty vials altogether. This was probably the same vaccine Roberto had at El Corazon. It wouldn't cure Lily, but having it for the people at Base Camp and at the Farm in San Angelo would help. Except how the hell would I decide who to give it to?

"Darren, leave this to us. Go see if you can find a cooler. We'll need something to transport these in. There's got to be one somewhere in this lab."

Dawn glanced over at the tray of vials I'd set aside. All she did was raise an eyebrow.

"It's a vaccine. For the Tick virus. Only twenty samples,

but—" I shrugged. "I don't know how we'll decide who gets the vaccine."

"Forget giving it to anyone. If it works, we need to replicate it."

"Can you do it?"

"Me, personally? No. But there's got to be someone out there who can."

It wasn't a solution, but it was a step. Yeah, maybe being an *abductura* didn't mean I had to do everything alone. Maybe it wasn't my job to make every decision.

I went back to the fridge for another tray of vials. When I came back, I noticed Dawn frowning at one of the small glass tubes.

"What is it?" I asked.

"I'm not sure," she said. "Nothing I recognize."

She handed me the sample. I had to squint to read the printing on the label.

It read simply: "NT QUAR 371X."

There were three vials of it.

"Do you recognize it?" she asked.

"No."

Darren had come back carrying a pair of Styrofoam coolers. "You found it? Cool!"

"No," I pointed out. "We didn't find it. We don't know the working name of the cure. Maybe this is it. Maybe not." I pointed to the tray, where all the vials were grouped by threes. I picked up another. "NT QUAR 371T." "NT QUAR 371S." "NT QUAR 371W."

I carefully slid the vial I held back into its empty slot, even though I was so frustrated I wanted to sweep my arm over the table and knock all of them off.

This was impossible. Thousands of vials. Any of them could be it. Or maybe none of them were. And we were running out of time.

"We're screwed," I muttered.

"No," Dawn said. "These are all variations of the same thing, right? You said Sabrina's doctors were trying to re-create the cure and hadn't yet. These are their attempts." She ran a fingertip along the tops of the vials. "Look, here's 371N. Here's 371P. All the way down to X, the first one I found. All we have to do is find the one without a letter."

Darren was back at the fridge pulling out more trays before she even finished talking. Almost immediately he held up a vial. "Got it."

Dawn and I both rushed over. "We can't know for sure—" I started to say, but before I could, Dawn took one of the tubes.

"Look! Look at the label. It's from a different printer!"

"How can you tell?" Darren asked.

"No. She's right." All the lettered variations of 371 were labeled with plain white stickers, bare except for the black type. This label had a pale orange border. Although the font was similar, there was a tiny logo before the name NT QUAR 371. A logo that looked like a double helix flowing through a G. "This is Genexome's logo. This is the sample from Genexome. This is it."

And for the first time since Lily had been attacked in that gas station in Sweetwater, I felt hope.

CHAPTER THIRTY

CARTER

"This is easy," Darren muttered with a grim finality.

Darren—the eternal optimist, the most cheerful guy I knew—did not sound pleased about this.

And yeah, he was way more optimistic than I was.

We had made it out of the lab without seeing any of Smart Com's security staff. In the time it took us to pack up the cooler with ice, the cure, and the vaccine, Marek had just sat there, like a drooling happy baby. His twin hadn't shown up with Dr. Dudzinski. No one from security had come running. Apparently, we hadn't set off any alarms. Raised any flags. In fact, we'd strolled out of Building C without even the gardener giving us a curious glance.

Now, true, while Dawn and Darren had packed the cooler, I'd taken Marek's uniform—thank God for heavy doses of ketamine. The pants were cuffed because they were too long and folded over at the waist since Darren and I had mutilated them to get the clip off. I'd even found a stock of tranq rifles. Once I pulled on his jacket, I almost looked like I was one of the guards. As long as no one looked too closely.

But that was the problem. Sabrina and all of her top people knew we were here. Even if she thought she'd won me over, she

206

would be cautious. Even though it had been less than twenty minutes since we'd taken out Marek, someone should have found him by now.

"This whole damn compound should be looking for us," I muttered, scanning the compound from my spot by the rear of the Hummer. "Someone should have seen us by now."

"You're complaining no one's shooting at us?"

"Not complaining. Just wondering what angle she's working."

"Okay, Sally Sunshine, you worry about Sabrina's motives. We'll worry about finding a ride." Dawn kicked her foot toward Darren. "How's that lock coming?"

"Almost," he muttered just before the lock popped on one of the Smart Com Hummers. He swung the door open and sketched an elegant bow. "M'lady, your chariot awaits."

Dawn smirked. "If the battery isn't dead."

"And if it has gas," Darren added.

"And if we can hot-wire it."

"And here you were worried this was going to be too easy."

Dawn slid into the driver's seat and got to work on the steering column. For two kids from what I gathered was a very conservative family, Dawn and Darren had mad skills when it came to car theft.

Of course, everyone I knew now had stolen an abandoned car at least once. The people who hadn't learned those skills hadn't survived long on the outside. There were tricks to stealing a car. Anything manufactured in the past decade was a lot harder to hot-wire. Anything that had been sitting too long, the battery would be dead. Hopefully, stealing one of the Hummers meant we wouldn't have to worry about the battery—there were Hummers all over the campus, like Sabrina had given them out as Christmas bonuses—but all the Hummers were newer models and therefore harder to hot-wire.

While Dawn was still trying to pop the key assembly out of the steering column, Darren reached past her to snag the keys out of the cubby in the door. He held them up for her. "That was easy," he said again.

The perfect escape vehicle? Gassed up and ready to go? It was like the Smart Com valet service had parked it there for us.

Dawn looked up at me. "You want to drive?"

"Yeah." She scooted over and I slid into the driver's seat. I scanned the parking lot. Cars were dotted around, but there were plenty of empty spaces. In the Before, Smart Com had employed thousands of people and its parking lot would have put Disneyland to shame. At the far end of the lot, there was the standard triple row of chain-link fences topped with razor wire. "Make sure your buckles are on."

"Why?" Darren asked, sticking his head forward between my seat and Dawn's.

She gave his head a light slap. "Why do you think, doofus?"

"I don't know. That's why I asked."

I ignored their bickering, but kept an eye out for any sign that the alarm had been raised. The fact that I didn't see anything wasn't particularly comforting. I circled back around to the front of the parking lot, giving myself as much room as possible between the car and the fence line.

"You buckled yet?"

"Yep," Dawn said.

Darren grumbled under his breath and then I heard a click. And then I floored it.

The tires squealed against the pavement as the engine strained to keep up. Still, by the time we reached the fence, we were going over a hundred.

"Whoa!" Darren yelped from the backseat. "You're not going to—"

The Hummer slammed into the fence. And then the next. And the next. The sound of crunching metal and the twang of snapping wires filled the air. One whole panel of fencing broke free and molded itself around the nose of the Hummer. The SUV bounced over the curb on the road just beyond the parking lot. We skidded to a stop in the middle of the deserted road.

In the rearview mirror, I could see Smart Com's cluster of buildings. The lights flickered and went out. Then, a second later, surged back on. I didn't really believe our escape had gone unnoticed, but now? There was no damn way they'd missed this.

"Holy crap!" Darren said from the backseat, his voice a mixture of elation and terror.

I slammed the Hummer into reverse and tried to back out of the fencing clinging to the nose. Looking over my shoulder, I drove backward, again with the pedal all the way to the floor. The roar of metal grating across the ground blocked out whatever obscenities Darren was yelling at me. I heard more wrenching metal and felt the wheel jerk in my hand as the fencing pulled free.

"You're good. That's it," Dawn said.

I slowed and only then did I turn around. The crumpled fence lay in the middle of the road. I glanced back at Smart Com, where the lights were still flickering. A siren was going off somewhere. I squelched the sick feeling of guilt in my gut.

Sabrina might be a monster, but there were plenty of humans living here who weren't. Yeah, I'd just gotten my people out, but

I'd endangered a whole hell of a lot of other people to do it. Dusk was maybe five hours away. I just prayed they'd get the fences back in place by then. And that we wouldn't be here to see it.

I put the Hummer back in gear and floored it again, swerving to miss the fence.

I took the first turn and just kept driving.

"Why are we alive?" Darren asked from the backseat.

Dawn twisted to glare at him. "What?"

"Those fences were electrified. Why didn't they toast us?"

"Rubber tires," Dawn snipped. "Didn't you pay attention in science? No, wait. Don't answer that. I don't want to know."

"When we stop the car," I said, "make sure you jump free of it when we get out. I don't know how long the car will hold a charge, but I don't want to find out the hard way."

"When are we going to stop?" Dawn asked.

"Not until we have to."

CHAPTER THIRTY-ONE

CARTER

We headed south, back toward Roswell, driving fast and not looking back, always waiting to see headlights in the rearview mirror. Because we should have seen them.

There was no way in hell Sabrina would let us just waltz out of there. But other than a single standard patrol we had to dodge on our way out of Albuquerque, we didn't see anyone. It was almost as if Sabrina hadn't even noticed us leave.

At some point, Darren took over driving so I could sleep. A couple hours later I woke with the same thought running through my head: this had all been too easy.

I stopped saying it aloud, because Dawn and Darren were so excited about our escape they were practically bubbling. I got it. I'd been there before. There was a high that came from breaking out of a place. A thrill that came with subverting the system that's designed to keep you in. I didn't want to take that away from them.

If Sabrina had let us go only to screw with us farther down the line, we'd find out soon enough.

On the outskirts of Roswell, I directed Darren back toward the bag of supplies we'd stashed on our first trip through. Then I started looking for another car. I couldn't get out of this Hummer fast enough. We found a beat-up Dodge in a neighborhood just south of town. All the houses seemed abandoned. None of them looked like they'd been that great to begin with.

While Darren popped the lock and jumped the battery, I pulled Dawn aside.

"You comfortable searching the house while I stand guard?"

I wasn't sure she'd be okay with this. After all, I'd first met Dawn when a team from Base Camp had been searching her house during a supply raid. All the food we had at Base Camp was stuff we'd found in abandoned houses. It wasn't fun digging through the belongings of people long dead, but it was better than starving. You got used to it. I just wasn't sure Dawn was there yet.

But she nodded gamely. "Look for the standard stuff? Food, bottled water, that kind of thing?"

"Sure, but your first priority is finding new clothes. Everything new from the bottom, up, for all three of us."

She raised her eyebrows. "Oookay."

"And a pair of coolers for the samples of the cure. Everything that was with us except for those three vials stays in the Hummer."

It only took Dawn a few seconds to figure it out. "You think she put some kind of tracking device on us?"

"I think we got out of there entirely too easily. Either she's incompetent or she's playing us. And the incompetent vampires don't live this long."

Dawn nodded, and went off to search houses. Thirty minutes later, we had two working cars, complete changes of clothes, three coolers, and three boxes of Quaker Chewy Granola Bars. It wasn't much, but it's more than we had before, so none of us was complaining.

I divvied everything up—two coolers and two boxes of granola bars in one pile, one of each in another pile.

"What are you doing?" Darren asked, confused.

"He's leaving us," Dawn told him before I could say anything.

"What are you talking about? That doesn't make any sense. Why would he—"

"Because we're being tracked," I said. "There's no way we're going to make it to the Farm in San Angelo in this Hummer. Not when they're following our every move. And we sure as hell don't want them following us back there anyway."

"So we ditch the car." Dawn crossed her arms over her chest and attempted to stare me down. But I've been in staring contests with monsters a lot scarier than her, and I didn't flinch.

"Then they'll know where to start looking for us. There's no way you'll be able to get away."

"What are you going to do?" Darren narrowed his eyes suspiciously at me.

"I'm going to take the Hummer and head out in the opposite direction. They'll follow me and you guys can get away."

"You don't really think we're going to do that, do you? Just drive away knowing they're going to catch you? Knowing you're going to die if they do?" Dawn looked furious.

"You don't have a choice."

"What about Lily? What happens to her if you get caught?"

That was the one thought that scared the hell out of me through all of this. The idea that I wouldn't get to Lily before she became a Tick. But I couldn't let myself dwell on that because if I did, I'd be paralyzed. I'd start making really stupid decisions and then we'd all be screwed.

"That's what you're for. That's why you need to get through to

San Angelo. If something happens to me, Ely will find her and he'll know where to take her. You'll have gotten through with the cure and then Lily will be safe and so will everyone else." At least that was my plan. My hope. My mantra.

I hung on to it like a burr, refusing to even imagine things going any other way.

I reached into the car, pulled out the cooler that held the vials. I took two vials—one for Lily and one for Marcus—then handed the last one to Dawn. I put my vials in one of the coolers, packed ice around them, then watched as Dawn did the same.

"I don't like this, Carter." Darren looked more troubled than I'd ever seen him.

"There's nothing about it to like or not like," I told him. "Jesus, Darren, when's the last time there's been anything in this whole damned mess to like?" I shook my head. "This isn't about doing what we want to do— it hasn't been for a long time. This is about doing what has to be done."

And I had to get the hell out of there. We were burning time, burning daylight that we couldn't afford to waste. Besides, if Sabrina was tracking the Hummer or something in it, we'd been sitting in one place for way too long.

It was finally Dawn who moved things along, giving her younger brother a nudge toward the driver's door. "You want to drive or what?"

Darren gave me one last worried look, and then said, "Hell, yeah."

I gave Dawn a quick hug before she climbed into the passenger side of the car. She winced a little, which I didn't like at all. When I crossed around to Darren, I shook his hand. "Head east, toward Lubbock, but you'll want to skirt around the town itself. There's a pretty big Farm there, one of the biggest in the state. There are plenty of smaller towns around there where you can find gas for the rest of the drive to San Angelo." Then I added more softly, "When you get back to the Farm, make sure she sees a medic or something, okay?"

He nodded, looking way more serious than he usually did. He may be Dawn's goofy younger brother, but he had her back.

What was that like? Having a brother or sister that you could count on to be there no matter what?

It was hard to watch them drive away. I liked Dawn and Darren. I trusted them, which in this world was all too rare. Even if they were a bit naïve, they were both smart and skilled. They would be okay on their own. Then again, it was the only reason I was even considering this. Because I knew they would do everything they could to get the cure where it needed to be while I did all I could to get to where I needed to be.

For a moment images of the helicopter crash bombarded me. I didn't see it, but I'd watched enough movies in the Before to know what it had probably looked like. That was what haunted me. Pictures of Lily lying battered, bloody, broken, with no one around to help her.

For long seconds, the thought paralyzed me. But I shook it off. That was the thing about the world we lived in now. If you thought too much about it, you'd freeze up, wouldn't be able to do anything. You had to keep going, keep moving to stay ahead of the monsters. Not just the actual monsters, but the emotional ones—the fears and doubts that would devour you more completely than any Tick.

Instead of giving in, I climbed back into the Hummer and headed south again, this time toward Alpine. I still wasn't sure if I trusted Sebastian, but I wasn't above borrowing his wheels.

Besides, every car he owned was faster than this one. Around dusk, I stopped in Carlsbad to search for another car.

Dusk was prime hunting time for Ticks. They were just waking up. They were hungry. And if a pack of them found me, I was totally screwed.

By myself, there was no way I could fight off a whole pack.

But I stopped at dusk for a reason. If Sabrina was tracking this Hummer, she probably assumed I was stopping for the night. If looking for a car now bought me a few hours' lead, then it was worth the risk.

I drove up and down the dusty streets until I found one with five different cars parked out in the open to maximize my chances. There was a Ford and a Hyundai that I couldn't start. I passed up the VW Bug when I realized it was a diesel. It was hard enough finding regular gas. I struck gold with a Chevy. I started siphoning the gas from the Ford into the Chevy, and then went to clear out the Hummer. I carefully took the cooler with the two vials and placed it on the front-seat floorboard of my new ride. Then I pulled out all the clothes we'd been wearing and hid them behind a bush in a nearby yard. I didn't know where Sabrina might have put a tracking device, but if it was on the clothes, I wanted to make it hard on her.

This was paranoia at its finest. I didn't even know for sure that she was tracking us. All I had was this sense of impending doom, which may or may not have been brought on by the fact that my girlfriend was in a downed helicopter with her psychotic father and my best hope of finding her again was a guy who'd already betrayed us once.

Yeah, what's not to be paranoid about, right?

Besides, Sabrina owned Smart Com. If anyone on the planet had tiny tracking devices, wouldn't it be them?

I didn't bother trying to get gas from any of the other cars on the street. If I'd been in one of the cars from Base Camp, I'd have spare gas cans, but I wasn't and I didn't. Maybe one of the houses nearby would have one, but just as I was debating if I should look, I heard it. A howl in the night.

I couldn't tell from this distance if it was a Tick or some other animal. More howls joined the first. I told myself it could be coyotes, but it wasn't like I wanted to meet a hungry pack of them alone in the dark, either.

I grabbed the box of food from the Hummer and was just sliding into the driver's seat of the Chevy when I saw the shadows at the end of the block shift. I saw the movement rather than the shapes. I stilled instantly. Coyotes rely mainly on scent, but Ticks have great vision, too.

You'd think it'd be easy to tell one cunning predator from another. A Tick would have a hundred pounds on a coyote, maybe more. This creature kept low to the ground, but moved more slowly than a coyote. It was near the Ford, where I'd been not that long ago and where my scent probably still lingered. I slid into the driver's seat and shut the door. The movement or the sound caught its attention. It straightened to its full height. I couldn't see its face. I could only imagine the soulless hunger in its eyes. Another yelp echoed in the distance and this Tick answered with a long series of yelps and howls.

I fumbled to pull my flashlight out of my pocket, but the new clothes were unfamiliar and it took longer than it should have. I clicked it on and held it in my teeth as I grabbed the starter wire and the battery wire. I glanced up. Through the windshield, I could see the Tick charging the car. I had five seconds. Less.

I touched the wires together, but my hands were trembling and it didn't spark. Damn it! This car worked. I knew it did. I'd gotten it started just a few minutes ago. I'd turned it off because only an idiot kept a car running while siphoning gas.

I dropped one of the wires, gave my hand a shake, and tried again. This time, it roared to life. I dropped the flashlight into my lap as I jerked the steering wheel hard to the right and revved the engine. The Tick landed on the hood of the car.

For one brief second, we stared at each other.

The Tick was female, and her long scraggly hair covered much of her too-thin face. Ticks were usually more muscular than humans. More massive. This one seemed underfed and bony. Not that I was worried about her health.

She clawed at the windshield, seemingly baffled by the glass that separated us. Yeah, Ticks just weren't that bright. But she was determined.

She raised her hands, fisting them together. This was the Tick's go-to move. You slam your fists into whatever you wanted to crack open. Which meant I was about ten seconds away from being dragged through a hole of jagged glass.

I put the car in gear and slammed my foot down on the gas. She tumbled forward onto the windshield. Ten seconds later, I slammed on the brakes. She flew off the hood of the car and landed in front of me.

Two weeks ago, this is where I would have hit the gas again and crushed her with as much speed as I could. Two weeks ago, I never would have passed up the opportunity to do that kind of damage to a Tick. I might not have killed her, but wounded and broken, she probably wouldn't be able to kill me, either.

But now, with two precious vials of the cure in a cooler on the floor, I couldn't make myself do it. This Tick had been human once. Like Lily.

And if we pulled off this crazy gambit, if we actually managed to re-create this cure, then this Tick could be human again. Like Lily.

In that instant, my whole world shifted. I couldn't kill Ticks anymore. Not while there was the hope that we could save them. Not while Lily was out there somewhere, battling this virus.

I slammed the car back into reverse and floored it, driving backward down the street until I nearly reached the intersection. Then I spun the car around and drove off.

I could hear the Ticks behind me, not just the female anymore, but the others, too, their dissonant yips and yowls filling the night.

Somewhere out there, Lily was spending the night outside, away from safety and sanctuary. Was she huddled somewhere, hiding? Alone and afraid? I hoped so, because the alternative—that she was already dead—was unthinkable.

I didn't stop driving. I kept heading southeast, until the sun started to creep over the horizon. Only then did I stop to dig the sat phone out of the duffel.

Ely answered on the first ring. "I hope you have good news."

"I was going to say the same thing."

"Yeah," Ely said grimly. "I found them."

"Where are you?"

"Outside of some Farm near College Station. A couple of hours from Houston."

"Okay, then. I'm on my way."

"It's not that simple," Ely said.

Of course not. When was it ever simple?

"They've already turned."

My heart clenched. And I squeezed my eyes shut. I flashed back to that moment when the female Tick had jumped onto the hood of the car. That really could have been Lily. She could be that monstrous right now. That driven by blood lust. That hungry and afraid.

This was the thing she'd feared the most. Turning into a Tick.

If any part of her human brain still functioned and still remembered her life and who she really was, did she wonder why I'd let this happen to her? Did she curse me and hate me? Because I hated myself.

I'd let this happen. This was my fault.

"We'll get them back." Because I couldn't think of anything else to say, I added, "Did you find the crash site?"

"Yeah."

"Do you know if anyone else from the helicopter survived?"

"There weren't any other Ticks around. They must have cleared out before I got there."

"What about the doctor and her dad?"

Ely was silent for a minute. "There were remains, at the site of the crash and farther on. You don't want to know anything beyond that."

"I'm not—"

"No," Ely said harshly. "Look, we don't know how it went down. You don't need the details and I'm going to try damn hard to forget that it's my baby brother that might have done that."

I didn't press him. He was right. I didn't want any more carnage in my mind. And I didn't need the reminder that my Lily might be capable of it.

"Did you get the cure?" Ely asked.

"Yes."

"And it works?"

I nearly lied. If I'd been talking to almost anyone else, I

would have. But Ely's brother was out there, too. He deserved to know the truth.

"I don't know yet."

"What the hell is that supposed to mean?"

"What do you think it means? I don't have absolute proof that anyone has successfully been given the cure and turned back from a Tick into a human."

"Then how do we know it works?"

"We don't."

"Okay, why do we *think* it works?"

"Because Sabrina showed me footage they'd recorded of them dosing someone."

"You know they can fake those things, right?"

"I don't think this was fake. She seemed like she was on the up-and-up."

"We're putting our faith in a psychotic vampire?" Ely's voice sounded strangled.

Jesus. This was what it came down to.

"You gotta put your faith in something, right?"

CHAPTER THIRTY-TWO

MEL

When I wake, I don't know how long I've been out. I am still curled up beside Chuy, but I am no longer on the floor. At some point, Sebastian must have carried me into Roberto's room, laid me out on the bed, and covered me with a blanket. The idea of Sebastian gently caring for me is so antithetical to his nature I could almost more easily believe that Chuy suddenly started walking upright and carried me in.

I lie there in the bed, my hand propped on Chuy's gently rising and falling chest. There is something so peaceful about sleeping next to another living creature. How did I never know that before?

Eventually, I push myself to sit up. Chuy keeps sleeping on the bed as I tiptoe from the room. Sebastian is on the sofa, his legs stretched out in front of him, his eyes closed. He looks asleep, but somehow I know he's not.

Despite gorging myself earlier, I'm still hungry. Maybe this is part of being a vampire. Maybe I will never feel full again. The extra bags of blood I'd brought out from storage are no longer on the coffee table. Sebastian must have moved them to the mini-fridge, because that's where I find them. After I pull them out, I notice Sebastian has come to stand behind me. As always, he's fast and silent. I am used to him sneaking up on me, but I'm not used to the fluttering I feel in my stomach. His kiss is still fresh in my memory.

Maybe it will always be. I want him to kiss me again, but when I look up at him, his gaze is unreadably dark and I know that won't happen. Not with his words ringing in my ears—*I should be old enough to know better.*

"Mel—" he starts to say.

But I can't listen to him tell me how young I am. How silly or how gullible. I know these things. So instead, I thrust a bag of blood toward him.

"We should both feed again." I try to focus my attention on the other bag still in my hands. "There's plenty of blood, and once we're not starving to death, we'll feel better. Our judgment will be more sound."

"Ah, yes," he snarks, seeming suddenly like his old self. "Sound judgment. The Price girls' most distinguishing characteristic."

"Look, you may not be very invested in this particular venture, but I still care about getting out of here and bringing you to Genexome so you can unlock your vault or whatever it is you want to call it, and give me the cure." I say this to remind myself as much as to remind him. Somehow, between my thirst and my need, I've forgotten why I'm here.

"That's what you think? That I'm not invested in this?"

"Don't pretend you give a damn about what happens to anyone other than yourself." I pause to give him a chance to correct me. He doesn't. "You care about your own goals and that's it."

For an instant, he looks like I'd slapped him. Then his face settles into a mask of cool indifference. "That's what you believe."

"Yes! If you cared about anyone, then why haven't you released the cure before now?" The questions that had been simmering inside of me for so long just boil over. "Why have you let the world collapse around you? You've let countless people die. If you could have stopped it, why didn't you?"

"Because I'm an evil, selfish bastard. That's the only answer, isn't it?"

I search his face, looking, desperately, for some sign that I'm wrong. For some admission on his part that there is more to the story. Some scrap of information that will make this all make sense.

"I don't understand," I admit.

"There is nothing *to* understand."

"So you really do have the cure? You've had it the whole time, and you just let the world burn?" These are the questions I should have been asking all along, ever since he admitted he had the cure at Genexome, ever since he admitted that he *was* Genexome. But everything has moved too fast until now. My world has been turned upside down over and over again. And I no longer know which way is up. "Why?"

He studies me for a moment and then chuckles. "That's the question you're asking? Why I betrayed the world, not why I betrayed you? You're not even remotely curious why I sent you here, to your death?"

I blink in surprise. "No. I understand that."

"You understand that?" he asks archly.

His tone annoys me—he somehow implies that I'm a child and can't possibly comprehend his motives. I bump up my chin. "Yes. I do. You are not the least bit invested in me as a person. Me and my life and the lives of everyone I care about are completely expendable to you. We are all just pawns in this war you've waged against Roberto. I get that. I understand that

I was expendable, but I don't understand how the entire world was expendable."

Our fight must have woken Chuy up, because the dog creeps across the floor to stand by my side.

Sebastian stares at me for a long moment. He's studying my face, almost like I've been speaking another language, one that he's trying frantically to translate into his own. Finally, he shakes his head.

"Well then. I suppose you're right. If that's the case, then I am truly a despicable bastard."

I realize suddenly that I'm holding my breath. That I'm waiting for him to deny it. I'm hoping he will. That he'll offer up some explanation. Some story that will help me make sense of how this man—this man who has apparently destroyed the entire world—could be the same man who has cared for me and mentored me for the past nine weeks of my life. How the man who sent me to die at Roberto's hands could be the same man who kissed me so tenderly.

I have no answers and he's not giving anything away.

I whirl away from him, frustrated. "Why did you even bother saving me?"

"It seemed like a good idea at the time." He's back to his usual sarcasm. "Then again, Carter was standing there, ordering me to do it and lots of things seem wise when an *abductura* is pushing you around."

"Not then." I turn back to glare at him. Maybe I should be rejoicing that he appears to take my questions seriously at least for a few minutes, but instead I'm just furious at him all over again. "This morning. When you came out onto the porch with the crossbow."

"What was I supposed to do? Let them devour you? That wouldn't have been a very intelligent game plan, now would it?"

"I was doing fine." My protest sounds more scared than angry, which I guess it is.

"You're exhausted and hungry. You were barely holding your own."

"I don't need you to rescue me. You've done that already and it hasn't ever turned out good for me."

"Very well. Next time I'll just let you die. Protecting you is a full-time job and it's one that's gotten rather dull, what with the endless moral inquisition."

"You don't have to protect me. Because, quite honestly, you haven't been doing that good a job. Seeing as how you sent me unprepared into the lair of the most dangerous vampire in history, trying to protect me now seems a bit disingenuous."

"I wasn't trying to protect you. I was saving my own ass. This morning you were the only thing standing between me and a slow painful death by starvation."

"Right. How had I forgotten, even for a minute, that none of this is about me?"

Anger burns through my veins, so sharp and heated I think that my blood must surely be near boiling.

All this time, I've been holding one of the bags of blood and now I toss it at him. "Here. Now I'm not the only thing between you and starvation."

He grabs the bag in midair and eyes it, smirking. Then he looks up at me, a lascivious gleam in his eyes as he drops his gaze pointedly to my chest. "Sure you don't want to warm this up for me?"

Suddenly, I'm furious. Not just because he's the mastermind behind the destruction of the world, or even because he's betrayed me, but because he's not the man who kissed me so tenderly. That man doesn't even exist. That tenderness was a figment of my imagination. The product of my optimistic, swooningly romantic foolishness.

The real Sebastian is a sadistic bastard.

As if sensing my mood, Chuy bristles beside me. He lets out a low, rumbling growl. That's all the encouragement I need.

I slap Sebastian as hard as I can. Which it turns out is pretty hard. His whole head snaps to the side. I'm shocked by my own violence, but not worried. I know I can take him. Except instead of hitting me back, he jerks me to him and kisses me.

But this kiss is nothing like the previous one. This is rough and dark and the most dangerous thing I've ever done. If the other kiss had been heaven, then this is pure hell. It makes my blood pound and it terrifies me all at once, because I don't want just to kiss him. I want to possess him. And something darker, too. I want to hurt him. Like he's hurt me. I want to wound him. I want his life. His blood. His very soul.

Somehow, I know instinctively that he feels the same way. His tongue in my mouth seems to be pulling me, the essence of who I am, from my body. He is pulling the air from my lungs.

I am drowning in him.

And I can't breathe.

Literally.

His hands have slipped from my jaw to my throat. His thumbs press into my windpipe, cutting off my air supply, even while he is kissing me still.

My hands slip up to cradle his face. I want to go on kissing him forever. Almost as much as I want to kill him.

I thrust my arms out, breaking his hold on my throat, and suck in a desperate gasp of air. He stumbles back, but I follow, spinning on the ball of my foot to kick him in the chest. He backflips away from me, landing on his feet, hands out in front of him.

For a long moment, we both just stand there. Staring at each other, sucking in deep, rage-filled, fear-fueled breaths. Chuy is growling at Sebastian again, poised to pounce.

It is the vampire berserker rage. I understand that now. But how had it come on so quickly? I thought it had passed. That it was gone. I'd been an idiot.

Apparently being surrounded by a horde of monsters wasn't intense enough, now I'm trapped in a locked safe house with a man who wants to murder me.

There is no way this is going to end well.

And then Sebastian tears his eyes away from me to scan the room. I see his gaze land on it. A painting by the door. It's something impressionistic and iconic that I feel like I should recognize. I don't get why he's looking at it, but then he lunges for it, ripping it off the wall. He smashes it against the floor and the wooden frame shatters, throwing out shards and splinters. We both lunge for different pieces. Unsure what to do, Chuy yelps, throwing himself between Sebastian and me.

The one closest to me is bigger. I go into a slide, my arm outstretched. My hand is just closing on the wood when Sebastian grabs one of the other, smaller pieces.

He wields it out in front of himself like a dagger. I scramble to my feet, putting as much space between us as I can, brandishing my own clumsy splinter.

And then he does the unthinkable.

He thrusts the stake into his own heart.

CHAPTER THIRTY-THREE

CARTER

"Are you sure they're there?" I asked Ely.

"Yes."

There was the remains of a frat house, a dozen or so blocks from campus.

Ely had been scouting the house for the past day and a half. I had no idea how he'd spent thirty-six hours this close to a nest of Ticks and survived, but somehow he had. He was like a frickin' ninja when it came to this crap.

He'd found a house across and just down the street with a third-story window that looked out on the Ticks' nest. I'd nearly puked going in, because he'd littered the first floor with garbage. Not just trash, but the really foul stuff, animal feces and molding vegetables, decomposing medical waste. And—when he'd given me the directions over the sat phone—he told me to wrap myself in plastic bags before walking through the house. It was all about covering the scent, he claimed.

I figured there was a chance he was just messing with me, but I did it anyway. And now we sat up in that third-floor bedroom watching the Ticks' house through binoculars.

It was nearly two in the morning, and though we could see the movement outside the other house, it was nearly impossible to distinguish one Tick from another.

"You've seen them both?" I asked.

"What do you want me to do, swear on a stack of Bibles? They're there. I've seen them. I've watched them for the past couple of days while you've been off getting spa treatments."

"It was a shower. Not a spa treatment."

"Whatever."

Yeah. I guess I shouldn't have mentioned the shower, not when he'd been wallowing in trash for the past few days. It wasn't like I'd been bragging. I'd just told him what had gone down in Albuquerque.

Somehow, in addition to finding Lily and Marcus, and getting this house set up across from the nest, he'd also snuck into the nearby Farm and stolen half a dozen tranq rifles.

"I wish we had night-vision goggles," I muttered. Ely was the best there was at surviving on his own—clearly—and he was smart. But how sure was he that Lily really was in there? Did I want to see her? Was I ready for that?

I'd seen a lot of Ticks. I'd seen their eyes glazed over with mindless hunger. I'd breathed in their rotting breath. Seen their teeth, too big for even their massive jaws.

Would I still be able to love Lily, after I'd seen her like that? Would she ever be the girl I'd loved again?

The thought of her as a Tick made my innards squelch. The thought that I might not be able to move past it only made things worse. I *had* to fix this.

"If you have some magic fairy who's granting wishes and you fucking waste one on night goggles, I'm stabbing you," Ely said from behind me.

I closed my eyes for a second and nearly laughed.

"Okay. Let's talk about what we do have."

Ely reached over and took the binoculars from me and then

stared out through the window himself. "What we do have is at least five Ticks in the house. Maybe more."

"So three other than Lily and Marcus."

"Yeah. And one of them is this huge guy. I think he's the alpha."

"The alpha?" I asked.

"Yeah. With pack animals, there's always one that's dominant. The alpha." I raised my eyebrows and Ely shrugged. "What? I watched a lot of nature shows."

"Okay. Do we know where they're nesting?" I asked.

"As far as I can tell, they all sleep in the front living room. The one with the curtains."

"But there are curtains, so you don't know for sure."

"Actually, my buddy Superman came over and checked things out with his X-ray vision. No, I don't know for sure. But I've surveyed the perimeter of the house and that's the only room with curtains still up, so yeah, I think that's it."

"And there's not a basement or a cellar or anything? Some place it would be completely dark during the day?"

"No, you dipshit. This is Texas. No one has basements in Texas. Didn't you grow up here, too? Why don't you know that?"

Actually, I'd spent a lot of my childhood and adolescence in boarding schools back East, where everyone had a basement.

Instead I asked, "Are all the tranq rifles you stole fully loaded?"

"You think I'm dumb enough to steal empty rifles?"

"Stop being pissy. Lily and Marcus's safety is my priority here."

I didn't trust him. I would never trust him again. But there was no way I could do this alone.

I blew out a breath. "Okay, so that makes eighteen darts

231

total. That's six darts for each of the Ticks. Which may or may not be enough to take them out."

Ely stood up then. "Don't forget, we still have to tranq Marcus and Lily, too."

"Don't forget, we can't tranq them. Sabrina said the Tick they tested the serum on had been tranqed and he reacted poorly. He died."

"So we're trusting the word of a vampire now?"

"We trusted Sebastian. You trusted Roberto."

"Which is what got us here in the first place."

"Look, we have exactly one shot at this. If we tranq them and then give them the cure, they will die."

"Maybe, but—"

"Maybe?"

"Maybe," he said again, talking over me. "But if we don't tranq them, then we die. Even if we take out all the other Ticks—which we don't know for sure we can do even with the eighteen tranq darts—but if it's just them, you're talking about putting ourselves in a room with two Ticks. That's the point I think you're missing. They are Ticks. They are not the people we love." Ely thrust a hand out toward the house across the street. "That is not Lily in that house. That is not my brother across the street. That is a monster and he will kill me if he gets a chance. I'm not going to give it to him."

"What are you saying? That we don't treat them? 'Cause that's not really a solution, either. Even if we could do more testing on the cure, we can't just leave them like this. They're not safe. The Ticks may have seemed impossible to kill ten months ago, but people are wising up. They're getting creative about ways to kill Ticks."

And I'd been one of the people who spread the word about

how to kill them. I had killed countless Ticks myself. I had stabbed them in the heart, blown holes in their chests big enough to toss a pumpkin through. I'd chopped off their heads.

Yeah, every time I'd killed a Tick, it had been my life or theirs, but now that there might be a cure, I couldn't help . . .

No. I couldn't think that way. This situation was too messed up as it was. I wasn't going to haunt myself with that crap.

"We can't leave them as Ticks," I insisted.

"Well we can't just go in there, shoot them up with the cure, and expect them to sit around playing Go Fish with us, either. We have to find a way to subdue them while we wait for this to take effect. Do you even know how long it will take?"

"No." The video Sabrina had shown me had been sped up.

He was right. We couldn't just dose them and hope that the inhumanly strong monsters didn't mind when we jabbed them in the arm. Besides, this wasn't the ketamine that Dawn had used on Marek. This had to actually go into a vein.

"Okay. Then we need a plan. We go in when they're sleeping, we tranq everyone, and then we remove Lily and Marcus to some other location. Somewhere we can keep them safe while we wait it out. Somewhere they can't kill us."

After a second of consideration, Ely nodded. "Where's that?"

"I have no idea," I admitted. "You got a map?"

Ten minutes later, we were poring over an old paper map of Texas that Ely had spread on the ground in front of us. He tossed a gum wrapper in the middle of the eastern part of the state to mark our location.

After a few minutes of searching, I put my finger down on a spot north of Houston. "Here. We bring them here." The spot on the map read "Texas Department of Criminal Justice, Huntsville Unit." "To the state prison in Huntsville."

CHAPTER THIRTY-FOUR

CARTER

"Do we have a backup plan?" Ely asked five hours later. "In case things go badly."

"Nope."

We had spent most of the past few hours planning the raid on the Ticks' nest and waiting for dawn. Once everything in the house had been quiet for a couple of hours, we'd crept out of our hiding spot and crossed the street. In the front yard, Ely slung off the backpack he'd been wearing and dropped it by the pathetic remains of the landscaping.

"Based on the pattern of movement at the windows . . ." Ely said as we stopped on either side of the front doorway. The door itself had long ago been ripped off its hinges. Ticks weren't big on doorknobs. "They sleep all together in the front living room on the first floor. We should be able to walk right in and start firing."

I nodded, not bothering to mention that he'd told me this already. We each had two of the tranq rifles strapped to our backs and one ready to fire.

"We go in, we shoot everything that moves until they stop moving."

I nodded again. My heart was thundering so hard I was surprised it didn't wake up one of the Ticks. I'd fought and killed my fair share of Ticks in the past ten months, but I'd never walked right into one of their nests.

I counted down on my fingers from five and then Ely and I both swung through the doorway. The foyer, which we'd been able to glimpse through the open door, was empty. To the immediate left was the living room. Heavy curtains hung on the windows and the only light came in through a thin gap in them. My eyes darted around the room and I fired automatically as I found the huddled shapes. On my right, two shapes curled on what looked like a sofa that had been torn to shreds. I darted them, twice each. The soft phffft, phffft, phffft of my rifle firing was matched by identical sounds from Ely.

Ely and I both pulled out our flashlights and held them up, surveying the room.

"I only see four," I said.

As I spoke, one of the Ticks on the sofa twitched, then gave a whole-body shiver that was almost violent. It reared up, howling drunkenly. I fired another dart into it at the same time Ely did. Then he spun around, putting his back to mine as we both scanned the room.

"I still only see four."

"Agreed."

"Is there any chance you miscounted?" I asked.

"No. There were definitely five here as of yesterday. I don't see the alpha Tick."

Together we turned slowly, watching the other Ticks in the living room for signs they might wake.

"Are we sure they all came back last night?"

Ely cursed.

"I'm going to take that as a no. Okay," I said, my mind racing. "We've got two options. We grab Marcus and Lily and get the hell out. Or we split up and one of us goes to find the alpha Tick."

From deep within the house came a low rumbling growl followed by the creaking of floorboards and the sound of wood splintering.

We automatically both turned toward the sound.

"Option one is looking a lot less possible," I commented.

"You want to go find that beast or should I?"

Behind us, one of the Ticks made a snuffling noise. I whipped around, looking from Tick to Tick. One of the ones in the corner shifted and then stilled. Somewhere else in the house, the other Tick howled again, a long low-pitched cry followed by several short yips. Like he was calling for the others. When he didn't get a response, he howled again and this time another voice joined his. There were two of them. And then they both fell silent. But I could hear them moving somewhere in the house.

Just from where we stood, I could see hallways and rooms shooting off in several directions. Back in the Before, when I'd been at all those East Coast boarding schools, my friends and I had crashed a couple of frat parties. We'd been young enough that we'd been kicked out on our asses pretty fast, but still, I'd been inside some frat houses. They were always big and labyrinthine. These Ticks could be hiding anywhere and they could be damn hard to find. They'd stayed alive this long, which meant they were smart—for Ticks.

"I'm tired of waiting. Get your rifle ready." I propped my own rifle against my hip and pulled out my pocketknife. I used my teeth to open it while I rolled back my sleeve. "Hey, buddy," I called out. "You gonna come find us or what?"

"What the hell are you doing?" Ely demanded.

"Are you ready?" I asked Ely. He nodded and I ran the knife across the outside of my forearm, keeping the slice nice and shallow. It still hurt like hell. "'Cause here he comes."

I swapped the knife to my left hand and grabbed the tranq rifle in my right, propping the barrel on my left wrist. The cut was throbbing and I could feel the blood oozing from it. One drop ran down to my elbow and then fell to the floor.

"Come on!" I yelled again, but I didn't need to.

A roar came from within the house and then the thundering sound of a huge creature tearing its way past cheap furniture. I started firing before it even made it through the doorway. Phffft, phffft. Ely was firing too. Phffft, phffft, phffft. And still it came barreling toward us.

The darts didn't seem to faze it at all. He just ducked his head and rammed me. I flew through the air and landed on my back, his massive weight on top of me. I still had one tranq rifle strapped to my back and it bit into my shoulder as I landed. I tried to roll with the impact, but the alpha Tick was too strong. I slammed the rifle I still held into his temple, but he didn't seem to notice. Hell, maybe the five tranq darts had just deadened his pain.

He howled again, not in anguish but in fury, and bared his huge teeth at me. I grabbed the rifle in both hands and shoved it up under his jaw, straightening my arms to keep his snapping mouth away from me.

"A little . . ." I never got the word *help* out.

"Busy," Ely grunted back. Only then was I aware of the bangs and crashes coming from his direction.

The Tick on top of me grabbed my ear and started to pull.

237

His arms were way longer than mine. And stronger, too. My muscles started shaking. I could not hold this beast off for much longer. And if I could, he would actually rip my ears from my head. His claws were digging into my skull and I could feel the blood seeping from beneath his fingers.

My left arm started to give out and the rifle tipped down. He lunged forward toward my shoulder in the same instant that Ely thrust a stake through his back. A jagged piece of wood pierced his heart and came out through his chest, stopping five inches from me.

He roared and rolled to the side—thankfully losing his grip on my ears. I gave one last push and thrust him off me.

Sucking in deep, ragged breaths, I pushed myself up onto my knees, bracing myself on my good arm. I looked around. Ely stood a few feet away, his last tranq rifle held ready, pointing at first one Tick and then another, occasionally looking past me to the Ticks that were already knocked out.

At his feet lay what I took to be a female Tick, several tranq darts in her chest. A stake there, too. For an instant, my heart stopped. What if—

But, no. Her hair wasn't the right color. And her clothes, the tattered remains of a flowered dress, were all wrong. Lily had had on jeans and a gray hoodie. A lot of Ticks stopped wearing clothes altogether. When they still wore them, it seemed like an afterthought, like something they just never bothered to take off. Still, the idea haunted me. Had Ely known that? He'd seen Lily recently. He would have known what she was wearing. Maybe. Maybe he just hadn't cared, when it had been his life or this Tick's.

I couldn't think about that.

God, there were so many things I couldn't think about. Like

the fact that these two Ticks were now dead. If things had gone differently, they could have lived long enough to get the cure. And in some weird way, I knew I owed this Tick. He'd kept Lily alive long enough for me to find her.

I used my good arm to push myself to my feet and wavered as my head swam. I put my fingers to the skin behind my ear and they came away bloody.

Ely glanced at me. "You okay?"

"I think I need a hepatitis shot."

"You had one."

"What?"

"It was one of the vaccines we all got before Sebastian let us into the academy." He didn't stop surveying the room as he spoke.

"We should have known then this was fucked up."

"No shit."

My breath was still coming in bursts and every muscle in my body was shaking from the aftereffects of the adrenaline. And to be honest, I totally wanted to puke. Or sit down and cry. Not that I had time to do either of those things.

I looked around at the six Tick bodies littering the floor. Given how hard it had been to knock out the two Ticks who'd been awake, we were damn lucky the other four had been asleep.

I looked over at Ely, who was only now lowering his tranq rifle, even though I was pretty sure it didn't have any darts left in it. "Five Ticks, huh? You do know how to count to six, right?"

"Screw you."

I pulled the tranq rifle off my back and held it out to him. "You want to stand guard while I grab Lily and Marcus?"

He looked at my hands, which were shaking visibly, and nodded. "Sure."

I might not trust him and he was such an ass sometimes, but I was glad he didn't call me on the shaking hands.

I turned back to the living room, where two Ticks still lay on the sofa nest and the other two still lay in the corner, curled up like dogs. I gave a passing glance at the two on the sofa. One was a male that looked underfed, the other a female with a thick lock of gray in her hair. They were both sleeping soundly thanks to the darts, so I moved past them to the pair of Ticks in the corner. To Lily and Marcus. Even though he's bigger than her, Marcus was tucked into the corner. She was in front of him, draped over him, almost like she was protecting him. Her dark hair was a tangled mess and I reached out a shaking hand to brush it back and look at her face.

I've seen so many Ticks up close, but I'd never seen a person I loved transformed into a Tick. It was impossible not to catalog the changes. Her eyes—closed, but twitching restlessly from the tranquilizer—appeared more sunken. Her cheekbones more prominent. Her teeth had grown. She now had massive incisors that barely fit in her mouth. They were like the teeth of a lion, meant for tearing flesh and crushing bones.

Instinctively, I gave my shoulder a roll, imagining the damage that alpha Tick could have done if Ely had been just a few seconds slower.

Tentatively, I picked up her hand and felt its deadweight in mine. She was really out of it. Thank God. Because she would not have liked what I had to do next. I picked her up gently and carried her out onto the front lawn and laid her down on the sidewalk. Then I went back for Marcus. And finally, I collected the backpack Ely had dropped and pulled out the zip ties and the duct tape.

I worked quickly and not just because I didn't know how long the tranquilizers would last. I've done a lot of shit in the After that doesn't sit well with me. I've stabbed monsters, I've hunted animals, I've had to decapitate the mutilated bodies of my dead friends—shit that really messes with your head and doesn't ever go away. Shit you never forget.

Somehow, this was right up there with the worst of it. Zip-tying my girlfriend's hands and feet. About a dozen times. Duct-taping her mouth. Jesus.

Maybe five minutes later, Ely and I carried Marcus and Lily away from the house. My car was just two blocks down the street. By the time we loaded them in the back, my hands had stopped shaking. Suddenly I felt exhausted and thirsty. And just . . . tired of this whole damn situation.

"How far away is this place?" Ely asked.

"Less than an hour."

"And how long do you think they're going to stay tranqed?"

"I don't know," I lied. I did some mental math. I had tranqed Lily before. Back when we were first trying to get off the Farm in North Texas. I had done it to protect her, because it was the only way to get her to safety. But I still felt shitty about it. Worse still, when I thought back on it, Lily hadn't been out that long. "Hopefully more than an hour," I told Ely.

He scrubbed his hand down his jaw. "'Cause I seem to re-member that everyone metabolizes those tranquilizers differ-ently."

I glanced over at him. "What are you saying? You think she's going to wake up first?"

"I'm just saying I sure as shit don't want to be trapped in a car with a couple of Ticks when they wake up. I don't think all the zip ties in the world are going to hold them for long."

"You got any better ideas?"

"No."

"Because this is Lily we're talking about. And your brother. If you do have any better ideas, tell me now."

"I'm just not a big fan of making a pointless sacrifice."

"What? You want me to drop you and Marcus by the side of the road and let you figure something else out?"

"No. But I do want you to drive faster."

"Then stop distracting me."

* *

In the Before, Huntsville Unit A had been the site of more state executions than any other prison in the United States. I'd learned that in the ninth grade when my English class had written editorial essays and I'd been assigned the topic of capital punishment. I don't know why that one random fact stuck in my head, but it did.

It's why I'd thought of bringing Lily and Marcus to the prison—because I'd seen pictures of solitary cells on death row. No, I didn't like the symbolism of locking Lily up on death row and then shooting her full of a serum that might or might not kill her and might leave her suicidal if it didn't, but there wasn't a lot to like about this situation.

And that was all before we actually saw the prison.

Whatever awful and horrific things had happened in this prison in the Before, it was nothing compared to what had happened after.

Ely and I stood right outside the fences, staring at the dead bodies littering the yard. There were a lot of them. Some looked like Ticks, some looked like they'd been killed by Ticks. There were piles of bodies near the fences, like people or Ticks had tried to climb over them and the fact that they were electrified hadn't stopped them.

"What the hell do you think happened here?" Ely asked half under his breath.

"I think whoever was in charge panicked when the outbreak happened. I think the warden just fled and left the inmates locked up. The virus spread within the prison and the prisoners had no way to escape or defend themselves."

"Jesus," Ely muttered. "You'd think that was illegal."

"Yeah. I'm sure wherever that guy is, he's standing trial right now."

"Is the plan still a go?"

I studied the fences and the walls, considering ways in. The prison was right in the middle of town, just a few blocks away from what had clearly once been a college. This was one of the things I loved about Texans: their total disregard for logic in zoning. The two institutions were separated by a single row of buildings and what had once been a lovely oak-lined park. I guess I should just have been glad that this college hadn't been turned into a Farm. It had probably been too close to the shit storm in Houston.

"Yeah," I said. "We don't exactly have a lot of options here. This is still our best bet."

I crossed the street back to the park and searched the ground until I found a branch, which I then tossed at the fence. There was no spark. No sizzle. I walked closer. No hum of electricity. Even with the razor wire, Ely and I could probably climb it, but how would we—

"I've got wire cutters in my bag if that helps."

"Yeah, dumb-ass, that helps."

Twenty minutes later, we had a hole cut in the fence big enough for us to carry Marcus and Lily through. More importantly, they were still out of it, breathing fitfully but deeply. Their pulses slow and even.

"Do you think there's anything still alive in here?" Ely asked as we went in.

This was the question I'd been asking myself ever since we drove up. "It's been nine months since things went bad here. That's long enough even for a Tick to starve."

"Or to just be really, really hungry."

"Nah," I said with more confidence than I actually felt. I nodded toward some of the corpses. "Those bodies are human. And they still have their hearts in them. If there'd been Ticks starving in here, they wouldn't have been picky about what they ate."

I squelched the nausea climbing up my esophagus and tried to block out the sights in the prison yard.

As we crossed the yard, Ely asked, "Has it occurred to you that there might be Ticks out there somewhere, and that come dark, they could use that hole we just cut into the fence to come get us?"

"Yes," I said honestly.

"So what's to keep them from doing it?"

"Hope." I eyed the guard station. "And probably some assault rifles."

"You really think they left that stuff behind when the guards abandoned this place?"

"This is a maximum-security prison smack in the middle of a town. I'm guessing they had a lot of ammunition."

"Which the inmates probably already found and used." Ely glared at me. "And if you tell me that you hope they didn't, I just might hit you."

I thought back to the night we'd rescued Mel from the Dean who'd kidnapped her. He had strewn the church with dead bodies to ward off the Ticks. "I think Ticks are going to steer clear of the prison. Too many rotting corpses. Besides, if we don't get them"—I pointed to Lily and Marcus—"into solitary confinement soon, the Ticks outside the prison are going to be the least of our worries."

CHAPTER THIRTY-FIVE

MEL

At first, I can only stare at him. What's he done?

Why?

Why would he . . .

Then, as I watch, helpless, he crumples to the ground.

I gasp and my hand flies to my mouth. I drop the shard of wood I'm holding and dash across the room. Sebastian writhes in agony on the floor. I pull his head onto my lap.

"Sebastian?" I gasp. "Say something!"

For a second he just lies there, sucking in deep breaths like he's trying to get a handle on the pain. Then he reaches up and brushes my hair out of my eyes. He tries to tuck it back behind my ear, but it is too short and a lock of it falls forward again, which makes him smile, almost. "We were out of control, Melly. It was either this or kill you." His hand drops back to his side and agony twists his features for an instant. "I couldn't risk that."

Tears choke me. "I don't understand."

"When I was wounded. When I was dying, we weren't at each other's throat." Still looking pained, he raises his hand to my neck and lightly traces the spot where his fingers had bitten into my flesh. "Don't you see? It's the vampire rage. We can't be near one another. I told you that."

And so this was his solution? To stake himself again?

"But earlier. I didn't want to kill you then."

"Exactly. Because I was already dying."

"No." I shake my head so hard my hair flies in front of my face, which is just as well because I don't want him to see the tears that are suddenly filling my eyes. "I don't accept that."

"I told you. It's not something you can control." His hand drifts down to rest right above my heart. "You didn't really think we were special, did you?"

"I . . ."

I want to argue with him. Not in anger this time—that was all gone—but in fear and in panic.

Everything in me rebels at his words. I won't believe it, even though it makes sense somehow. When he was dying, when he was too weak to be a threat, it hadn't mattered that we were both supreme predators. Once the stake had been removed and he'd fed, his strength had returned, and with it, both of our baser natures.

So this is it? I will lose him forever. I will be alone. Forever. I am not sure which idea disturbs me more, and that is terrifying.

Even though he'd explained the rage when he'd first turned me, I hadn't felt it firsthand until a few days ago. I hadn't believed how strong it would be.

"So what? You're just going to die? I don't accept that!"

I finally have the answer to that question about what kind of man he is. A bad man pretending to be good would never have stabbed himself to save another.

No, Sebastian is a good man. Tortured, but good. And I may never get to know him any better than this, even though I fear I already love him.

He smiles. "Nothing so dramatic, Kit. We leave the stake in. You bandage me up again. And we keep going."

"How long? How long can you live like this?"

"Long enough to get to Genexome and open the vault for you. Then you take what you need and leave. It's all good."

"No," I say. "None of this is good."

His lips twist in a smile that's a little amused and a lot pained. "You were right, Melly. I should have distributed the cure sooner. I should have made sure it was in the right hands before I went after Roberto."

"Why didn't you?"

"Wouldn't have made any difference, with Roberto in control."

I don't know what to say to this. I no longer know what to believe. This didn't seem like the time to argue with him when he'd just stabbed himself to save my life.

I trace my fingers down the perfect, beautiful lines of his face, relishing the faint stubble under my fingertips. My thumb brushes across his lower lip and he sucks in a breath. I don't think it's from pain.

"It's no good, you know, mooning over me like this. It will never end well."

Impulsively, I bend down and press my mouth to his. It isn't anger or hope that fuels me this time, but fear. Because with Sebastian I've felt things I'd never felt before and I don't want to lose that. I can't lose it.

I pour my desperation into that kiss and I feel it in him, too.

I lift my head just slightly. "No. I don't believe that," I say. "I've seen a lot of nature programming. And, yes, a lot of apex predators are extremely territorial, but they still . . ." Embarrassment floods me and I feel my cheeks turning red. Who knew vampires could blush? I swallow and push through. "They still mate. Maybe not often, but they do. And they don't kill each other doing it. We can—"

He cuts off my rush of words by pressing his fingertips to my lips. They are cold again and the thought chills my heart. "Nice try, Melly, but you can't argue your way out of this."

"But—"

"If we were creatures of nature, that would probably work. But vampires don't reproduce through sex." He chuckles, but it must hurt, because he winces on the end. "Which isn't to say it's not a worthy diversion, but it's not how we procreate. We don't need another vampire to make more vampires. We need humans."

"But—"

He brings his hands up to my face, and cups my jaw. "Listen to me. This isn't going to work. There's no scenario where we get to be together. Do you understand me?"

I try to shake my head, but he doesn't let me move and so all I can do is close my eyes and refuse to look at him.

"I need you to understand this." His voice sounds broken, desperate. I open my eyes and search for that same emotion in his face, and to my shock I see it there. "We can't be together. We try it again and either I'll kill you or we'll kill each other. Either way, no one wins. So whatever sentimental fantasy you're cooking up in that girlish heart of yours, you have to put it away. You have to think about yourself now. You can't have me. Not now or ever."

CHAPTER THIRTY-SIX

CARTER

Lily woke up just before dusk and I couldn't help wondering if she'd been out so long because of all the darts or because Ticks were naturally nocturnal. That was probably just a way of making myself feel better. Ely and I had secured two solitary cells at opposite ends of the block from each other. We'd found chairs to strap Lily and Marcus to, Hannibal Lecter–style. We'd secured them and waited.

I couldn't make myself watch, but I could hear her. At first, it was just groaning, because she still had the duct tape on her mouth. At some point, she must have worked it off, because she started making anguished yelps. Those howls of pain and distress that sounded like nothing a human would make. Yet somehow, terrifyingly, she still sounded like Lily. I could hear her voice in the crazed keening. This was horrifying, blood-chilling proof that I would know her anywhere. In any form.

She wasn't herself, and yet somehow she was. Somehow, my Lily was still in there. I could only pray that I'd be able to get her out.

And that's what I did. I pulled a chair out of the guards' station. I set it down right outside her cell and I listened to her desperate cries, the lonely yips and howls of a pack animal all alone. Confused and afraid. After maybe an hour, she broke free of the chair. I heard creaking. And then the pound of wood on concrete, then wood shattering. At some point, she started pacing. I heard the shuffling awkward gait as she moved from one end of the cell to the other. Her long legs and powerful muscles weren't meant for this confined space. Her pace picked up as her howls got louder and more desperate. She was scared. And alone. And the sounds of her fear tore at my heart.

Screw this.

Was it time yet?

How could I be sure?

I started pacing, myself. Down the length of the corridor and back.

I couldn't dose her too soon. I had to be sure the tranquilizer was out of her system. And I had no way of knowing when that would be.

I had promised myself I wasn't going to watch her. That I was going to stay nearby but out of sight. But maybe I could calm her down. Maybe seeing me, hearing the sound of my voice, would help?

I crept over to the door.

"Lily, it's okay," I said softly as I slid open the metal hatch covering the Plexiglas window.

She whirled around, her nose tilted up, like she wasn't responding to the sound of my voice so much as to my scent. Her posture straightened, and for an instant, she looked almost human again, despite the tangled mass of hair around her face. Then she drew in one long breath. Through her nose. Like a connoisseur sniffing a fine wine.

And she launched herself at me.

She hit the Plexiglas so fast and so hard that the sound of her collision reverberated in my ears. The impact split open her forehead. She stumbled back, her brow knotted with confusion and maybe pain. Blood trickled from the cut down into her eyes. Then she breathed in again. And launched herself at me a second time, teeth bared and snarling. She bounced back more quickly this time. Frenzied and starved, she threw herself at me again and again.

I backed away slowly, heart pounding, fear pulsing through my veins. This was Lily. The girl I loved more than my own life. And to her, I was just food.

CHAPTER THIRTY-SEVEN

MEL

Nothing ends a conversation like having the guy stab himself in the heart. In terms of embarrassing ways to have a guy reject you, this has got to be some kind of record, right?

I should have known better than to open myself up to him. To trust him. To . . . love him. Oh God, I love him.

No. I will not be that stupid. I abjectly refuse to be stupid enough to fall for a guy who would kiss me and try to kill me in the same breath. And I refuse to romanticize the fact that he stabbed himself to keep from killing me. Because I'm tired of him pushing me away. I'm tired of being treated like a child. Tired of him telling me what I can and cannot do.

I can't be with him. I don't want to be with him. He's infuriating and domineering and . . .

Oh, who am I kidding? I do want to be with him. So much it hurts. But he's made it perfectly clear that he's not even going to try to make it work between us.

We don't talk for a while after that. I'm too pissed, too hurt, and Sebastian is in too much pain. Which he totally deserves. He's lucky I don't ruin more priceless art to stab him again.

Instead I find a dagger in one of the drawers and go to work ripping the fine linens into shreds so that I can rebandage his wound. Then I feed Chuy again, because I don't wholly trust myself to be too close to Sebastian. Or maybe I just want him to be in pain like I am.

I think he feels the same way, because when I approach him and reach for the bandage, he waves me off.

"No. Let me do it."

"I can do it," I say.

He strains to push himself up so he's leaning against the sofa, his legs stretched out in front of him. "No thanks, Florence."

"I'm not letting you bandage yourself. And you're too weak to stop me anyway, so get over it."

I kneel beside him on the floor. His hair is hanging in his face again and I want to push it back, to really look at him, now that we're not trying to kill each other. But I don't, because I know he'll just give me another lecture. Instead, I use the dagger to slice off my original bandage. It's tricky work, pulling off the old bandage, some of which is deeply embedded alongside the stake. I know the pain must be horrible. I hear it in the forced steadiness of his breath, which is far too rhythmic to be natural.

To distract myself I ask, "Who's Florence?"

He laughs then, a low, pained sound that's as desperate as it is amused. "Florence Nightingale."

"And I'm supposed to know her because . . ."

"A famous nurse from the Crimean War. All the men fell in love with her. What are they teaching you in school these days that you don't even know who Florence Nightingale is?"

Annoyed by his reference to my schooling, I'm tempted to tighten his bandages a little more. Instead I say, "Apparently not that. I don't even know where the Crimean War was." Once I've got most of the bandage off, I try to examine the wound. This shard of wooden frame seems so much worse than the stake from earlier. This is jagged and dusty.

"You are so young," he says, almost accusingly.

He's right, of course. I don't feel young. I have never felt young, but right now—swooning over the hot guy I can never have—I am acting very young. Well, I'm done with that. No more swooning for me.

"And you are so stupid," I mutter under my breath. "This looks horrible. You couldn't find a rusty nail to stab yourself with?"

"As a matter of fact, I had some barbed wire I thought of using but it just wasn't handy."

"No, instead you decide to impale yourself on a jagged piece of lumber."

"This? It's barely a splinter."

I snort. I don't want to be amused by him. I'm furious. And insulted. And Sebastian is dying by inches. Nothing about this is funny.

But his attempts at humor only endear him to me.

I start wrapping him in the bandage, hoping that maybe I can stanch the flow of blood enough that he won't get that much weaker. But he's weak already. I know this. I can feel it in my own blood.

Once I've got the bandage on, I push myself to my feet and go look for more blood to feed Sebastian. A minute later, I toss another bag at him.

He sets it onto the sofa a few inches from his head. "No thanks. I just ate."

"Drink it," I order. "If I can keep you drinking, maybe you'll be strong enough to make it all the way back to Genexome."

"No thanks," he says again more slowly. "You know vampires. Can't hold our liquor."

Of course, we're at cross-purposes here. I'm trying to save his life, he's deliberately throwing it away.

I cross back to his side and stab the dagger into the bag. "Drink it or I will pour it down your throat myself."

His eyes follow the dribble of blood leaking from the puncture in the bag. "It will only—"

"It will only keep you alive. Now drink it, because I'm not dragging your sorry corpse halfway across the state."

I don't wait to see if he follows my directions. Instead, I walk to the door and move to open it.

"You don't want to do that," he says.

"Well, someone has to check to see if the Ticks are still out there. So it's either this or we die in here."

"Roberto would have security cameras and a live feed to one of the channels on the TV."

Still facing the door, I cringe. I should have thought of that. I'm the child of the digital age and I'm tired of being one step behind a two-thousand-year-old vampire.

But I try not to let Sebastian see my frustration. The last thing I need is more of the *you're-so-young* conversation.

Instead I cross to the media center. Even here I'm at a loss. Mom was never big on TV in the Before. She was always convinced I needed more human interaction, not less. So we'd had just the two TVs in the house and little beyond basic cable. Forget DVRs and gaming systems and live security feeds. All of which Roberto does have.

I grab a remote that's the same brand as the TV and start pushing buttons. Not much happens.

"Better bring that here, Kit. You seem to be technologically impaired."

I grab an armful of remotes and dump them on the ground next to Sebastian, who quickly picks up the correct two. A moment later, the TV flickers to life and he's navigating the menu system.

"Seriously?" I ask. "It's that easy for you?"

"I have a similar system myself."

"Oh, so all vampires shop at the same electronics store? Because you never mentioned that in my training."

He almost smiles. "It's more that all vampires like the very best. Of everything."

"Oh, and you have—what is this? Three different gaming systems? You have all that also?"

"Of course."

I roll my eyes at the vulgar display of testosterone that is the media center. "You have immortality and outrageous wealth at your disposal and you choose to spend your time playing video games?"

He shrugs, clicks more buttons on different remotes. "What would you have me do?"

"I don't know. Something that betters mankind. Create great art. Write music. Research global climate change. Cure cancer. Play dominoes, for God's sake. Just do *something*."

"Well, as you recall, I took a stab at that whole curing-cancer thing. Didn't turn out too well."

I swivel to look at him. "Was Genexome really working on that? I thought that was just a ruse to get the Tick virus out there."

He shrugs. "Potayto. Potahto." Then he points at the screen. "And here's the security feed."

Part of me wants to ask more questions, but I don't. Getting out of El Corazon, that's what's important. Searching for ways that Sebastian might just be misunderstood is simply pathetic.

The screen divides into six little screens, each showing the feed from a different camera. One is clearly a wide-angle lens showing the view overlooking the town from the front of the house. Two more are of the exterior. The remaining three are within the house itself. All but two show Ticks stumbling around.

I stand up and walk closer to the screen, trying to place where the three interior cameras are. "I think that's the hall from the living room into the kitchen." I point to the edge of the screen. "The door down to the basement should be just off-screen here. I think I remember there being a hallway to the garage in this direction. So that means—"

But before I can finish the thought, Sebastian asks the one question I never saw coming. "Are you in love with Carter?"

CHAPTER THIRTY-EIGHT

CARTER

My hands were shaking so badly I could barely load up the syringe. Dawn's hurried instructions were running through my brain. I had to tap out the air bubbles, because if I shot air into her veins, it would kill her. Of course, if I didn't wait long enough for the tranquilizer to wear off, it would kill her as well. If I'd grabbed the wrong serum, that might kill her. There were a lot of *ifs* here that all ended up with Lily dead.

"You sure you know what you're doing?" Ely asked, watching me warily.

"Do I look like I do?"

"No." Ely's voice was a mixture of deranged laughter and total disbelief.

He and I were in the corridor outside Lily's cell. She'd calmed down. A little. I could hear her pacing, punctuated by the occasional sound of her throwing her body against one of the walls. She seemed to be tiring. Seemed to be less frenetic. Or maybe that was just wishful thinking.

"Okay," I said, trying to sound more confident than I felt. "You shut the door behind me. I don't want her escaping, because I've only got one shot at this."

"Trust me, *miho*, I got plenty of reasons to get that door shut once you go in."

"But be ready to open it again so I can get out after I've given her the shot. I was given the vaccine at El Corazon, so I shouldn't be in any danger."

"Unless she rips your heart out."

"Exactly."

Ely shook his head, like he thought I was crazy. He was probably right. But what was I supposed to do? If there was any chance that this cure would work, I had to try.

I held the syringe pointed up, gave it one more tap with my finger, and nodded at him. "Let's do this."

Lily spun on me the second I stepped into the cell. She moved incredibly fast, throwing herself through the air toward me. I ducked and rolled under her, cringing when she hit the wall behind me. She whirled back around before I could get my feet under me. She pounced on me, slamming me into the ground. The impact knocked the syringe from my hand and it skittered across the floor. She pounced on my chest. God, she was strong.

As a human, Lily had been lean and tenacious as hell, but now she was all muscle. She was speed and hate bundled together in one unstoppable package. I tried to knock her off me, but she swatted my hands aside. I flung out a hand, reaching for the syringe.

"Lily, it's me!" I gasped. "It's Carter! Don't!"

I felt my fingertips skim the side of the syringe. I stretched, reaching. Desperate. And felt it spin out of my grasp.

For an instant, she sat poised above me, her teeth bared in animalistic rage, a thread of drool spilling from her lips. Her inhuman eyes met mine. I searched for any sign of recognition. Of humanity. I saw none. As she raised her hands above her, she tipped her head back and howled.

I knew what was coming. She'd slam her fisted hands down onto my chest. My rib cage would crack open. She'd peel back my ribs like she was shelling a nut. Then she'd rip my still-beating heart from my chest and devour it.

This was it. I was going to die. I'd failed at everything. I couldn't save her. I couldn't save myself.

Then, just as she was starting to bring down her hands, Ely stepped up behind her and slammed the chair into her temple.

Her hands still hit my chest. Hard. But not hard enough to crack anything. She whirled around, confused, then wavered. And fell to the side.

Ely stood there, over her, chair still in his hands, chest heaving as he waited to see if she stirred. Then he looked at me and blew out a shaky breath.

"I know you said she couldn't be tranqed when we dosed her, but"—he set down the chair and sank onto it—"shit, she was going to kill you. And you didn't say we couldn't knock her out."

I pushed myself to my feet, pulling in one breath after another as adrenaline coursed through my veins. I rubbed my chest where she'd hit me. My ribs were still sore from the fight with Marek and pain sliced through my chest. She might have broken something after all, but my heart was still in my chest and that's what mattered. Anything else I could handle with Ace bandages.

I nodded, scanning the ground for the syringe. "Good call."

I found it, against the wall. It hadn't broken. Thank God. My hands were trembling as I picked it up. I tapped it for bubbles again, mostly to give myself something to do while my hands were still shaking so badly.

"Let's get this over with." I crouched down next her, rolling her over onto her back so her arms splayed out to the side. I ran my thumb over the skin of her inner elbow. My hands hadn't steadied yet and I couldn't even see a vein. Shit. I looked up at Ely. "You know how to do this?"

"What, you think just because I'm Mexican I know how to shoot someone up?" Then he laughed. "Nah, I'm just messing with you." He took the needle from me. "I can't make any promises, but I've watched *Trainspotting* like a dozen times."

Between the two of us, we got it done. We hoped. Knowledge of heroin use was not something I'd thought I'd need to survive the apocalypse. Then again, I never would have imagined my girlfriend trying to eat my heart out of my chest. Go figure.

A moment later, Ely and I stood outside the cell, watching Lily where she lay on the ground, her chest slowly rising and falling.

"What now?" Ely asked.

"Now we wait."

"How long?"

"I have no idea."

I didn't say it aloud, but I had already started praying.

CHAPTER THIRTY-NINE

MEL

I pause, hand raised to point out where I think the garage is, and for a second it's all I can do to even breathe, I'm so surprised by Sebastian's question.

I turn slowly to look at him. "Why would you ever ask if I'm in love with Carter?"

"Curiosity. Boredom." He lifts a hand and points to the TV. "Nothing good on TV anymore."

"Well, I'm certainly not going to answer." I'm not going to spill my guts just to satisfy his curiosity.

"I answered your question."

"Which question?"

"The one about Genexome doing cancer research."

"'Potayto, potahto' is not an answer."

"I'll give you a real answer if you'll give me one."

"Tit for tat?" I ask. "Okay, Hannibal. Answer my question first."

"Yes, Genexome did cancer research. And Alzheimer's research. And worked on a host of other medical problems. Vampires don't age and don't get diseases. Using vampire DNA to cure human ailments seemed like a natural solution."

And just like that, my mind is racing from one medical problem to the next. Yes, cancer and Alzheimer's, but there were plenty of other degenerative diseases as well. Multiple sclerosis. Lou Gehrig's disease. There were so many things that our DNA might be able to affect. "That is incredibly forward thinking of you."

"Don't romanticize me. Biomedical companies have reasons to order bags of human blood by the truckload."

"Really?" I shoot him a dark look. I'd wondered what exactly he'd done for food in the Before. "And none of the humans thought that was strange?"

"I paid them to overlook it. The medical research industry is extremely lucrative."

But there is something in his voice that tells me he wasn't only in it for the money. Or maybe that is just me romanticizing him again.

"So if it started as pure research, how did it go so wrong?"

He wags his finger at me. "Oh, no, you don't. You haven't answered my question yet."

"I was kissing *you*. Not fifteen minutes ago. Why would I do that, if I was in love with Carter?"

He smiles and there's a hint of cruelty to it. "I was kissing you fifteen minutes ago. And I was strangling you fourteen minutes ago. We both know kissing has little to do with love. Right, Kit?"

Bile rises in my throat. Of course.

Of course, this isn't really about curiosity or boredom. This is him putting me in my place again. Him reminding me that whatever else that kiss was about, it wasn't about romance.

I lash out. "You must think I really need these lessons in romance. Because I'm 'so young.'" I throw his phrasing back at him. "But trust me. I don't."

I want to say something more. Something more painful.

Something brutal. But if there's one thing I have even less experience in than kissing, it's delivering a hurtful setdown.

So instead of hurling the perfect insult at him, I retreat to Roberto's bedroom and scrounge in the closet until I find a duffel bag. I use some of Roberto's fine Egyptian cotton towels to line it and then bring it back to the kitchenette to look for ice.

"You never answered my question," he says smoothly when I reappear.

"Carter is my sister's boyfriend."

"That doesn't mean you don't love him."

Of course I don't love him. Carter is . . . just Carter. A friend. He's always been that. And nothing more. And I could tell Sebastian the truth, but I'm tired of him pushing me away and putting me in my place. And I'm so damn mad at him.

Sebastian's voice turns suddenly serious. "Listen to me, Kit. I know you think he loves her. I know he thinks it. But you're a vampire and he's an *abductura*. You are by nature a most perfect pair. Made for one another. It might be easiest if you just accept it."

And now I'm more than mad.

"Fine," I snarl. "Yes. I love him. Why wouldn't I? He's the perfect guy. He's totally hot and he's actually trying to save the world instead of destroy it. So why wouldn't I stab my sister in the back to get him?" Sebastian's mouth twists, but I can't tell if it's a smile or a grimace. Maybe I should take it easy on him. He's in pain. On the other hand, I feel like he's actually answering my questions. I may never have the chance to get this information from him again. So I ask another one. "What were you trying to do with the Tick virus?"

"I was trying to create a cure."

"For what?"

"For everything. Cancer. Alzheimer's. Even vampirism. I thought I could fix the flaws in our personalities."

"The flaws?"

He meets my gaze now. Serious and steady. "Our natural territorialism. I thought I could tweak our DNA just enough that we'd be able to be with one another. It's our one great flaw. Our solitude. It's no fun to live forever if you're always alone."

I rock back on my heels as shock slams into me. I know instinctively that he isn't talking about me here. All of this—all the research, all this yearning for another vampire—that happened long before he'd met me. Which means there's someone else he loves. Which is so much more painful than him merely not loving me.

"You're in love with Sabrina," I say stupidly, because the answer comes to me so fast and so hard that I can't not say it aloud. "You must have fallen in love with her when she was still human and your *abductura*. You turned her into a vampire, thinking you'd be able to control yourself."

That's what all those warnings to me had been about. He knew firsthand that there was no way to overcome his vampire berserker rage, because he'd tried to do it. He'd fought against his nature and failed. He knew it couldn't be done.

"Oh, no, you don't," he clucks. "It's my turn to ask a question."

"That wasn't a question," I point out, stifling the pang I feel when I remember his words. An *abductura* and a vampire are nature's most perfect pair. Was that what it had been like between them? Perfect?

"It's still my turn. Why go to such desperate measures to find the cure for your sister? Why not just bite her and turn her into a vampire, too? That seems to be Carter's solution to everything, surely he suggested it."

"I never had a choice," I say. "I wouldn't force this on her. Not if there was any other way." It's a simple answer, but it's the truth and I'm glad he accepts it for what it is.

When he nods, I think of my next question. There's no point asking anything else about Sabrina. My gut tells me he won't answer me anyway. Besides, I can extrapolate from here. There was tension between them, but not yearning. Whatever they had once, she's over it and he's too hurt to try again. I can't say I blame him. After this, it's not like I'll be eager to take another stab at love.

I decide to go back to asking about the virus. "If you really have the cure at Genexome—"

"I said I did."

"Then why not distribute it sooner? Why just sit on it?" Because this is the one thing I can't reconcile. The one thing I can't wrap my brain around. "You could have gone to the government right away. You could have stopped this before it got to this point. You could have saved hundreds of millions of lives."

"Like your hero Carter?" he asks, with a little bit of a sneer.

"Yes!"

"Are you sure you're being honest with yourself? About why you won't turn Lily."

"What?" I'm so startled by his words I hardly know how to respond.

"Oh, respecting her free will is all well and good. And that's very noble. But surely you've thought of the natural consequences, haven't you?"

"What do you mean?"

"You refuse to bite Lily, she eventually turns into a Tick.

That's awfully convenient for you, the girl who's in love with her boyfriend."

Suddenly I want to kill Sebastian all over again, and for reasons that have nothing to do with vampire berserker rage.

"That's ridiculous. And insulting." I push myself to my feet and whirl away. "I would never sell my sister out to get her guy. And he wouldn't want me if I did."

"Are you sure?" Sebastian pokes. "You are twins. He might not even notice the difference."

"God, you are such an ass."

"Just pointing out the obvious here. I mean, you don't seem like you're in a big rush to get to—"

"Shut up," I snarl. "Or I really will chop you up and use your body parts like passkeys." But even the threat isn't enough to calm me down, so I ask the really big question. The one I've been working up to. The one I know will hurt him to answer. "Why did you hate Roberto so much?"

He looks bored. "You mean besides the fact that he was vile?"

"Obviously. Did he turn you? Is that why you hated him?"

"He did turn me. But that's not why I hated him."

"Then why? Why the multiple assassination attempts? Why the elaborate plans to bring him down?"

"Are those separate questions?"

"You used me to get you into El Corazon." I hurl the words at him. The pain is fresher than I thought. "Without me, he wouldn't be dead. I think this one should be a freebie."

"Very well." Sebastian's expression is unreadable, but something tells me he is telling the truth now. He speaks slowly, revealing very little emotion. "He did turn me, but that's not why I hated him. I told you a vampire's nature never changes? Well, it was Roberto's nature to be a willful, truculent child. He was greedy and self-indulgent and constantly in need of entertainment. He ate wherever he wanted with no thought to the consequences. To make matters worse, he was a Centurion in Augustus's army."

"The Roman emperor?" I ask, because my history knowledge is sketchy at best.

Sebastian nods, seeming almost distracted as he continues. "Roberto used to hunt on the battlefields of the empire. Picking off victims in battle. That's where he turned me. But then he left before he even knew I had regenerated. I had no training. No knowledge of what I'd become. Unfortunately, when I awoke, I was not far from home. Everyone I'd fought with had either died or been captured as slaves. So I went home to my wife and children. The results of that visit were . . . not something you'd ever forget. Not in a thousand years."

Suddenly I am sorry I asked. My imagination is too vivid. I remember myself in those early days. The confusion. The bone-deep hunger. The lack of control. If he'd returned home to his wife and children after being turned . . .

Bile crawls up my throat.

He would have unwittingly butchered them. Except they were *his* children, with his genes. Some of them would have regenerated. And at first, maybe he thought it was going to be okay . . . well, not okay. But maybe he thought he could live with those vampire children. That he could take care of them. That he would still have some kind of a family.

Except that wasn't how it worked, was it?

At some point, the vampire rage—which Roberto had not told him about—would have kicked in. And it would have hit him before it hit any of his children. He would have killed them all. And he would never be able to forgive himself.

269

Sebastian's face is pale, his gaze almost blank, like he's cut himself off from the words he'd been saying. I know, instinctively, that he will say no more. I can't blame him. I turn away then. If I had a history even remotely like the one I'd just imagined for him, I wouldn't want to talk about it, either.

CHAPTER FORTY

CARTER

The sight of Lily writhing on the floor tore at everything inside of me. I wanted to be brave enough, strong enough, to be there for her. To make myself watch her, even though it was impossible. I just . . . I couldn't.

She had to live through this and I couldn't even make myself watch.

I turned away and pressed my back to the wall just outside the door. After Ely and I dosed Marcus, I stood there outside Lily's cell for a long time—maybe hours, maybe only minutes; I had no way of knowing. I just listened to the sounds of desperate keening and tortured pain. Until slowly, finally, her cries faded to whimpers. I made myself look through the Plexiglas again and saw her, curled in a fetal position, shivering. Massive tremors shook her whole body. Like an electric shock. Like she was suffering from hypothermia or something. God, she looked so cold. If I could just hold her, I could warm her up.

I reached for the key. Before I could even twist it, she sprang from the floor and launched herself at the door again, hands raised, fingers curled. She clawed at the Plexiglas, and snarled.

I stumbled back, knocking over the chair, my heart pounding panic through my veins.

I didn't look again. I couldn't. Whatever she was going through, I wasn't strong enough to watch.

Instead, I just sat there, on the floor, trying to think about anything other than the bone-crushing transformation Lily's body was going through.

"I never meant for this to happen," I said.

Inside the cell, Lily's anguished cries quieted.

"Does this help?" I asked. She gave a low moan, but at least she wasn't howling anymore. So I kept talking. I told her about stupid crap. Things from the Before. The different schools I'd been in. The things I'd done to get kicked out. And then I told her about Elite. About how lonely I'd been. Some things I'd never told anyone.

"I guess Merc was the first friend I made there. Of course, he kicked my ass the first week I was there. And the second. I didn't bitch about it, though, because I figured, hell, I'd asked for this. I was the one who'd screwed up my life in Richardson. I'd made the mistakes that had landed me at Elite. If the result was getting my ass kicked week after week, it was still better than losing you. And I'd already lived through that."

I heard a sound almost like a sigh. Instead of looking, I just kept talking.

"I thought about you a lot when I was at Elite. Mostly when I was alone in the shower." Shit, that made me sound like a total perv. "Just because that was the only time I was alone. That and at night." Like that sounded any better. "It hadn't been like that. Okay, it hadn't all been like that. Sure, I'd had this one running fantasy where you just stepped into the shower with me—" Yeah, this was *so* not helpful. I dropped my head back against the wall and closed my eyes. "What I mean is, I had this fantasy, in the Before. About you and me together. Not like that. Just together. I'd pull up to your house on a motorcycle—don't ask me where I thought I'd get a motorcycle, that's not the point—anyway, I pull up in front of your house and you come running out, this big smile on your face, and you climb on the back and we just ride off. That's the whole fantasy. Just the two of us, riding off . . . I don't know, into the sunset or something, I guess.

"And, I mean, it was great, but it wasn't real, you know. It wasn't really about you. It was just about getting away. Getting out from under everything. And now that I know you—now that I really know you—I know that fantasy isn't ever going to happen. You'd never just ride away from everything. Even if we could. Even if there was somewhere we could go, just the two of us, you wouldn't do it. You're too smart and strong and fierce. You're too stubborn, that's for sure. I guess what I'm saying is, I don't have that fantasy about the motorcycle anymore."

I almost laughed at myself, because this all sounded so friggin' stupid to say aloud. And saying it didn't even begin to cover how I really felt. How much I needed her. "I mean, I guess I still think about that shower thing sometimes. But I don't dream about riding off with you now. Now? Jesus, all I want now is just to be worthy of you. I know, I won't be. That I can't ever be worthy of someone like you, but that's what I'm trying to do. That's what I'm going to try to do every day for the rest of my life. And I just hope to God you're around to give me hell if I slack off. . . ."

My voice trailed off and I sat there, my back to the wall just outside her cell.

And that's how it felt. Like my back was truly to the wall.

Because if this didn't work, I had nothing. If this didn't cure her, if she didn't survive, then I was done.

Somehow, I'd keep it together. Somehow, I'd keep fighting. Maybe.

But I knew this: if I lost Lily, I'd lose myself as well. I wanted to be strong enough to do this without her, but I was a realist. Without her, I didn't have what it took. Without her, I'd never scrounge together the hope that humanity would pull itself out of this mess of shit.

And if the cure didn't work on her, then chances were good that we didn't really have a cure at all. If the cure didn't work on her, then we were all screwed anyway.

Who was I kidding, even *with* the cure, we were—

"Did you say something about a shower?"

Her voice from behind me was so faint, I almost missed it.

I whirled around. I saw her through the Plexiglas, sitting on the floor of her cell, her back to the wall, too, her knees pulled up to her chest. Her hair was a wild tangle of knots around her face, dried blood caked to her temple and cheek. But her eyes looked human.

I sucked in a deep breath. "Lily?"

Hope roared through me. Please. Dear God. Please.

She raised her gaze to mine. "Carter?"

The fear and doubt in that single word slashed through my heart. I plastered a palm to the Plexiglas. "Lily. You're all right."

"I—" She frowned and bit down on her lip. "I think so."

"You're not going to try to yank my heart out?"

"No!" The horror in her voice said it all. She was human again. She was herself. "God, did I try to do that? Did I try to—"

"No," I lied. "You would never."

I slid the key into the lock and opened the door to the cell. In an instant, she flew across the room and into my arms. She ran to me. At normal human speed. And I just held her. So close I wanted to absorb her into my body. I wanted to shelter her. Always.

I wouldn't let go. Ever.

CHAPTER FORTY-ONE

MEL

I don't know what to say to Sebastian anymore. I can't ask any more questions. If there's more to this dark story, I don't want to know. I can't take it. Our game of quid pro quo has flayed me and left me bare. So I turn back to the security screens. The Ticks are moving around the house. This could be our last chance to get out of here.

I stalk back over to the duffel bag and zip it closed. "Get up," I tell Sebastian. Then I call to the dog. "Come on, Chuy. We're getting out of here."

Sebastian gestures to the TV screen. "There are still Ticks out there."

"So? I'm in the mood to kill something. Besides—" I point to the screen with the shot from the garage. "Look at this. Why does he have a security camera with a view of the garage?"

"Because he really likes his cars?"

I smirk. "Or because it's showing the view right outside a secret doorway. Besides, who builds a fortress with no way out? There's got to be a back door out of here somewhere, right?"

Sebastian smiles and I realize that he'd reached this conclusion earlier and had been waiting for me to catch up. "Good girl. Now, where do you think it is?"

After thinking about it for a second, I say, "It wouldn't have to be hidden on this side, only on the exit. But he would still want it out of the way. Maybe that pantry in the kitchen?"

As soon as I have the idea, I dash off to check, and sure enough, it isn't even in the back of the pantry. There *is* no pantry. Just a plain door, and two steps in, another more secure door. Thankfully opening it from this side doesn't require Roberto's corpse.

I go back into the living area to get Sebastian. I sling the handles of the duffel over my arms and wear it like a backpack. I hand the katana to Sebastian and arm myself with the dagger. It's the shorter of the two weapons, but right now I'm more mobile than he is. I wedge my shoulder under his arm and with Chuy by my side, we head for the back door.

He pauses at the "pantry" door. "It lacks the elegance of . . . oh, say, a sliding fireplace, like you see in the movies, but I suppose it will do."

Even though there are Ticks in the house, we don't see or hear them until the secret passage ends in a door that opens out into the garage, where we find a pair of Ticks huddled around a bottle of something I don't recognize.

Beside me, Chuy tenses, letting out another one of those low growls. The Ticks turn at the sound. I hesitate, but Sebastian doesn't. He steps away from me with surprising speed, and with two quick slashes of his katana, he's killed one of the Ticks. The other rears back a step, then roars and throws itself forward. Two more slashes and that one, too, goes down in a blur of red blood and blue liquid.

He stands there for a second over their bodies. Then he turns back toward me. He looks shaky and pale and he reaches out a hand to the counter that runs along the back of the garage. At first I think he needs to balance himself, but he just grabs a rag and cleans off his blade.

"Don't go weak on me now," he says.

"I'm not." I bump up my chin. "But now that I know there's a cure, I can't help but think—"

"It wouldn't have worked on them anyway."

"What? How do you know?"

"They were drinking antifreeze."

I look at the blue liquid slowly glugging onto the ground from the bottle Sebastian inadvertently sliced open. "Seriously?"

"Animals are attracted to it because it's sweet and it smells good, but it's poisonous. They would have been dead regardless." He turns his back on me and surveys the garage. "Now let's pick a car."

Roberto's garage is the size of a Jiffy Lube and probably better stocked. There are seven different cars. I don't know cars, but they all look expensive. And rare. There's everything from what looks like a Model T, to a couple of classic muscle cars, to several that just look new and modern and fast.

"I have no idea," I admit. "Pick out whatever you can hot-wire and let's go before more Ticks find us."

"Hot-wire? Please." Sebastian moves to a cabinet mounted on the wall. The cabinet is locked, but he slices off the lock with the katana. The door swings open to reveal a row of car keys hanging from hooks. He snags a pair. "I think today we'll go green."

I follow him over to a sedan at the end of the garage. "But it's red," I say as I open the door for Chuy. He hops into the back and sits on the floorboard.

"'Green' as in ecological," he says as he slides into the driver's seat. "It's an electric car."

"Is that smart? What if we run out of . . . charge or whatever?" I ask once I'm seated beside him with the duffel bag stashed between my feet—just in case Chuy gets hungry.

"It's just under two hundred miles from here to Genexome. We can recharge there. Besides, this is one of the fastest cars on the market and it's not a gas guzzler. Now be a dear and see if you can find a garage door opener. I don't want to chip the paint."

"Shouldn't I drive?" I ask once I've found the opener. "Since, you know, I'm not bleeding to death?"

"I'm not sure I trust you with a car this nice. Besides, I'll be fine."

"You'll bleed all over the driver's seat."

"And if Roberto complains, I'll pay to have the car detailed."

CHAPTER FORTY-TWO

LILY

Once, not long after Dad left, when Mom was big into therapy for the whole family, a psychologist said my need to protect my sister bordered on pathological and was my way of expressing my fear of abandonment in a socially acceptable way.

I called the guy a nut job—because, hello? . . . siblings were supposed to look out for one another. And I guess Mom agreed, because when I refused to go to him again, she didn't make me. Since the guy had been the last therapist on our insurance plan, that had been the end of family therapy.

Now, all these years later, I finally see the guy's point.

Sometimes, it's easier to worry about other people than it is to even think about what's going on inside of you. And sometimes, the shit going on inside me is too dark to even think about, let alone analyze.

"You sure you're going to be okay?" I ask Marcus for . . . oh, about the hundredth time.

We are standing out on the street outside the prison. Carter and Ely are maybe thirty feet away, over by the Chevy.

Since I came to, Carter's been treating me like I'm fragile. Something delicate.

Like the china-head doll my Nanna used to keep on the bed in her guest room. No matter how many times Mom had warned me to be careful when I played with the doll, it didn't stop me. I played too roughly one day and cracked her head. She didn't break, but the cracks spread out from the back of her head like a spiderweb. I never picked her up after that for fear she'd shatter. That's how I feel now. Like I might shatter, even though from the outside I look okay.

I guess Marcus knows that, because he asks, "What about you?"

"Yeah. I'm good." I don't believe it when I say it any more than I believe it when he does.

Neither of us is good. Neither of us is fine.

We're breathing. We're thinking. We're human. That's something, right?

But we're both . . . haunted by the ghosts of who we were.

I don't know how long we lived like that. Just a few days, Carter says. But it felt so much longer. I lived for years in that too-big body that was mine and not mine. And in those yearlong days, Marcus was family.

"Don't let Ely bully you," I tell Marcus.

Marcus just shrugs. "Ely's not a bad guy."

I don't argue. I don't tell him that I know a side of Ely he never will. I don't tell him that Ely thinks love is weakness and empathy is for suckers.

Instead, I pull Marcus into my arms and hug him tight. Ely may be his brother by blood, but Marcus and I share something more than that. We lost ourselves together.

"It doesn't seem real," Marcus says. "When I think about it, I mean."

"I know."

"Do you think we'll ever forget? What happened? What we did?"

I take him by the shoulders and hold him out away from me. "Listen to me. What happened out there? That wasn't you. That's not who you are. You are better than that. You are more than that. And you are going to be okay. Do you understand me?"

He nods, eyes slightly wide. And I keep talking. I barely know what I'm saying, but I say it over and over again until the words almost aren't words at all. And while I'm talking, I can feel the connection between us, because we were pack mates. He submitted to me, just like I submitted to the alpha. And I know—without even knowing how—that the alpha is dead. That the rest of the pack is gone. That it's just Marcus and me now.

Even though we're human again. Even though he can think for himself. Even though we're parting ways and I don't know if I'll ever see him again. Despite all that, I know there's a part of him that will always submit to me. And if I order him not to think about the things we did, if I order him not to worry about them, not to be haunted by them, then he will bend to my will. Not because I have any latent powers as an *abductura*, but because we were pack mates. Because it's the natural order of things and because it's easiest.

So I do it. I make him believe.

And when it's time to leave, time to go back to Carter and climb into a car and drive away from this place forever, I can still feel the connection between Marcus and me. And I know I did the right thing in making him set his guilt aside.

It's that pathological need to protect people again. Because if I can worry about Marcus, if I can take care of him, then I won't have to think about myself and I won't have to keep wishing that the alpha was still here to tell me the same thing and make me forget.

Because I want to forget so many things. The joy my strength brought me. The thrill of running through the night, the ground pounding under my feet, my muscles springing beneath my skin.

The salty blood on my tongue. The way it coated the inside of my mouth. The exhilaration of bones cracking in my fists. But most of all, the sweet bliss of submitting to the alpha. The euphoria that came from handing over all my thoughts, my decisions, my will to him. The absolute peace I felt under his command. The sheer, unmitigated ecstasy of mindlessness.

It was an illusion—that sense of peace and belonging. It was a lie, but it was a lie that I loved believing in. And it's a lie that I'll miss forever.

Before I was exposed to the virus, before I became a monster, I'd feared it. I'd known for months that I had the genes to become a Tick. That I had that potential sleeping inside me. I'd been so terrified of what I might become and what I might do. It had never occurred to me to fear who I already was.

CHAPTER FORTY-THREE

CARTER

We said good-bye to Ely and Marcus just outside of Huntsville—the town, this time, not the prison. There were plenty of cars around, so finding an extra ride wasn't a problem. Classic Ely—he managed to hot-wire a well-stocked Mercedes sedan. We found enough gas to siphon from the abandoned cars that at least we wouldn't have to worry about fuel for a long time.

When it came to good-byes, Ely and I both made it quick. Neither of us was good at them. It was different for Lily and Marcus. They stood together, off by the Mercedes for a long time, talking quietly. I couldn't imagine what about. They'd known each other for only a few days. Their relationship could be counted in hours. Long, tortured, dark hours that I couldn't imagine. But still, only hours.

Even though Marcus was just a kid—he was what? only fourteen or fifteen—he didn't look like a kid anymore, and when Lily stepped close to hug him, I had to bury a jab of jealousy.

"What do you think they're talking about?" I muttered aloud.

"Do you really want to know?" Ely asked.

"No." I guess I didn't. There would always be parts of Lily I didn't know and didn't understand. Parts I'd never lay claim to. Whatever Lily had done when she was a Tick—whatever she'd done to survive—that was hers. Those were her memories. Her secrets. Until and unless she wanted to share them with me, they weren't mine to even question.

I'd thought she'd end it with the hug, but they kept talking. I didn't want to rush her—because, hadn't she been through enough in the past twenty-four hours? So I turned to Ely. "You sure you don't want to come with us to San Angelo?"

He chuckled. "Yeah. That would go over great with Lily."

"Good point." After a minute, I admitted, "I thought she was going to kill you when she first saw you outside the cell."

Ely scrubbed a hand across his jaw. "Yeah. I get that a lot."

Thankfully, neither of us brought up the fact that I had nearly gotten him killed just a few days ago. "Where do you think you're going to go?"

"Mexico probably."

"Oh, that plan," I said. Ely had first lured Lily to Texas with the possibility that there might still be some form of civilization in Mexico. "You really think Mexico is still standing? All because Homeland Security built that wall along the border?"

"I don't know. Maybe. Don't you think it's worth checking out? Besides, I have a theory that Latinos are less susceptible to the virus."

I gestured to Marcus. "All evidence to the contrary."

Again, Ely laughed. "That's the thing. Didn't I ever tell you that my mom married a gringo after my dad died? Marcus is half white."

"Huh. I did not know that."

"Yeah. It's not like I brag about it. Hurts my street cred." After a minute, Ely asked, "What about you?"

"Nah. I never had street cred. Just rebellious rich kid crap."

"No, I mean, you sure you're going straight to San Angelo? You're not even going to try to go to Genexome to find out more about the cure? I mean, come on, we *know* it works."

"My first priority is to get Lily to safety. I'm not dragging her halfway across the state when we still have no way to get into Sebastian's vault. I'm not putting her at risk like that."

"If Mel talked Sebastian into coming back and opening up that vault, then you can get in."

"That seems like a pretty big if to me."

"We're talking about saving humanity here. I can't believe you're not even going to try."

And just like that, Ely turned his back on me and walked away, shaking his head in disgust.

Ely, the guy who had betrayed my friendship. The guy who'd tried to kidnap my girl. The guy who'd left a baby to die. And I disgusted *him*.

I stalked after him and caught him after maybe three steps. I grabbed his shoulder and whirled him around to face me.

"What the hell was that?"

"What?"

"How dare you act all high-and-mighty? Like I'm the asshole here? Haven't I done enough?"

"I don't know. Have you?"

"For close to a year now, I've held together this rebellion with little more than a roll of duct tape. I've fought for people. I've saved people. Hell, I've even killed people. I've buried the bodies of people I cared about. I've seen and done things I will never be able to forget. All with the hope that someday, somehow, we'll be able to pull a miracle out of our collective asses and we'll turn the tide in this war. But you know what? So far, in the miracle department, I ain't seen jack. So excuse me if for once I'd like to take a break and just enjoy the fact that at least one person I care about is alive."

Ely just stared at me in silence and it took me a second to realize how complete that silence was. Lily and Marcus had stopped talking to stare at us. Lily looked a little drawn. And a lot nervous.

Not that anyone could blame her. She gave Marcus another hug and walked silently past Ely to reach me. I didn't even look at her until she touched my arm.

"I think it's time to leave," she said softly.

I nodded, making myself look down at her. She was just as pretty as ever, but she looked worn. Tired. And older than her eighteen years. She looked like one of those women who's lost too much weight too fast. And, sure, everyone who was still alive had lost too much weight too fast. That was a given. But I knew her face pretty well and she'd lost at least ten pounds. In the past three days alone.

And that was why, even though I was looking at her, I still couldn't meet her eyes. Because who the hell was I to bitch about the sacrifices I'd made. Nothing compared to what Lily had been through.

"Yeah," I said finally. "Let's head out."

Lily waited until I'd navigated through Huntsville and was out on the highway before she asked, "You want to talk about what happened with Ely?"

"No."

"Hey, don't get me wrong, if you were giving him hell for trying to turn me over to a bloodsucking monster, I'd be all for that, but this sounded different."

"He's pissed that we're not going to Genexome."

"Why wouldn't we go there? That's where the cure is, right?"

"No. We don't know that."

"But is that where the cure came from?"

For a split second, I thought about lying. Because I didn't want to have this discussion now and because I could make her believe it if I wanted to. But the thing was, I didn't want to.

"Yes. It is. I stole the cure from a vampire in New Mexico named Sabrina. She stole it from Sebastian. But that doesn't mean there's more of it at Genexome. Dawn and Darren had one sample left. They took it when they headed back to San Angelo."

"So you had exactly three doses of the most important medicine in the history of the world and you wasted two of them on me and Marcus?" She frowned at me. "Are you kidding me?"

"What did you want me to do, Lily? I was out of options. I didn't have a way to save you. I—" My hands were clenching the steering wheel, my foot heavy on the gas pedal as the Chevy crept toward ninety. "Look, I'm not going to argue with you about this. What's done is done. And there's still one sample left."

She opened her mouth and then shut it again. She nodded and said, "Okay. What's done is done. But that is all the more reason we need to get back to Genexome. If there's any more of the cure, it'll be there. If there's information about how we can make more, it'll be there. At the very least, there's equipment."

"Yeah. For all we know, it is there. But that doesn't mean we can get to it. Mel and I went to Genexome. It was the first place we went after—" I broke off, because I realized there was so much she didn't know. She'd been sick—really sick—when we'd been at El Corazon and she'd been in a coma part of the time. So I quickly filled her in on the highlights. The only thing I left out was the revelation that I was an *abductura*. "But whatever Sebastian has or doesn't have, it's locked up tight. There's no way we're getting in."

"And you can't just get him to let you in?"

"Not if he's dead. And even if he isn't, did you miss the part where he set your sister up to be the fall guy?"

"No. And I also didn't miss the part where you let my sister go off to find him by herself. If Sebastian is really the evil bastard you claim he is, then why is Mel facing him alone?"

I didn't bother to point out that when it came to Mel and Lily, it had never been an issue of letting them do anything. They were both smart and strong-willed and determined. Still I couldn't help thinking I should have tried harder to convince her. I could have made her stay with me.

Guilt choked me and the silence in the car was so thick I had trouble talking past it. "Look, I know this is probably hard to hear, but Mel isn't . . . she isn't Mel anymore."

"What's that supposed to mean?"

"It means she's different."

"Not-autistic different? Because we knew that might happen."

"No. Just different. Tough. Predatory." Even as I said it I struggled with the words. But they seemed too harsh and completely inaccurate at the same time. Mel was both more and less than she'd been.

"None of that means anything to me," Lily said fiercely. "She's still Mel. I don't care how tough she is now. She's still my sister. I'm not going to turn my back on her."

"Hey, calm down," I said soothingly. "It'll be okay. I promise." Ah, hell. I'd known all along Lily would never be the kind of person to just ride off into the sunset on the back of a motorcycle. It was one of the things I loved about her. "If you want to go to Genexome and find her, that's what we'll do."

She looked up at me, hope battling the exhaustion in her eyes. "Okay."

I blew out a breath, and kept my gaze on the road. "Next time we stop, I'll set up the sat phone. We'll try to call her. If we don't reach her, we'll keep heading for Genexome. We know that's where she's going."

Lily just nodded, looking out the window until she fell asleep. Me? I just kept driving, heading toward all the things I didn't want to face. All the things I hadn't told her yet.

Once we met back up with Mel and Sebastian, Lily would find out I was an *abductura*. Maybe it was no big deal. Maybe she wouldn't care at all.

Or maybe it would freak her out knowing that I had the ability to control her emotions. To make her feel anything I wanted her to feel. And maybe she'd never want to see me again after that.

And maybe that was the least of my worries, because I was starting to wonder exactly what had happened to Mel. I had been trying to call her on the satellite phone for days now and still hadn't reached her. And I was starting to run out of excuses. Maybe she didn't know how to use the phone. Maybe Sebastian hadn't taught her. Maybe she hadn't even realized the phone was in the car with her. Except I didn't really believe that was true. Which left me with the only other maybe.

Maybe something else had happened. Yes, she was a vampire. Yes, she was tough, but that didn't mean she was impossible to kill. If something had happened to Mel, Lily would never forgive me. And I would never forgive myself.

CHAPTER FORTY-FOUR

CARTER

We stopped the car a couple of hours west of Huntsville, just outside the tiny town of Junction. It had seemed like as good a place as any to search for more gas and food. I loaded up the gas cans while Lily searched the house for food. When the cans were full and she was still loading up supplies, I set up the sat phone and called the Farm in San Angelo.

"So the cure works?" Joe asked, when I explained why I'd called. Then I heard him repeating the news to other people in the background. A cheer went up. A few more long seconds passed before I could hear him again.

"The cure works?" he asked again, sounding dumbfounded.

"Yeah. It does." My mind raced just thinking about it. A cure. I'd seen it work with my own eyes and even I almost didn't believe it.

"How much of this stuff did you say you found?" Joe asked.

"Three vials."

"And you used two of them already?" Joe muttered a curse on the other end of the phone. "Which means we can cure one more person. That's just great."

Surprised by his attitude, I said, "It is great. We can use that sample to—"

"To what? We can't magically replicate more," he pointed out.

"We have no idea how this stuff was made. And even if we did, we don't have the facilities to do it."

"So we'll figure it out. We've got a ton of smart people here. We can do this. Just give us a minute to celebrate, jeez."

But even as I said it, in the back of my head, all I could think about was Sabrina's to-do list that she'd rattled off. All the things that needed to happen before that cure made it into the hands and the bloodstreams of the people that needed it most. And worst of all, I thought of the haunted look in Lily's eyes.

She'd only been a Tick for a few days. I didn't know what happened in those days. I didn't want to know. I'd seen Ticks. I'd seen the way they ate and killed. I'd seen what they were capable of. Would I want to live with those memories?

It killed me seeing her look so fragile and broken, but there was nothing I could do but be here for her. And be waiting on the other side.

As if he could read my mind, Joe said, "Having the cure and curing people are two very different things."

"I get it. We've been fighting a long time. And you're tired. And you just want this to be done. But you've got to let us have a moment here." Who was I trying to convince: him or me? "For the first time in almost a year, we have something to hope for. Your daughter might grow up in a world where the Tick virus is just part of our history. A horrible, bloody part. But part of our *history*. Think about that for a moment. We need this. I need this."

"You're right," he said after a minute. "Okay, where do we go from here?"

Right now we had the cure. We had something that could change the course of human history. Something that would ensure there was a human history. A single glass vial of magic.

And if we messed this up by pretending we had everything

under control when we really didn't, if humanity crashed and burned because of our mistake, then it was all on us.

"Look, here's what we need to do," I said. "We need to go back to Genexome. See if there's any more of this stuff in that vault. More importantly, we need to find the research notes. But here's the thing—" I paused. "If Lily and I don't make it, then you've got to protect that one sample like it's the Holy Grail, okay? You've got to do anything you can to keep it safe. To find someone, somewhere, who can use it to make more. I wouldn't trust the vampires if I was you. I wouldn't trust any of them. Maybe if you can get back to Base Camp, you can find someone in Utah who can tell you what to do." I thought again of that dead body in the hall outside of Genexome. I thought of Sebastian and Mel and whether or not we could trust them. Frankly, right now it all seemed completely undoable. "If you don't hear back from us, then you move heaven and earth to get that sample into the right hands."

"Okay," Joe said seriously. "I'll do it. Just get me the sample and I'll do whatever needs doing."

It was like every cell in my body came to a screeching halt. Like I just stopped living for a second.

"I don't have the sample," I said slowly.

"What? You said we had one sample."

"Yeah. The one sample Dawn and Darren had. The one they brought you from New Mexico."

Suddenly my heart was pounding and my blood racing. Like someone had slammed a shot of adrenaline right into every single one of my dying cells. And I knew what he was going to say before he said it.

"Dawn and Darren never made it back from New Mexico. I thought they were with you."

I couldn't speak. I couldn't even breathe.

Two good people were lost. Just gone. I knew—somehow, inexplicably—I just knew that they were gone. They were gone because they'd come with me to New Mexico. I knew they'd been inexperienced and I'd still asked them to come. And now they were missing, most likely dead. And with them was the last vial of the cure.

The phone slipped out of my hand and tumbled to the ground. I slammed my empty fist on the trunk of the car. Again and again, until pain pulsed through my hand and up into my arm, but it still wasn't enough. It could never be enough to blot out the anguish.

And then I saw Lily, staring at me, aghast, standing maybe ten feet away, a box of canned food in her arms.

I tried. I tried so damn hard to swallow all the rage inside of me. All the anger and doubt and grief, but the emotions won. Over and over again they won out. I wasn't just battered by my grief for Dawn and Darren. It was all of it. My rage at Sebastian. My guilt because Sabrina had tempted me. My long-suppressed terror that I would lose Lily forever. My emotions crushed me. I bent over at the waist, bracing my elbows on the hood of the car and pressing my forehead into my palms as I tried to get my emotions back under my control.

I sucked in breath after breath of icy air but I couldn't get ahead of it. What was the point? What was the fucking point of even trying to beat this thing when time after time it won?

From my peripheral vision I saw Lily set down the box and walk over to me. She didn't even ask what was wrong. She just picked up the phone. I think she talked to Joe for a bit. A moment later, I felt her beside me, wrapping her arm across my shoulder.

Only then did I force myself to stand. Instantly, she was in my arms, just holding me, and still I couldn't get it under control. Because now I was crying. For Dawn and Darren. For the family that I had taken them away from. I thought of their brothers and sisters. Their father. The man who had fought so damn hard to keep his family alive when the world was collapsing around them. And somehow he had done it. Until I came along and lured two of his kids away with the promise they'd make a difference in the battle against the Ticks. And now they were gone.

And along with them, the last best hope for humanity.

"You don't know that they're dead," Lily said softly.

"Come on, Lily. You know what it's like out there. You know how hard it is. You barely made it—hell, you didn't make it. And you had way more experience than they did."

"That doesn't mean—"

"We both know that if someone goes missing, they are probably gone forever."

"Joe wasn't."

"Joe was a frickin' miracle."

She didn't bother to argue with me because she knew I was right.

"Here's what we do," she said, her voice calm and confident. The voice that I loved. "First off, we don't panic. Not yet. They had a sat phone, right?"

I nodded and she must have felt it against her shoulder.

"Okay, so we call that phone and we keep calling it as long as we can. And we call their dad back in Utah. They might have gone there."

"That wasn't the plan."

"No. But we all know that plans don't always work out. There's a chance they just needed to go home."

Logically, I knew she was right. And logically, I also knew that there was a good chance—far too good a chance—that we would simply never know what had happened to them. There were more than five hundred miles between San Angelo and where I'd parted ways with them. There were five hundred ways to die out there. None of them peaceful. Most of them horrible.

And I would live the rest of my life wondering what had happened to them and what I might have done to stop it.

CHAPTER FORTY-FIVE

MEL

It's not that I'm sad to leave El Corazon. *Sad*'s the wrong word altogether. But I am . . . conflicted about it. So much has happened here. I can't help but feel as though I've lived more of my life here than anywhere else.

Nanna—the only one in the family who'd really loved to travel—had kept a map of the world on her bedroom wall, with pins for all the places she'd been. Most of the pins were just sewing pins, the ones with brightly colored heads. But a few of them—San Francisco, Prague, Omaha—were pinned with big pushpins. When I asked her why, she'd told me those were the places where big things had happened—where she fell in love for the first time. Where she met Grandpa. Where her kids were born. Those places felt bigger to her. They had more gravitational pull.

That's how I feel about El Corazon. Like I could leave here, but it would always be pulling me back.

We are almost to the outskirts of town when I jerk up in my seat and say, "Wait! We have to turn around."

Sebastian slams on the brakes. "Please don't tell me you left the oven on."

"Not back to the house. To the car. The one I came in. There was a satellite phone in the car."

"Now, see, that might have been useful to have when we thought we were trapped in Roberto's safe room for the rest of our lives. Shame you didn't think to bring it with you."

"Well, I wasn't exactly planning on being stuck there forever. How was I supposed to know you'd want it?"

He smiles. "I might have wanted to have a pizza delivered."

Sebastian circles back through town. Thankfully, we don't see any more Ticks. Maybe they're all back at the house getting drunk on Roberto's blood and leftover antifreeze. It only takes a minute for me to retrieve the bag that Carter had stashed the phone in, which is a good thing, because I'm not sure that Sebastian wouldn't drive off without me if he had a chance.

As he drives back out to the main road, I dig through the bag to find the phone. It has an antenna, which is bulky, but I manage to get it set up in the backseat. It doesn't work as well as it would have if the car wasn't moving, but it should be good enough. I feel like I should check to see if there've been calls, but I don't know how. I push a few buttons but can't get anything to work.

"I don't understand. It worked before."

"You might try plugging it in."

"Oh." I frown at it. "You think the battery's dead?" I dig through the bag until I find a cord and get the phone plugged in.

"You really are worthless with electronics," he says.

"Sorry, some of us weren't busy prepping for the apocalypse in the Before."

"Yes, but what about your uncle? Rodney, the nut job. Didn't he prepare you for this kind of thing?"

"Maybe he did that with Lily. With me, we just listened to Elvis songs. I—"

I break off when the phone finishes powering up and emits a beep. And then another. And another. And another.

"Is it supposed to be doing this?" I hold it out to Sebastian.

"You have missed calls."

Thankfully Sebastian dials down the snark as he talks me through it. I listen with a growing sense of dread, despair, and disbelief. After the last message from Carter, I put down the phone.

"The cure works."

Sebastian shoots me a look. "I told you it did. Did you need to see the FDA testing results?"

I ignore his smartassery and tell him about the helicopter crash and how Carter had to track down Lily and administer the cure.

He's silent for several minutes and I'm grateful for it, because my mind is reeling. I'm still not wholly used to the full brunt of the emotions I feel now that I'm not human anymore and the last thing I need is to try to deflect Sebastian's sarcasm and process my grief at the same time. "What about your father?" he asks quietly.

"Dead. Carter didn't—" The words choke me, but I push them out anyway. "Carter didn't see the body himself, but someone else did."

Sebastian doesn't ask the question that's on my mind. If Lily had turned after the crash, was she the one who'd killed him? I know she's human again and I can hardly imagine what that would be like. To be human and live with the memories of a monster. Maybe with the memories of killing a loved one. It's bad enough living with the memory of my father the last time I saw him—at El Corazon, looking so . . . cocky. So full of energy

299

and confidence and total belief in the rightness of whatever part of the apocalypse had been his doing. Bad enough trying to sort through my new hatred of him and my grief. Because despite whatever horrors he'd caused, he was still my father. He was still the only one I'd let hold me when I was a child and I was upset. He was still the man who'd read *Goodnight Moon* to me every night until he left when I was ten. He was still the hand I wanted pressed to my forehead when I was feverish.

Knowing he was a monster made me hate him more, but it didn't make me love him less.

Knowing he was a monster only made me question my own wickedness. If I forgave myself, did I have to forgive him, too?

I'm already drowning in my thoughts when I feel a hand on mine.

"I'm sorry about your father," Sebastian says.

I shrug. "He was an asshole."

Sebastian is silent again for a long time as he winds his way down the two-lane road that leads off of Roberto's property and we approach the gates to the world outside. They're still open, which is how I left them when I came through. There was no point in shutting the gates when a huge swatch of the fence was down anyway.

Sebastian slows the car to drive through them and says softly, "I still remember when my parents died."

I suck in a breath, because I've never heard him talk about his life before he was a vampire. "That was . . ."

"Hispania. A very long time ago. Before I was turned. There are some things you never forget. No matter how long you live. No matter how much you might wish you could."

Will this be me, in two thousand years? Wishing I could forget the loss of my family? My father who is dead. My mother

300

and uncle who are lost. I'll probably never know what happened to them. Even if the world is restored tomorrow, I'll have no idea how to find them. And no matter what happens, I'll lose Sebastian. Which means the only person I really have left is Lily.

Who, if Carter's messages are correct, is frantically wondering if I'm even still alive.

I tell Sebastian the rest then. About how Carter and Lily are going to Genexome to try to get into the vault to get the rest of the cure.

"Wait," he says, interrupting me. "If Carter hasn't gotten into the vault yet, then where did he get the cure that he used on Lily?"

"From Sabrina."

"He went to Sabrina's? On his own?"

"Yes. He didn't have any other choice."

Sebastian mutters a curse.

"What?" I ask, panic tripping up my heartbeat. "Please tell me that the cure you let Sabrina find wasn't somehow . . . not the cure. I mean it worked, right? So it wasn't somehow poisoned or something."

"No. It's fine. I just would have preferred that Sabrina not know about Carter."

"Because he's an *abductura*?" I ask, even though I know the answer.

"Yes. For the past twenty years, Sabrina's *abductura* was Paul Workman."

"The computer guru? But he died right before the Tick virus was released, didn't he?"

Sebastian shakes his head. "I think she probably reported he'd died, but I sensed him when we were there. He was still alive, but just barely. She needs another *abductura*."

301

"But Carter got away. She didn't try to keep him there."

"If he got away, it's because she's going to try to grab him somewhere else. In that last message, did Carter say where they were?"

"Just outside of someplace called Junction, but I have no idea where that is."

"That's just south of here. Call him back and tell him to stay put. Wherever he is. We're coming to get him."

"Can't we just meet them at Genexome?"

"No. I want him under our protection as quickly as possible. I don't trust Sabrina."

I can't help but feel a little stab of anger at that. "I thought she was the love of your life. The one person you were willing to do anything—even give up some of your powers—to be with."

"Exactly. Which is why I know her best."

CHAPTER FORTY-SIX

LILY

Reunions are supposed to be cheerful things. Or at least emotional.

This one isn't.

Maybe we're all too tired. Maybe Mel and I just don't know what to say to each other.

I don't even recognize her when she climbs out of the car with Sebastian. A dog hops out after her—something large and covered with long brown fur. It looks more like a bear than a dog.

I tense, because Mel has always hated dogs. Their exuberance scares her. And they smell. When she was a kid, just the sight of one could send her into a full meltdown. But before I can rush over to distract the dog and steer it away from her, it sidles right up next to her and her fingers curl into the fur at its shoulder.

Everything in me rebels.

This girl standing between Sebastian and a huge dog can't possibly be my sister. Her hair is cut into a sleek short bob. Her lips look unnaturally red. And weirdest of all—even weirder than the dog—she looks right at me.

In the Before, she almost never did that. She'd look through just one eye, in a birdlike way.

But now she looks from me to Carter and then back, eyes directly on mine.

Unsettled, I link my fingers with Carter's, seeking his strength and comfort, needing it so badly that I almost miss how tense he is. He nods stiffly in Sebastian's direction by way of greeting, but doesn't say anything, which surprises me, because they used to be . . . well, maybe not friends, exactly. But they used to get along.

Carter squats down and calls to the dog. "Come here, boy. Come on, Chuy." The dog hesitates, looking up at Mel, before trotting over to Carter. Carter scrubs his hand over the dog's head as Chuy greets him. "Thanks for taking care of him."

Mel nods stiffly, but she looks almost hurt that the dog is with Carter now.

Carter stands, barely glancing at Sebastian as he turns to grab the bag with our supplies. "I figure I'll drive since you—" He nods vaguely in Sebastian's direction. I can only guess that he's referring to the stake that's still in Sebastian's heart.

He's explained that the stake is allowing him to be around Mel without stirring up any territorial disputes.

"Right," Sebastian drawls. "Since I'm not at my peak right now."

"You good to navigate?" Carter asks. "You know this part of the state better than anyone else."

Sebastian arches an eyebrow. "I'll try to not die long enough to get us there."

"Yeah. Do that."

Which puts Mel and me awkwardly in the back. We've spent a lot of long silent car rides together in the backseat of a sedan, since Nanna lived up in Nebraska, a fourteen-hour car ride from our home in Dallas, and Mel could never fly.

So in a way, this is familiar, even though there's this dog in the backseat between us. And I'm able to pretend that this new silent and angry Mel is no different from the silent and aloof, autistic Mel of our youth.

It helps that I'm tired. That I'm recovering. That I'm only newly human again. Soon the shush shush shush of the tires on the road lulls me to sleep and I dream of Slinkys and of Mel humming Rachmaninoff and of Mom stroking my hair when I'm feverish.

I wake up, dizzy and disoriented and alone in the car. I can't help remembering the last time I woke up like this in a car. When Ely had tranqed me. I expect a blast of nausea to hit me, but it doesn't. I stumble out of the car to find Carter, Sebastian, Mel, and Chuy staring off in the distance. We're in the desert somewhere, deep enough into West Texas that there are mountains on the horizon.

"What is it?" I ask.

Carter turns to me. "It's not good." He points to the west. "Is that a car?"

"Looks like it," Sebastian says, lowering a pair of binoculars. "Everybody back in the car."

I shuffle behind the others, still feeling disoriented. Carter takes off almost before I've got the door closed. "Maybe it's someone from San Angelo," I say hopefully, but I know Carter doesn't believe it. He must have his foot all the way on the gas, because this car is going race-car fast for a sedan. "Or maybe it's Dawn and Darren."

"It's not," Mel says grimly.

"How do you know?" I ask.

Sebastian looks back at me and I can see him exchange a look with Mel. Something passes between them. Something that's not wholly sexual, but not really innocent, either. Something that's dark and a little angry and full of verve, but devoid of joy.

After a second, he looks away to stare out the front window and answers in a stiff voice, like it's taking all of his restraint just to be here, "Because we're already in my territory. And if that was just some humans in a car, I wouldn't have noticed them."

My mind is still sleep-befuddled and it takes a second for his words to sink in and for me to remember what I know about vampires and how territorial they are. "So that's another vampire?"

"Yes. More to the point, it's Sabrina."

"But I thought you were allies with her?" I try to lock eyes with Carter in the rearview mirror, but he's so focused on the road he doesn't meet my gaze. "Carter, isn't she the one that gave you the cure you used on me?"

There's a long stretch of silence where I can tell everyone is trying to figure out how and what to tell me.

Finally, it's Mel who answers. "Actually, he stole the cure from her."

"You stole it? From a vampire?"

"What was I supposed to do, Lily?" He glares at me in the rearview mirror. "She had the cure. I needed it for you."

"Okay, then." I give Sebastian a poke on the back of the neck. "You know her. How bad is it? How much trouble are we in here?"

"She and I aren't exactly close."

"But you know her, right? Is she going to play nice? I mean, you have more of the cure in the vault at Genexome, right? If you just offer her more of the cure, will she let us go?"

"That's the plan," Carter says, but I don't think anyone in the car is fooled.

Sebastian slants me a wry look. "Oh, is it? I didn't realize we had a plan."

"Yeah. Me neither. You got any better ideas?"

"Nope."

It may have been the plan, but it didn't sound like a very good one.

CHAPTER FORTY-SEVEN

MEL

I know there are things left unsaid between Lily and me, but none of them are things I want to say in front of Sebastian and Carter—certainly not now that Sebastian thinks I'm in love with Carter. And once we reach Genexome, there isn't time. But maybe that's the great thing about sisters: a lot can go unsaid. At least that's the great thing about Lily and me. We're old pros at that not talking business. I think of all the times—back when I was autistic—when I simply didn't have the words to tell her what I was thinking or how I was feeling. All the times I did the best I could with a few bars of humming and the slink of my Slinky, which had always been my comfort toy.

I long for those days. For that ability to say so much with so little.

Now I have all these words and no way to put them together. And no time to speak them anyway if I did.

Carter pulls to a halt in front of one of the seven gray buildings that make up the Genexome campus. I'm glad Carter can tell one building from the next, because they all look identical to me. Still, it must be the right one, because Sebastian—hobbling along with Carter's help—guides us into the building and down the stairs to the hallway leading to the vault. Once we're there, it all starts looking more familiar.

Unfortunately, even the cool air hasn't done much to slow the decomposition of the dead bodies in the hall. The stench grates on my already jangling nerves, making the last pint of blood I drank slosh in my belly. I can feel it climbing up my esophagus. Maybe twenty feet from the door, Lily stops to puke, which only makes things worse. I look back over my shoulder and see that Carter is still helping Sebastian down the stairs.

"Any chance you can hurry this up?" I ask, burying my fingers in Chuy's fur, partly to steady myself and partly because dogs are less picky about the age of their food and I don't want Chuy getting too close to the bodies.

"Do you want to carry him?" Carter shoots back.

"As a matter of fact—"

"Stop bickering, lovebirds," Sebastian interjects as he pushes Carter away. "I should go on from here by myself anyway."

Carter and Lily stand back. He's shuffling his gear around, like he feels as nervous as I do. Chuy stays close to my side while we wait for Sebastian. Carter's got his arm around Lily's shoulder and she's resting her head against him, like she's still weak. Which I'm guessing she still is. I'm shooting mental daggers at Sebastian's back and just glad neither Carter nor Lily noticed the lovebirds comment. I focus on the warmth of Chuy's skin under my fingertips. It is almost enough to soothe me.

I really want to kill Sebastian and I'm not sure if it's because we're in his territory now or because he's been acting like such an asshole.

He steps up to the LCD panel and pushes a button. A Plexiglas gate slams down, blocking him off from the rest of us. For one horrible moment, it occurs to me that this could all be some sort of trap. He's cut off from us. He could disappear back into his own safe room and leave us out here at the mercy of Sabrina.

I can't think of why he would actually do that, but there are so many things about Sebastian that I don't understand. That I'll never understand.

My heart pounds as I watch him typing some kind of code into the keypad. He's close enough for the retinal scanner to do its thing and then he presses his palm to the screen, and a second later, the computer emits a peppy beep and the door slides open. A few seconds later, the gate does, too.

And then a siren goes off. A screeching, annoying whaa-wa, whaa-wa, whaa-wa loud enough to pierce my eardrums. Chuy flinches and whimpers.

"Get in," he orders.

We rush forward, carrying what gear we've brought from the car or collected on our way through the building.

"What is that noise?" Carter asks.

Sebastian gives him a condescending look. "That's called an alarm."

"Obviously," Carter says through gritted teeth. "Why is it going off now? Did you trigger it when you opened the vault?"

"Not at all," Sebastian says, busy at the LCD screen on the inside of the vault now that we're all in. He punches a series of buttons on the panel and once again presses his palm to the screen. The door closes behind us. "Sabrina triggered it on her way into the building."

Carter shoots me a look, his expression puzzled, like he's trying to figure out if we'd triggered an alarm and he hadn't noticed. "When Mel and I were here earlier, we didn't set off any alarm."

I just shrug, because I don't know what's going on.

"Of course not," Sebastian says smoothly. "No, Sabrina did that on purpose. She wanted to make sure we knew she was coming for us."

CHAPTER FORTY-EIGHT

CARTER

I followed Sebastian down to the lower level.

"What do you mean she wanted to make sure we knew she was coming for us?"

He ignored me at first, instead heading for a doorway at the far side of the living room. I followed him into a much smaller room. Two of the walls were lined with weapons storage lockers. The room was a veritable arsenal. The third wall was dominated by a media center with a computer desk and large flat-screen TV. I gave him a chance to pull up the security video feeds. He studied the screens for a few minutes. And still didn't respond. I cleared my throat. And got nothing.

Finally, I got right in his face. "What the hell?"

He glanced at me, like I was some kind of insect he wanted to squash. Then he gave a beleaguered sigh. "She's baiting us. Trying to draw us out."

"To what end?"

He kept his attention on the TV as he used the remote to pan through the screens, sparing me only enough attention for an eye roll. "If I had to guess, I'd say it's so she can kill us."

Yeah. His attitude was really starting to piss me off. I took a step closer, blocking his view of the screen. "Look, we're in this together. If you want to be a dick, do it sometime when our lives aren't on the line."

Sebastian looked at me then, his expression smug and condescending. "Ah, such words of wisdom from one so young."

I had to clench my fists to keep from punching him. "Look, I'm not any happier about this collaboration than you are, but if I can put up with you to get this worked out, then you can damn well do the same."

"Sorry my secure fortress, lifesaving supplies, and world-changing cure are such a burden."

"Yeah. Your constant stream of lies and deception have been a real friggin' help. Thanks."

"Have I hurt your feelings?" Sebastian sneered in a tone he'd use to speak to a child.

"You might have told me."

"Told you what?"

I tapped down my irritation. If the past few days had taught me anything, it was that losing my temper made every situation worse. "Oh, I don't know. About Genexome. About the Tick virus. Maybe about the fact that I'm an *abductura*. That might have come up sometime in the past two years."

When Sebastian looked at me, his expression was devoid of that wry sarcasm that I was so used to getting from him. Instead, there was a kind of cold anger glazing his eyes. "What would have been the point?"

"Oh, I don't know. It might have been nice to be a little prepared."

"It wouldn't have changed anything," he said dismissively.

"Bullshit. It—"

He whirled on me, and in an instant slammed me up against

313

the wall and held me there by the throat, my feet dangling a couple of inches from the floor. I didn't fight back. He was faster and stronger than I could ever be. Even wounded, he'd beat me. So I didn't give him an excuse to try. I just prayed that he'd calm down and realize what he was doing before he strangled me.

"It would have changed nothing. You still would have wanted to save Lily. You still would have searched the Farms until you found her. You still would have done everything you could to keep her safe, even if it meant manipulating other people. The only difference is you would have felt guilty about it and I would have had to listen to you bitch."

"You still"—I choked out—"should have told me."

He dropped me, turning away. He let out an audible, shuddering breath as he pressed a hand to his chest, where the stake was still lodged. When he turned back to face me, I could see the blood seeping through his shirt.

Despite the pain he must have been in, his expression was cold and blank. "What exactly do you think you would have done differently? If you'd known?"

He was right, of course. The bastard. He was always right.

Even if I'd known what I knew now, I would have tried to find Lily and Mel. I would have wanted to make sure they were safe. Would I still have started the rebellion? Yeah, I probably would have done that, too. Because no matter how I looked at it, we needed to fight. I would never have been okay with humanity just lying down and accepting defeat.

But when it came to my relationship with Lily—well, there I might have changed things.

"If I had known—" I said aloud. "I might have saved Lily, but I wouldn't have pursued her so hard. I would have given her a choice."

"A choice?" Sebastian sneered. "You think she ever had a choice when it came to loving you? None of us have a choice when it comes to love."

That's when it hit me. Sebastian's pissy attitude. His anger. It wasn't because he was in pain. It wasn't his normal disdain. It wasn't even the remnants of his territorial rage.

"So that's how it is," I said softly.

"That's how what is?" he snarled.

"You're in love with Mel." He whirled on me, but I held up my hands. "Hey, I'm sorry, man. I didn't know."

Jesus. No wonder he was so pissed.

"It's not like that." He turned his attention back to the security feed, but I didn't think he was really seeing anything.

I didn't believe him. Not for a second. It was exactly like that. He was in love with a girl he could never have. Despite everything Lily and I had been through, despite my gift and despite her exposure to the Tick virus, in the end, at least we had each other. Sebastian and Mel would never have that.

There wasn't anything I could say that would make that gig any better. So I turned my focus to the screen, trying to make sense of the images there.

After a minute, Sebastian whispered, "She's in love with you."

I glanced at him. Surprised, because reassurances weren't really his thing. "Yeah. That's what she keeps telling me."

"Not Lily. Mel."

I rocked back on my heels.

Before I could say anything, Sebastian continued—without even glancing my way, like this was totally no big deal. "I know you'd never leave Lily, but just don't . . . don't hurt Mel."

"Is that what you think? That she's in love with me? Because

315

you're wrong." He started to say something, but I didn't give the dumb-ass a chance. "Think about it. In the past two months, she's been in my company for less than twenty-four hours. Total. Before that, when she was still human, she was an *abductura*—and way more powerful than I am. I think one of us would have noticed if she'd been in love with me then."

For a long moment, he didn't say anything, just kept staring at the TV screen. Then finally, he pointed at a shot of the exterior of the building.

"Sabrina's retreated from the building and is setting up camp right outside. I don't think we're going to have to worry about her trying to break in. At least not in the immediate future. She'd rather just wait us out."

For a second, all I could do was gape at him. Then it occurred to me that it didn't really matter to him if Mel was in love with me or not. He couldn't have her either way. And maybe it would have even been easier on him if he'd thought she didn't love him.

Of course, unless we could figure out a way to defeat Sabrina, this wasn't going to end well for any of us.

"Okay, then," I said, "what do we do?"

"For now, we wait for her to get cocky and screw up."

CHAPTER FORTY-NINE

LILY

Once the door closes behind us, locking us in, the blaring sound of the alarm isn't quite as nerve grating. Even better, the stench of rotting flesh dissipates, even though I'm pretty sure those scent molecules have buried themselves so deep up my nose I'll never not smell it.

But maybe my sense of smell is just different now. Now that I've been a Tick. Maybe I'll always hate the smell of dead things and crave the scent of fresh blood, even when it's in polyurethane bags, buried in an insulated suitcase.

For now, I'm just glad to be out of the car and away from the dead bodies and—for the moment anyway—safe.

The guys seem deep in some conversation near the entrance. Something about levels of security and whatnot. Me? I want to get as far away from that door and the scent of death as possible.

On the other side of the door, the hall had been stark and utilitarian. Gray cement walls and cheap fluorescent lights. On this side, it's a whole different world. The walls are paneled in dark wood. Elegant frosted-glass sconces dot the hall. This isn't a bunker. It's the foyer to an underground mansion.

Ahead, the hall opens up and leads to a grand staircase, one that goes down rather than up. Off the side there's a library with bookshelf-lined walls and a pair of sleek modern chairs in front of a cold fireplace. On the other side, there's an office. From where we are, I can see the room at the bottom of the stairs. It's a living room with a media center on one side and an open kitchen on the other. Somewhere, either on this level or the one below, I assume there are bathrooms. And probably freezers of food. Most likely blood, but I try not to think about that.

Mel and the dog have wandered into the office off to our right and I follow them through a pair of open French doors. Across from the door, mounted on the wall, there's a whole collection of swords and daggers. There are even a few older-looking pistols. I'm oddly drawn to the weapons. Weapons have never interested me, but history always has. These are old. Some of them look ridiculously so. For us, they're part of the distant past. Even the most recent look far older than the gun my great-grandfather carried in World War II. That's the oldest weapon I've ever seen in person. The only thing I know about Grandpa Rosen is that he enlisted so his parents wouldn't have to feed him at the end of the Depression, and served in Italy. In my life, that's practically ancient history. In Sebastian's life, it's so recent it doesn't warrant a place on his wall.

He's been alive impossibly long. If he had family or siblings, he probably doesn't even remember them now. And someday, that's what I'll be to Mel. A blip. A ghost. Someone who lived for a fraction of a moment.

I think of the pink backpack I left with Sebastian after she became a vampire. A small stash of things left over from our life in the Before—a stuffed toy squirrel. A Slinky. The lovies she cherished most when she was human. The things that brought her comfort.

I have no idea what happened to them after we parted ways back in Decatur. That was eight weeks and a lifetime ago. Mel and Sebastian probably changed cars too many times and he wouldn't know how important it was and she wouldn't remember how desperately those things had mattered to her, and if she did remember, maybe she wouldn't care. Maybe I was the only one who cared about those lost lovies.

And then, inexplicably, when I turn to look at the bookshelf behind the desk, I see a collection of toys. A wooden toy phone, a toy car, one of those birds that bobs for water, and a Slinky. An old-fashioned metal Slinky exactly like the one Mel used to have. Except it can't be hers. This one is shiny and new and looks like it's been here for months. Is it possible that Sebastian brought Mel's Slinky here or did he simply have one of his own through some bizarre twist?

Entranced, I walk over to it and run my finger down the outside. I pick up the Slinky and turn to see if Mel has noticed it, too, but she's not even looking at me.

By the doors, there's a coat tree with a navy pea coat hanging off it. Her hand is on the sleeve of the coat, her eyes are closed, and she's leaning slightly toward it, like she's breathing in its scent.

And just like that, I understand. The dark tension between them isn't that vampire territorial thing Carter has told me about. It's something else. Something romantic and maybe sexual, and it hurts me to think of Mel that way. Because I'm not yet used to thinking of her as an adult. As this other person who is at least as grown up as I am and who doesn't need a stuffed animal or a toy, but who does need to breathe in the scent of the guy she loves.

And also because of the swords on the wall. Sebastian isn't just old. He's violent. I've seen him kill. Ticks and humans. I've seen him fight. I've seen him struggle to control himself and I've seen him lose. And every cell in my body, every molecule in my brain and firing synapse, yells that she is *not* for him.

But this isn't my decision. I've made one decision for her already and I don't know if we'll ever recover from that. So I set the Slinky down where I found it and I walk around the desk back toward the door, not looking at her. And she is so focused on Sebastian's jacket that Chuy is the only one who notices me leaving.

"I'm going to go downstairs to see what I can find in the kitchen," I say stupidly. She just gives me a blank look, so I add, "I know you and Sebastian brought your own . . . food. But we should check and see if there's anything for Carter and me to eat."

She nods, but before I can leave, she stops me with a touch to my arm. "Actually, I want you to help me find the cure."

"Yeah. Sure, we can ask Sebastian—"

"No. Before he notices we're looking. While he and Carter are still fussing with the security system."

"I'm not sure they would like that you're calling it fussing—"

"I'm serious."

"Okay. What for?"

"If it works the way I think it works, then I think it can cure me."

"Cure you?" And then I get it. "Oh. Oh, Mel."

"No, it's not that. I'm not—" She turns away and I'm not sure if it's because she can't stand to look at me or if she doesn't want me looking at her. "I'm not mad anymore. In fact I'm even used to being like this. To the things I can do."

There's a note of pride in her voice, and for the first time, she sounds to me like the old Mel. The way she used to sound when she talked about music and math.

"Then why?"

When she turns back to me, her eyes are blazing with determination. "Do you remember what Sebastian said about vampires being territorial?"

"Yeah, of course."

"Haven't you wondered why he and I can be together right now? Why we're not trying to kill one another?"

"Aren't you his apprentice or whatever?"

"No. It's not that. He still has a stake in his heart."

My stomach gives a sickened squelch. "I knew he was wounded, but I thought he was just recovering."

"No," she says. "I bandaged over the stake. It's the only reason we aren't trying to kill one another. But it's slowly killing him."

"And so you want to take the cure? To save him? That's ridiculous."

"Not just to save him. To save everyone. You and Carter. And everyone else." She starts pacing like her thoughts are racing more quickly than her words. "Don't you see? Sabrina is out there. Someone has to fight her."

"Then we'll fight her!"

"No. The only one of us who can win is Sebastian. This is his territory. He is stronger here than anywhere else. I can feel it. Even wounded, he's the only one who can defeat her. But she's powerful. And the only way he'll be strong enough to fight her is if he takes that stake out. He's not going to take it out as long as doing so would put me at risk. That means I can't be here. Not like I am. The only solution is for me to take the cure. If we're lucky, I'll become human again and he'll have time to recover at least a little bit before Sabrina breaks through the security system."

My gut tells me that this is a bad idea. A horrible idea. But I don't know how to argue with Mel's logic. "Maybe she won't."

"She will. She's going to do everything in her power to find her way in. And if she does, she's either going to take Carter and kill you and Sebastian or she'll do those things and then destroy the cure."

"You don't know that she wants to destroy the cure," I point out.

"It's a safe bet. Don't forget, I've been to her compound. She's been doing well since the fall of civilization."

"Carter says she hasn't been doing that well. She has no kine left."

"She had plenty of kine when we were there. At least it seemed like she did."

"Why would she lie about that?"

"To him or to us?"

"To either of you."

Mel takes a step closer to me then, looking more determined than ever. "This is why we can't trust her. Why we can't leave it to chance. Why you and I have to do something to fix this."

"So you're just going to give up all your strength and all your power to protect him and you're just going to trust that Sebastian is going to protect you?" This goes against every feminist bone in my body. Our mother would be horrified.

But Mel's lips just curve into a smile. "You forget, I had power and strength before. It was a different kind of power and strength, but it was mine. It's the power I was meant to have."

"But you said you liked the person you are now."

She shrugged. "Well, maybe when this is all over, when we've defeated Sabrina and any other vampire that comes along, maybe after we've cured the Ticks and the world is back the way it's supposed to be, maybe I'll take a tae kwon do class or something."

I feel a hysteria rising up in my chest, because I so can't imagine Mel taking tae kwon do. In fact, I can't imagine how this person in front of me is Mel at all.

But, somehow she is. And she's just as stubborn as she's ever been.

I throw out one last protest, because I can't just let it go. "We don't even know for sure if the cure would work on you!"

"I know it will. It's what he originally made the cure to do."

"It could kill you."

"It won't. It'll work."

CHAPTER FIFTY

LILY

Mel and I find the vials of the cure downstairs, stored in a refrigerator full of blood and dangerous chemicals. I recognize it because I remember the bottle that Carter used in Huntsville. I remember seeing it discarded on the floor of my cell. This one is identical. We find a syringe in a first-aid kit in the downstairs bathroom. The room isn't big enough for both of us and the dog, so Mel tells Chuy to wait out in the living room. I wish there was somewhere else we could put him because I'm afraid he'll give us away, but she doesn't seem worried.

I have to use the stretchy rubber bandages to tie off her arm before I can dose her.

"I'm surprised you can do all this," Mel says, watching me work. "Do you remember it from when Carter dosed you?"

"No. I'm just going by what I've seen on TV." I don't want to think about the memories I do have from my time as a Tick.

"Do you remember very much?"

"No," I lie, poking at her arm with my fingertip to find a vein.

"Do you think I will?"

I stop prodding her arm and look up at her, studying her face. The face of my twin. I never felt like she looked like me until now.

And yet we still look different. It's not like keeping up

appearances has been a top priority, but I am aware that I'm looking pretty bedraggled. My hair is shaggier, because two days ago I was a wild creature running through the desert and I've only finger-combed my hair since then. I feel like I have a mile of dirt coating my body. My clothes don't fit well because they aren't really my clothes. They're clothes that Carter got me from somewhere after the whole Tick thing and I don't even want to think about what happened to my old clothes. I know how bad I look. And I know that Mel doesn't.

Somehow being a vampire agrees with her. Her short, chopped hair accentuates her delicate jaw. Her skin seems to glow. And her eyes . . . God, her eyes.

In all the years we lived together . . . In all the years she was my sister and my best friend and the best parts of me . . . In all those years, she never once looked me right in the eyes like she's doing now. Of course, her eyes aren't human eyes. They are vampire eyes. Her pupils are scalloped around the edges, like a chameleon's. They are both beautiful and creepy as hell, but they are still hers and they're focused directly on me.

And it breaks my heart that after I give her this shot, she may never do that again.

And then I realize that she's waiting for me to answer. That she thinks I'm not answering because I can't tell her the truth.

I set down the syringe and I grab her hand. "Do you want to remember?"

She thinks for a second and I can almost see tears pooling in those eyes. "I want to remember some of it. And I want to forget some of it."

I give her hand a squeeze. "Okay, then. You decided. You pick right now which parts of it you want to remember and which parts you want to forget. And you file away the good parts in your mind. You make yourself remember all the things that happened that were good and you set aside anything that wasn't." She nods, pressing her lips together, like she's trying not to cry. "All you ever wanted was a choice, right? So this is your chance to decide. You're in control of this, okay?"

She nods once more and my heart breaks all over again, because right now, in this moment, she is more and less my sister than she's ever been. And this person, this person she is now, is someone I'll never really get to know. I can know who she was and who she'll be, but this person will be gone forever.

I drop her hand and pull her into my arms, squeezing her tight. I don't want to let go. Ever.

Before I can make myself let go, there's a knock on the door.

"Lily, are you in there?" Carter asks.

I pull back. Mel's eyes are wide and worried.

"Yes."

She looks at the needle. "Do it now," she whispers.

I don't have time to think. Don't have time to mourn. I pick up the needle and grab her arm. Even as I'm sliding the tip through the whisper-thin skin at the inside of her elbow, I hear Sebastian coming up behind Carter.

"Are they in there?" He practically roars the question.

He knows.

I push down the plunger on the needle.

From outside the bathroom, it sounds like all hell is breaking loose. Carter and Sebastian are yelling. Furniture crashes and shatters. I block it all out.

I pull the syringe from Mel's arm and let it fall to the floor. Mel sucks in a deep breath, clutching her arm. I catch her as she goes limp.

A moment later, the door slams open and the chaos from

outside pours into the room. It rages around me, but I can't make myself respond. I can't make myself talk. I can't even let myself cry. All I can do is hold my sister and cling to the memories that I'm deciding to keep, because they are precious and too few and they may have to last me forever.

At some point, Carter must calm Sebastian down. At some point, he comes and takes Mel from my arms. At some point, I let him. And then Carter holds me while I cry. And then finally, when my tears are gone and the memories are tucked into my mind, I pull myself out of Carter's arms and I go upstairs to the office by the entrance. I collect the Slinky from the shelf and the pea coat from the rack by the door. And then I go to the bedroom where Sebastian has laid out Mel. She is sleeping. Chuy is beside her on the bed, his chin resting on his paws. I lay the coat on her chest and I climb into the bed on her other side. I stay there all night, passing the Slinky from one hand to the other, taking what comfort I can from its soft slunk, slunk, slunk.

CHAPTER FIFTY-ONE

CARTER

I've never seen anyone lose their shit the way Sebastian lost his shit when he realized what Mel and Lily had done. For several terrifying minutes, I couldn't control him and I was certain he would kill us all. And that there was nothing I could do to stop it. That this was it.

After everything I'd done to get us there. After all the sacrifices I'd made to keep Lily alive, after all the people who'd died to get the cure, Sebastian was going to kill us all and the cure would disappear with us.

That fear, all-consuming, overwhelming, soul-swallowing, magnified his own despair. I felt it like a feedback loop I couldn't break out of.

But then, somehow, some shred of calm snuck in. Some shard of peace and logic and serenity crept into my subconscious and through me to Sebastian. By the time he broke the door down, he was actually almost composed.

He scooped Mel up and carried her off while I held a sobbing Lily. She was so upset it took nearly a half hour to get the whole story out of her. By the time she was done talking, she was just done. She disappeared for a minute and then returned with a Slinky—where had she gotten that?— and a coat. She found the bedroom where Sebastian had laid Mel down and she climbed in bed with Mel. It didn't take her long to fall asleep. After that, I alternated between monitoring the security system and checking in on Mel and Lily.

I didn't know what to say to Sebastian. So I just stood nearby, waiting for him to talk. Except he didn't. He just sat by her bed, watching her, as silent and as still as Chuy.

I moved closer, got right in his line of vision so he couldn't ignore me.

"This isn't helping."

I got nothing from him.

"I've been watching the security system."

Finally he looked up but said nothing.

"It's holding Sabrina at bay. For now. But we can't stay in here forever. Even if Sabrina doesn't figure out how to sabotage the air filtration system, Lily and I need food."

And Mel would, too, when she woke up. If she woke up. But I couldn't bring myself to say that aloud.

Sebastian still said nothing, but at least he was listening now. Showing some flicker of interest.

"You know why she did this, right? She did it so that you could take that stake out of your chest. So that you would be at full strength when you fight Sabrina. She did it because she knew you would have the best shot of any of us at beating her. Don't waste this. We've got to get that stake out of your heart and we've got to do it now or we're all dead. You know I'm right."

"So that's the role I get to play? The wounded warrior who sacrifices himself for the woman he loves?"

"I don't know. She is the woman you love, isn't she?"

He made a sound that was halfway between a strangled sob and a laugh. Then finally, he stood, slowly unbuttoned his shirt, and started unwinding the bandage around his chest. I went off to the bathroom to look for—I don't know—some Bactine or something. By the time I got back, his shirt and the yards of bandage were in a blood-soaked pile on the floor. I walked in just in time to see him wrench the jagged spike of wood from his chest. He doubled over in pain as the stake came out. It was maybe six inches long and covered in so much blood it was stained red. This was no stake. This wasn't a piece of smooth maple, honed to a point. This was a crude hunk of one-inch pine. Yeah, it was broken at an angle, so there was sort of a point to it, but for the most part it had been jammed into his ribs. It splintered on the way in, leaving slivers of wood behind. It had broken bones. The hole in his chest was almost two inches across and the blood that pumped out of it was already tinged pink with pus. I dashed across the room and caught him just before he collapsed on the floor.

Even though he hadn't made a sound pulling the stake out, Lily woke up. Hell, I probably made more noise than he had.

"What's hap—" Then she saw him. She took it all in: the blood, the stake, the wound. She hopped off the bed and ran for the bathroom. A second later, I heard the sounds of her puking. If I hadn't been supporting Sebastian's weight, I might have puked, too. She was back by the time I'd moved him to a bed in another room. "What do you need?"

"More bandages. Towels. A magnifying glass and tweezers. Hell, maybe pliers."

She nodded and disappeared, leaving me alone with Sebastian. Until she got back, there was nothing I could do but stare in horror at this wound.

This is what he'd done to himself to stay by Mel's side. This was the pain he'd been in for her.

God, I felt like an ass for asking if he loved her.

CHAPTER FIFTY-TWO

LILY

I don't have the stomach to watch Carter cleaning Sebastian's wounds. All that blood brings up memories that will haunt me forever.

I want to shut the door on that part of my mind. To close myself off from it. But unlike the solid steel door on the vault, no part of my mind can be completely shut off. The memories and doubts seep in around the doorframe.

Moving helps chase them away. Action.

So I keep moving, wandering through the living room and then scavenging in the kitchen a bit. There's no real food. No human food. Not that that's particularly surprising. So I find a granola bar in one of my bags. It's crumbly and stale, but I scarf it down anyway. I'm licking crumbs off the package when Carter finds me in the galley kitchen.

"We need to talk," he says, sounding stern. I know this voice. It's his Leader of the Rebellion voice. It's the voice he doesn't bring out unless something serious is going down.

Fear tiptoes down my back. He was up in Sebastian's office just now—where the security monitors are.

"What's up?" I ask, bracing myself for even more bad news. What it could be, I can't imagine. What could be worse than we're-trapped-in-an-underground-vault-with-a-scary-ass-vampire-on-the-other-side-of-the-door?

He moves to stand just across the counter from me. His expression is so tense—so serious—I want the comfort of his arms around me before I have to hear whatever he's going to say, but he doesn't open his arms to me and so I don't move toward him.

Instead, he braces his palms on the six-foot expanse of granite countertop that separates us and ducks his head, like he can't even look at me when he delivers this news. Which is maybe my tenth clue that this is bad, but my first that it's actually about me. And all I can think is that this must be about the cure he delivered back in Huntsville. Maybe that it doesn't actually work. Or that it's only temporary. Or that it will kill me in the end. Because that's the one thing worse than scary vampires at our gates: me a Tick again. Me human just long enough to inject my sister with a serum that will ultimately kill her. Yeah. Either of those two things would be worse.

Suddenly I'm glad he's not looking at me, because then he won't see the way I'm holding my breath, because if I have no air in my lungs, I can't sob.

Still looking at the counter between his hands, he says, "When we were at El Corazon, after you'd been sedated, Roberto told me something. Something that hadn't even occurred to me." He looks at me then, with his head still ducked, so it's almost like he's looking at me from under his lashes.

"What?" I whisper. *Just tell me!* I scream in my head.

"I'm an *abductura*."

For a moment—for a long moment—I don't even comprehend his words. It's so not what I expected to hear that it's like

332

he's actually spoken some other language that I can't understand.

"You're a . . ." The sentence started as a question, but I finish it as a statement. "Ooooh. You're an *abductura*."

"Yes." He looks up at me again, almost hesitantly, like he's waiting for the backlash.

"You're an *abductura*," I repeat stupidly. And then with more confidence. "Of course you're an *abductura*." This was his horrible news? This? I actually chuckle in relief. I am practically giddy. "Gosh, how did I not see that?"

"I'm an *abductura*. Doesn't that bother you?"

He sounds so . . . offended I almost have to smile. I can't even look at him for a solid minute.

Then I just shake my head. "It bothers me that I didn't figure it out. Does that count?"

He makes a low grumbling noise—almost like a growl—as he pushes himself away from the counter to pace the length of the kitchen. "That's not what I mean. I'm being serious."

"Well, I'm being serious, too." I follow, not letting him get too far away from me, not letting him put too much space between us. I rise up on my tippy toes and cup his jaw in my hands. "If I'm going to pride myself on being smart, then I need to step up my game, because I should have seen this coming. Sebastian started Elite Military Academy because he knew that kids like you—rebellious, strong-willed, smart kids—were statistically more likely to be *abducturae,* and that's where he found you, befriended you, and took you under his wing. You are incredibly charismatic and a natural leader. Honestly, I do not know why I didn't see it before."

"Would you please take this seriously!"

"I am. I just don't know what you want me to say."

"I want you to be pissed." He whirls back around. "Obviously you haven't thought this through, because you should be mad. You should be furious!"

"Well, I'm not." I can't do anything except shrug. "Why exactly should I be furious?"

"Because I love you."

My breath flutters around in my chest, because—holy crap—that's the first time he's told me that in a long time. I just wish he hadn't hurled it, like an accusation. Or maybe *confession* was a better term. Somehow, loving me pisses him off. I'm just not sure why. "I love you, too," I admit. "You know that, right?"

"Exactly," he says in that same terse, angry voice. "I love you. I have the ability to mold your emotional experience. Therefore you love me. You love me because I *make* you feel that way. For all we know, you don't actually give a damn about me at all."

"When you say it like that, it sounds like *you* should be mad at *me*, not the other way around." But he isn't mad at me. I can tell that. He's mad at himself, and frustrated with me for not understanding why.

"Don't you get it? I made you fall in love with me. I never gave you a choice."

"No. I don't get it," I tell him. "I don't understand. In all the months we've been together, I never felt like I was forced into anything. I just felt lucky, because you're the smartest, strongest person I know. And I get to be with you. That's not anything I'm going to complain about."

"Even if you don't have a choice?"

334

I try to see it from his point of view, try to understand his logic. And, yes, I get it. When he'd first come looking for me after the Tick-pocalypse, he thought I was the *abductura*. He thought I had the power to control his emotions and it had made him feel powerless. He hated it.

Again, I walk over to him and wrap my arms around his waist. I feel the familiar tingle of excitement at being so close to him. I relish it, because when I'd turned—when I'd been a Tick—I thought I'd lost it forever. I thought I'd never feel that way again.

It still scares me, because Carter has pushed me away before. When he got freaked out by the idea that he might not be able to protect me, when he thought being apart from him was in my best interest, he'd pushed until I'd left. Or I'd run. I wasn't really sure anymore who I blamed for that. It didn't matter. What matters now is that we are back together and I'm not going to let anything—even his doubts—get between us again.

"I do understand why this bothers you. No one wants to be in a one-sided relationship. But you're thinking about this the wrong way. You're forgetting all the very real reasons I have for loving you."

I lean back and look at him, taking in the signs of exhaustion around his eyes that somehow only make them look bluer.

When I first met him, I was drawn to his charisma and—yeah, sure—his hotness. But I didn't know him. I didn't have any real reason to want to be with him. But now? Now that I really know him?

"Yes, I do love you purely because you love me, but not in the way you think. Mel and I were on that Farm and might not have made it out if you hadn't come for us. You searched Farm after Farm until you found us."

His back and shoulders are covered in scars. Places where he'd had tracking chips inserted subcutaneously and then later sliced out. One for each Farm he'd broken into and out of while looking for me.

I slide my hand up under the hem of his shirt and trace the lean muscles of his back until my fingers find them.

His eyes flicker closed at my touch, but then open again when I say, "You put yourself at risk over and over again. For me. You never gave up on me. Even after I turned into a Tick, you still fought for me. You found the cure. You saved me. Carter—" My voice breaks, and for a second, I almost can't go on. "And, yeah, when I'm with you, I can feel how much you love me, but maybe I need that. I'm a naturally cynical person. I was abandoned by my father and emotionally shut out by my mother. I don't know, maybe if I couldn't feel how much you love me, maybe I'd have trouble believing it myself."

I don't know if I've convinced him, but he drops his forehead to mine, just resting against me for a moment before breathing out a slow, tired breath. His breath smells slightly spicy from the gum he's been chewing. He feels warm and solid beneath my hands. And good.

Then his mouth is on mine and he's kissing me. A deep, soul-searing kiss that I feel from my skin all the way to my bones and in every cell in between. His hands are holding me so close, like he can't bear to let me go, like he needs me as desperately as I need him. Maybe there are more things we should talk about, but for now, this is enough. Even though just kissing him will never be enough. But, in this moment, it almost is.

It's almost enough to block out the memories from my time as a Tick. There are things I know I'll never share with him. Things that will haunt my thoughts and terrorize my dreams. Maybe forever. But I have no intention of letting those nightmares destroy this. Because I could get lost in them or I could get lost in this. And I choose this moment.

CHAPTER FIFTY-THREE

MEL

It's dark when I wake up, but I don't know if it's because it's night or because the lights are off. I'm in a bed that's unfamiliar but that smells divine. My mind feels spongy and dense. Like my thoughts keep burrowing for warmth instead of traveling a straight path through my brain. And, somewhere off in the distance, from far away, I can hear music playing. Rachmaninoff's "Rhapsody on a Theme of Paganini," which has always been one of my favorite songs.

I breathe the music in, loving the sleepy, dreamy, perfect way it makes me feel, and the air is scented with a smell that's both comforting and exciting and new and familiar all at the same time.

Instantly I know where I am. I'm at Sebastian's.

And I know why I'm here and what I've done. My thoughts are now rabbit quick, moving through the burrows of my mind. Scurrying away before I can catch them. I am not Melly anymore. I am not Sebastian's Kit. I'm not Mel yet, either, but someone in between. A half vampire and half-autistic girl. I don't want to lose either. I want to be both.

But that's not possible. This isn't a destination, it's a hub. I haven't arrived, I'm merely changing planes. Though while I'm here, I intend to see more than the terminal.

I force my eyes open, push myself up on a shaking elbow, and look around the room. Sebastian is by my side, vampire fast.

"How do you feel?"

Like my soul has been ripped out. Again.

"Fine," I say. I reach for his hand before I think too much about it. "Carter and Lily?"

"They're okay. They're resting in the other room." He tries to pull his hand away, but I hold on to it with strength that surprises even me.

"Sit with me?" I ask. He hesitates. "Please."

There's a chair by the bed and he sits on it, knees right against the bed frame, elbows on the mattress. There is a tension in his body that I don't understand. It's not bright enough in the room for me to really see him like I want to. I know he won't look any different when I'm Mel again, but these are the eyes that fell in love with him and I want to hold these memories like Lily told me to.

"Turn on the light?"

He blinks, clearly surprised, but gets up and does it anyway. When he comes back to the chair, he sits with his elbows propped on his knees and his expression perfectly blank. Too blank.

"I don't understand." Maybe the cure is messing with my head, muddling my thoughts already, but I can't make sense of the tension radiating from him. "You're mad at me?"

He pushes up from the chair by my side and stalks to the other side of the room, not moving vampire quick, but taut with vampire anger. "Yes, damn it. I'm mad at you. I'm furious because you risked your life taking a cure that hadn't been tested enough. We had no idea for sure what it would do."

"Of course it wasn't properly tested. It's not like there are enough vampires around to run FDA-sanctioned tests."

"You could have been killed." He whirls around and practically growls the words at me.

"But I wasn't. And neither was Lily. If it was safe enough for her, then it was safe enough for me."

"Yes," he says, his voice suddenly cold. "But do you honestly think I care whether one more mewling human lives or dies?"

"No. I don't think you care." His words are like a scalpel carving out parts of my soul. Because that's what I am now to him. Just another mewling human. Yet another worthless creature he can never care about. "But I do."

"Oh, yes. I know that. You *care* so desperately for them." He sneers.

Them? Does he mean Carter and Lily or does he mean all of humanity?

Before I can ask him, he continues. "Don't you get it? You are worth more than them. You could have been the best of us."

Just when I thought his words couldn't possibly hurt me more, the scalpel digs deeper. This time, it's not the scorn that hurts, it's the hint of admiration. It's his love of all the darkest parts of my soul. All the parts I want to hide or forget. "I could have been the best?" I ask, with a hint of scorn. "The best murderer? The most brutal? The most vicious? Because of my 'killer instinct'?" I throw his own words back at him.

And just like that, his anger is gone. His eyes close and regret passes across his face, leaving grief in its wake like the debris from a flash flood. And then he's back in the chair by my side, his head cradled in his palms. "No, Kit," he murmurs. "Because you could have been the *best* of us. The strongest. The wisest. The most benevolent." Then he takes my hand in his. "For far too long, this world has been ruled by vampires who were selfish

340

and cruel. Who were interested only in accruing power. You could have been different. Instead you sacrificed yourself. And for what? Lily and Carter?"

"And for you," I say softly.

He laughs, a sound so bitter it makes me ache. "Right. So I can kill Sabrina and save the world."

"I know that's not what you want." The words hurt, but I push them out.

"I could have done that without taking the stake out."

"Maybe," I admit. "But you wouldn't have lived. We both know how strong she is. You may have been able to kill her, but the damage she would have done to you . . ." I shake my head, unable to talk, unable to pretend that he could have walked away from that battle. "You have to survive this."

"Melly—"

"No! Promise me," I demand fiercely. "Promise me that you won't go into this fight expecting to die."

"I've been alive two thousand years. Death isn't such a bad deal. Frankly, these past few days have just been borrowed time." I must look confused because he explains. "I went after Roberto. I always knew that was probably a battle I wouldn't come back from."

"Don't say things like that." I clutch his hand, desperate now. "I didn't do this only to save Carter and Lily. Or even to save all of humanity. I also did it to save you. To save your life."

"Melly, don't—"

"I know you think you're not worth saving, but you are. And if you want there to be a vampire in the world who is strong and wise and benevolent, then that vampire should be you. That vampire already *is* you."

He tries to pull his hand away, but I don't let him.

"If you love her and you don't want to kill her—"

His head snaps up. "You think I'm still in love with Sabrina?"

"It's okay," I say softly. "I understand that you loved her and then had to give her up once she turned. I understand that that's why you didn't want to turn me. But she can't be trusted and she has to be stopped. You understand that, don't you?"

"Yes, I understand that. I'm not an idiot, Melly. Despite all evidence to the contrary." He brings my hand up to his lips and presses a gentle kiss to my knuckles. "You were never in love with Carter, were you?"

The moment for lying or pretending just so I can protect myself has passed. "I will always care for him because he loves Lily, but I've never loved him. Not like that. He's a great guy, but he's no vampire."

He presses my hand to his cheek and then leans forward and kisses me. This kiss is not fueled with vampire passion or vampire rage. It is simple and sweet and kind. It is as delicate as the way his eyelashes flutter when he closes his eyes to kiss me.

Later, when he sits back down, I say, "For a man who's two thousand years old, you are very stupid."

His smile makes my heart sing—which sounds so trite, but really isn't. Not when I hear music in everything.

"Yes," he says. "I suppose I am."

He leans over to kiss my hand and winces as he straightens.

That's when I realize he's changed his shirt. And probably his bandage, too. That's when I notice that his skin has lost that sickly green tinge it had on the drive here.

"You took the stake out."

"Carter said it was what you wanted."

I nod. "So you can fight Sabrina. I know you'll be stronger than her. Here on your own territory. She can't possibly win." I squeeze his hand more tightly, until he looks up at me. My mind feels foggy with sleep and with the serum that's pulsing through my blood. Suddenly I can't remember if I said this before, so I add, "You can't go into this fight expecting to lose. Do you understand me?"

"I wouldn't dream of it," he tells me.

And I want to believe him so badly that I decide to. I choose that belief. That he will be okay. That he will choose to win.

After a moment, I ask, "So now that the stake is out, do you still want to kill me?"

He smiles—another rare smile! "Melly, when I thought you were dead, I wanted to kill everyone."

For a moment, he merely looks at me, his expression unlike anything I've ever seen. Then he closes his eyes and presses his forehead to our joined hands. I feel him suck in a deep breath, feel the way it shakes his whole chest, like maybe he's crying, and my heart feels so full that I can't breathe. I believe that he loves me. Right now, just like this. I know it can't last. That the vampire girl he loves will be gone soon. I know this because I can feel the old Mel sneaking back in, and I can hear it in the way his breath hisses out like a sonnet. In the way his dark silence fills up all my empty spaces. Soon, Melly Kit will be gone forever and with her, his love. I can make peace with that.

If I save Lily and Carter. If I save Sebastian. If I do all that and still get to have this one moment of happiness, then that's what I will take even if it's all I will ever have.

CHAPTER FIFTY-FOUR

CARTER

I waited until Mel fell back asleep and Sebastian came out to feed again before I gave him the bad news. In fact, I waited until he'd drained most of the bag and was feeling pretty relaxed before I even walked into the same room as him.

He just gave me a droll look. "You might as well tell me how it is. I can feel you stressing out from half a building away."

"Okay. I've been watching the security feed. As far as I can tell, the building is completely surrounded."

"By who?"

"I don't know," I admitted. "I guess by Sabrina's people."

"Give me specifics."

"I've counted fourteen armored vehicles. And twenty more cars."

"And these armored vehicles . . ."

"Are basically transporting an army. She's pretty much set up an RV park at our front door."

"Are you sure it's her?" Sebastian asked.

"She's not trying to hide. She's right out there in the open. She wants us to see her."

"You said she'd lost a lot of kine," Sebastian pointed out.

"You said she was well stocked when you were there just a few days before I was, why did you assume I was right and you weren't?"

Sebastian clenched his hand into a fist, like he wanted to

slap me upside the head. "Because you're the *abductura*, you idiot. I will almost always believe you. So please be more careful with your fact-finding in the future."

"Yeah. When we get out of this mess, I'll make that my top priority."

"If she has an army, why didn't you see it?"

"Off the top of my head, I'd say because she didn't want me to." Feeling frustrated, I started to pace. "She knew we were coming. She had her guys pick us up in town. She had plenty of buildings to keep all of her people under wraps while we were there. I had no way of knowing how many people she actually had, and frankly, I was there to talk to her and get the cure. I wasn't there for recon."

Before I knew it, Sebastian and I were standing nose to nose, glaring each other down.

"This isn't helpful," Lily said from the other side of the room.

We both backed down.

"I know. I'm sorry." I dropped to the sofa and put my head in my hands, trying to think. "I need to be better about this shit. I need to—"

"Stop being so dramatic," Sebastian drawled. "You're young. Practically a child. Given recent research about the development of the frontal cortex, it's a miracle you can function at all."

Lily glared at him. "Given the enormous stick up your ass, it's amazing you can function, too."

Sebastian just arched an eyebrow, looking almost amused. "Oh, and that is helpful? Thank goodness you came along to put us on the right track."

"Look," I said. "The point is, we've got to find a way out of here that doesn't involve trying to fight our way past a hundred armed soldiers."

"Nonsense. We won't need to fight our way past them. We just have to give them what they want. Which is you, my dear boy."

"Excuse me?" Lily asked. "That's your plan? Hand Carter over to them?"

"Obviously Sabrina needs an *abductura* rather more desperately than we thought. She will most likely be willing to trade our freedom for him."

"Again," Lily asked, "that's your big plan?"

"No, of course, that's not my *big* plan. That's my petite plan." Lily nearly launched herself at Sebastian then. I stood up and grabbed her by the arm. Sebastian clucked disapprovingly. "The petite plan involves offering him up in order to get us safe passage so I can talk to Sabrina. Then I kill her. That second part is the big plan, in case you missed it."

All the fight went out of Lily and she sagged against me. "I do like that plan better. But it's still dangerous."

"Yes, well, no plan is perfect."

"So when do we do this?" I asked.

Sebastian glanced back toward the bedroom where Mel was still asleep. "Soon. Certainly before Mel wakes up and starts getting her powers back, because she'll undoubtedly try to go instead of you."

* *

It didn't take us long to get ready to go out there. We each selected a gun and a blade, both small enough that we could conceal them in our clothing. Neither of us thought we'd get close enough to Sabrina without being searched to actually use the weapons, but they made us feel better.

Sebastian's selection of weapons was far greater than just the ones he had displayed on the wall. He had a whole closet full of them. Everything from shotguns to crossbows to samurai swords. I left the crossbow out where Lily would see it when she came out. She was sitting with Mel now. She had refused to say good-bye to me, saying instead that she'd see me in a few.

Sebastian noticed my placement of the crossbow. "Good idea," he said. "She won't need it, though."

"She better not."

Sebastian talked to me the whole time. He was in full-on professor mode, like he could teach me to be this super *abductura* in ten minutes or less.

"You need to stay focused."

"Got it."

"And stay calm."

"Okay."

He slid a dagger into the holster by his boot. "You should try to visualize yourself somewhere you feel at peace. Like a clear green meadow."

"How long have you lived in Texas?"

"Three hundred years. Why?"

"You live in the desert, man. How many clear green meadows do you get out here?"

He almost smiled then. "I've seen pictures."

"Okay," I said, tucking the pistol into the back of my pants. "Focus. Check. Calm. Check. Scenes from *Bambi*. Check."

"Unless you want to create chaos," he added. "Which might be useful at some point. In that case, you should visualize yourself doing something disruptive. Like being in a fight."

"Actually, I'm doing that right now," I told him with a fierce grin.

"Yes. I can tell."

We paused by the door. It killed me, leaving Lily and Mel in there by themselves.

"If we don't come back—" I couldn't even finish the thought.

Sebastian, the bastard, just shrugged. "If we don't come back, they'll just wait until this is over and sneak out the back way."

"Wait. There's a back way?"

"Of course. Every fortress has a back way out."

And it was at moments like these that I really did wish I was strong enough to kick Sebastian's ass. "If there's a back way out, then why are we marching out the front door to face the army of hundreds?"

"Because if we didn't eventually walk out the front door, Sabrina would be suspicious. Besides. She's here to pick a fight. If we let her, she won't bother looking for Lily and Mel."

"Where does this back way out lead?"

"There's an underground tunnel leading to one of the other buildings."

"So you told Lily about this back door?"

"No. But Mel will figure it out. She did at Roberto's. Once she wakes up, she'll realize it pretty quickly."

"Not too quickly, I hope," I said. "I don't want Lily trying to do something brave."

"That's why I didn't tell her."

"Okay. Let's do this."

"Yes. Let's." He stopped me at the very last minute. "By the way, if I do happen to die horribly out there, try to slice out my eyeballs, will you?"

You'd think after a full year of the Tick-pocalypse, nothing would gross me out. But that did. "Is that some weird vampire ritual?"

"No. It will keep Sabrina's people from breaking into the vault." He pulled a face. "My goodness, what kind of monsters do you think we are?"

CHAPTER FIFTY-FIVE

CARTER

There were guys waiting for us on the other side of the door. Sebastian managed to get it closed before any of them could wedge a boot in or anything. They raised their guns, and he just held up his hands, smiling.

I couldn't help it. As I raised my hands, too, I said, "Take me to your leader."

They brought us out through the building to the parking lot where—I'm not even kidding—someone had set up a tent. Not like a camping tent. Like a friggin' pavilion. It was set up beside a spindly oak tree on the dry patches of dirt that served as landscaping in this part of Texas.

They'd already searched us, so one of the guards—someone I didn't recognize and hadn't seen before—raised the flap and gestured for us to enter.

The place was like something out of *Arabian Nights*. The tent was made of patterned red fabric. Inside there was a thick rug and an enormous stack of pillows in one corner with a blanket thrown over it. There was a table and chairs and incense burning, something overly sweet like patchouli, but it didn't quite cover a lingering unpleasant smell. Marek was standing in the corner, his arms crossed over his chest, looking as stoic and freezerlike as ever. And there was Sabrina. Looking serene and lovely. And dressed in tan jodhpurs and riding boots, like she was going on safari or something.

She smiled broadly when she saw us. "Ah. Welcome to my home!"

"Your home?" Sebastian asked with an arched eyebrow. "Don't you mean my home? And for that matter, aren't you going to formally request sanctuary in compliance with the Meso-Americana Accords of 1409?"

"Oh, I definitely would have if you'd arrived"—she looked pointedly at her watch and tipped her head to the side—"two hours and nineteen minutes ago."

I looked at Sebastian. "What's she talking about?"

Sebastian pinched his mouth closed in a straight line. Under his breath he said, "I'm not sure, but now would be a great time for a visit to Bambi's meadow."

Sabrina looked from him to me and back again before giving one of her cackling laughs. "Shall I tell him or shall you?" Then she waved her hand and added, "No, no. Let me do it. I so love a twist in the plot." She slithered over to him. "According to the Meso-Americana Accords of 1409, of which Sebastian is a signee but I sadly am not, a vampire may establish territory—even within the boundaries of another's borders—by establishing a home, holding it securely against invaders, and making a substantial blood sacrifice."

As she said this last, she strolled back to the area with the pillows and whipped off the blanket. Lying there, arms and legs splayed out, eyes open and sightless, throat slit, was the fragile body of Paul Workman.

That's when I got it. The fancy tent wasn't just for show. It was a home that she'd established here. The incense was covering the scent of Workman's dead body, which had been lying in his blood, his shit, and his piss for . . . oh, I'd guess the past two hours and nineteen minutes.

Except that didn't quite make sense, because he smelled worse than that. Like he'd been dead for days not hours. But he'd been slowly dying for months. Maybe this was just what death smelled like when you did it by inches.

Beside me, Sebastian was all but trembling with rage. I could almost see it rising off him like heat off the Texas blacktop. I knew it was all his, because my own emotions were still firmly entrenched in the disgust and horror range. As for him? I got the feeling it was all he could do not to launch himself across the tent at her.

Since he was apparently too angry even to speak, I said, "Let me guess: two hours and nineteen minutes ago, you murdered Paul Workman?"

The pillows were stacked almost waist high and Workman's body was angled so that his head was tipped back over the edge of one of them, the stringy wisps of his hair dangling. His blood was drying on the edges of the pillows below him and puddled on the ground. She lovingly stroked Workman's hair back into place.

"No. I sacrificed dear Paul almost as soon as the tent was pitched. That was almost a full twenty-four hours ago. No, the two hours ago was when I fought off the invaders."

Invaders? What the hell did that mean? I gave Sebastian a look, but he didn't even notice.

Sabrina must have seen the question in my eyes, because she crossed to one of the open flaps of the tent and called out to someone. "Bring in the other."

A moment later, a guard pushed someone through the door.

At first, I didn't recognize the hunched shape because he had on a hoodie and it was pulled up over his face. But Sabrina strolled over and whipped the hood back.

Marcus.

Shit.

He looked terrified.

I took an instinctive step toward him. Marek had come up behind me and clamped a hand down on my shoulder. "Marcus, what have you done?"

Marcus gave me a defiant look and bumped up his chin. "Yo."

Sabrina threw back her head and cackled. "I know! Isn't it a delicious twist? Here I was, camp all set up, waiting for one of you to put in an appearance so I could solidify my claim to this patch of land, and then he shows up and tries to sneak into my tent with a—" She was laughing so much she could hardly speak. "With a tent stake! Taken from my own tent! Isn't it delightful?"

I felt the hand on my shoulder tighten and it was the only thing keeping me in my place.

"Enough," Sebastian barked.

Sabrina's laughter vanished. "Isn't it, though? Isn't it exactly enough for me to establish my own tiny swath of territory?" She slithered right up next to him and traced a hand down his cheek. "And so close to your own. Oh, it must be driving you batty." She laughed again and turned her attention to me and winked. "Get it? Batty? Oh, I do love a good pun."

The sight of that wink creeped me out. Was this more of her showmanship? Was she really this crazy, or was it all part of her act? Did it matter whether she was unhinged when she was gearing up to kill us all?

"Sabrina, no one here believes you actually want this territory or are prepared to defend it to the death." Sebastian's eye twitched as he spoke.

"No. But I am prepared to make more blood sacrifices until my hold on it is firm enough to defeat you if I should need to." She smiled at Marcus, who looked like he might wet himself.

"What is it you actually want? Is it the boy? You need an *abductura*?" Sebastian put a hand between my shoulder blades and pushed me forward. "Then take him."

"Ah, so generous of you," Sabrina purred as she crossed to stand before me. She ran a gentle hand down my cheek as she studied my face. "He is just adorable, isn't he? So earnest. So serious. He would be so much fun to play with." Then she gave my cheek a tap. "But, no thank you."

"But—" I started to ask.

"I'm afraid I don't actually need an *abductura*."

"But Workman—"

"Was fabulous. The absolute best I've ever had. But he was only one of many." She tilted her head and considered Sebastian. "This is the problem with men. They never think far enough ahead. I've found women are much better at planning long term. I haven't had just a single *abductura* since that awful flu epidemic in 1918."

I felt oddly calm, despite the fact that our plan was crap and the situation was spiraling rapidly out of control. Despite the fact that Sebastian was about to crawl out of his skin. And that was when it hit me. I suddenly understood why I felt so oddly detached.

Marek was an *abductura*. I didn't know why I hadn't felt it before. He was subtle and he was good. It was just the faintest trickle of soothing green meadow and frolicking butterflies.

Sabrina clucked her tongue, as if chiding Sebastian, and then turned back to me. "No, Carter, my dear boy, I don't need you. If, when this is all over and I've murdered Sebastian . . . if you survive and would like to apply for the position, we'll talk. But until that time, I'm afraid you'll have to offer up something just a little more valuable."

CHAPTER FIFTY-SIX

MEL

When I wake, my brain is no longer rabbit fast, it's roadrunner fast. Too quick to catch, too speedy for even the wiliest of coyotes.

I find Lily pacing in the living room, like Wile E. waiting for the package from Acme.

She is lost and worried, about me, about Carter, even about Sebastian, whom she has never liked. She tells me the plan, which is good, even though I know it won't work. Plans never work, not the way you expect them to.

I know what we need to do. Exactly what we need to do, but the words get stuck in a logjam and this time even my nursery rhymes fail me. I've been away from them for far too long and I've lost them like kittens and mittens and now there'll be no pie.

Which might work if pie was what I wanted. When what I actually want is Lily . . . Joan of . . . "Robin Hood," I blurt out, because he's the archer I want. "Like Mulan with the apple on the arrow."

I can see she's got it now. The idea of the arrow at least, but she's shaking her head. "Even if I can still use the crossbow in Sebastian's office, I'm not sure that shooting Sabrina will do any good." She's pacing now. "I mean, an arrow through the heart works great for a stupid Tick, who doesn't think to pull the arrow out, but for Sabrina . . ."

And I know she still doesn't get it. "It's not the arrow that will kill her. It's the blood."

"The blood?" Lily asks. "I'm supposed to get her to feed from someone? Someone whose blood is poisonous? How can I do that?"

"Don't feed her. Inject her."

"Inject her? With the cure?" Lily's eyes light up. "Right. Because it will knock her out. And take her out of the equation. Probably forever." She grabs me in a quick hug. "Mel, you're a genius."

Which I already knew.

"A bird in hand is better than two in the bush, but two in hand is better still," I tell her, and I believe she understands because she gets me even when I'm at my most difficult.

CHAPTER FIFTY-SEVEN

LILY

I test out the crossbow first, shoot an arrow right into Sebastian's office chair. If we make it out of this, I will happily buy him a new one. If there's anywhere left that still makes office chairs. If not, maybe I can learn to sew.

The good news: the crossbow works. Which I suppose I should have expected, since the weaponry here isn't a display, it's an arsenal.

I'm at a loss about what to do next, but Mel must have it all worked out, because when I emerge from the office with the crossbow and four arrows, she's waiting at the kitchen table with the first-aid kit and four vials of the cure. She wears the new Slinky on her wrist like a bracelet.

We carefully wrap the tips of the arrows in gauze bandages and tie them on. Then I slide the vials of the cure into the pocket of my hoodie. We'll put those on at the last minute. I stash the arrows into the duffel bag as well as a pair of binoculars I found and sling it onto my back like a backpack, with the bag open at the top and the arrows sticking out. The crossbow has its own strap and I sling that over my shoulder as well. Then I look at Mel.

"Okay. I assume that if you came up with this plan, you had

some idea how to get out of here and to a location where I can shoot these."

She nods, smiling slightly, and gestures for me to follow her. First, she takes me back up to the office, where she shows me the live video feed from the security cameras outside. We can see Sabrina's army out in the parking lot. We get that view from about five different angles. She's got this crazy, bedouin-style tent set up in the middle of the lot. One of the cameras is right outside the vault. In that one, I can see the utilitarian hallway, the smear of blood where the dead bodies lay for days—but apparently now have been taken away—and a cadre of Sabrina's men. Another camera shows the front entrance of this building. I recognize the sprawling copy of Picasso's *Guernica* over the reception desk, which seems like pretty grim lobby art. And then there's another shot of a different lobby. Not this building. The reception desk is similar, but instead of the Picasso, there's a banal landscape of a pond and willow tree.

Mel points to this picture. "'One of them leads to the castle at the center of the labyrinth, and the other one leads to . . .'" she says in an odd voice.

I shake my head. "I don't get it."

She repeats the phrase and then adds, "'B-b-b-BOOM!'"

"Oh. It's a quote from . . ." Dang it. What movie? Something we watched as kids. "*Labyrinth*! 'One of them leads to the castle at the center of the labyrinth, and the other leads to . . .' 'B-b-b-BOOM'?"

"'Certain death,'" she supplies.

"Nice." I look at the screen again. "Okay. The hallway just outside that door, which leads to the lobby with the Picasso, which leads to the parking lot and Sabrina's circus of horror. That's the way to certain death. Obviously. So this other lobby, that must be the castle at the center of the labyrinth." I turn to Mel. "So how do I get into the labyrinth?"

She takes me to the library right across the hall. She stops in front of that ridiculous fireplace and reaches for the sconce on one side. She tries to turn it, but it doesn't budge. I realize what she's doing and start helping. The mantel is an ornately carved monstrosity, full of Gothic gargoyles and . . . weirdly, a willow tree. I plant my palm on the panel with the willow tree and press. Voilà! The entire fireplace slides open.

Mel steps aside and gestures to me. "'One of them leads to the castle at the center of the labyrinth.'"

I make it three steps into the hallway when I realize Mel is right behind me.

I turn around to see her standing there, watching me with her head tilted, looking at me in that familiar birdlike way.

"Wait a second. You're not coming with me." She just looks at me and I feel a sense of calm and purpose, but I fight against it. "No. It's too dangerous for you. You should stay here. You'll be safe."

She shakes her head and points toward the door and I know that sense of calm is so strong it must be deliberate. It's her way of reminding me she's an *abductura*, too. She has her own job to do and she can't do it from the safety of the vault. Even though Mel doesn't like hugs, I launch myself at her and hold her tight. And even though Mel doesn't like hugs, she holds me tighter.

When I pull away I look her in the eye. And she meets my gaze. "Okay, but we stay together. At all times, no matter what."

She nods, smiling.

It feels like it takes forever to get through the labyrinth and I'm incredibly thankful for the yellow security lights mounted on the walls every fifteen or so feet. Eventually, we reach a door that opens right into the willow-tree lobby.

I creep to the front windows and peek out. Though the parking lot is full of hundreds of soldier types, none of them are looking at this building. We could walk right out in the crowd and probably no one would notice for a while. But we'd never get close enough to Sabrina without being disarmed, and firing a crossbow through a crowd is a good way to shoot a lot of people you don't mean to hit, but not the person you need to kill.

We find the stairwell and head up to the roof. On the roof, six stories up, the wind is fierce, loud, and bitingly cold, but the view is perfect. I set the duffel and the crossbow at my feet and get out the binoculars.

When I see it, when I actually see it, despair fills me. Sabrina's tent is so far away.

I drop the binoculars and sink to my knees, scrubbing my hands over my face. "It's an impossible shot. I can't make that. No one could make that."

Then I feel Mel's hand on mine and her will in my brain. I drop my hands and look at her. I draw in deep breaths to fight the panic, which threatens to overwhelm me, despite what she's doing to help.

"Okay," I say finally. "I can't make that shot. But maybe we can together." Maybe if she keeps me steady and keeps me calm. Maybe. And maybe is the best we can do.

Working side by side, we pull out the arrows. I carefully break the vials open onto the gauze coverings, dribbling the serum slowly until it soaks into the cloth. I kneel by the edge of the roof, bracing my elbows on the half wall that surrounds the roof. Then I load one of the arrows and raise the binoculars. Mel is beside me and I purposely match my breathing to hers. We have the perfect shot. Now, if Sabrina will just leave the damn tent.

CHAPTER FIFTY-EIGHT

CARTER

"I'm tired of your games," Sebastian snarled from beside me. "If you don't want the boy, then what do you want?"

"Isn't it obvious?" she purred. "I want power and control forever and ever. It's as simple as that."

"Power and control are never simple."

"No," she agreed, almost sounding sad. "I agree. Especially not when one's pesky ex-boyfriend is moping around begging you to take him back."

"I never begged. I merely offered you the option."

"The option? The option of giving up immortality and riches and infinite power merely so I could be with you? What kind of ridiculous woman would give up all that . . . for you?" Then she gave his cheek another one of those patronizing taps. "Don't take it personally. I wouldn't give this up for anyone."

I slanted a look at Sebastian. "Seriously?"

I left the *this is the crazy bitch you loved?* as an unspoken addendum.

And sent a powerful shot of calm, peaceful meadow along with it. It must have reached through the haze of his anger, because he almost smiled back at me. "She was a lot more fun before Roberto mentored her. And prettier before the Botox."

Sabrina lunged forward and made a furious hissing noise.

And this, I know, is real anger. Maybe the first real emotion I've felt from her.

Marek stepped out from behind me and caught her. "Remember the plan, Mistress."

Her gaze hardened as she glared at Sebastian. Then she wiggled out of Marek's grasp and stalked away from him. She smoothed down her dress before turning back to us. "Yes. The plan."

Either Sebastian was really pissed off, or he was enjoying baiting Sabrina, because he said, "The plan? You have a plan? That's rich. Because if I remember right, you've never been very good at following plans."

"Of course I have a plan! You don't think I came all this way—" She broke off and gave herself a little shake, like she was having trouble keeping herself under control.

I watched her, taking in the way she kept twitching her shoulders. Like her safari outfit was too scratchy. The way she was pacing more quickly now, like a dog in a kennel. Maybe that peaceful meadow wasn't quite what we needed here. I threw in a dose of busy subway station with a dash of amped-up Times Square.

"I, for one, would love to hear about this plan of yours," I said.

She whirled on me, hunched over slightly, her gaze hard and sharp. "Are you being uppity?"

I shrugged. "No, ma'am. You said you were going to tell us your plan. I said I wanted to hear it. Nothing uppity about that."

She straightened, shrugging back into her royal queen posture. "Yes. The plan." Her mouth pinched in as she turned back to Sebastian. "The plan is simple. If you're going to stay in my territory for very long—and I dare you to try to leave—" She made a sweeping gesture toward the guards. "Then you'll once again have to formally seek sanctuary from *me*. Once I have granted it, I have the right to demand a boon."

"And if that boon isn't my *abductura*, then what is it?"

"The cure. I demand all the samples you have of the cure as well as all the research."

"Oh," Sebastian drawled. "Is that all?"

"Is that all?" she snarled. "Yes, it is. Make no mistake, I will destroy all the evidence that this silly cure of yours ever existed. I will wipe it from the planet. Vampires have more power than we have ever had and I will not have you messing it up with your silly ideas about human equality."

Sebastian just looked at Sabrina, giving her a moment to simply seethe. Then he said smoothly, "You've forgotten one important thing."

"I haven't," she screeched. "I haven't forgotten anything."

"Yes. You have. I can formally request sanctuary from you because I'm a signee of the Meso-Americana Accords of 1409. And when you're in your own territory, you can certainly grant it and you can demand a boon from me. But you weren't alive in 1409. You're not a signee of the Accords. My power trumps yours. Always. You don't have the right to establish a territory within my boundaries, no matter how many invaders you fight off or how many blood sacrifices you make."

That was why Sebastian had lectured me about being so calm and so controlled. That's why he wanted me to Bambi's-meadow the shit out of this place. He must have known this all along. He'd needed me to fool Sabrina into thinking her bid for territory had worked.

Now I ratcheted up the Times Square and threw in a dose of rave.

She stared at him for a moment, eye twitching. "You're wrong!

I know that you're wrong! Every time you have visited me in my own territory, you've formally requested sanctuary. If we're not all bound by the Accords, then why did you formally request sanctuary? Why did you grant me my boon?"

"Because I'm polite," he said tersely. He took a quick couple of steps toward her. "Because it's good manners."

Sabrina paused for a moment and then launched herself at Sebastian. He knocked her back and then sent a kick to her ribs that she easily spun away from. The flurry of moves that followed was almost too quick to even see.

Marek moved to grab Sebastian and give his mistress an edge, but no guard, no matter how well trained, is a match for a vampire, and he couldn't even touch Sebastian. I threw myself in front of Marek, slamming my hand into his solar plexus. The guy was huge, but I hoped it would at least wind him. It didn't. He grabbed me by my shoulders and slammed his forehead down onto mine. My brain actually rattled inside my skull and my vision blurred around the edges. Before he could hit me again, Marcus jumped onto his back. Marek reared away from me, trying to get his fingers under Marcus's arm where it was crushing his windpipe.

I whirled around to check out the rest of the tent. The guards looked as confused as I was. They didn't know if they should help Marek or Sabrina. I added to their confusion, pumping out a steady stream of chaos.

Sabrina seemed to be holding her own against Sebastian. There wasn't anything I could do to help Sebastian.

Jumping into the fight with Marek was the obvious choice, but I didn't have a weapon. And, yeah, I could fight, but I couldn't go up against a trained mercenary. Not if I wanted to have any hope of walking away. And I did want that.

Instead, I looked around the tent and my gaze fell on Paul Workman, the poor bastard. And there, laid out on the cushions as part of the gruesome tableau, was the knife she'd used to slit his throat.

I grabbed the knife. I made it halfway across the tent before one of the guards launched himself at me. I slashed out with the knife and then dropped into a spinning kick.

In my head, I was going to bob right back up from that, but there were so many damn pillows around, my legs got tangled in one and I fell flat on my chest. The guy I'd cut grabbed my ankle. I kicked him in the jaw, but he didn't let go.

I looked up just in time to see Marek reach behind and grab hold of Marcus's hoodie. He actually pulled Marcus up over his head and flipped him over backward, throwing him across the tent. Marcus landed against one of the tentpoles, making the whole tent wobble. Marek stumbled backward, roaring in anger. I struggled to get my arms under me and get out of Marek's way, but the guard kept pulling on my ankle. Marek took one more step backward and I lashed out desperately, and for once, luck was on my side. I caught him on the back of his calf. Sabrina's knife sliced right through his Achilles tendon. He went down, reaching out for anything he could grab hold of and bringing the whole tent down with him.

CHAPTER FIFTY-NINE

LILY

From our position on the rooftop, we can't see what's going on inside the tent. We can only wait and watch and pray that we'll have the chance to help.

Turns out, waiting, watching, and praying are not my strong suit.

Sitting up there, I think of all the times Carter told me to wait for him to do something and I didn't listen. Sometimes it created more chaos. Sometimes it helped. Maybe I should have "learned my lesson" by now or something, but I haven't. All I really know is that I'm not going to stop trying to help. I will try, though, to always be smart about it.

So now, even though I want to do something crazy and reckless, I want to run down there and kick some ass, I realize I can do more good here. Maybe. If someone—anyone!—would just take the fight outside the tent!

Off in the distance, more vehicles are arriving. A lot more. Reinforcements, but I'm not sure for whom. Sabrina, I guess. Who would come for us? Yes, we have friends in Utah, but they're too far away. The Farm in San Angelo is barely holding its own. And it's mostly untrained Greens anyway.

Maybe I should abandon my post. Go down and warn Carter

and Sebastian. But what good would that possibly do? So instead, I stay on the roof and I watch. And wait.

Then the tent shakes, which makes me think maybe something is about to happen. I hold my breath. I wait some more. And then the whole tent goes down. People are moving inside the tent, struggling to get out. Sebastian is the first person to stand. Then, out of the folds of fabric, pops a woman. Sabrina. Even though I've never seen her, I recognize her instantly.

Beside me, Mel says simply, "Now."

And I let the arrow fly.

CHAPTER SIXTY

CARTER

I stumbled out from under the tent just in time to see the arrow pierce Sabrina's heart.

For a long second, no one moved. Sebastian was maybe five feet away from her. He looked battered. His lip had been bloodied and four deep scratches marred his cheek. This was his territory, but he clearly hadn't fully recovered from that stake in his heart when the battle had started.

Of course, the arrow through Sabrina's chest had slowed her down. It hadn't improved her mood, though.

She whirled around as if looking for who had shot her.

I knew it was Lily, but I had no idea where she was. Somewhere safe, I hoped.

Then Sabrina ripped the arrow from her chest. And hurled it away from her.

"You idiots! Did you honestly think it would make a difference having some sniper in a building to take potshots at me?" She leaned and hissed like a feral cat. "I'm not some mindless Tick who doesn't know how to take out an arrow."

One of her guards stumbled out of the tent and she pounced on the man. With a slash of her pointy nails, she sliced open his throat and started guzzling his blood.

Lily fired another arrow. This one pierced Sabrina's neck.

Again she pulled it out. This time she hurled it at me. Before I could even pick it up, another arrow flew through the air. If I didn't know better, I would have thought that Lily wasn't even aiming for Sabrina's heart.

Then I grabbed the arrow off the ground and looked at it. Lily had blunted the point with something. White gauze, maybe. It was covered in blood now.

I stared at the arrow in confusion as Sebastian and Sabrina circled each other. Then I looked up. Lily was firing from one of the rooftops. She had to be, given the angle the arrows were coming down from.

I held my breath until I saw a glint of metal from the nearest building.

How many more arrows did she have? At least one more if I could still see the glinting light off the crossbow. She had to still be in position.

The only problem was, she was shooting arrows dipped in the cure and Sebastian was between her and Sabrina.

They circled each other slowly now. The battle wearing them both down, but for different reasons.

I didn't know if Lily's trick with the arrows would make a difference. I didn't know how long it would take even if it did. Mel had passed out within seconds, but she'd had a full vial of the stuff shot right into her arm.

I crept around, trying to stay close to Sebastian. Then, when Sabrina was facing Lily's building, I launched myself at him and brought him to the ground. Lily fired another arrow. This one landed right in Sabrina's heart.

She reared back again, clawing at the arrow. "What is it with you people and these arrows?"

Somewhere off in the distance, I heard gunfire. In the tent, there was more scuffling. I just prayed that Marcus wasn't hurt. I had no idea how Sabrina had captured him, but I sure as hell didn't want to explain to Ely that I'd gotten his brother killed.

Sabrina ripped this arrow from her chest also. This time, she held it out and looked at it, swaying on her feet. "What is this?"

She sucked in a deep breath. Then another. Her hand seemed to spasm around the arrow shaft. Then her eyes rolled back in her head and she collapsed.

* *

Things happened fast after that.

Sebastian tied her up, though in the end he didn't need to.

I found the knife and cut through the tent fabric until I found Marek, who had been writhing in pain, useless to his mistress.

I wanted to believe that everyone deserved a second chance. That everyone who made a mistake would have a chance to redeem themselves. I just didn't know how to give Marek that second chance. Not when he'd worked for Sabrina. Not when he'd stood by while she'd tortured and killed his predecessor.

I hoped that someday we'd once again live in a world where those kinds of second chances were given and where those kinds of decisions were made by someone wiser than I was. But today wasn't that day and I was the only one standing over Marek with a knife. And if I let him live now, I had no idea what chaos he might cause with just his mind alone. So I killed him quickly and hoped that no one saw me throw up afterward.

* *

Once Marek was gone, most of Sabrina's people fled. Some stayed and fought. At first, I thought they were fighting one another. It was maybe ten or fifteen minutes before Lily made it to my side.

By that time, I'd fished Marcus out of the tent. I'd helped Sebastian tie Sabrina up with strips of red silk and I'd puked again.

Sabrina was writhing in pain, but still unconscious.

Marcus was sitting by the tent, clutching a pillow and looking like he was ready to puke, too. Lily hugged me. Hard and like she didn't want to let me go. Like she didn't actually have control over her arms. Then, without saying a word to me, she went and sat beside Marcus, pulling him to her and rocking him slightly, like he was small kid, even though he was taller than she was.

I crouched down in front of them. "You want to tell me how the hell you ended up here?"

Lily looked up at me and smiled. "You talking to me or to him?"

I nearly laughed. "Hey, I saw that fancy shooting from the other building. I know how you got here."

Marcus looked like he might cry, I couldn't blame him, since I was pretty sure he'd been damn close to being Sabrina's next blood sacrifice. But he shrugged Lily off and said, "We needed a distraction and I don't speak much Spanish. So I volunteered to come in."

"We?"

That's when Ely walked up, flanked by two very serious-looking Latino guys holding automatic weapons. "Yeah. We."

I stood up and shook his hand. I kind of wanted to hug him, but I still wasn't sure about those guys with the guns. "All along, you've been saying this wasn't your fight. Isn't that what you've been saying since you left the rebellion?"

"All along you've been saying this was everyone's fight."

"Good point." I looked at the guys and then out at the rest of the parking lot, where the fighting had stopped. And where more guys with more guns were rounding up the last of Sabrina's people. "So. You went to Mexico, huh?"

He grinned. "Yeah. Turns out, I was right about that wall keeping the Ticks mostly out. They've been struggling, but hell, at least there's some government still standing. And when I told them about the cure, they were pretty interested."

By now, Lily was done babying Marcus. Or maybe Marcus was done being babied.

She came back to my side while I spoke with the Mexican officials Marcus had led here. Once we were done and she and I were alone, I just held her for a long time.

When I glanced around, at first I didn't see Mel. I felt a burst of panic until I realized that she was with Sebastian, tucked up against his side so close she was almost invisible. I nudged Lily and nodded in their direction.

Her gaze followed mine and we both watched them, frowning.

"Is that weird for you?" I asked after a minute.

"Seeing my sister that physically comfortable with anyone? Yes. Seeing her like that with Sebastian? Doubly so."

"Are you okay with it?" I asked.

She seemed to consider it for a moment and then said, "She's my sister. It's not my place to not be okay with it. He just better treat her right. I'd hate to be the one to end his two thousand years of life."

"Yeah. Me, too." I was surprised to realize I meant it.

After a while, she looked up at me and said, "About giving the cure to the Mexican government . . ."

"Yeah?"

"I hope you don't think I'm being paranoid, but we can't let them have all of it. All the information. Some of the samples, sure. But we need to duplicate all Sebastian's research and try to get it up to Canada also. And back to Utah. Anywhere and everywhere we can think to send it. It's not that I don't trust them, but this is too important. It needs to be in the hands of as many people as possible. As soon as possible. Maybe that's paranoid and crazy, but . . ."

"But we just defeated a crazy, power-hungry bitch. I'm okay being paranoid for a while."

She rose up on her toes and kissed me. "After we're done being paranoid, maybe we can just be happy for a while, okay?"

"Yeah. I think I can manage that. Let me tell you about this great peaceful meadow I've been visiting. . . ."

CHAPTER SIXTY-ONE

CARTER

"So what do you think is going to happen?" Lily asked, whispering.

"I don't know," I answered honestly.

We were back in the underground vault beneath Genexome. Sabrina lay on the bed sleeping fitfully, her hands and feet zip-tied as a precautionary measure. Lily and I had agreed to take the first watch. The sound of piano music drifted in from the other room, but I couldn't tell if it was from the sound system or if it was Mel playing.

Outside the vault, things had settled down eventually. Sabrina's people had scattered or been arrested. Some of the Mexican army had decamped, and the few troops they'd left behind were camping out in the parking lot. Sometime during the next few days, Sebastian would hand off the samples of the cure, along with the protocol for making it. We weren't handing over Sabrina. Mel and I had convinced them to let us keep her. And maybe they didn't want her anyway.

Not that we knew what we were going to do with her.

"If this were a movie," Lily said, "when I shot her with the cure, there would have been some awesome special effect of her aging rapidly until she reached her real age and then crumbling to dust." She paused to give me a chance to answer. "Do you think that's what's going to happen here?"

"Don't know. Mel's the only vampire who's ever taken the cure. If she did the rapid age thing, it was only nine weeks in ten hours, not a hundred and fifty years." I looked down at Sabrina's form. It had been over six hours. Her physical appearance hadn't altered at all. "It doesn't look like she's going to rapid-age. Maybe she'll just be . . . you know, human."

She looked at me. "And still a very powerful *abductura*."

"Yeah. She'll be someone we have to watch out for." I knew how strong she was. How persuasive, even without her powers. Sabrina could be a very dangerous person. "Do you think we should have handed her over to the Mexican government?" I asked Lily.

"No," Lily said simply. "She's our problem. We'll find our own way of solving it."

On the bed, Sabrina's legs twitched. She groaned and rolled over, her eyes flickering open. She blinked for a second before using her bound hands to push herself up. In the other room, the music stopped abruptly. A second later, the door opened and Mel stepped inside, Sebastian right behind her.

Sabrina's eyes were wide, terrified. Her gaze darted away from Lily and me, as if we were of no interest at all. She barely glanced at Mel. It was Sebastian she couldn't take her eyes off. I could see her waiting for the vampire berserker rage to kick in. I could feel her panic when it didn't.

"What have you done?" she gasped at him. "What have you done?"

"The cure doesn't work only on the Ticks, Brina," he said, more gently than I'd have thought possible. "It works on us, too."

"You—" She glanced around the room again, as if searching for confirmation. "You cured me?"

"We didn't know what would happen," Sebastian answered. "You had to be stopped, Sabrina. And this seemed better than killing you."

"Better?" Her voice rose sharply and she waved her bound hands. "This seemed better to you? Bound like a criminal? Trapped here? This seemed better?"

"You're not a criminal, Sabrina," he said soothingly. "You won't have to stay here. I don't think we can let you go back to Smart Com, at least not right away, but—"

"Here in this *body*," she hissed, interrupting him. "I'm trapped here in this puny human body." She sneered the last few words, lashing out at us all with a burst of hatred. "You made me your *kine*."

"No, Brina," he said again. "I don't have kine. I haven't had kine in a hundred years, but I wouldn't expect you to understand that."

"I can't do this," she said desperately. "I can't go back to being human."

"You'll adapt."

For an instant, her gaze darted to Sebastian's. "And you and I can be together again? I can be your *abductura*. I can—"

In two quick steps he crossed the room and sat on the bed beside her. He took her hands in his and leaned close, whispering something none of us could hear.

Her gaze met his and then jerked away. She blinked so rapidly I almost didn't see the tears.

She took several deep breaths, sucking air in through her chapped lips in an audible hiss, like it took every ounce of her will to not fly apart. Then she said stiffly, "I can't live like this."

And then, more panicked, twisting her bound wrists in front of her. "I can't live like this. I can't live like this." She wrenched at her hands, frantic now to free them. Her arms contorted as she tried to break the zip ties. "I can't live like this," she said over and over.

"Calm her down," Sebastian barked. I wasn't sure if he was talking to me or to Mel. Or even to both of us. "Use your powers to calm her down!"

I tried to order my own thoughts, but I couldn't wade through her panic and fear to even get to them. Beside me, Mel dropped into a crouch, hands curled over her head, and let loose a low, sorrowful keening noise.

"Calm her down," Sebastian ordered again.

I took a step forward, but before I could reach Sabrina, Lily dashed past me. Too late I saw the scissors in her hands. A massive pair of metal shears.

"I'll take the ties off," Lily said, rushing forward.

But Sabrina was still looking down at her hands, trying to break free. Then, at the last minute, she looked up. I saw the gleam in her eyes. Saw her intention, but somehow her will trapped mine. I couldn't stop her even though I knew exactly what she was planning. I was simply frozen, unable to protect her from herself.

As soon as Lily had snipped the zip ties, Sabrina grabbed the scissors. And stabbed herself in her heart.

CHAPTER SIXTY-TWO

CARTER

Sebastian and I buried Sabrina later that night, on a gentle rise, a few miles away from the Genexome headquarters. According to Sebastian, it wasn't far from where she'd been born nearly two hundred years before.

Sebastian had his strength back, which made my being there to help pretty pointless, but I felt oddly compelled to stay. As though Sabrina were a stand-in for all the people I'd lost that I hadn't been able to bury. McKenna. My parents. My friends from the schools I'd gone to. Lily's mother, whom I'd never even met. Dawn and Darren, who we hadn't heard from yet, though Lily still held out hope for them.

We didn't have a ceremony. Sabrina's death felt no more or less tragic and meaningless than any of the other things that had happened in the past year.

When we'd sifted the last shovelful of dirt onto her grave, Sebastian straightened and said, "You know this isn't over, right?"

"What do you mean?"

"There are still vampire empires out there. A lot of them."

"So?" I asked.

"Lily and Mel won't be safe—not really—until all the vampires are dead."

I looked at him, trying to gauge his mood. He'd been oddly quiet. I'd thought it was because he was burying one of the few friends he had, but maybe I'd been wrong.

"What's your point?" I asked.

"You should kill me," he said simply.

I let out a laugh then stopped. "Wait. You're serious?"

"It's the only way to protect them. As long as I'm alive, something could happen. I could infect one of them. I could lose control. It could be bad."

"So you want to die? To make some sort of grand gesture?"

He blinked in surprise. Maybe at the scorn in my voice. "I want to protect them. I thought you would—"

"You thought I would kill you?" I asked. "Don't get me wrong, it's not that I haven't wanted to, but now that Mel's in love with you, I figure you two are a package deal. There's no way I'd kill you. The last thing I need is Lily pissed off at me forever because I killed the guy Mel loves." Then a thought occurred to me. A pretty unpleasant one. "Unless you've decided you don't love her. Now that she's autistic again."

And just like that, Sebastian had his hand around my throat. Slowly he pulled me right up to him until I was dangling a few inches from his face. "Do not be any more of a fool than you have to be."

He thrust me away from him and I stumbled back several steps before catching myself. Well. I guess that was that.

Obviously, he still loved her. So much he was stupid with it. I knew the feeling. The world was a crazy, terrifying place. And the fear that you couldn't protect the ones you loved could eat away at you.

"Look," I said. "If you're worried about protecting them, the best way to do that is for you to be here. In the fight."

I added that last bit pointedly, because I'd seen the looks he'd been giving the supply of the cure that was stashed in the refrigerator. Like he was thinking of taking it himself.

"You are our best defense against other vampires. You know their empires. You know how they work. You'll know if any of them come after us. And I figure they will come after us. Sabrina won't be the only person threatened by the idea of a cure."

He seemed to consider this for a moment before saying, "If I stay a vampire, I can't be with Mel."

"Because you're worried about turning her?"

"Because the vampire/human thing just doesn't work out. Ever."

"Says who?"

"Says everyone."

"Everyone is full of crap. I think you'll just have to stay a vampire long enough to kill the others, then you can do whatever you want with that cure."

After a moment, he nodded.

"By the way, I've been wondering what you said to Sabrina." Sebastian threw me a look. "When she offered to be your *abductura* again. What was your answer?"

He looked away. "I believe that's between me and her."

"Which I would totally respect. Except you're with Mel now. And the way I see it, I'm the closest thing she has to a brother. It's my job to look out for her. She doesn't need to be anyone's second choice."

He looked at me then, his gaze flat and expressionless and oddly deadly. For a second, I thought he wasn't going to answer me. For a half second, I worried he might do worse.

Then he sighed and looked away. "Your generation has no boundaries, do you know that?"

"You gonna answer or not?"

"I reminded Sabrina that ten years ago, I went to her and offered her the cure. I offered to take it first, in case there were ill effects. I offered her the chance to be with me for the rest of our lives, however long that might be. For my insolence, she had me beaten and dumped at the edge of her territory. My forgiveness extended only so far as not doing the same to her."

That would have been good enough for me. I turned to leave, but before I could, Sebastian said softly, "Mel isn't my second choice. She's my only choice."

MEL

When I was a vampire, when I lived in a world of silence and blood and death and life like I'd never known, I used to wonder sometimes what I would have sounded like to the old Mel, to the Mel who heard music in everything.

Not just what I would sound like, but Sebastian, too. He had been silent to me when I first met him. When I was a vampire, when I knew him, would he have finally sung for me? Would we have resonated together? Those times he kissed me, what would the music be then?

I wondered if it would be Rachmaninoff, which is how Lily and Carter always sounded to me. My very favorite music—deep and lush and swooningly romantic.

I've heard people talk before, about blood singing. That's how I felt. As though Sebastian made my blood sing, and it broke my heart that I would never hear it.

Now I do.

It isn't Rachmaninoff. It's something new. Like the sweeping swell of music at the end of a movie. It is indescribable and unique. It would fit nowhere, but it fits here. And it is all mine. All ours. And it is all the sweeter because we were both so silent before.